THE SCOURGE OF SCAPA FLOW

J. FARRAGUT JONES

A DELL/BRYANS BOOK

Published by
Dell Publishing Co., Inc.
1 Dag Hammarskjold Plaza
New York, New York 10017

ISBN: 0-440-17701-4

Printed in the United States of America

First printing—August 1981

LIKE A GREAT KILLER SHARK,
THE MASSIVE U-BOAT GLIDED
STEALTHILY NEARER ITS MASSIVE
PREY....

"Tubes one, two, and four ready, sir!" The helmsman's eager tone startled Kapitänleutnant Prien. He shot a glance at his torpedo officer.

"Slow ahead both."

The conning tower could now make out the battleship's gun deck deadlights. It was all or nothing. The alternative was to die without a reason, or to slink out—beaten....

"Range two-six-zero-zero . . . spread, point-zero-four." The dreadnought's tripod mast was dead center as he pressed the burnished brass button:

"FIRE!"

THE SILENT SERVICE SERIES

WATERS DARK AND DEEP

FORTY FATHOMS DOWN

THE SCOURGE OF SCAPA FLOW

THE SCOURGE OF SCAPA FLOW

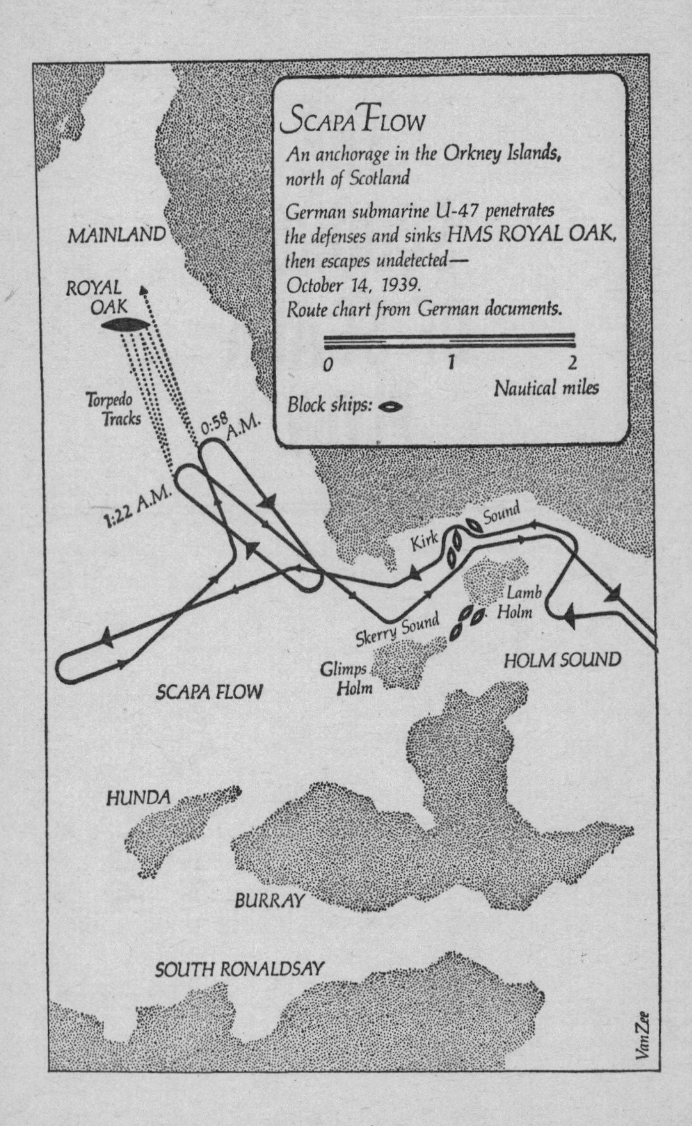
SCAPA FLOW
An anchorage in the Orkney Islands, north of Scotland
German submarine U-47 penetrates the defenses and sinks HMS ROYAL OAK, then escapes undetected—October 14, 1939.
Route chart from German documents.
0
1
2
Nautical miles
Block ships:
MAINLAND
ROYAL OAK
Torpedo Tracks
0:58 A.M.
1:22 A.M.
Kirk Sound
Lamb Holm
Skerry Sound
Glimps Holm
HOLM SOUND
SCAPA FLOW
HUNDA
BURRAY
SOUTH RONALDSAY
VanZee

Prologue

"Your father will be very proud of you." Oberleutnant Schutz squinted into the milky fog as *UB-116* cut a white mustache bow wave in the glasslike bottle green sea.

"Of *all* of us, Rudolf—*if* we make it." Kapitänleutnant Hans Joachim Emsmann let his binoculars hang against his brass-buttoned watch jacket. It was enough to have Seaman Berckheim worry about drying *his* objective lenses. It was an afternoon for naked eyes. "Berckheim, sweep for'd as well as aft," he ordered quietly, then turned to his swarthy first officer. "What time was the last fix?"

Schutz riffled through a small note pad. "Pfeiffer shot the sun at fifteen-twenty, sir."

"*Donnerwetter*—almost two hours ago." The pallid officer fingered the tarnished gold embroidery on the bill of his blue cap, a nervous habit unbecoming to the son of a commodore in the German Navy. He wanted to open his leather jacket; it was warm for October—and ghostly calm. He leaned to port, over the tower railing to see past the helmsman at his pedestal station. Was that a rock . . . the gray beyond the mist-shrouded bow?

"But for the pea soup, sir, we'd've dived and picked

up Duncansby Head on the scope like we did Rattray's."

"We've logged almost eighty miles since that land fix. . . ."

"And another twenty on dead reckoning, sir—but then you're one of the best navigators in the flotilla."

"There's always a *first* time, Rudolf; the Pentland Firth tides run up to nine knots. Our course over the bottom may not coincide with our calculations. Take over while I recheck the tide charts—and let's go to slow ahead."

"Aye, sir . . . we'll keep a sharp lookout for reefs and Englishmen." As the commander descended, he noticed the naval ensign, hanging limply on its mahogany staff atop the aft tower rail. He'd expected that the mission would be rousing and knightly—a Teutonic charge at the enemy's bastions. No . . . the flag symbolized the fatherland: tired, hungry . . . and defeated.

Emsmann spread the North Sea chart on the navigation table in the tiny control room. He checked the tide tables once more: the eccentricities of flow from the Moray and Dornoch firths and the effects over the shallows at Moray Bank, the invisible moon's caprices, and the earth's magnetic deviation. He poised his china marking pencil on the celluloid overlay and traced the course. There were notations along the red line: "25/10, Schillig; 26/10, Dogger Bank; 27/10, Halibut Bank; 28/10 . . ." The commander took his cap off and unbuttoned his coat. The German Navy was not noted for being overly concerned with its crews' physical comfort; the enemy's submarines, if not as efficient, were certainly better ventilated. He drew a line along his parallel rule edge; it ran at 334 degrees from Rattray, on the northeast shoulder of Scotland, to a point west of the Pentland Skerries—a deep-channel area. Then he sectioned the course line with equal turns of his compass dividers—one turn for each ten surface miles and two for each ten submerged—over the last day's leg and compared it with his previous pilot's reckoning. It checked out; *UB-116* was two miles west of Duncansby Head and ten miles south-southeast of Hoxa Sound, one of the five navigable entrances to the Royal Navy fleet anchorage in Scapa Flow. But his boat was positioned on paper only. He would need a tactile fix; the fog ruled out a land fix. There was no sun, nor would there be stars later for a celestial fix according to the barometer.

There was only one way. Dive and sound with the patent lead; run slow and sound; then compare the findings with the chart depths. No need for the tallow insert or Kelvin tube in this case. Too complicated anyway. He pulled out the Orkneys chart.

The contour lines indicated a fifty-meter-deep channel that ran NNW for six miles, starting a mile northeast of Duncansby to within a mile of Swona, a small island in the firth that shallowed fast on its south side. The perspiring fingers drew dotted lines left and right around the island, both routes converging over a deep hole one half mile above its northern tip. The commodore's son, a graduate of Flensburg, where navigation was taught with great pride and German precision, opted to *feel* his way along the sandy bottom to the island and then run to port and north, sounding the shallows until he reached the fifty-meter hole. From there he would take his final underwater bearing on the gyrocompass and set a course directly through the mile-wide Hoxa narrows. Done!

He climbed into the conning tower and peeked through one of the open rectangular ports. Still pea soup. Leaning to the voice pipe bell, he called the control room, "Prepare to dive," then poked his head through the bridge hatch and ordered the watch to stations as the bosun shouted below, "All vents open . . . clutches out . . . switches on . . ."

Topside, the ribbon-capped helmsman took his wheel off the pedestal and clambered over the bridge railing to follow Leutnant Schutz and Matrose Gefreiter Berckheim down past the conning station, where the ports were being secured, to the *Zentrale*, the brain compartment of Blohm und Voss's steel bantling. Smyzec grabbed the spoked wheel and corrected his course, having swerved several points during the change of stations.

Emsmann watched the hatch dogged and waited at the grid panel, should one of the compartment-keyed bulbs flash, indicating an unsecured fitting or malfunction.

"Go to forty meters . . . both slow ahead on three-three-four . . ."

"To forty, sir," replied the bosun from below.

Taking a last look, the commander watched as white froth gave way to transparent green in the conning ports. Satisfied that the tower was secure, he set his jaws taut and skittered down the ladder to a position next to Berckheim. Bracing his arms on the gyroscope housing, he marveled at this latest advance in German science—a compass that always read true north, unaffected by terrestrial and local or stray magnetic fields. If his reckoning had been correct, the gyro, a mechanical brain spinning at 20,000 revolutions per minute, would be infallible in the final approach.

The pressure depth meter hovered at forty meters as the bosun, Chief Petty Officer Konrad Bauer, corrected the trim with minute adjustments, the blowing and flooding of the bow and stern ballast tanks, much as a high-wire performer with his bamboo balancing pole.

"Schutz, we didn't hit bottom. . . ." The commander exhaled.

"I guess we're in the Pentland deeps; you're a genius, sir—"

"Perseverance—and faith in our purpose . . . plus luck."

"Bauer"—Schutz took over—"prepare for lead line soundings at five-minute intervals. . . . Motor room"—he whistled into the voice tube—"four minutes slow ahead both . . . and two minutes clutches out. Commence at eighteen-fifteen hours . . . report as you go. . . ."

The 180-foot-long submersible crept northward at a jellyfish pace—blind except for a twenty-eight-pound lead weight suspended from a watertight gland adjacent to the ballast keel by a stainless steel wire. Steuermann Deppe called out the depths as he braked the slackening wire and reeled it in.

"Twenty meters . . ." The quartermaster gulped and wondered if his brother, a machinist on *U-93*, wasn't better off as a prisoner of war, having been captured after tangling with a square-rigger that proved to be an armed Q-ship the year before.

"Hard right; come to zero-six-two. Both slow ahead."

"Twenty-five . . . thirty . . ." The wire reeled off.

"Left rudder, come to zero-zero-five." Emsmann

slipped out of his coat; the room thermometer read 105 degrees. He counted minutes, then seconds on his stopwatch as the rudder angle indicator above the helm responded.

In fifty-five minutes *UB-116* was over the fifty-meter channel.

The commands flew: "Battle stations . . . rig for depth charges . . . flood tubes one, two, three, four . . . periscope depth—easy . . ."

"Blimey." Hydrophone Operator Herbert Potter adjusted his earphones and tuned his wireless to the listening station at Harrabrough, across Hoxa Sound.

"Cantrick station calling, come in please." Potter slipped one earphone off and turned up the wireless volume while still listening on the hydrophones with one ear.

"Harrabrough calling Cantrick; Haycox here." A chatter of static. "Come in, Cantrick . . ."

"Donald, m' boy, it's Herbie—on the *civilized* island. I'm picking up screws at our one-fifty degrees. Sound increasing . . . but can't see fer the bloody fog. Do ye have any pickets out? . . . Over."

"Hold on. Potter . . . negative on pickets at this hour . . . I'll sweep your bearing and get back to you. Out."

Soundman First Class Haycox, a transfer into the new branch called ASDIC, lined up a tracked rod over his harbor defense chart from the Cantrick station to a 150-degree bearing. He turned his hydrophone receiver to full volume and electrically rotated the underwater sensor head to sector yellow at the intersection of the Cantrick bearing. Yellow was the outer of four 1,000-yard-wide arcs across the sound.

The island of Swona was within yellow's boundaries. Concentrically north, the next two arcs were called green and blue. The fourth arc spanned the Hoxa narrows from Switha Island on the west to Herston Head on the east. It was called sector purple; it was a minefield.

Haycox heard faint propeller noises in yellow. He rotated into green, then called the duty officer. If all the pickets were accounted for, the screws could mean only one thing.

It was the day that Austria had surrendered by "accepting" all of President Wilson's conditions, and a day that London saw the "doom of Germany," and Paris, "the end very near." The hydrophone operator snapped off the calendar sheet: Tuesday . . . large "29" . . . small "1918."

He crumpled it into a little ball of paper and dropped it into his overcrowded wicker wastebasket.

Emsmann, cap backward, grabbed the rising periscope handles as the gleaming clocklike counterweight descended into a well behind him. The cable wheels squeaked to a halt, and the commander's eye bulged into the rubber ocular. Blackness!

"Periscope clear," reported the chief engineer.

A small blurry glow appeared on the starboard beam . . . a ghostly necklace off the port bow. The captain squeezed a rubber bulb; jets of alcohol sprayed onto the scope's lenses and prisms, evaporating the condensation; blurs sharpened into bright coruscations, the necklace sparkled and was reflected on quiet water. Without turning the periscope, Emsmann could see forward, to the sides, and behind. German optical technology had triumphed again! The much-awaited 360-degree panoramic head was now functioning. No more would U-boats be surprised from astern by fast-closing English destroyers. Inside the fish-eyed perimeter image appeared a normal front field. The captain waited patiently and focused on the narrows dead ahead. His stomach rumbled as his fingers slid from sweat on the metal handles.

The patchy fog closed in again, lifted in spots, hung low over the dark shoreline. An occasional streetlamp, then a phantom halo, then nothing. Nothing but the thrumming of electric motors as the intrepid cyclops minnowed on its wide-eyed track. . . .

Invisible to the enemy—but very much followed.

The crew, to a man, was quiet; they knew that in five minutes they'd surface—take the English by surprise. A carnival shooting gallery waited against the night glow of Kirkwall, capital of the ancient archipelago. *UB-116* headed unerringly into the sea dragon's den—fired with a Teutonic fervor destined to restore the lost pride of Empire.

"Tubes one to four ready . . ."

The brass knob turned, focused on Hoxa Head as a swirl of night fog parted and rose, revealing the busy Nevi Skerries beacon and the tranquil flow beyond.

"Full ahead both and ready on diesels . . . bridge watch, make ready. . . ." Emsmann steadied his steel steed, lances poised, as blurred lights flew by—left and right—streams of fog and luminescent ribbons toward the vanishing point like meteor trails. . . .

Leutnant Schutz, the sole volunteer on the mission, braced his callused palm crablike over the torpedo firing buttons, his Prussian brain agog at the impending encounter with the British flotilla that lay around the bend. . . .

* * *

"Closing . . . closing . . . Lieutenant Commander Roskill pushed a silver shilling piece slowly across the gridded chart, his staff gathered around the table, tensely staring.

"Closing . . . now blue and closing . . ." The operators kept up a steady stream of position calling and coordination with the other stations, all hooked in like a spider's web feeling the tugs of the trapped insect. "Closing . . . sector purple, repeat, *purple.*"

The myriad black mines strained their chains below the surface of quiescent Hoxa Sound, a forest for migrating herring. The deadly horde leaned with the tide, a garden of ominous blossoms—leaned toward the streaking, bubbling gray shark. . . .

The galvanometer needle dipped; the chattering among uniforms subsided and stopped. The final silence of war. The needle wavered and was drawn point down where it shivered and shone. Commander Roskill's eyes were shut.

Petty Officer Rheem slammed the double-yoked brass switch home. A rumble of thunder. Rheem excused himself and went to the WC, wherein he privately crossed his heart.

Early the next morning, according to various accounts, a Royal Navy picket rolled two depth charges into an oil-slick center of the sound. An immense bubble gurgled to the surface, accompanied by a brass-buttoned leather watch coat. A few days later a team of divers located the wreck and burned their way into the mangled hull. They worked their way aft past tumbled torpedoes, torn bodies, and gear to get at the control room.

Two bare arms, crushed at the elbows, jutted like alms takers from an aperture between the pressure door and the frame. One was swathed in seaweed, fingers in a beckoning gesture.

It is not known what intelligence, if any, the Kaiser's Navy possessed of the disposition of the Home Fleet that precipitated the doomed sortie, but it is a fact that the British fleet had moved to Rosyth, near Edinburgh, a month earlier and that Scapa Flow was empty when *UB-116* met its *Götterdämmerung*!

November 1918

The bulbous kite-balloon hung 1,000 feet above and to seaward of its puffing gray master. Its shadow, flung westward on the water, mingled with that of the Firth of Forth Bridge. They were headed toward the Isle of May, guardian of Edinburgh and the fleet anchorage at Rosyth.

In the wicker gondola, Lieutenant Bryan MacQueen took another look through his binoculars, then anxiously rang up the phone, the line of which ran down the tether to the radio room of HMS *Cardiff,* a light cruiser.

Aboard the battle cruiser *Königsberg,* a nineteen-year-old-midshipman, Theodor Drahn, stood on the bridge. He turned, shielding his eyes from the hazy sun, and looked aloft at the towering superstructure. At the summit a white flag hung like a shroud above the German colors. Grim, bearded Rear Admiral Meurer stared ahead like a zombie. Four bells rang out.

A crowd had gathered on the Kellie Castle green overlooking Fife Ness and the ancient fishing villages of Pittenweem and Anstruther. The townspeople were eagerly waiting their turn at the three-inch brass refracting telescope that Angus Erskine, science headmaster at the University of St. Andrews, had "appropriated" for the occasion.

The Dundee *Record* lay billowing on the grass among a scattering of textbooks. Under the masthead date, 15 November 1918, appeared the banner headlines:

ARMISTICE IMMINENT
KAISER FLEES!
High Seas Fleet Mutinous

At approximately eight bells, or four in the afternoon, Admiral Meurer led his staff of six up the gangplank to the deck of *Queen Elizabeth,* battle cruiser and flagship of Admiral Beatty, who would receive the surrender. There were snappy salutes from the British deck officers.

Theodor Drahn, yeoman, was the last to be piped aboard.

As it turned out, young Drahn, who was to function as a messenger and recorder of the event because of his bilingual prowess, sat behind a screen with his notebook and fountain pen. Next to him, representing the crown, sat Sir John Lavery, distinguished artist and member of the Royal Academy. Theodor watched in awe as Sir John squeezed his watercolors onto an enamel palette. As if it were all at some fair! Or on a stage!

Drahn's hand shook his pen and dribbled ink. Not so with Sir John, who drew boldly with charcoal sticks on his easeled Strathmore paper block. He roughed in the figures: seven in all athwart the long table, backs to a bulkhead festooned with elaborate framed engravings and photographs. Five German officers on the near side. A British officer standing at the porthole wall and two seated against the right wall, hands ceremoniously clasped on their vertical sword hilts. The table was strewn with rolled-up charts and papers. Drahn's view was inferior to the artist's, so he relied on the painting as proceedings wore on rather than bump Sir John for a better view.

On one of his occasional glimpses he was struck by the sorrow in Meurer's face. Admiral Beatty read the terms like an automaton. Stiff and unflinching. Unyielding. Sir John brushed in roseate faces on conquerer and conquered alike. Drahn's heart was so heavy he could scarcely write. Only six months out of Flensburg Navay Academy, he was witnessing the death of his fleet. How excited he'd been—then. Assigned to a fine ship, only to have as his first action its demise.

Two bells! Curious, thought Drahn, enemies with the same clocks, the same hours and minutes. He thought of Heidelberg and saw his father's watch-repair shop. Myriad timepieces: gongs, bells, tinkles. Springs and geared wheels. Cuckoo clocks and collectors' rarities. The medieval clockworks in the town square. The bronze figures would be striking the huge bell five times—five o'clock. Should he have stayed? Become a loop cyclops like his father?

Sir John took delight in dabbing the gold stripes on Admiral Beatty's sleeves. Might as well have been a human camera for all his feeling. "A lucrative commission," his peers would whisper. "Get more commissions out of *this*." Theodor retched within. The clocks whirred and spun for him. Time became eternity as the names of the German vessels echoed through the sumptuous cabin: sixty-nine men-of-war to their funeral. First the battle cruisers: *Hindenburg, Derfflinger, Seydlitz, Moltke. . . .*

All with white flags!

31 January 1920

My dear Father and Mother:

Your son Theo is on his way home!

Yes, I can finally write without censorship. I share the transport ship with eighteen hundred defeated German sailors. It will take me three days to muster out in Wilhelmshaven and arrive by train in Heidelberg. The authorities have graciously arranged airmail service for our letters, so this will precede my return and prepare you for my apologies.

Please forgive me for making such a foolish move and not waiting before enlisting at the academy. You were right; all was already lost. At least I got my wanderlust solved!

I hope you will be pleased that I have been active during internment in Kirkwall as camp watchmaker. I've been allowed access to a shop in town, the proprietor of which is not in the best of health. Aside from fixing the watches of British fleet officers, I have worked on those of the townspeople and have gotten plaudits and even an offer of employment, should I ever want to return. The offer is attractive especially because of the shopkeeper's lovely daughter, who has been very kind.

It would be difficult to recount all the misadventures I've endured since the surrender of our fleet at Rosyth over a year ago. The humiliation of Admiral Meurer! We did everything to the letter and were treated in contempt for it. I don't know who was worse: the Bolshevik traitors or the British captors. But we all knew it was over. The first thing our sailors did upon anchoring in Scapa Flow a year ago last November was to *fish*. They were so hungry! The British thought it was not befitting the auspicious ritual of capitulation. To *fish*!

Discipline got so bad during the next few months while the Allies were trying to make up their minds as to which of them would receive our ships as booty that the crew of *Friedrich der Grosse* found roller skates somewhere and repeatedly skated on the iron decks over the officers' heads. The British damn near drove us all mad. We are Navy like them. Would they have liked such treatment had roles been reversed?

I am very lucky to be coming home at all. What you didn't hear in the official accounts of the scuttling of our fleet last June was that the British, who had been out of the flow on torpedo practice, were so enraged at seeing their booty capsizing that they indiscrimiantely fired at our lifeboats and killed thirteen of our sailors. I was in one of those boats, and we were unarmed! I shouted at the British. Four men in my boat had been hit. They didn't seem to care and ordered us back to our sinking ship. Luckily we made shore in the confusion. I will never forget that bloody day!

Please give my love to Helga, and spare her my details.

Your loving and repentant son,
Theo

It was a hot morning in August. Theo had worked on the watches and clocks all the previous night. Mr. Robertson's daughter had called the internment officer and gotten Theo a leave of three days to work on her father's premises. Second heart attack. He would have to stay at Balfour hospital for a few more days. So Theo fixed the backlog of orders and fell asleep on his workbench.

He woke up at noon, still in the shop on Albert Street near St. Magnus Cathedral.

"Theo, I've been waiting for you to wake up." The delicious aromas of bacon, coffee and fresh buns accosted him. Shook away his nightmares of the scuttling.

"You don't have to go back yet—even if you've finished the watches. I saw Dad this morning, and he says there'll be more work coming later on this afternoon. Seems that the doctors', nurses', and patients' timepieces all need help." Claire Robertson, in her exuberance, accidentally brushed her body against his hand—his delicate, sensitive hand—as she set the breakfast tray on the workbench before him.

It was the first touch of a woman for him in two years. It was the first time a woman's breast had ever touched his hand, or vice versa. And no man had ever touched her breast. She was only seventeen.

He blushed, and she made excuses about the coffee and ran to the back where she now lived alone, her mother having died when she was ten.

After collecting her wits, she returned with a tin coffeepot, and she hid behind the steam. She stuttered in concealing her tinglings.

"Drink some, so I can pour you fresh and hot." She blushed when she saw he hadn't touched his food. He was looking at her eyes. She affected a stance much as she remembered her mother would do, and it saved her from embarrassment. "You know how difficult it is to get bacon—"

Theo apologized and dug in with such gusto that they both had to laugh. Even Carrie, the cairn terrier, wagged her tail.

"She doesn't wag much. I guess she likes you." Claire was careful how she poured the coffee.

Theo leaned away, gave her more room than before.

"It's a beautiful day for a walk. That is, I usually walk Carrie. Would you like to come along?" Claire petted her terrier. "We usually walk up to the sycamores near Grain House."

"Isn't that near one of the ancient mounds? Second century; I've read in the guidebooks about your antiquities." Theo, though famished, stopped in the middle of a chew and watched her . . . her sparkling white blouse billowing as she petted her dog. She answered him without looking up—allowing him time, though she was unaware of such things, to peek with pounding heart at her young breast, to focus and caress with his famished eyes.

"I guess I'm just too used to Grain House to see it that way."

He coughed as the bun went down the wrong way, and he felt a warm surge through his body. "I would like to . . . very much." Was there too much inflection in his 'much'?

So they went to the sycamore grove.

The next day they left Carrie home and took an early bus toward Stromness, and Theo marveled at the view from the heights overlooking Scapa Flow.

Several destroyers were beached, but the battle cruisers had all sunk. He'd last seen them floating keel up. There was activity in the straits around Burray. Perhaps a salvage crew?

"That's Hoy." Claire was pointing south. "You should see Dwarfie Stone. It's supposed to be the oldest of the tombs."

They got off at Maeshowe and crawled through the four-foot-high opening of a 3,000-year-old priest-king's burial chamber. Once in the large domed vault, electric-lighted, the guide pointed out runic inscriptions by Viking vandals who had broken in during the Crusades. He snickered as he translated in musical rote: "Thorny was bedded. Helgi says so. . . . Ingigerd is the best. . . ."

Claire pretended not to listen.

Then they walked the mile to Stenness to look at the henge stones and the Ring of Brogar.

"Like a small Stonehenge," Theo marveled. Something compelled him to look at his pocket watch. He lined up the tiny digit 12 with the largest of the twenty-seven standing stones, all taller than a big man. "Something must have happened here." He laughed. "Perhaps it was a large clock of the seasons, you know, like a sundial. Probably set up to coincide with the solstices—"

"The whats?" Claire was trying.

"Solstices are the times of the year when the sun has no apparent motion, either northward or to the south . . ."

She smiled quizzically.

"It's also called Midsummer Night."

"Like the Bard?" She brightened. "The twenty-first of June or thereabouts. When *wild* things happen. All kinds of sacrifices . . ."

The twenty-seven stones turned into ships for Theo. Nose-down ships. Sinking on the twenty-first of this past June. A chill went through him. The High Seas Fleet in stone! The graveyard markers for *Friedrich*, for *König Albert*, *Moltke* . . . and his own *Königsberg* and all the rest . . . Altogether, he calculated from the layout, there must have been . . .

He looked at an information sheet. Sixty stones originally. Six divisions of the 360-degree circle. How many ships were on the bottom of the flow? He would go mad if there were exactly sixty.

"What's wrong, or are you getting messages from the past?"

"Sorry, Claire. It's nothing." Theo lied. He'd never experienced anything so consuming in his life.

They corresponded regularly. Claire bound Theo's letters in groups of twelve. One every month, with specially bought lilac ribbon.

He wrote about his father's shop and the more unusual watches and clocks that he worked on. He wrote about life in Germany and the party program of a Mr. Hitler from Munich. He explained the Kapp putsch and its failure and sent her a clipping photo of the mass Nazi demonstration he had attended while on a skiing trip to Garmisch by way of Munich.

She answered with news of her father's deteriorating condition and reminiscences of their excursions to the Island of Hoy and Skara Brae and the Earl's Palace at Birsay . . . and their first walk with Carrie to the sycamores and how Carrie still cocked her head cutely at the mention of Theo. But it was Hoy that she dwelled on since it was in a passageway of the Dwarfie Stone, with its air of mystery, that he first kissed her. Lightly on the cheek; an expedient of close quarters . . .

He'd ask about the Ring of Brogar because "it had done something to him," and she'd scour the libraries of Kirkwall and Stromness for information, then copy faithfully each word, date, and thought on the ruin and post them to him. She even sent him a chip from one of the fallen stones, which he had imbedded in ebony. It hung, along with her photograph, where he would see it upon waking every morning.

There was plenty to tell about Germany. In 1922 Walther Rathenau, statesman of Jewish decent, was brutally murdered. Theo's sister, Helga, was married to a Heidelberg graduate in pharmacy. Now there'd be no problems regarding time and pills. He described the practice of dueling and importance of proper scars and the university's new prohibition of fencing on its grounds and the opening of the old prison jail for offenders. Then came the Ludendorff putsch and Hitler's arrest.

Claire was fascinated by the stamps on Theo's letters. Numbers into the millions of marks. For one letter! He wrote her about wheelbarrows of paper marks to buy a pair of shoes.

She countered that the richest man in England was no longer the Duke of Devonshire but a shipowner by the name of John Ellerman. That the cessation of war had changed people for the better; they were kinder to children and animals. Even the town game of ba' seemed less ferocious on New Year's Day of 1923 than the year before. Of the 150 or more participants in this no-rules soccer game, only a few were injured badly enough to go to the hospital. She told about the radio her father had bought so they could listen to Stanley Baldwin's speeches.

Theo's brother-in-law had joined the part-time storm troopers, and Ezra Pound had become a Fascist.

In 1925 German children marched with swastika flags in Munich, Mussolini was unopposed, and Lenin was dead.

The next year Clive Robertson died in Kirkwall, and Theo Drahn sold his prize Breguet chronograph watch and bought a diamond ring. He left Heidelberg and became the proprietor of Robertson's shop and beloved husband of Claire.

Robertson & Drahn prospered and hired apprentices. Theo became a respected townsman and naturalized subject of the king. He played ba' on New Year's Day and became an expert at the dart board at the Toddy Pub in Finstown, where he would stop off every time he visited Brogar's standing stones.

Though at first they talked of having children, neither one complained when they didn't. Theo would take long walks by himself on the Orphir Road, with its ominous panoramic views of the flow and Hoxa Sound. He watched the salvage operations of Cox & Dank's Metal Industries Ltd. Particularly interesting was the patching of 700 openings on the battle cruiser *Hindenburg*, which took five months. Once floated with compressed air, she promptly sank again and remained on the bottom till 1930.

Claire had lost the bloom of youth and taken to the delicious fudge chocolate of a relative in Stromness. She fast became plump and was content to do the books of the business with her clackety adding machine. Theo grew a thin mustache to cover his dueling scar and was happy to take the new ivory Morris Garage sports car to Stromness for fudge after first stopping off at the Toddy for darts and Irish whisky with beer chasers. He took a fancy to Jenny, the barmaid, who fell for his ivory car and would go on wild full-moon rides along A966 to the Brogar Ring, paying "a reasonable fare" of such variations as Theo asked, "provided the top was up" and "there was no chance of *anything* happening."

When he was alone at Brogar, he would go into a trance, self-induced with the help of Jameson's whisky. One by one, in the midnight sun's glow, he would incant the names of the sunken High Seas Fleet ships and caress the stones until he had accounted for the entire fleet, which, indeed, he managed to equate in numbers to the 2,000-year-old megalithic array.

His imagination bounded into sacrificial orgies such as he'd read about in *The Golden Bough* and heard about from the old dart throwers of Finstown. At the apex of his trance he would imagine entering Jenny at all orifices on the sacrificial stone during a thunderstorm, cleaving her with a bronze ax, and planting her pieces among the stones' bases . . . then collecting her blood from the stone and flinging a haggis bag of it into the flow below Orphir's heights.

Then he would think about revenge for the forced unchivalrous demise of his fleet.

Jenny's hair was the color of almond and wafted the aroma of highland clover. Her young head rested back, eyes pleasantly closed, on the tan leather bucket seat of Theo's MG, hair splayed like a fan and the corners of her sweet mouth curled into a distant smile.

What ho, daughter of whisky! Theo had trouble keeping his eyes on the bumpy road. Yer in a classy vehicle now; bet yer parents never pictured you in such splendor. That's it, lass; stretch out yer glorious legs against the fire wall. Ah, thank you, lightning—Mr. Thor, or is it Jove?—for flashing on her lap with gossamer folds caressing her young belly. My God, child, I want to nuzzle into your breasts, those twin Fujiyamas from the gazetteer. Ye let me kiss ye on the cheek now and then for every ride ye get. Even allow me a quick pinch o' yer bottom, but when I touched yer tit once, ye screamed bloody murder. . . .

So t'night we're drivin' to Leith. Hah, that's a laugh. I only said so because ye were leavin' fer Canada to stay wi' yer aunt. Godforsaken Manitoba in the middle o' nowhere. Shouldna done it, I know, but ye teased me about maybe stayin' over in a fancy hotel in Aberdeen with me, an' seein' what might happen. Damn the grog I had t'night. But I played it right, damn ye. Ye said yer byes to the boys at the Toddy, an' ye went t' yer room and packed an' met me on the Stromness Road. Maybe I'll put ye on the boat to Scrabster; I've got m' reputation to think of . . . besides, I've got a big day on the links with some important people; buyers they are, for His Majesty's Navy. Curious things always seem to happen on the first day of summer.

Summer! Theo swerved and corrected. Good, she still slept. He looked at his luminous-numbered wristwatch: almost two in the morning. Above, the sky was torn with racing clouds against the eerie glow of the midnight sun in the west, over the ocean, the sea that would soon separate them. Rain pelted like pebbles on the convertible top, and he pushed the windshield wiper lever to its maximum speed.

Summer! A series of lightning bolts illuminated the landscape and Jenny's heaving Fujiyamas. 'Ow 'bout a wee kiss, he thought, in honor of midsummer's night and the kaiser's fleet? Why, I'll bet ye was still in primary school when we scuttled ten years ago tonight. I was only nineteen myself. What's say that I'm yer boyfriend? Theo turned off the main road and drove up to the Brogar Ring and shut the engine off.

The wind became the ancient Druid priest's chanting. Theo couldn't make out the words, but he was driven by them, possessed by them. He hovered over her, inhaling her youthful fragrance. Then he turned the dashboard light on. She was lighted with a green cast. He studied her sleeping body, ran his hands up and down it only an inch from her dress, her breasts, her legs. He put his mouth close to her breasts, then her belly, and he shivered excitedly. He felt himself. Hadn't had a cockstand like the present since he'd first met Claire, so many years ago.

Dare he do what he'd always wanted? Jenny had joked about the gearshift knob. It was lewd, she once said, and snickered. Perhaps that was what she wanted, too. Lightning flashed as he unbuttoned his trousers and freed the steed. Ah, even a young man would envy this one. It glistened green.

He took her slim right hand in his and curled it around his pulsing shaft. I must be dreaming, he thought. Then he spoke softly. "Now slowly up and down with me." Her hand was inside his. "That's it, my love. Easy . . . easy."

Her eyes blinked, and her lipsticked lips parted in horror as the realization set in. For a moment she was afraid to look; then she screamed and was drowned out by thunder. She tried to pull her hand away, but it was firmly stroking, both of Theo's hands holding her to the job. She bolted forward and tried to bite the hands only to become the recipient, albeit an inch off the mark, of a torrent of warm lava.

Theo, spent, relaxed his grip, and Jenny, screaming, bolted from the car, clawing at her violated face. She stumbled and ran madly among the standing megaliths, hiding first behind one and then the next away from the ivory automobile.

The Druid's chant was now clear to Theo. He reached behind the seat, under some gear, and drew out a canvas-wrapped object. The dull bronze of a ceremonial ax glinted green. He undid the canvas and leaped out into the rain. Was this the reason he'd bought the ax from a farmer who'd plowed it up near Loch Swannay? Similar artifacts in the library encyclopedia were dated 1500 B.C. and valued a thousand times the quid he'd paid.

Of course, this must be a dream. If it be, let's make the most of it. Theo ran in the drenching rain, looking behind each stone in turn, brandishing the ax before him. Then he saw her run for the woods. In his madness, he fell into a shallow ditch, and sputtering like a wetted fire, he tore his muddied shirt off and went after her again, snarling with the druidic chants of the elements: sac-ri-fice . . . sac-ri-fice . . .

Jenny ran and ran, then tripped over a fallen stone and lay, sobbing, in a fetal position, face in the wet grass. He was upon her like a bear. He grabbed her arm and turned her to face him. She saw the ax and screamed, but the sound didn't come. She whimpered and pleaded at his feet, and he ripped the dress from her back. She kicked and squirmed as he tore off her underwear and threw it with the wind.

He picked her up and half dragged her toward the mute stones of Brogar, ax high over his head and chanting over and over, "Sac-ri-fice . . . blood . . . honor of the High Seas Fleet . . ." She fought and bit him, and it only excited him more. Another cock-stand. He was proud of his prowess. Now he would have her—on Midsummer Night, when all kinds of *wild* things happen.

He set her down on a flat, fallen stone, and she tried to run away. This time he hit her in the face and forced her to lie flat. He put the ax down and forced her legs open, hitting her each time she screamed or resisted. One hand on her breast, squeezing and holding her writhing body down, he ravaged her, snorting like a wild boar, chewing between her flailing legs. Wet and salty like eating seaweed. He put a finger into her, and she arched into his mouth, and he bit her savagely. Suddenly the fight was out of her, and he drew her knees up and thrust deeply into her, chanting, "Sac-ri-fice . . . you bitch, you bitch."

"Please, I'll go. I won't tell anyone. Really." Her eyes were closed and her thin hands praying, like a medieval stone sarcophagus. "Please," implored Jennifer Kathleen Cotrell, "by all the saints that are holy. Please let me go. You won't have to worry; I'll be in Canada . . . . I swear by God, Oh, please, Mr. Drahn."

"Oh, please, Mr. Drahn is it now?" Theo took hold of the ax handle leaning on the stone. "It's too late for *that* now—you cock teaser." He buttoned up his trousers. "Jennifer."

"Sir." She trembled.

"What year is it?"

"Year of our Lord?" She fluttered her lashes.

"Year of our Lord, and shut your eyes." Theo

moved behind her reclining head and raised the ax high with both hands.

"Nineteen twenty-nine, sir.'" She had hope now.

"Fifteen hundred *before* Christ," he thundered.

"But, sir—" She opened her eyes.

And saw the ax descending.

Her brown eyes bulged, and she tried to scream.

No sound . . .

Theo saw a dart board with her turned-up nose as center.

Moltke was an eye; *Derfflinger,* her mouth. Then a fog descended. German ships metamorphosed into His Majesty's battlewagons: HMS *Renown* . . . HMS *Repulse* . . . the mighty *Hood*!

Then the ships became stones. In a circle.

Brogar Ring!

Blood spurting.

Catch the blood—

from the stone . . .

There! In a sheep's stomach.

Now tie the opening

and—THE BODY!

Rain and wind had wakened Theo.

He hacked methodically at the body. Next, he dug a deep hole slantwise under the flat rock, then deposited Jenny's pieces into it.

The storm was over.

Four thirty by his self-winding Harwood wristwatch!

Hurriedly he undressed and threw his clothing, including shoes and socks, into the wet hole, over the severed body. Then three feet of earth, and he stomped it down. Her dress, her underwear. All had been recovered and buried three feet under.

Theo put on fresh clothes and golfing shoes out of his suitcase. Then he drove south and along the flow to a vantage overlooking the anchorage. He put a rock into the bloody sheep bag and flung it into the harbor. It sank, oozing red.

Then he rinsed the ax and drove toward Kirkwall.

Once home, Theo unbelted Jenny's steamer trunk from the rack over the back bumper and carried it carefully into his cellar. It would be all right in the cellar, near his workshop. After all, Claire never ventured into the cellar. Rheumatism and damp air, you know. He wanted something to remember Jenny by.

Besides, Theo was curious about the intimate personal effects—panties, bras, and who knows what—of voluptuous young ladies. And shoes! He liked girls' shoes.

Especially patent leather ones, with buckles.

The next day, on the Stromness golf course, he played as if nothing had happened. Indeed, Theo told himself it was only a dream. And he, save for nightmares, convinced himself.

In 1929 the barmaid Jenny Cotrell just *disappeared.* The dart players all agreed that she'd gone to Canada—as she'd said many times she'd do. Soon there was a new barmaid, a younger one. Prettier and blonder!

In the pubs they discussed the horrid pornography of those writers Joyce and D. H. Lawrence from samples that appeared in the Orcadian rotogravure supplements and nodded when the government took steps. They derided the distortions and excesses, the life-styles of art, theater, and dissonant BBC music. They took Wodehouse into their homes and left Waugh in the libraries and scoffed at Trotsky. The Orcadians raised chickens and Black Angus beef to Ramsay MacDonald's refrain—"Up and up; on and on . . ."—as the Depression descended on the Orkneys as well as on Oklahoma. Two million unemployed on the "sceptred isle"! The American loans had stopped. Tariffs rose on the Continent, and Britain had no choice but to acquiesce. The Liberal party foundered, and so did free trade and the gold standard. Pounds sterling it became. Hunger marches were staged, and the hand of socialism reached across the Strait of Dover.

In 1933 Hitler was maneuvered into power, not in the least part by chameleon members of the old governing classes. No dictator had ever before been so much desired.

Dietrich Drahn sold his business and moved to Switzerland before the Nazis found out some embarrassing facts about his lineage. He died shortly after, his will providing well for the surviving family.

Theo leased a small building and produced timepieces and invested in the Highland Distillery above Kirkwall. One of the by-products of this last venture was the occasional company of its former owner, Mr. W. G. Grant, who'd become a prominent excavator and authority of Orkney's Neolithic treasures. He had built, for his pleasure, a scale model of the Brogar Ring to support a theory that it may have been a gigantic sundial.

When the Germans demonstrated their technological prowess in Spain, Theo was secretly pleased, as were many Englishmen who detested the dirty rabble of the workers' organizations. He was an adherent of Houston Stewart Chamberlain's philosophy of Nordic racial superiority.

With the Nazi march into the Rhineland, a glimmer of pride rose within him. Germany, protector of the West against Soviet communism.

In March of 1938 *Anschluss* destroyed a plebiscite for Austria. Then Sir Neville and Munich. Then Czechoslovakia.

And the pogrom of November: *Kristallnacht.*

The firm of Robertson & Drahn was given an order for chronographic watches by the Royal Navy. Theo bought a mint ivory 4½-liter Bentley, complete with Roots blower and Van den Plas coachwork.

For the yearly pacification of rotund Claire, they went to Aberdeen, car and all, first by way of car ferry to Scrabster, then, after taking the Thurso Road south across Caithness to Latheron, on the magnificent coastal highroad, along the North Sea past Dornoch Firth and around to Inverness, where they stopped for famous finnan haddie at a tavern on the river.

The splendid vehicle next pulled up at a prehistoric stone circle at the hamlet of Daviot near Inverurie. Past three on the afternoon of June 21! Sun cast long shadows from the standing stones upon the gently sloping green to the north.

Theo felt a strange elation at being alone with Claire for the first time in years. He rummaged under the jump-seat tonneau canvas for his camera. Claire was reclining on one of the fallen stones, eyes closed in the sun: a fat lizard swathed in pinkish taffeta. He felt a familiar shape, wrapped in cloth and tied securely. The ceremonial bronze ax! He gripped it and watched Claire stretching and cooing in the sun.

Writhing on the rock. The Neolithic ceremonial rock . . . The sacrificial altar? The Druids' voices again. Yes, it was like that other night . . . with Jenny Cotrell. Theo unwrapped the ax, put it under his jacket, and walked over to his wife. He looked around and, satisfied, circled around her stone and stood behind her arm-propped head. Slowly he raised the ax with both hands. It would be a neat cleft, dead center of her forehead at the hairline. Her eyes flickered, but she didn't see the blade over her head. Theo faltered. It was then that he heard the motor of another car. He stealthily rewrapped the ax and opened the bellows camera. His wife obliged with a coy smile as she posed on the megalith.

Aberdeen was only an hour's drive away. They would stay at the Station Hotel because it had a fine restaurant and Claire felt that the highest-priced hotel was always the best. Theo noted in his guidebook that it was close to the waterfront and planned to take a walk after dinner. Alone.

ONE

"You sure now that you didna win th' Lonsdale Trophy, Mr. Drahn—did I pronounce it right?" Sandy Macpherson plucked his darts disconsolately out of the riddled board.

"One more game? The little lady will be wondering where I am." Theo smacked his lips on the whisky glass, then set for his first throw.

"Not mine. She's glad to be rid o' me." Sandy sat wearily on a stool near the bar. Rain patted on the front window around the green neon sign that proclaimed the establishment, off Blaikie's Quay, to be Jack's.

"Thought of entering the Lonsdale, but living in the Orkneys . . ." Theo opened with a double twenty. At the mention of Orkney a bearded seaman rose from his booth, leaving his partner, and watched the dart game from a closer vantage. Theo won again, then drained his beer and paid his part of the bill.

"Might I buy a whisky for an Orcadian?" The offer came in a thick German accent. It was almost more an *order*. Theo felt an automatic response. He clicked the heels of his mind, then sat down at the dark wood booth next to a young seaman at the behest of the elder.

"This is my son, Kurt. I'm Gerhardt. Gerhardt

Graeff." The young man toasted nonchalantly with his foam-rimmed pint of Belhaven Light, then doused his blond mustache into it.

"Drahn here; D-R-A-H-N. Call me Theo." Graeff . . . Graeff. He pondered the name.

The bearded sailor motioned for the barmaid. "Give my friend Theo a double Jameson's."

"But how did you know?" Theo lit a Players.

"Wouldn't have, except that you are such a marksman with darts—with an accent that's familiar to me. South German?"

"Close. Heidelberg."

"And when I heard 'Orkneys' "—Gerhardt chuckled —"I made it a point to watch your bottle. Irish whisky, German, marksman, and Orkneys!" He downed his Steinhäger and followed with his pint. "I'm originally from Nuremberg. Klaus attends the university there; he's a deckie on my trawler for the summer."

"German trawler?" Theo was confused.

"I fish for profit, and there's more money here. Besides"—Gerhardt tamped his short meerschaum—"travel broadens."

"There's only one other German boat in Aberdeen out of three hundred trawlers." Kurt waved smoke away from his eyes.

"He's already homesick."

"I understand. Nuremberg is—an unusual city these days."

"It's very *exciting*. . . ." Kurt's eyes blazed.

"If I'm not too inquisitive, what is your interest in the Orkneys?" Theo held his whisky up to the petal-shaded light bulb on the paneled wall, then looked at his watch and shrugged as he thought of Claire.

"Been through Scapa Flow many times, past few years. Better passage in winter than Pentland Firth. Those nor'easters off the sea are murder through the firth. . . ." The word sent a shudder through Theo. "Best way is in through Hoy and hug the mainland after Scapa Bay, then kiss St. Mary's village and set course out of Holm Sound right off Rose Ness or Burray Ness depending on whether you're going off Norway or into the Skagerrak—"

"Father has seen some—"

"Last month I picked up Kurt at the station in Edinburgh. Saw the sights, as it were. Tell Herr Drahn what we saw in Rosyth. . . ."

"The destroyers—all lined up—"

"*Nein! . . . Der Schlachtkreuzer—*"

"*Derfflinger. Ja, Vati—*"

The sudden sharp staccato of German turned Scots' heads in the surrounding booths, and Kurt lowered to an excited whisper close to Theo's ear.

"My English is not good." Kurt continued in German. "The twenty-seven-thousand-ton battle cruiser *Derfflinger* was floating upside down next to a dry dock. As long as a city block, a rusting, dirty keel, covered with mussels and thick barnacles. The seaweed stems were as thick as your wrist; had to be chopped away with axes. The metal was eaten through in places. Such a proud ship it had been"—Kurt slammed his stein down on the table—"and now they're going to break it up. We looked inside. Fish were trapped and swimming in the upside-down cabins. To make matters worse, there was a tin house built on the keel. We had such beautiful ships—"

"You'd think that Kurt had been a sailor aboard the cruiser, yet it went down before he was born."

"If war came again, I would join the submarine service. I'd get even with–"

"Careful, Kurt. We're surrounded." Graeff laughed. Theo stirred uneasily, looked around sheepishly, then grinned.

"Maybe I'll stop and look at it. We're driving to Edinburgh anyway. My God, look at the hour . . ."

"Were you in the war?" Kurt asked suddenly.

"Yes, but only for a short time. It was practically over. I was about your age."

"The High Seas Fleet? You were probably in the Navy since you now live in the Orkneys."

Theo nodded politely and thanked Graeff for the drink. He offered money for the ritual round but was waved off by Graeff, who relighted his meerschaum pensively.

TWO

On the following day Theo drove to St. Andrews, where he registered with Claire at fashionable Rusack's on the Links. They lunched at a greens restaurant, and as promised, he gave her ample cash and traveler's checks to squander in the resort shops full of nightgowns, summer jumpers, and fancy cakes.

Scarcely had the cab borne Claire out of the hotel grounds when he skipped across Links Road and cut through the green toward that venerable gray-stone building known worldwide as the Royal and Ancient Golf Club of St. Andrews. Claire had agreed to meet him back at their rooms at six.

It was only one. Five hours without her!

Clapping his hands in glee, he strode up the granite steps and into the Silence Room, a sort of museum of golf that he'd read about. Momentarily distracted by the charms of a group of distaff graduates of the adjacent university, wearing scarlet gowns, he paid homage to the glistening exhibits in a glass display case embedded in an old wall.

Silver golf club, with the inscription "1754. First St. Andrews trophy club given by noblemen & gentlemen being admirers of the ancient and healthful exercise of the Golf."

Then there was the gold medal given by William

IV in 1837 which officially proclaimed the club as "Royal and Ancient," but spelled "golf" as "golph."

Theo winked at one of the girls, and her group scurried out lest he be an official of this most mannish club. He felt a surge of primeval vigor that led him to the bar.

Most of the plush barstools were vacant. And why not? A fine afternoon to be out *there*. Ah, but he wanted to play a round. But no partner! Boldly—and he surprised himself—he pulled up a stool next to a man in uniform. Possibly the chap was a transient and was also without contacts. Only a few hours, and he would certainly make the best of it. Theo pretended his stool choice was determined by the location of a tray of cheese and crackers. He then ordered—so as not to seem queer—a Scotch and soda. What a strange uniform, he thought. Certainly not one of us. He knew it was naval—but thank God it wasn't German! Enough at the pub in Aberdeen.

The officer was youngish, blond, and athletic-looking. A bottle of Danish Tuborg beer stood on the polished wood bar before him. He had just put down a copy of the Dundee *Record*. Theo couldn't help glancing at the front-page picture: German soldiers goose-stepping past admiring townsfolk. He put on his half-frame glasses and strained at the caption: "CONDOR LEGION RETURNS FROM SPAIN."

"Pardon me, sir"—the man had a Scandinavian accent—"would you have the correct time?" He shook his wristwatch irritably and listened to its ticking.

Godsend! Theo, with a flourish, pulled out his conversation-piece antique pocket watch and held it in front of the officer. An unusual watch, it featured a miniature sculptured golf caddie holding a putting iron in one hand and a driving wood in the other. To the right was an arc of finely engraved numbers, 1 to 12; to the left, a minutely calibrated arc reading, top to bottom, 0 to 60. The officer blinked in amazement.

"Watch closely," Theo said proudly. He pressed a button, and both of the caddie's arms swung briskly up, indicating the minute and the hour—accompanied by a chime.

"In Sweden we say *blandning*. It's something more than your 'dazzling.' It includes 'charming' or 'delightful.' And how very appropriate. Collectors' item?"

"Are you an enthusiast?"

"Yes, of golf, but, as you can see, not of wristwatches."

"In your country, in Stockholm to be precise, there's a famous horological society."

"Yes, the Watchmakers' Guild. I'm from a town north of Stockholm." The Swede extended his hand. "My name is Peter Nielson."

"Drahn, here, Theo." He spelled it as usual. "I'm here on a holiday—from the Orkneys." He folded his glasses and tucked them back into a leather case."

Nielson sputtered over his beer. "Excuse. It went down the wrong way. You have to keep after it?" He pointed at the watch as it lay in front of Theo.

"As a matter of fact, I do. I'm a watchmaker."

"Then perhaps you could recommend a watch for me to buy when I go to Edinburgh. This one has given up the ghost."

"Too bad I don't have my tools." Theo squinted closely at Nielson's wristwatch. "You might take a look at a Harwood self-winder while you're in Britain. A few swings, and you're all wound."

"Yes, I've heard of it. I will, thank you."

"But then you may want a chronograph since you're in the service." Theo leaned over the bar and looked at Nielson's service insignia pinned to his jacket.

"Submarine branch. Just returned from America, where I was an observer. I'm on a sort of holiday before the next assignment. A British officer was kind enough to give me a few names here."

"Have you played yet?"

"Arrived yesterday. I'm a bit rusty, so . . ."

"Would you go a round with another rusty duffer? I'm here only for the day—and my wife's shopping."

"What better reason, *Theo?*" They both laughed.

"I've got clubs in my car."

"Fine, I'll get us on Old Course, and we'll meet in the locker room in fifteen minutes. Anything you need?" Nielson shook his watch. "If it lasts fifteen minutes." Theo was already through the door.

During the game they exchanged stories and a few jokes about women. Both were afraid that the other was a better golfer. By the back nine they'd accepted each other as fairly equal. Nielson edged ahead with a par on the Heathery In and a respectable five on the thirteenth. He was certainly headed for a 95, no matter what.

Theo, two strokes behind, bounced one off a tree on the fourteenth, and it rolled onto the green instead of going over the stone wall, turning a sure nine into a respectable seven. On the infamous seventeenth he lofted his fourth shot into the road bunker, but it miraculously squirted out, against all rules of physics, and came to rest inches from the most famous hole in golfdom. He carded a 94, one stroke ahead of the astonished Swede.

They took showers in the locker area, and Theo couldn't help marveling at Peter's physique. He tried not to look but, like several other men present, was amazed at the size of Nielson's member, especially in relation to his own, which hung limp and inconsequential in the mirror over the basins. Of course, he's ten years younger, Theo thought, and not a child of the century like me. It seemed that Nielson was oblivious to the attention and just went about as if he were alone. Theo wondered how well the Swede did with the ladies, especially the hungry ones in Britain.

Theo ordered Scotch again. Straight this time. He was flustered and wondered why. Surely it wasn't—he wasn't. No, it was just that he'd been so insulated since Jennifer . . . what with Claire asking questions all the time. . . .

Nielson tantalized Theo with his accounts of sexual orgies after sauna baths in northern Sweden. "We were taught by the Finnish girls. I loved to be birched by a beautiful woman, so much so that they called me the equivalent of Birch Boy."

He found himself talking about his service in the German Navy. Was it some kind of primeval kinship with the blond Viking image that loosened him? Was it the Scotch whisky? He wasn't used to Scotch whisky. Were the ancient Druids directing him again? He noticed that Nielson was still drinking beer. . . .

"Nosirr, ya wouldn' get *me* on a submarine." Theo was slurring his words and made special efforts to correct the fault. "We're driving down to Rosyth tomorrow to see the *Derfflinger*. Battle cruiser, floating upside down, I hear. My ship was anchored near her in Scapa Flow. Proud ship she was, back in nineteen; now she's waitin' to be broken up for scrap and melting down. . . ."

Nielson had stopped drinking. He ordered another for Theo. His eyes narrowed, and he searched for ways to keep Theo talking.

"You could have fooled me; why, you're as British as anyone I know. But living in the Orkneys . . . *Brrr*. So desolate and unsheltered." He lit a cigarette. "I wonder how those sailors can take it, day after day . . ."

"Oh, you mean the fleet? Nice fellows, all so young. We do have some nice wenches to keep the fleet busy." Theo felt dizzy and suggested a game of darts. Always a good way to clear the head. Would have to, before meeting Claire–in an hour.

"You get more watches to fix when the big boats are in, I'll bet." Nielson threw a center fifty.

"More than I can handle. *Courage, Renown, Repulse* . . . they all come to Theo Drahn with their watches. . . ."

After ordering a last drink, Nielson thought fast. "Nothing like an impregnable anchorage for good sleeping."

"What?"

"I mean Scapa Flow."

"It ain't so impreg–" Theo was drunk. He licked a bar pencil and scrawled a map on a paper napkin. "You come in here, by Rose Ness, and ye hug the coast til yer past St. Mary's. There's fifteen feet at high tide, and more with a good moon. . . ." Theo drew an erratic dotted line.

"But the blockships—"

"They're out farther; ya gotta almost touch th' beach. . . ."

"So you said." Nielson acted nonchalant. "By the way, Theo, what was your last name again?"

Theo scribbled it below the map and added "Kirkwall." Then he excused himself to go to the bathroom.

While Theo was gone, Nielson dabbed at his mouth with a paper napkin and stuffed it into his jacket pocket. He was practicing darts when Theo returned.

They played one more game. Theo was still dizzy. The dart board spun crazily each time he threw. "I suppose if I were an admiral . . ." His mind fused the map he'd subliminally held in his brain with the circular dart board. He envisioned the High Seas Fleet on the board . . . then the stones of Brogar's Ring in place of the numbers . . . then the British fleet: *Courage, Renown,* and *Repulse*. He threw his last three darts so hard that he had to jiggle them out.

They bade each other farewell, but Theo stayed at the bar. He ordered black coffee and bought a bag of strong mints.

THREE

Observer Corporal Horst Pfeiffer leaned forward and tapped Flight Sergeant Alfred Kittel's shoulder. The pilot looked back and nodded approval as Pfeiffer pointed excitedly downward. The pontooned *Arado* gunned its BMW radial engine and banked over the teeming fleet: an infinity of ships.

A thousand feet below, on the calm, summer waters of the fickle Atlantic, a phalanx of slim white wakes were headed toward the afternoon sun. Seven gray stilettos sliced effortlessly through the shimmering green sea. Pfeiffer's heart strummed with pride at the sight. The famous Flotilla Weddigen!

To the north of the surface-running submarines, a column of hulking battlewagons trailed low clouds of steam: *Deutschland, Admiral Scheer, Gneisenau, Graf Spee,* and *Scharnhorst.* To the south were the heavy cruisers led by *Blücher,* then the fast light cruisers of the *Leipzig* class. Destroyers of the *Roeder* and Z31 classes steamed lithely on the horizons, covering the heavy units.

The corporal pushed back his goggles and slid the plastic canopy forward as the reconnaissance craft dipped closer to the submarines. He pressed his Zeiss 10 by 80 binocular eyecups snug and focused on one of the VIIB U-boats.

A large white "47" was painted on the side of the conning tower. The other boats in the line were in numerical sequence, but 49 and 50 were missing. In a few seconds the young airman would get a close look. As a child Horst was torn between two loves: Von Richthofen and Weddigen, aces of the Great War; one in the sky and the other, underseas. Back home in Karlsruhe, a model of the Baron's Red Fokker triplane hung over his bed, while Weddigen's *U-9,* which had sunk three British armored cruisers within one hour, reposed on a mahogany stand on the windowsill. Secretly he admired submariners more than fliers. It took more courage to serve aboard a U-boat.

The *Arado* swooped in close, and the corporal focused on the horseshoe-shaped conning tower. Almost directly above it, he focused on the captain, the officer under the sparkling white cap. In that instant, the man in the white cap looked up, a broad smile on his elfish face, and waved. Pfeiffer spun and refocused. The others were also waving, the aft skywatch, too.

"Engelbert"—Kapitänleutnant Günther Prien chided his first watch officer and exec, Oberleutnant Endrass, as Oberleutnant zur See Amelung von Varendorff looked on, amused—"I'm glad that was not the enemy."

"I'm glad we're not at war"—Endrass rubbed his pocked right cheek and squinted—"yet."

"Sir." Forward lookout Gustav Werder shielded his eyes and checked his binocular lenses. "Do you think there's going to be a war?"

The commander puckered his rabbit mouth. "Son, I think our leaders will do the right thing." He turned and watched the battle cruisers. Soon the *Bismarck* would be commissioned. He had taken a look at her, tied up at Hamburg. The latest radar was being fitted on the behemoth. At 45,000 tons she was the biggest battlewagon afloat in the world. Painting gangs had been winched all about her hull and structures and given her a dazzling camouflage that resembled huge black and yellow corporal's stripes. Finally the German Navy would have fifteen-inch guns; most major navies had had fifteen-inchers during the Great War, twenty years earlier.

Scharnhorst was bringing up the rear of the column, allowing the older boats to set the speed. She displaced only 35,000 tons, and her main guns were only eleven-inch. Could she stand up against the *King George* class with their fifteen-inchers? She was rated three knots faster than her potential adversaries. That would help.

Prien thought about the *Arado* that had buzzed them. It was now just a speck, headed back toward its mother ship. It seemed primitive that this plane would land on the water and require its ship to stop and winch her aboard and onto the catapult track. Not that other navies didn't do the same, but other navies had aircraft carriers, could launch a swarm of dive bombers and fighters in the middle of an ocean. The British had four carriers and had started construction on six more.

The *Ark Royal* had just finished her shakedown cruise in the Mediterranean. She could launch sixty aircraft as well as several catapult planes.

And the *German Navy*? Zero, except for slow, clumsy pontooned craft. And why? Reichsmarschall Göring would have to answer that. Would have to explain to all the next of kin, as well as to the Führer, why Germany did not have any carriers—after one of our ships was torpedoed by an airplane in the middle of the ocean; explain why there were no German fighter pilots to tangle with the enemy. So he was an ace, had shot down twenty enemy planes, but the world had changed since 1914. He had no use for the Navy. Prien recalled the story about Göring aboard the cruiser *Königsberg* on similar maneuvers just two years earlier: Göring got seasick and called a launch to take him ashore. Probably had stuffed himself at the captain's mess. *Ugghh*! Revolting! A junior officer aboard the cruiser had nicknamed him *Reichsfischfuttermeister!* So the vain, fat one liked the Navy even less now.

Then Hitler and his tight circle were from the mountains in Bavaria. No maritime comprehension. Göring told Hitler that any future war would be won in the *air*. What about the air over the *water*?

So Hitler decided that since air power would win, he'd cut back on submarine production and impress the world with huge battleships. Word was that the new "Z" plan called for six H-class battleships of 60,000 tons each. The *Bismarck* cost about 200 million marks already! And only ninety new U-boats! Seventy-five U-boats could be built for the same price as one of those H monsters! And more yet. Fifteen new battle cruisers of over 20,000 tons each!

Prien conceded that four aircraft carriers, included in the plan, were better than none. But a carrier took at least two years to build, and the "Z" plan target date was 1947. At the latest, 1948! That meant two carriers by 1944, if all went well—and why should the first carriers function well? They'd never built one. Besides, they didn't have any airplanes on the drawing board. Special designs had to be worked up: folding wings, carrier landing equipment, and so on. Prien shook his head in disbelief at the enormousness of the undertaking.

Submarines were what they knew best. He checked the compass repeater before him. Due west. To port and starboard, the flotilla glided unrelentingly toward the lowering sun. The best submersibles the world had ever produced, and the most experienced crews. For a moment Prien's imagination ran away. He saw the boats as a phalanx of Roman sea chariots, officers and lookouts silhouetted against the sky, charging full speed across the arena, and spurred on by the ovations of hundreds of thousands. Like at the Berlin Olympic Games in '36. *Sieg Heil . . . SIEG HEIL . . . SIEG HEIL . . .* Weddiger Flotilla . . .

"Half ahead both." Endrass's command startled Prien out of his reverie. "We've got to let the destroyer screen across," he added.

"Very good, Bert. Anything more on the wireless?" The commander knew that the message had to have been radioed and relayed up to the bridge. He hadn't noticed any visual signal.

"Only that we've just crossed fifteen West at fourteen-seven, about."

There were instant cheers from the bridge watch. This was the longitudinal meridian that started the western zone of naval operations, and as such, it meant a 50 percent pay increase for service time.

"With over ten thousand men involved, I don't think the admiral will stay too long." Prien's eyes twinkled. He hadn't been this far west since he'd got his seaman's papers in 1926 and pulled his first real duty on the *Pfalzburg,* a rusty freighter bound for South America.

"If we stay on this course," Varendorff bantered, "we can go ashore and see the World's Fair."

"You can go to the fair, Amelchen. I'll go to Yorkville and find me a nice German American girl." Endrass tilted his cap to a rakish angle.

"Ah, the sailor's dream: a bride in every port," The captain chuckled. "I get more of a kick out of a good naval exercise. . . ."

"Well, of course. You're *married,* sir—I mean . . ." The bridge watch stifled their amusement and looked seaward.

"I walked right into that, Bert." Prien laughed heartily, and the rest joined in.

It was that kind of boat.

FOUR

LT P NIELSON BOQ TRANSIENT 12 KM KIEL: 14/8/39 RETURN STOCKHOLM TEMP LEAVE MRS NIELSON ILL LUFTHANSA ARRANGED

Peter Friedrich Nielson studied his reflection in the rectangular port glass of the JU-52 trimotor airliner. The engines were sputtering, and the corrugated aluminum skin vibrated in concert. A gasoline truck sped over his squarish chin. In the bright summer sky a converted Dornier with swastikas on its twin tails banked into his high fair forehead. Peter's flaxen hair was thin and merged with his face, giving him a striking radiance when he took his service cap off. His mouth was tight, but wide, and the corners were slightly upturned: a permanent semismile. He tried to picture Lars Nielson, the father he'd never met, the four-masted schooner mate who had married his mother when she was only sixteen, then sailed away, never to return to the seaport of Umeå in Sweden's northern province of Lappland.

The wheel chocks were pulled, and the "Auntie Ju" spun toward the main runway and taxied across the smooth blacktop.

There were frocked civil servants jabbering in many languages, bemedaled Admiralty officers, and a few gross business types. The pilot announced that the weather was fair in Stockholm, they'd be flying at 3,000 meters, and oxygen would be available for those who requested it. The 800-kilometer flight would take about three hours and would arrive in time for dinner. A muscular stewardess clumped through the aisle, checking the safety belts, and the old Junkers strained its engines and took off.

Peter looked down at the harbor as the plane banked into its northeasterly course. He spotted the famed Germaniawerft shipbuilding yards and could just make out a submarine on the ways, ready for launching.

At 1,000 meters the low coastline of southern Denmark was already visible. It was only 75 kilometers from Kiel, three hours by steamer. Peter settled back in his seat. He'd brought a book, *The Riddle of the Sands,* but it lay on his lap, and he couldn't help looking back at the curious events of his twenty-five years. . . . Was this *it*? How seriously ill would he find her? She was only forty-two. But to be called home by his commanding officer . . . She *did* always cough a lot. Smoked too much. Inhaled yet. He shook his head and breathed deeply. At least he was in perfect health—except for that minor, ridiculous affliction that had prevented him from attending the Naval Academy at Flensburg. "Paranosmia" was the medical term for the state of confusing one smell with another. For instance, the patient might sense the tartness of an apricot when, in fact, he was sniffing a rose. Rare malady and, in Peter's case, very transient. He remembered only two instances in his life when he was aware of it, and both were after the examination. Perhaps it was the exam that did it!

The electric-shock machine . . . Peter was seventeen when he took the tests. They ran for two weeks just before Christmas, seven years ago, 1932. It was snowing.

Two eager applicants gripped opposite ends of a steel bar. Thirty others were waiting their turn. The psychologists sat mutely, pens poised over complex ruled forms with myriad little boxes and circles. Then the current was turned on. The applicants could not let go once the current flowed. Pens dipped onto the forms, scratched busily. The amperage was increased. One of the boys screamed. Peter wanted to, but bit his lip and swallowed the blood. He remembered the smell of electrical sparking and sizzling; then the pain subsided, and he thought he'd sensed a deep forest musk that increased as the current got stronger. When the eternity was over, the musk was gone, and he smelled the pungent electricity once more.

Then the vision, hearing, and other senses, the odor and fragrance test . . . A thick-spectacled scientist-doctor hissed at one of Peter's responses, then mumbled to himself and thumbed through a ponderous book. He jotted something down on his forms, then sniffed at one of the sample vials.

"Interesting," was all he said, and finished his examination without another word.

In early January a letter arrived in Umeå. Ulla Nielson waited expectantly as her son carefully opened the official-stamped envelope. There was no question in her mind that Peter had excelled in the examination. After all, he'd attended the best secondary school in Germany and had graduated early, in an accelerated program for gifted students. He was captain of the sailing team and had been offered a university scholarship in Berlin. He held the letter up to the lamp. It was noon, but the sun was only partially visible over the icy Baltic.

"Oh, no." Peter flung the letter onto the lavish Kashan purple and madder bird-tree rug.

So he went to Berlin and studied engineering, with a possible future in the development of Sweden's mineral resources. His mother had been adamant about her "contacts" in mining, especially a "friend" in Kiruna that he would eventually meet. After an enviable university record, which included leading his 1936 Olympic sailing team to the 6.5-meter championship, he entered compulsory service as a midshipman in the Royal Swedish Navy.

The question of paranosmia never came up, and he applied for submarine service. In November '38 he was given his first assignment—on the new *Sjolejonet* class 600-ton boat *Seahound.* The following March Peter Nielson was chosen to go to the United States as a naval observer for the submarine arm.

He'd made his report, a bit early, as a result of the *Sebago* sinking. His recommendations to develop a diving bell similar to the one designed by Commander Ben Mount that had saved half the crew, as well as the CO and himself, were being acted upon.

After a few days in Scotland he went home and was reassigned to Kiel as observer.

He unfolded the telegram and reread it: "14 August 1939 . . ."

Rudi Grunberger said there'd be war by late August or early September. He'd visited Uncle Helmut and Cousin Karl. His mother's family. Eckhardt. Berliners! But she had run away with a Swedish sailor when she was barely sixteen. She'd had enough of her father's puritanism. She liked the wildness of the Northmen, the outdoors, the deep, brooding forests. And she looked like a Viking. It was true; the earliest family records went back to the eleventh century —on her mother's side. Björnson, Child of the Bear.

Who was the Bear? Probably a sea raider from the Ume and Vindet rivers that flowed south past the town of Umeå into the inland sea. A bear from the deep forests of birch and scotch pine, where oak could not survive. The land of lichen, bear, wolf, elk, and the arctic fox. The land of the lemming hordes that descended from the snowcaps of Sulitjelma to march to the sea—only to be devoured by the owl, by the golden eagle, and by wild dogs.

Ulla Björnson went back to her ancestral land.

With Lars.

Then Lars went to sea,

and left his name for Peter.

And Ulla worked as a *statare,* a person without property. Lower than those who eked out a living from their stony land.

But Ulla was a beauty. She soon got a job as a domestic in the booming industrial capital of the north. Kiruna, 500 miles north of Umeå in the heart of Lappland.

Peter lived his first years in the shadows of Luossavaara and its brother, Malmberget, the "Mountains of Iron Ore." Then he suddenly had to leave his friends Birgit and Erik. And they moved to Stockholm, to a fancy pink house. It had central heating. He didn't have to gather birch for kindling anymore. He sorely missed his elkhound, Rokig, and his mother promised to take him to the zoo every Sunday to make up for the dog.

The loudspeaker blared. "Look to the right, we're passing over Copenhagen." Several naval officers leaned into the windows. The stocky stewardess poured coffee for the pilot, then carried the pot aft, looking right and left. Peter hailed her.

As he swallowed the thin, lukewarm liquid, he thought of the gallery. They lived above it . . . until he went off to private school in the Alps near Munich. The store was stocked with dinnerware and lightwood furniture. There were strange, contorted drawings and sculptures. There were coffee afternoons with colorful, tasty cakes. Rolls-Royces and Daimlers were parked outside. At night there was laughter and shouting from the exercise room in the cellar. He wasn't allowed to go into the cellar. It was locked. One had to have a special key. One day he found a key, so he sneaked downstairs and looked. There was a room with slot machines and a whisky bar. Another room was all in redwood, with seats and a box of stones. It was moist and hot from the night before. There was a room full of ice barrels. Peter didn't know what to make of it. He was eleven. He started up the stairs and noticed something strange in a locker. The door was slightly open. He tugged at it, and a barrage of birch branches fell upon him. As he was putting them back in the locker, he drew back in fright. On the inside of the locker door hung a black whip . . . and shiny black leather shorts with metal studs embedded around a hole. . . .

Peter ran, horrified and frightened of being caught. He dropped the funny key where he'd found it, went to his room, and crawled under the bedcovers.

Eventually he began to wonder about his mother. They weren't rich like some of the fancy-named boys in his classes. He was not a Saxe-Coburg, or a Hohenlohe-Langenberg, or a Zitzewitz und Knoll, yet they *always* had everything they needed or wanted. He'd seen the books. Very few sales; certainly too few for such sumptuous living. Ulla would spend time at Mediterranean resorts, follow the sun and have a tan in winter. She'd send postcards to his school from exotic lands.

When, at fifteen, he asked her, she told him that she had a secret benefactor, a sort of rich uncle. The gallery was "an investment."

So he stopped asking; he parried the inquiries of classmates and became immersed in his studies, avoiding idle pursuits and curious chatter.

He never got up the nerve to go into the cellar again. During semester breaks he would spend a day or two at home, then the rest of the time at a friend's house in the university town of Uppsala, an hour's train ride north, where he could use the famous library and study for his exams.

One Christmas, when his mother was in Cairo, "attending a business convention," Peter was invited to stay at a classmate's schloss, high in the Bavarian Alps overlooking the Chiemsee.

It was a stone nest of young Nazi-oriented students. The classmate's parents had gone to Berlin for the holidays and left the castle fully staffed for the enjoyment of a group of "picked" students. There were girls, daughters of party functionaries, with chaperones. There were Hitler Youth leaders.

There were no Jews.

One evening certain girls slipped past their chaperones and lit candles to read the little maps they'd been given at dinner earlier. It had been a strenuous day of skiing and communion with the great German outdoors.

Now it was time to commune with the Teutonic gods and the future of the Third Reich. The girls, dressed in white medieval gowns, stole quietly down the stone stairs into the dungeon behind the armory. It was cold and dank, but there were stalwart young men posted at intervals with blazing torches to help them on. Then they were met by a youth leader and escorted into a warm antechamber, where they quickly huddled around a huge, crackling fire. Originally the armorer's workroom, it had been converted into a comfortable living area complete with bear rugs and animal-skinned couches. On the heavy-planked walls hung colorful banners: Franco-Prussian, Afrikaner, Great War . . . and Nazi. There were tenth-century helmets and crossed broadswords, chain mail, Byzantine wall carpets, a tattered naval ensign from Tirpitz's Jutland flagship, paintings of Moltke, of Hindenburg and Ludendorff . . . of Kaiser Wilhelm . . . Mackensen with his skull and crossbones embedded in a high fur hat. There were photos of Krupp's Big Bertha *Kanone* and the Condor Stukas over Spain. . . .

Peter couldn't take it in all at once. Powerful marching music on the gramophone. Now a change of record: light Bavarian folk music. A girl got up from her couch and started to dance toward an armbanded young man. Peter, like the other men, was wearing, as prescribed, Bavarian lederhosen with suspenders, white socks, walking shoes, and white shirt with black four-in-hand. Tyrolean hats had all been hung on pegs by the dozen young men as they entered prior to the girls. One by one they paired. Several brands of the best German beers were on tap. A wide planked table was overflowing with Munich's renowned delicacies of the *Fasching*: poached plover, quail, and gull eggs topped with caviar from Dallmayr's, blue-cooked trout, a suckling pig, and roast furred rabbit as centerpieces, roast beef fillets, meat and goose liver pâtés, parsley veal sausages, and fruits and vegetables from the *Viktualienmarkt*. Twenty-four places were set, each one with a small swastika flag on a pedestal.

The girls accepted wine in metal goblets from their partners and danced to tunes made popular by Marlene Dietrich and Lale Andersen. After a rousing polka, they took their seats, and the host, Bruno von Hassel-Berndorff, toasted "the young intellectuals of the Third Reich." His sister, Luise, sat quietly, envying the prettier girls, while Bruno talked about the Nazis. Luise noticed that Peter was not paired with anyone. He listened courteously as his classmate gestured, then clapped politely. Luise made up her mind.

During the wild carnival carousing that followed the late meal, Luise managed to trick Peter into drinking pear brandy—his first schnapps. Then she got him to try Steinhäger. She was not pretty, but she was not plain either, and she was a very brilliant scholar. Peter's natural enthusiasm for her favorite studies impressed her. He was not like the foppish and vain nobility that was part of her existence through her family's position. Here was a man who treated her as an equal. She felt comfortable with Peter. She got no vibrations of sycophancy, and she planned to seduce him.

Luise knew the castle well. They called it the castle because the lodge had been built on the foundations of a twelfth-century castle. Only one stone tower remained standing. It had a marvelous view, overlooking a bend of the Inn River and the village of Neubeuern. Bruno had his armory room, but

Luise had her *Romanzezimmer.* For many summers and skiing vacations the Hassels had brought their two children to Ausblick. Indeed, it was an overlook, a magnificent view of the mountains and the Inn Valley and the flatlands to the north. The tower was called *Spionchen,* or little spy. During the summer Herr von Hassel set a powerful telescope on the battlement. The family would enjoy alfresco lunches on *Spionchen,* would study the horizon as far as Munich with the telescope. Herr von Hassel was fond of looking northeast at the Chiemsee. The instrument's eighty-power lens allowed an exciting view of Herrenchiemsee, the palace built by Ludwig II, the "Mad King," in the Franco-Prussian War years. Bruno, a philosophy student at the Berlin Academy, had been mesmerized by the opulence of Ludwig's palace. The Mad King had emulated Louis XIV, two centuries too late. He had even seen himself as a Sun King and had had a gold sunburst installed over his bed. He had copied the French fountain of turtles at Versailles and impressed his guests by pressing a button and having his ornate dinner table submerge into the cellar, then emerge with clean plates and the next course. Emil von Hassler assured Bruno that he would be as affluent as Ludwig in the new German hierarchy. Bruno also admired Ludwig, in spite of his eccentricities, because the king had been an important patron of Richard Wagner; he had built the Festspielhaus in Bayreuth for the prime purpose of playing Wagner's music. Bayreuth had become famous. Wagner had become the inspiration for Germany's rebirth.

Let Bruno put on his Wagner recordings, mused his twin sister. She led the tipsy Swede along a catwalk to her childhood lair in the tower of *Spionchen.* For years she had, like a mother bird, feathered it against the cold for the time when she would meet her warrior . . . and it was a time to sire heroes. The carnival. The youthful abandon, the mountains with their presence of Teutonic gods. It was Luise's Valhalla.

Quickly she started the fire. She had done this many times, but this night would be different. She would be the aggressor.

Peter snuggled under the black and white animal fur pelts and fell asleep, a smile on his lips. Luise waited, put heavy, dry logs into the huge fireplace till it was so warm that Peter threw the pelts back. He squirmed comfortably and mumbled about never having another drop, and then he lay still . . . on his back, the fire flickering on his handsome blond hair, his smooth, muscular chest, and his slim, heaving belly. He had on only a pair of cotton shorts.

Luise leaned over him like a hungry lioness and kissed his cheek, his chin, his lips, and his belly. He giggled and said he was ticklish, then fell off again.

Luise drew a dagger, emblazoned with a swastika, and hovered over the sleeping Viking. The blade glinted in the firelight. What if she'd stolen it from her brother's collection? He had many more. She stuck the sharp point under the hem of Peter's shorts and, in one upward stroke, slit the fabric. It fell away, and he was exposed to her hungry eyes. She then cut the leg hem, and Peter was totally nude, like a baby. But he was no baby. Luise kissed his belly and kissed until she had kissed the end of his ample endowment. She loved the curly blond hair, for she, and her family, were all brunette. Then she gobbled it into her mouth and fondled it with her voluptuous lips and tongue. The body stirred but was too tired to resist, to defend. That's what Luise thought.

Peter Friedrich Nielson felt a warmth in his loins as he relived his first affair: a delicious, tingling warmth. He handed his empty coffee cup to the stewardess, then closed his eyes and picked up where he'd left off.

Yes, he'd let it happen, but he'd been afraid that he was in no condition to be successfully amorous with this girl. He'd never . . . He hadn't ever had a waking orgasm before. Only wet dreams. So he let her do it. He got hard, very hard, and she was going up and down rhythmically with her mouth, and he thought he'd burst, but it still didn't explode. He nearly went berserk when she took her mouth off him for a moment.

Then a strange, cool sensation. She was slipping something under his pelvis. He was afraid to look, but he raised his head slightly and saw what it was.

Leather. With shiny metal studs.

Luise slipped it behind him, then laced up a series of thongs. His gleaming column rose out of a black platform. He peeked again. She had slipped out of her lady-in-waiting gown and was adjusting a leather apparatus over her breasts. The nipples extended through holes. His eyes opened wide as she stepped out of her panties. She looked at him and smiled.

"Are you all right? I was worried." Luise leaned over and gripped his sex tightly. She wore black kidskin gloves and manipulated him smoothly. He said nothing. It felt so good.

"I hope I'm not shocking you." She kissed him on his lips, then moved down over his belly again. This time he put his palms behind her head and pulled her down on him. He arched into her, and she made animal sounds. She drove him to a frenzy, and he felt all choked up inside. It was as if the floodgates were jammed. He throbbed as she slid her body over his, spread her legs, and sat on him. She took him to the hilt, and she screamed with delight, spinning half a turn on him, balanced on knees and hands. He still couldn't, was still hard and vertical.

Luise got up.

She returned from the fireplace. There was a branch in her hand, silhouetted against the fire. She handed it to him and lay down on the pelt in front of him, legs toward him. Then she raised her buttocks, propped herself up on her elbows, and told him to strike her with the supple branch. He sat up, looked at her. Feet still in slippers, high in the air like a ballet dancer . . . Firelight dancing between her legs. All of her . . . not a meter from his eyes. "Do it, please," she implored again and again. "I want you to do it." He was still woozy, but his senses were improving. Peter leaned close and looked at her. Soft hair between her legs . . . and then he dared look lower. He moved the bedside candle, held it within inches of her. He'd never seen—except in medical books. The valley. The crevasse. The wet, dark landscape. He devoured it with his eyes and felt weak inside. "Do it," she sobbed.

He swung the branch lightly against her backside.

"Harder," she cried.

He swung harder, heard the slap against her white skin.

"Harder," Luise ordered.

He obliged and swung harder than he meant to. Something made him do it. He hit her again and again, and she squealed with delight. Each squeal made him more excited. He was a man, a hunter. Was this his heritage? His mother's through the son. He'd become, he'd envisioned himself as, the *Björn,* the Bear of the North.

"Once more, just once more," Luise bleated.

Then she emitted a tremendous sigh and shook and throbbed all over. Her legs spread apart toward him, and knees high, she reached for him and pulled his body onto hers. Her deft hand guided him, and soon he was undulating rhythmically with her.

He felt something slashing at his back, at his legs. It hurt, but it made him explode inside her.

That was the first time.

Now he had lost count.

Not only of Luise, but of her circle of wild friends.

Berlin. Rome. Marrakesh. Athens.

He was not afraid of his mother's cellar anymore.

The cab drove past the Kungsträdgården. The park was crowded with young people. It was summer, and soon, too soon, the sun would disappear into winter. The fishermen were stowing their nets along Lake Mäarlan's banks after a good day's catch. The lights were on in front of City Hall, its deep red façade topped by three gilded crowns. Already twilight.

Peter called from the airport, and the maid said that Mrs. Nielson was in a private room at the city hospital. The doctor told him on the phone that it didn't look good.

He had a feeling that he'd come home for a reason. His commander must have known when he sent the telegram. They all must have known. It was that way with death.

Peter stopped at the confectionery store and bought

a box of her favorite candy: chocolate-covered cherries filled with brandy. He bought an arrangement of bright yellow and white asters, then went to the hospital.

He'd never been comfortable in hospitals, especially hospitals with light green walls. The reception nurse sent him in to see Dr. Thorwaldson. He was told that his mother was inoperable. It was a matter of days.

She lay, propped up with a copy of the *Svenska Dagbladet* spread across her lap. She'd lost weight; in fact, he didn't recognize her for an instant.

"This is the right room!" His mother was one for jokes.

Peter shook off his embarrassment and sat down beside the bed. A nurse came in and tended to the flowers.

"Thought you might need a drink." He handed her the unwrapped box of chocolates.

Ulla smiled. "You never learned how to wrap gifts, but you know, Peter . . . I love you for it." She reached out weakly with both arms. He embraced his mother somewhat awkwardly. But at least it was an embrace. Peter had a fleeting moment of shame—about Luise and her sadistic tutors, those friends of Bruno. Then he remembered the strange paraphernalia in the cellar under the gallery.

"Perhaps it's better this way." Ulla coughed.

"Just what do you mean, Mother?"

"My son"—she reached for Peter's hand—"there's going to be war. I can just feel it." Her hand tightened on his over the newspaper. There was a photograph on one page of massed German tanks on maneuvers. She continued as an enigmatic smile crossed her face. "I know that I don't have much time—" She stifled a cough deep in her chest. "At least I won't be around. Who wants to watch a war anyway?" She tried to laugh. Peter looked down at the newspaper. He wasn't good at such conversation.

"I *know,* Peter." Her eyes blazed, and she had difficulty moving her body upright. Peter put another pillow behind her.

"Thanks." She plucked a chocolate from the open box and smacked her lips before popping it in. "Can't smoke so . . ." She didn't finish the sentence.

"Mother, we've got the best doctors . . ."

"*Merde.*"

It was the only French word she used, and she used it humorously. Peter chuckled.

"Might as well tell you a few things. Poor dear, you must have wondered about many things. Haven't you?" He avoided her eyes, and she continued.

"Peter, your father did not sail away!" It hit him like a bolt. He felt a dryness in his throat. "What I meant to say, and God knows I've tried to put in into better words, is . . . that the man who sailed away was not your father. Yes, you have his name. I have his name. But your father is alive . . . and doing *very* well!" Ulla wiggled back into her pillows and grinned mysteriously. She sipped some water through a bent straw.

"I know there's going to be a war, and I'll tell you how I know."

Peter unloosened his service tie.

"That's it. Stay awhile." She joked. "In 1913—" She stopped and motioned Peter to close the door. He did, and she continued. "Lars Nielson and I broke up. At first it was a night here, a night there.

Then a few days, a month, and then he left. In the meantime, I had to support myself. I couldn't go back to Germany and face your grandfather.

"I was pretty, or so people told me, and I got a job as a maid in a hotel in Kiruna. I'd met the manager in Umeå. I'd been working part time in the market. He was very nice to me. I was promoted to be a hostess in the hotel restaurant. Businessmen from all over the world would eat there. We served delicious venison. I got generous tips. As you know, every country wanted Sweden's iron ore . . . even then.

"It was late in September. Already getting cold. I remember that the staff had just stacked all the firewood to dry in the waning sun. The manager called me into his office. He told me that the hotel owner, Mr. Lundquist, needed a woman to act as hostess at his hunting lodge north of the city. There were going to be important guests, and it would mean a great deal to the profits of the hotel—and my future."

"You went . . . alone?"

"At first, no. The cook and his helper came along. There were three businessmen. They'd brought much equipment and the finest gun cases. Polished brown leather with gilt hand tooling. There were manservants, and I'd never seen so lavish a table. Nils, the manager, and Mr. Lundquist took the party hunting the first day. It was my job to see that the guests were comfortable. I then realized why Mr. Lundquist had wanted me. The guests were German and spoke no Swedish. It was easier for me, too.

"The next morning two of the businessmen had to leave. I knew them only as Uncle Hans and Uncle Detlaf. They left with a Swede whose name was

Lager-gren. I think he was an official from the mines–"

"What about the other businessman?" Peter fingered a cigarette package in his jacket pocket.

"I was getting to that. It had started to snow. Nils called me to his room and told me that he wanted to drive the help back in the Daimler and he'd come back out the next day with the sled to pick up me and Uncle Axel, if I wouldn't mind. Axel was the most important of the guests and wasn't feeling well enough to make the trip. He'd asked if I could stay another day. I agreed; there was no other answer for me. Uncle Axel was the least raucous of the three. In fact, he was almost timid. He was balding and wore a big, bushy mustache. Besides, he was in his room most of the time anyway.

"The light snow turned into the first blizzard of the season. It snowed for two days. The telephone was out of order as well. The first day with Axel was uneventful. I cooked hot meals that he requested and ate alone, which was correct. That evening he spoke his first personal words other than 'thank you' and 'please.' 'Miss Nielson'–his voice was high-pitched–'do you plays cards?' Somewhat stunned, I answered, 'poker.' "

" 'That will have to do.' He started shuffling and bade me sit down across the table. We had a surprisingly good time. For a timid man he was really very entertaining. You could tell that he had been brought up well. He talked about his travels and how the demands of his business kept him from having fun. He said he had to maintain the aura of perfection so that others would emulate him. This was the first time in years, he told me, that he wasn't looking at his timetables.

"After a few games, he took out an enormous cigar and lit it, exclaiming, 'Nobody would believe this!' Then he got up and brought a bottle of cognac over from the bar. 'And they wouldn't believe *this* either.' He poured two generous dollops and drank it in one smiling gulp.

" 'Nothing like a snowstorm to bring out certain qualities in people, eh?' I nodded approval.

"Axel tended the fire as if he were playing with a toy. 'In my house I never get to do this.' He put on each new log with relish and a flourish.

"We finished the bottle. After that I don't remember much, except I woke up in his bed. I could hear him whistling a tune. Then I smelled bacon. He was in the kitchen, cooking.

" 'You don't know how much you've cured me,' he told me over coffee. 'We should do this more often.'

"And then I realized. It was a bad time. The worst. I hadn't intended . . . the blizzard . . . the cognac. And he *was* fun. He was really like an uncle—outside of our indiscretion.

"Nils drove us back in the troika. It was a beautiful, bright day . . ."

"A day to sire heroes?"

Peter's mother nodded pensively.

"So my father was really a businessman named Uncle Axel."

"Yes and no. As we were sleighing back to Kiruna, my mind cleared up. I recalled some of the things that had happened, especially after Axel smiled and told me that his back still ached deliciously. I had vague recollections that I'd fired up the sauna—and we'd taken it together. It was his first time, he told me. I must have given him the whole treatment in my drunkenness. I'm ashamed to admit it, but I was a pretty wild young girl. One thing that Lars did do well was the sauna. His mad friends from Finland . . . they were like Mongols . . . you can imagine a hybrid of Swede and Russian Eskimo! We took turns at 'entertaining.' It was a two-hour ride to Vaasa in a motorboat. Every weekend that summer before he left. I guess I'd become one of them—an animal, especially after a few drinks . . ."

"It must have been very difficult for you, Mother."

"At first, but one gets used to anything. Anyway, Uncle Axel had been tipsy, too, and he said a few things. His father had been a rascal. Had cavorted with young boys in Capri. Family scandal and all that. His father even organized a club for these activities. All the members had personal keys to his villa—"

Peter remembered the key he'd found when he was eleven but said nothing, and she continued.

"—Uncle Axel went back to Germany. I should have suspected, but several months went by before I went to a doctor. I knew it couldn't be Lars's child; he didn't . . . couldn't very well. But I thought that it might make him come back. At least people would think the child was his.

"One day the following spring, when I was eight months pregnant, Nils drove me out to the lodge. I'd offered to make some suggestion about redecorating, especially with some of the fine new furniture that Swedish designers were becoming famous for internationally. It would also keep me on a part-time payroll for a while. I'd also wanted to sew some new drapes. Mr. Lundquist approved, especially since business was going so well, not in the least due to my *help*. The iron ore trains were full, going both ways:

to Narvik for the Atlantic route in the winter, and then to Luleå as well, soon as the ice broke up.

"I did, however, have another motive for going back to Vargsätt—the lodge. The longer I carried you, the more curious I became about Uncle Axel. When he left, he told me that war was inevitable, and it was beginning to look as if he was right. Military officers came to Kiruna. Russian, German, and English, too! He'd shown me something that night during the snowstorm. It was on the table when we were playing cards. I last saw it among the poker chips. It was a key that had belonged to his rascal father. It was on a gold chain, and there was a curious medallion with it.

"It was there, in the chips caddy drawer. Luckily no one had played poker in the interim. Once back in Kiruna I locked my door and studied the unusual medallion. It was gold, elliptical in shape, and had, of all things, a bas-relief of two crossed dinner forks. I hid it.

"Hardly a month after you arrived, Franz Ferdinand was assassinated and the war began. The Germans were ready: their armor, their guns, their terrible heavy guns made with Swedish iron. Bought by German businessmen in Kiruna!"

Ulla Nielson sank back into her pillows and gasped for breath. Peter tried to stop her, have her rest, but she was adamant. "You don't want me to stop before the good part, do you?"

Peter shook his head benignly and ate a chocolate.

"I'd made up my mind," she went on. "Who was this Uncle Axel? How could he have been so sure about the war? What was the meaning of crossed dinner forks on a key chain? Except for his mention of scandal and Capri, I had nothing to go on. But I would find out. In September I went to Stockholm to look at furniture for Varsgätt, as well as for the new wing at the hotel. I took the 'evidence' with me.

"I went to the museums and libraries and searched for a similar coat of arms. The forks may have been Axel's family crest. No luck. I went to the jewelry marts in Old Town and Skeppsholmen and Dyurgården. Nothing. I found crossed swords, batons, keys, lances, and axes. But no forks . . ." His mother was talking in spurts, getting weaker, but Peter knew better than to stop her now. How she had loved to tell long stories at bedtime.

"Nothing in Stockholm, so I wrote to Capri. I wrote the chamber of commerce that I'd found a key on the main street of Kiruna and asked if they could identify it so I could send it back to its owner. I said there had been a group of Italian businessmen in Kiruna that day, and I was also writing to Milan and Rome. I lied. Anna, an Italian maid, translated the letter for me. She was a dear; took care of you when I had to go away occasionally.

"When I received the reply, one word leaped out at me from the short paragraph. It was a word, and it was a name all at once. Like the American 'Kodak.' I didn't need a translation." Ulla beckoned for her purse on the white end table.

She opened it and drew out an envelope. There was a stamp with a green engraving of Mussolini on it. She handed it to her son.

Peter's hands trembled as he unfolded the note. She lay back, waiting expectantly for his reaction.

The letter, addressed to his mother, was written in formal, bureaucratic Italian and signed by one Marrone, director of registry. It described the complexity of the investigation into the ownership of the medallion and identified the owner as Signor F. A. Krupp, residing at Villa Hügel, Essen, Germany.

Peter's face blanched as he pronounced the name and address softly several times. He stuttered in his confusion and elation, then handed the letter back.

"Keep it. It's helped me for some years now, and it will help you . . . and please, light up a cigarette. I want to sneak a puff."

Peter inhaled on his cigarette by mistake and coughed violently, then handed it to his mother. She blew big clouds and closed her eyes in rapturous pleasure.

"You then contacted someone at Villa Hügel?"

"I was very discreet. I made a graphite rubbing of the medallion, the way people do with gravestones, inserted it into an envelope and mailed it to Villa Hügel, to the attention of Herr Axel. One morning a week later I was telephoned at the hotel and told to be at the Kiruna post office at noon sharp. I was to wear a green shawl, or carry one, and the caller, a woman, said she'd be wearing green shoes. It was still summery. Her code query was to be: 'Excuse me, did you lose this lipstick?' My reply was to be: 'Erika, what brings you to Kiruna?' This would establish us as old friends."

"Obviously it worked." Peter stubbed the butt out.

"We went to a tearoom and talked. She was like an automaton. She smiled and asked me what I wanted. Her jaws dropped when I told her I'd had a child by the man who owned the medallion. She became more friendly, almost amused, but regained her composure. I told her the medallion was in a safe-deposit vault at our bank, along with this letter. I showed her a copy, which she took and thanked me for. She told me not to say anything—for the good of the child—to anyone and she'd contact me again within a week.

"Next, she invited me to stay with her in Stockholm and 'talk business.' She'd found out about my artistic inclinations and was ready to offer me, for her *client,* a position as manager of a shop her *client* had planned to open in the most fashionable section of the city. So I played the game. . . ."

"That's how! That's where it all came from." Peter whistled in disbelief. "The car, the maid . . . the gallery . . ."

"And don't forget. Your education at all the best schools on the Continent." She closed her eyes again and handed Peter her cigarette. "*That* was my last one."

"Mother—"

"No scenes now; there's too much to do. Samuelsson has prepared the will and has all the necessary papers. They'll bring someone else in to manage the gallery; it's getting to be quite a clearinghouse for the Gestapo . . ." she whispered.

"I hear they've been putting pressure on the newspapers . . ."

She cautioned him with a finger to her lips, then motioned him to come closer. He sat on the bed and took her hand. It turned, palm down, in his. Her hand was coldish. He felt an object slide into his hand.

"I want you to have it."

He looked closely at the medallion.

"Take it with you, and don't worry. I'll be all right." She tapped him playfully on his arm.

"That's what I wanted to hear, Mother." He embraced her but didn't see her tears, which she hid very well. "I'll see you again tomorrow."

Peter's steps echoed in the marble hall as Ulla strained and reached into her bag. She groped around until she found it.

A seemingly ordinary pill.

FIVE

"I take it he's expecting you."

"Sort of . . ." Lieutenant Nielson read the prim but pretty receptionist's necklace name, "*R-i-k-e*."

"I'm sorry," she bleated through the circular opening in the textured glass partition. "You *have* to have an appointment."

"I'm a representative of the Royal Swedish Iron Ore Mines in Kiruna." Peter acted imperious, and the girl laughed, then stopped when she saw the black armband on his sleeve.

"I'm sorry." She covered her mouth with manicured fingernails.

Peter took an envelope from an inside pocket of his uniform jacket and handed it through the opening. "Look, beautiful, I'm in town for just a few days. How about me taking you to a flick?"

She took off her glasses nervously, then fumbled with the envelope. "What's this for?"

"It's a code name."

"Uncle Axel?"

"He's been waiting for this letter a *very* long time."

"But I can't just . . ."

"You don't want to get in trouble with him, do you?"

She shook her curly locks.

"Then have it put on his desk. I'll be back at two o'clock. That gives it almost three hours. I've heard he only spends fifteen minutes for lunch."

"One hour. It's fifteen minutes for *breakfast.*" She blinked and put her glasses back on, studied him for a moment.

"And what I said still goes."

"We'll see." She tried to act unconcerned.

Peter walked around the huge complex. He had no trouble clearing various gates and entering the clanging and humming buildings. His credentials allowed him into all but top secret installations. Soon he would be cleared for that, too. He had a plan.

In touring the works, Peter saw the most massive steel sheet rolling machine in the world, the famous 15,000-ton press. He marveled at the production lines of Panzer tanks, howitzers, navel cannon barrels, and armor plate. He felt proud—and a part of it. Even the name of the works—*Gusstahlfabrik*—gave him goose pimples. As a child he had seen the title . . . in books, newspapers, and cinema newsreels. It meant "cast steel factory." He was now part of the venerable Krupp Cast Steel Works, A.G.

Gustav Krupp von Bohlen und Halbach. Peter rolled the name around in his head. He had read up on the family of steel. Bertha Krupp, daughter of Alfried, was plain and lacked suiters. The kaiser's man was Gustav von Bohlen und Halbach. He was a "corseted" career diplomat at the Royal Prussian Embassy to the Holy See in Rome. Fräulein Bertha Krupp was twenty, and Gustav, thirty-six and a head shorter than his future bride. It was a blitzkrieg affair, and even Bertha's sister was bewildered by the galloping events. Kaiser Wilhelm decreed that little Gustav, in deference to all Germanic tradition, would inherit the Krupp name to "ensure at least an appearance of continuity of the Essen dynasty. . . ." The little civil servant would also be allowed to pass along the name and fortune to the eldest son!

How thoroughly German. How expedient! Peter wondered about Alfried, the eldest son. Six sons and two daughters! One son, Arnold, had died in infancy. Alfried, born seven years earlier than himself! A playboy racing around Munich in a red sports car, in Aachen with a supercharged Austro-Daimler. No. Peter would have skippered a yacht in the Olympics. But then Peter Nielson had no *blood*. Harald, Berthold, Claus, and Eckbert, the others *had* Krupp blood. All *he* had was the name of an obscure Krupp: Peter Friedrich Wilhelm, son of Jodocus Krupp, who had married a shrewd woman, Helene Ascherfeld. It was she who had started the Krupp empire at the end of the eighteenth century, by her manipulation of credit in the iron business after Jodocus's death. The Krupps, bubbling since the merchant Arndt Krupp was first registered in the records of Essen in 1587, came into their own. One of Arndt's sons married the daughter of an Essen gunsmith in 1612. The son, Anton, adopted his father-in-law's trade and turned out 1,000 gun barrels a year during the Thirty Years' War. And more wars followed!

Named after the son of an Ascherfeld! Why? Had Ulla read the Krupps' history? Had she envisioned herself shrewd like Helene Ascherfeld? Was he, Peter Friedrich Nielson-Krupp, destined to succeed where Peter Friedrich Wilhelm Krupp had failed? He had died at forty-two, a rifle-club layabout and errand-boy for his shrewd mother. But his son, her grandson, became the manager of the first Krupp works. *Ascherfeld*! he thought; sounds Jewish!

It was Friedrich who had usurped the well-guarded English rediscovery of the secret of Damascus sword steel. It was Friedrich who had founded the Gusstahlfabrik in 1811. It was Helene who had made the money that had made Krupp. Poetic justice!

"*Achtung*!" The loudspeakers reverberated through the dozen square kilometers of plants and outbuildings. "Herr Leutnant Peter Nielson, Royal Swedish Navy, will please report instantly to the administration building executive offices, third floor. . . ."

Peter stopped on the trolley tracks in front of the *Hauptverwaltungsgebäude*. He looked up at the ominous red brick building with its triangular peaked tower and uninspired lines. A bay window stuck out of the tower façade at the third-floor level. An old man with a rim of white hair and craggy features was looking down at him from the center window.

Gustav Krupp von Bohlen und Halbach settled down in his plush red leather chair to receive his guest. He almost always sat to receive. His chair was high, and sitting behind his desk, he appeared taller than his five feet six inches. He would be as impressive as possible before a son he'd never met. He picked up the sheet of creased notepaper and scrutinized the graphite rubbing of crossed forks from various angles by the light of the bay window behind him. He cocked his head this way and that like a balding turkey. Yes, he'd heard from his operative in Stockholm about the Nielson woman, but he'd not expected this—so fast. What was it going to be? Blackmail again? Not that it was originally blackmail . . . but a man in his position . . . and all those conniving have-nots out there . . .

Secretly he still had delicious memories of the snowstorm at, what was the place again? Wolfsschanze? No, that was the Führer's hideout. Ah, yes. *Wolfsweg.* Now, at sixty-nine, he was going to meet the offspring of his one and only *sixty-nine experience.* Gustav's loins tingled, as they had for all these years, when he thought of the sauna and the birch whipping he'd received from that northern child-witch. If only Bertha knew. All the children after Berthold—Harald, Waldtraut, Eckbert—were results of his image of wild Ulla. Superimposed on poor Bertha. Ulla's streaming blond hair, her face, her breasts and other privates. Just as he would superimpose images in his photography darkroom. In bed Bertha was Ulla. . . .

The cumbersome paneled door opened slowly. His secretary showed the officer in. Gustav waved her away, and she closed the door behind her. The blue-clad "Aryan" stood tall and quiet on the polished wood floor. His steel eyes met those of Krupp von Bohlen. The corners of his mouth turned up in a perpetual smile gave him an aura of confidence. He was his own man, and Gustav was one to notice that trait.

"May I offer my condolences." Gustav clasped his bony hands as if in prayer. "Please sit down; I've canceled a few things. We've got fifteen minutes."

"I don't suppose I should call you Father." Peter rubbed his hands together.

"I keep my office temperature down to fifty-five degrees when possible. It's precisely *that* outside today." Gustav evaded an answer to Peter's question.

"Well, I *am* glad to meet you, Herr Krupp von Bohlen."

"Yes, I can understand that, Leutnant Nielson. I hope that you are happy with the, ah, *arrangements* in Stockholm." Gustav toyed with a desktop thermometer. His face was streaked with craggy, vertical crevasses, almost a leather mask. His baldish forehead was ringed with white hair, somewhat disheveled over his protruding ears. His small white mustache and somewhat portly frame gave him the appearance of a retired butler.

"Aside from the obvious, is there any reason that you are here?" He smoothed down the rubbing of the crossed forks.

"Well, sir, there is one thing . . ."

"Do you have the medallion with you?" Gustav looked up sharply, and their eyes locked. It was Gustav who turned away.

"It's still where Mother—"

"No matter, what is it you want?"

"You knew about my failing a physical exam at Flensburg for a very minor affliction . . ."

"It's been so long . . ."

"Paranosmia, a rare aberration in my sense of smell."

"Yes . . . yes . . . We got the best specialists for you." A glimmer of interest betrayed the industrialist.

Peter sat erect and proper and delivered his request.

"My mother was born a German. Her father was an Eckhardt. Heidelberg stock. But *her* mother was from Sweden. Björnson. Child of the Bear. I've always thought of myself as mostly Swede—and a little German. Herr Eckhardt is a Berliner. But for some strange reason I've always admired Germany more than Sweden. The Germans are brilliant, exciting, and always on the move. The Swedes are the opposite: happy with their lot. Status quo! As a child I'd read about the Vikings, the longboats of wood out of Gokstad and Birka, which is now called Stockholm. The men of iron who sailed forth, like the animals we really are, and conquered—from the Caspian Sea in Russia to Jerusalem and Spain—infiltrated the rivers of France all the way to Paris, raided and left their seed in Scotland and Ireland. Then they colonized Iceland and Greenland before landing in Labrador and Newfoundland in America . . . and possibly even landed in the New World and fought the American Indians as far south as Boston. . . .

"I tried to like Sweden, but it wasn't aggressive enough for my heritage of the Bear. It was dying; it was weak; it was being used. Yes, by Germany, the Bear of Western Europe. Then another bear challenged us—from the steppes. Asiatic types. So we played it safe. Between two bears—and a lion.

"*Now* I know why I was impatient with Sweden. I am not Swedish; I am not a loser. I am *a German.* My father was not a drunken Swede. He is a *German.*

"Herr Krupp von Bohlen, I want to serve my country. I cannot do it as a mere observer for a neutral power. I want to show what I can do for the Third Reich—but I'll need help. . . ."

"Go on." Gustav added, "Peter."

"I am a submariner." Peter touched the insignia on his lapel. "I would like to take a more active part in the imminent struggle against our common enemies. As a neutral I'll be able to do things that I couldn't have—even had I passed the exam for Flensburg. What I haven't had in actual training aboard U-boats, I've made up for in various ways. I've been aboard the Cadiz boat; it's now in Turkey, called the *Gür*. Very similar to Type Two Germaniawerft designs. I have friends in Finland. I've seen the *Vessiko* in Turku and agree with Commodore Dönitz: too limited in range and hitting power . . . adequate for coastal patrols . . ."

Gustav pursed his lips and leaned back thoughtfully.

"But the boat that impressed me the most was the *Vetehinen.*" Peter observed Krupp von Bohlen's reaction before he continued, "nice boat, just a change here and there and we have the new VIIb . . ."

"Perhaps I can work out something." Gustav flipped through his index book.

"I was aboard the American submarine *Sebago* when it sank."

Krupp von Bohlen coughed and reached for the water pitcher. "Perhaps you should see someone at BdU, my son." He forgot himself and attributed it to encroaching senility. "Maybe we could work out something with the McCann-type rescue bell." Visions of a profitable order for such units danced in his head.

"I will be honored to talk to the right people about the device, but first I would like to get an assignment set up where I can do my part in what's coming."

"Just what do you mean?"

"A ranking officer in Berlin told me about Poland."

"I see."

"Can you fix it for me to see someone in Naval Intelligence? If he agrees with my plan, perhaps I can obtain a limited commission, one that will allow me to work on various projects."

"May I ask what your plan is?"

"To cripple the enemy fleet decisively."

"I can see that you are determined." Gustav twirled his mustache. "I must say that Germany needs men who are innovative." He opened his index book, then uncapped a gold-plated fountain pen and wrote a neat, terse note on his stationery. After signing it with a flourish, he handed it, along with an envelope to the lieutenant with the mourning band.

Nielson spent the night at Ulrike Knittel's tiny flat in the suburb of Bredenev. They had meant to go to a movie starring Ingrid Bergman, *The Four Comrades,* but somehow never managed to get out of bed.

SIX

The stenciled sign on the outside of the door was simple:

AMT AUSLAND/ABWEHR
Adm. Canaris

Peter waited patiently among a group of officers seated on pewlike benches around the perimeter of the high-ceilinged reception room in the eclectic four-story stone building on Berlin's Tirpitz-Ufer. There was a smell of fresh paint. One of the side doors was open. Workmen were installing directional signs in the corridor. A Luftwaffe colonel, next to Peter, was chewing on a spent cigar while immersed in a current copy of *Weltwache* magazine. The cover featured a photograph of Stalin, with a caption: "*Ribbentrop nach Moskau.*"

There were surprised glances when Peter's name was called. Such a young man, and only a *Leutnant*, thought the colonel grudgingly, and what's more, I've been waiting longer. He turned a page with such force that he ripped it halfway out.

An orderly led Peter past an army of uniformed clerks to an inner office at the end of a short corridor. He opened the mahogany door and announced the *Leutnant*'s name.

On the polished desk there were two salient objects that rose above the clutter of papers: a scale model of a warship and a bronze monkey trio, "see nothing, hear nothing, say nothing." Peter took the seat nearest the desk. He noticed that the plaque on the model's base was inscribed: "*Dresden*: a light cruiser." The other thing he noticed was that, like Krupp von Bohlen, the man behind the desk was small. It was something an athlete would notice regardless of a person's sitting position. The admiral's sparse hair was white. He had bushy white eyebrows, and his blue uniform was more wrinkled than one might expect of an admiral. An Iron Cross, First Class, was pinned to his tunic. Age? Old enough to be my father, thought Peter. There was a strange resemblance between Canaris and the American movie actor who was his favorite—who had starred in *The Petrified Forest* and that curious film with *die totenende Kinder*, "the Dead End Kids." He looked as though he were about to yawn. Peter noticed him put away a bottle of pills as he entered.

"I've heard good things about you, *Leutnant*." The admiral cleared a space between the books and papers on his desk, then arranged an easeled snapshot so Peter could also see it. "My best friends." It was a photo of two dachshunds. "I am also a submariner." He leaned over and studied Peter's insignia. "Managed to sink three ships in the Mediterranean—and *poof* the war was over." He rummaged through a desk drawer. "Here she is. *U-Thirty-four*. I had a temporary command. Then I was given *UB-One-twenty-eight.*"

"Fortunate transfer. *U-Thirty-four* was sunk by a Q-ship."

"Yes, our last loss of the Great War. *Leutnant,* you seem well versed in certain things—for a Swede."

"I tried Flensburg, but there was a minor problem."

"So I heard."

Peter was taken aback. Did his father care? Perhaps he did!

The admiral ordered coffee for two, and Peter told him of his plan to infiltrate Scapa Flow. Canaris made some entries on a personnel form and buzzed his adjutant.

"Colonel Jenke, may I introduce you to Oberleutnant Nielson, permanent rank. . . . Take the boy to One-M and set him up with BdU until further orders."

Jenke and Nielson saluted the admiral and left.

"Congratulations, *Oberleutnant,* on your promotion. The old man doesn't give field commissions very often."

"And it's not even wartime," Peter quipped, to the colonel's amusement. "*BdU.* That's headquarters for . . ."

"Commodore Dönitz," Jenke added matter-of-factly.

"Dönitz was in the Mediterranean in 1918, too. Did they ever know each other?"

"No comment" was the colonel's reply.

SEVEN

23 August 1939

Dear Theo:

As you can see by the postmark, I do get around. Kiel is a marvelous town for boat lovers. I've been out sailing and truly wish you could have been here.

Something has come up of the most urgent nature, and I know it will be of great interest to you, especially in relation to your business. I know that you will want to be part of this venture.

This is sudden, but I will arrive at Grimsetter on an unscheduled flight this Friday afternoon, the twenty-seventh. I've already confirmed a room at the Kirkwall Hotel and will take a taxi and ring you up when I'm settled. Perhaps we can do a round on your course at Stromness.

Looking forward,
Peter Birch Boy

Nielson licked the flap of the special delivery stamped envelope and tucked it into his inside jacket pocket. Then he chuckled over the St. Andrews paper napkin as he set his photo copying lights at the proper angle for his Zeiss Contaflex 35. Peter focused with a special magnifying attachment on the map of Scapa Flow that Theo Drahn had so conveniently drawn for him several months earlier at St. Andrews. He was immensely proud of the camera that the Abwehr had issued him. The first full-frame 35-millimeter reflex camera ever devised. It was now in limited production, and he envisioned an attachment for the submarine periscope ocular. He bracketed his exposure readings, took out the Adox film spool, and, whistling "Loch Lomond," secured his quarters, and got on the base bus.

Meanwhile, Canaris had given his blessings to SS General Reinhard Heydrich's plan *Grossmutter Gestorben* for August 31. His SD men would be disguised as Polish troops, occupy the German border radio station at Gleiwitz, and destroy the customs post. Corpses would be provided from Gross-Rosen concentration camp near Breslau to make the skirmish look "authentic." The mock Polish troops, already in uniform and learning Polish attack phrases, were at the SD leadership school in Bernau, under SS Oberführer Mehlhorn. Two top SS officers were already assigned as "attackers" and "defenders."

Hitler and Goebbels had already written their speeches!

EIGHT

On the bright eastern horizon a faint outline of the Cordillera Cantábrica was visible. Below those peaks, invisible for the earth's curvature, lay Cape Finisterre —"end of land" to the Spaniards of Galicia, the forelocks of the Iberian Peninsula.

Kapitänleutnant Prien leaned his white cap into the gusty northwester as he looked toward land. If Galicia was the forelocks, then Lisbon, the port of his hero Vasco da Gama, was located on the nose. He unfolded a pocket chart, creased it so the face of Portugal was prominent. *U-47* was surface running thirty miles off the coast. He noted the depth: 1,000 meters! As deep as the coastal mountains were high. The thought of sinking in such depths flitted through his nimble mind. The Americans had rescued half the crew of one of their boats from 70 meters with a diving bell. But 1,000 meters would be a different story. A boat would be crushed long before it settled on the bottom he was patrolling over.

The twin MAN diesels, each capable of 1,600 horsepower, with pistons as tall as a man, drummed the VIIB along at a cruising speed of twelve knots. The captain was secure in the knowledge that the engines were the world's best and proud that Rudolf Diesel, a German, had perfected them. He knew that weight for weight, his boat had no equal. Maneuverability, speed, range, and firepower—if it came to a contest, it would win.

Vasco da Gama! He saw the framed picture over his bed when he was a student at the Katerinien Preparatory School in Leipzig. The explorer with a plumed velvet hat who had discovered the sea route to India. The first to sail around the Horn, the man who had tapped the riches of the Far East. And with a boat half the length of the *U-47,* which was small enough! What was left to explore on this earth? Nothing but the ocean *depths!*

By the chart Prien estimated his position at about longitude 9°5″E. by latitude 43°3″N. He was 700 kilometers south of Ireland, two days' surface running, and in the shipping lanes, just as his orders had prescribed.

Prien's number one, Endrass, was leaning dreamily on the voice pipe to his right while two ratings manned their binoculars. In the event of war the watch would be increased to five.

But this was the third of September, and the heads of state had been jockeying for many months and could go on forever. The captain abhorred politics, especially politicians, and he was content to be at sea, far from the striped trousers and homburgs. From below, through the conning hatch, he could hear music; the control room watch was tuned in to Berlin on the Rundfunk. Prien marveled at the crisp reception, so long a distance. The announcer gave a time check: 10:00 A.M. He wound his Rolex chronograph wristwatch. He counted forty seconds by the sweep hand and wondered if, should the occasion arise, his crew could dive without something going wrong. The test dives had gone well—but an actual emergency?

"Sir, sir!" Seaman Gerhardt Hänsel pulled himself up through the hatch. "Signal, sir. War with England, sir!"

The words stunned the bridge watch. Endrass stood up erect and took a deep breath. One of the ratings lowered his glasses and quickly crossed his heart. Prien slid down the ladder to the control room as the war watch took stations.

The men were crowded around the wireless; rousing military march music echoed throughout the boat. Faces appeared, half shaven, in the compartment hatchways. The commander searched his crew's eyes for a statement. He waited for the quartermaster, Spahr, to answer.

"They're about to repeat, sir," whispered Spahr as he fine-tuned the knob. The martial bands faded out and were replaced by the matter-of-fact voice of an announcer:

"This is the German Rundfunk with a special announcement.

" 'The British Government has given an ultimatum to the German government demanding the withdrawal of German troops from Polish territory. At nine this morning the British ambassador in Berlin presented an insolent note informing our government that unless a satisfactory reply was received in London by eleven o'clock this morning, Great Britain would consider herself as being at war with Germany.

" 'The British ambassador has been informed that the German government and the German people decline to accept or fulfill any demands contained in a British ultimatum!' "

There was a silence as if an angel had, as the proverb went, flown through the room. An angel of death. The bands struck up once more, and Spahr turned the sound down. The message had been broadcast on the intercom the length of *U-47*. A seaman came out of the WC and was told the news. He thought it was a joke, then saw the captain working feverishly at the chart table, saw Sammann unlock the Schmeisser machine-pistol rack and check the weapons.

"Proceed to this point." Prien's index finger tapped the chart. "Go to two-two-zero." Prien eyed the control room compass, then set the parallel ruler on the new course.

Spahr nodded solemnly, then added a muffled "Two-two-zero, sir."

As Prien climbed resignedly into the tower, a voice from the officers' mess, forward of the control room, broke the silence: "God have mercy on those who started this."

Endrass looked tautly at his commander as the ratings scanned the horizon vigilantly with their rubber-covered Zeiss eight by fifties. Forward, in the tower's shadow, a detail checked out the 8.8.-centimeter deck gun.

"Well, number one, this is it." Prien gripped the wind deflector rail tightly with both hands and squinted ahead.

"Nothing to do now—but our best," Endrass replied.

Prien went over the war procedure, point by point, with his exec: Report *anything* and *everything* sighted . . . hit the klaxon on spotting anything in the air; better dive than find out a gull is a plane—too late . . . double the reload drills. . . . Endrass saluted as the old man climbed down.

Old man, thought Prien; he *was* old for a submariner. Born in 1909. Thirty years ago! He dug into his wall locker and took out a small leather-bound book. Suddenly he felt as if he wanted to be alone, and he reached inboard, slid the green curtain on its tracks. He wasn't sure how he would react to the situation, and he didn't want his men to notice. After uncapping his fountain pen, he turned to a blank page and wrote: "3 IX 39."

What would a numerologist make out of that? He continued, noting the times and coordinates, the weather, and a few personal observations. And then he slid into his bunk.

"Commander to bridge. Smoke off the starboard bow."

The shrill shout cut deeply into Prien's sleep. He'd jumped up and heard only the last words. The control room mate repeated it as the commander flew past him, cap in hand. Endrass pointed at a thin curl of smoke on the horizon. Prien focused on the wisp with the watch's glasses, heart thumping. Would it be the enemy? If so, he'd rather it be a freighter or tanker than a warship. He didn't want lives lost—was that it? Or was he scared, as he'd every right to be. Scared of making the wrong decision. Scared of something's going wrong despite him.

The plume pulled a tiny black spot over the edge where hazy green met hazy blue.

Prien looked down at the compass repeater. "Come to one-zero-eight. Group up, full ahead." Endrass flicked up the voice tube cap and repeated the orders. *U-47* shuddered with the burst of power and leaped into the swells—a dark gray cat after the smoking mouse. The wood-slatted deck disappeared under frothing geysers of bow waves—dipping and riding, yawing and righting in a broaching sea. At eighteen knots the 800-ton craft knifed toward the quarry . . . looming larger and larger in the oft-wiped binocular lenses. The steamer, heading north, appeared to be a freighter of medium tonnage. Upon making out the bridge structure, Prien called for a dive.

With top speed headway, *U-47*'s foreplanes bit into the brine, and she was under in less than forty seconds. The crew exchanged satisfied glances. Prien said nothing. He expected that of his men. The forward, or sky, periscope whined up over the humming of the electromotors. The *Kapitänleutnant*, cap turned aft, shifted a lever and activated a warming circuit to clear condensation mist from the complex prisms in the periscope head. Next, he adjusted the darkening shade, eye pressed to the rubber ocular, and rotated the instrument with foot pedals. Prien found the target close to the bearings he'd last had on the bridge by means of a calibrated ring on the shaft above him. He focused quickly, recognizing the Greek colors on her standards. Fine, a neutral! Then he pushed a lever with his right hand which angled the sky prism slowly upward as he swung around on a revolving stool that was welded to a ring on the housing. He turned to the stop, then spun the opposite way, each time increasing the sky angle until he was satisfied there would be no aerial surprises. Gripping the cross handle with his right hand, he operated a compensation knob which offset the pitching motion of his boat. Then he leveled the angle and switched from wide angle through 0.6 and refocused at 1.6 diameters magnification. The image was sucked into the Goerz instrument and devoured by the anxious commander.

"Is that *one*?" Endrass asked fervidly.

"She's Greek; a rusty freighter. About six thousand." Prien let his watch officer take a look. "Get ready for action; prepare signal flags and report when ready." Prien climbed into the tower, followed by the watch and gun crew. The belowdecks watch was stacking 8.8. armor-piercing shells in a rack below the ammo hatch.

All stations reported: "Forward torpedo, ready . . . Engine room, ready . . ." The tanks were blown, and *U-47* boiled out of the sea.

The gun crew scrambled out of the tower hatch and down the steel rungs. Willy Meyer snapped the tampion out of the muzzle as Dziallas slammed a round into the breach of the *Schiffskanon* C/35.

"Fire one across her bows." Prien studied the dirty old hulk through his powerful binoculars. He couldn't make out any name or port of call.

The gun ka-boomed sharply, reverberating throughout the steel ship. The shot dropped a boat length ahead of the freighter, sending a white spout high above the pallid green. Willy cheered at Chief PO Hans Sammann, sitting proudly in the gunner's yoke. Dziallas set another round in and tried to wipe the irritating blue smoke out of his eyes.

"Minimum ahead," Endrass ordered through the pipe. "Set up the aerial mast."

The crew of the freighter was scurrying fore and aft, tugging at the lifeboat covers and tackle. Slowing down, she blew off clouds of white steam, then lay still and helpless in the swells. Steinhagen semaphored with his *Flaggenwinken*: "SEND OVER A BOAT WITH YOUR SHIP'S PAPERS." *U-47* glided cautiously into hailing distance, gunners at the ready. There was no answer to the flag signal.

Prien shouted the order through a megaphone. Tawny heads popped up and down behind the freighter's gunnel and deckhouse. After a gravelike silence, a voice echoed from the hulk. "Okay, sir."

Suddenly the old scow became alive. Two lifeboats were swung out on davits and precariously lowered as crew members jostled into them. Tarpaulins and fenders went bouncing overboard. The oars were flailing before the boats were in the water, such was their occupants' fright. Submarines meant one thing. Torpedoes!

They pulled frantically away from the freighter—and away from the U-boat.

"Half ahead port." Prien's boat crept ahead and soon was abeam of the fleeing lifeboats. The crews, as one, pulled in their sweeps and held their hands high over their heads.

"Where is your captain?" Prien looked down from the conning bridge at the ragtag Greeks as Hänsel, a marksman, covered them from the *Wintergarten* with a Schmeisser machine pistol.

A tall, pale figure stood up in the lead boat; he nervously handed a brown leather briefcase on the end of an oar to the deck PO while the detail crew warped lines about the midships bollards, holding the lifeboats fast against the port saddle tanks.

Prien shuffled through the papers, then sent them back with an admonition for the Greek captain: "You must maintain radio silence about this encounter; if you don't, I'll consider it a hostile act."

The tall Greek officer broke into a smile and reassured the Germans above him that he would comply. Apparently the freighter crew did not understand what was happening; their hands were still in the air.

"You may proceed." Lines were cast off, and the lifeboats remained motionless as *U-47* picked up way. As a parting gesture of good faith the Greek captain raised his right arm in a Nazi salute.

"Neutral and cargo for Bremerhaven," Prien announced.

One of the lookouts, Gustav Böhm, piped up from his post. "Can we trust their scurvy words, sir?"

The captain dressed his artificer down neatly and nicely regarding his own experiences and insights as a past merchant skipper. In the distance, catching the oblique rays of late afternoon, the venerable Greek poured on the coal until her plates rattled, while the thankful crew broke out the ouzo and praised Jesus and Mary.

NINE

It was 0600. The commander had gotten up early and gone to the bridge. No bells at 0600 on a submarine, not as on merchantmen and surface warships, which still clung to the past—to the times when the only timepiece aboard was the prized chronometer, snug in its fitted and padded mahogany box below in the captain's quarters. Not on a submarine. No place for anachronisms. Prien chuckled at the wordplay. He loved *Wortspiel*; the English called it punning. Some of his favorite sea chanteys contained the attribute.

At 0600 it was the middle point of the morning watch. How he recalled the glorious sunrises at four bells. Sumatra . . . Good Hope . . . Hispaniola . . . Madagascar . . . And the storms . . . the ice . . . the biting spray. Now he was a commander; he didn't *have* to go on the bridge, but he *wanted* to. Good for the soul—especially now—on the third day of the war. He pulled up the collar of his sea jacket up, against a following morning breeze. Soon it would be time to find his scarf—the one Ingeborg had given him when he'd left Tirpitzmole a week earlier. He felt his face, wet from the spray. He wondered whether he looked more like a commander with a beard. The beard would *go* as it always did.

A blood red shimmering oval, the sun wavered through the low-hanging mist. Obersteuermann Spahr, the watch PO, was playing with his sextant. Prien looked up. Playing? No, Spahr was taking a fix on Venus, that bright sliver. The captain, though a whiz by "pants' seat" and dead reckoning, was happy to leave the sines and cosecants to those who specialized. He would, however, check the navigator's findings when a second opinion was needed. His forte was radio navigation, and he was proud of his "sparks" certificate, earned in the merchant marine.

Gradually the sun oozed clear of its progeny's limb, paling imperceptibly into an orange, incandescently edge-lighting a high procession of wispy, hooked cirrus as its rays broke free of the dense atmosphere. The morning planet star was now captive of translucent green veils. In the west Orion dipped, the herald of winter. Morning to history's seafarers came as close to paradise as anything imaginable, be it Valhalla, Olympus, or Christian heaven.

"Where are we?" the captain quipped, feigning a simpleton's demeanor to his highest-ranking petty officer.

The navigator obliged with his own joke. "About five hundred kilometers farther north than yesterday."

Prien smiled crookedly.

"All right," Spahr conceded. "Forty-six point zero-five north by ten point six-five west in round numbers."

"That's better." But they both knew that *U-47* with its full load of fourteen eels was halfway between Spain and the south coast of Ireland. The shipping lanes of war were not defined. But chances were that sorely needed cargoes from the Mediterranean for the British islands would not go farther out than the tenth meridian of longitude: their sector.

The aroma of real coffee was snaking up through the open hatch, tempting the men on the tower, when the starboard bow watch called out, "Smoke, dead ahead!"

Prien peered through his binoculars and followed the smoke. "Seems to be zigzagging."

"A bad conscience perhaps?" Endrass climbed up.

"Take her down, Bert, and put us on a crossing course." The captain disappeared, following his nose. No time for breakfast. A cup of night sentry would have to do.

Taking fewer precautions, having had the bit in his mouth, Prien chose the attack scope in the cork-lined tower. This instrument was more complex than the sky scope below in the control room. The saddle was fixed, aft of the well since usage precluded that the target was ahead of the boat. A zigzag was good indication of a belligerent, and chances of aircraft had to be taken. The attack scope head was smaller than its forward relative: less feather wake on the surface, less chance of being spotted. Maximum magnification showed gold letters on the bow. "*Bosnia,*" emitted slowly from the commander's tight lips. A short, squat freighter, her funnel was bright carmine red (unconsciously recalling his mother's paint tubes), the hull and bridgehouse black, and she rode somewhat high, showing a poisonous green from water to waterline.

Her nationality was indistinguishable, but the name sounded Slavic. The control room mate couldn't find it in the Weyer register and Obersteuermann Spahr suggested that it might have missed the current edition.

"Slow ahead. We'll let her pass and come up behind her." Endrass nodded approval. It was good tactics. The ship might be armed and could bring all guns to bear if the sub surfaced broadside, rather than just the fantail mount, or it could veer and ram, cutting the low silhouette in two. The periscope whined down.

Preparatory to surfacing, the electromotors were rung up to maximum speed. The stoker, Schmalenbach, poked his head through the control room hatch. "Diesels ready, sir." Prien snapped a glance at the sound man in his niche forward of the *Zentrale.*

"Bearing?"

Steinhagen closed his eyes, one hand on his cloth-covered directional wheel, the other pressing on his right earphone. "Screws dead on bow, sir."

"Take her up." The commander counted seconds on his watch.

Sammann, the chief petty officer, barked out routinely, "Open one, three, and five."

"Open."

Compressed air hissed into the buoyancy tanks, and the U-boat's bow responded to the hydroplane angles.

"Fifteen meters, sir." The control room mate read the Papenburg depth column. The bridge watch and gun crew were poised in the tower. Hänsel held the course steady with his steering buttons, eye on the conning compass repeater.

"Pressure equalized." A shout from aft.

Oberleutnant Hans Wessels, the engineering officer, twirled the dogging wheel on the underside of the conning hatch as the diesels started up and the dark gray tower broke through the waves. Aft, in the E-motor room, Hotzer and Römer had rotated the controls to zero and were pulling the switches.

As the gun crew took positions, *Bosnia* fired up her boilers, churning up a bubbling wake and picking up speed away from the surprised adversary. A shot was fired over her. The freighter ignored it and zig-zagged.

A second 8.8-centimeter shell dropped close off her bows, throwing a geyser on her decks. Still, she increased speed.

Hebestreit, the radioman, scrambled up the ladder and handed Prien a slip of flimsy. "They're sending, sir."

The commander's jaw tightened as he read the message: UNDER FIRE FROM GERMAN U-BOAT. MAYDAY SOS URGENT POSITION 46 DEGREES ZERO FIVE . . .

He handed it to Endrass, who'd replaced Wessels since the going had gotten rougher and experience was needed. Their eyes met and agreed. This was it!

"No more games," he shouted to the deck gun crew. "*Fire.*"

Bosnia was hit midships; debris scattered, and a puff of smoke obscured her lifeboats.

"Five rounds rapid fire," Prien ordered.

The garishly painted ship shook and floundered as the 3.5-inch high-explosive rounds tore into her hull and bridgehouse. The crew scurried like ants out of the hold. She wallowed and hove to, broaching in the swells.

A flash of flame licked out of the rent hull, aft of the funnel, then another on deck. Muffled explosions blew clouds of yellow smoke in all directions; then blue flame spurted from the main hatch decks. Soon a massive, swirling cloud of yellow smoke obliterated the sun. Lifeboats were launched, full of coughing and choking crewmen. Several were seen to jump, pushed by the ravenous, leaping flames behind them.

"Looks like sulfur smoke," Endrass observed.

"Smells like it, too," Prien added. "Half ahead both. Let's get to windward in case she blows up."

Seaman Hänsel sang out from his port sector, "Column of smoke, two points off—"

The captain turned and told the spotter to keep the intruder in sight. He didn't like the looks of it; if it was black and moved fast, it could be a destroyer responding to *Bosnia*'s distress call.

One of *Bosnia*'s lifeboats had snagged its lowering gear and swamped. Crewmen thrashed out of it to get away from the inferno above them. Soon the heat would be intense enough to cook anyone too close. The lines were frantically slashed, but the boat was too full; it slipped below the surface, leaving the crew hanging onto their oars.

U-47 inched in as close as it dared as Sammann and Dittmer clung outboard of the midship rail and reached down to the frenzied, haggard swimmers. Some shouted, *Kamerad*," and others, unintelligible foreign words. Several tried to call, coughed, and disappeared. Others swam toward the first lifeboat.

Sammann, stripped to the waist, hauled one of *Bosnia*'s crew aboard. The crewman, small and red-haired, fell, throwing up on the deck. His mates, washed back by a wave, struggled back and slithered up onto the saddle tanks as the Germans tried to grab them without success.

"Norwegian freighter, sir." Prien spun around and leveled his glasses. The intruder from the southwest lay high. She was in ballast and apparently had no cargo. She was in her right, thought the commander. It was right to save lives, and it would solve a sticky problem: what to do with the rescued crewmen.

Meanwhile, the red-haired boy had gotten his breath back and was standing at the rail with Dittmer. The commander ordered the boy to be sent up to the bridge. The boy told him that he was aboard as cabin boy and cook's helper. When asked, the boy said *Bosnia* had carried sulfur from Turkey. They were bound for Glasgow. Prien thought he had a London Cockney accent, similar to what he'd heard in his maritime travels. Hänsel wrapped a blanket around the youth's shoulders.

"You're afraid of us?" Endrass asked.

"No, just cold, sir." His thin, water-shriveled fingers held the blanket tightly about his neck.

"And your captain?" Prien spoke softly.

The boy motioned with his jaw toward the other lifeboat. *U-47* pulled up alongside, and Willy Loh threw out a line, led by a monkey's fist weight. The spliced weight hung across the stern, and *Bosnia*'s cox'n hauled in on it. Loh turned away momentarily at the sight of a blistered, reddened body slumped over a thwart.

"Which of you is the captain?" Prien was using the megaphone.

A man with an officer's coat struggled to his feet and pointed to the blazing inferno. "He's still aboard."

"Probably destroying the ship's papers."

The commander nodded to Endrass. They both had to admire such courage. It was beyond war and winning.

"What is your rank?" the megaphone boomed again.

Tipping his torn cap, he shouted, "First officer, sir."

He was motioned up to the bridge as orders were given the helmsman to steer toward the approaching steamer. The deck crew called the bridge's attention. They'd spotted a survivor. He was floating and seemed unconscious. The U-boat veered off course, and he was hauled aboard and carried below through the ammo hatch. The commander and *Bosnia*'s officer went below to see if they could help. Sammann had laid the limp body on a bunk and stripped off his wet clothes, bundled him in a dry blanket. He was thin, his emaciated ribs outlined with wet and caked coal dust ground into the skin. Dittmer began artificial respiration.

Bosnia's officer spoke in broken German: "German Navy—we happy you good hearts people, sir." Prien stared at the officer: fat and pulpy, well fed. Quite unlike his stoker.

Steinhagen signaled the Norwegian vessel to take the English crew aboard. She lowered a boat which came alongside and picked up the three crew members and then went after the other lifeboat. Suddenly a figure jumped from the bow of *Bosnia*. It was the captain. He swam toward the rescue boat, waving and shouting. *U-47* waited impatiently until the launch had finished her task and been winched aboard. After lowering her flag in a salute, the empty freighter turned back on her northward course.

The entire crew save those who wouldn't wake up came out of the hatches, fore and aft, to witness the maiden torpedo shot. To their surprise, the coup de grâce did not make *Bosnia* stand spectacularly on its tail and whoosh below. There was a muffled thud, and the ship bent in the middle and went down slowly, leaving a few wooden crates and boards bobbing in her stead.

U-47, like the Krupp steel that had gone into her at the sprawling Germaniawerft yards at Kiel, was now tempered, toughened by the unrelenting North Sea, strengthened by its first victories, and hardened by the stench of death.

The British, in desperation, developed the armed convoy technique. With no less than 2,000 tankers and freighters plying the shipping lanes on any given day, Britain was vulnerable. And Commodore Dönitz knew it. The Empire's arteries fanned around the globe, but one thing was certain: They all entered the heart, and it was around the Hebrides, the Orkneys, and the Channel that the majority of little pins on a chart in the operations room in Kiel that bore the designation *Befehlshaber der Unterseeboote* were stuck.

Korvettenkapitän Victor Oehrn, staff officer, Operations, plucked one of the black ball-headed pins from its place and moved it north on the wall map. "We've got to watch this fellow," he commented to the others in the room. The officer, with a firm push, stuck the pin into a grid area west of the Hebrides, a Scottish island group in the Atlantic Ocean.

The balding commodore looked up from a series of position plots that had been given him by his communications officer, Stockhausen. He rose from the cluttered desk and studied the wall chart. His aging eyes had trouble reading the little number inscribed on the pinhead. He moved back a bit, hoping the younger men hadn't noticed. He would remember the number: 47. Then, as if drawn by a magnet his eyes rolled farther north, across the Highlands of Scotland . . . and stopped at Scapa Flow.

"ANY SHIP IN CONVOY GOES TO THE BOTTOM." The captain, or *Kaleu,* as commanders were called by their crew, printed the phrase carefully in his diary. It was the order of the day. Late in the atfernoon the watch had been glad to go under. Even autumn off the Hebrides could feel like winter. Also, there was no point pushing luck within range of a Blenheim bomber.

"Captain to the control room!" Prien was somewhat relieved: a good reason not to have to do his homework.

The third watch officer proudly proffered the ladder to his commander. Prien knew the import of this. The attack scope! He gingerly turned the scope and saw what looked like a forest of toothpicks dancing vertically. The sea was rough and sloshed over the objective lens again and again.

Prien counted twelve steamers and an escort of five destroyers. The large ships were zigzagging while their nimble guardians steamed in wide circles.

The U-boat changed course and headed directly at the convoy. But the wind into which she now headed made visual observation impossible as the scope was buffeted and swamped again. They followed the convoy, waiting for the right moment.

By nightfall their courses had intersected. Prien picked a fat tanker against the western twilight. He remembered Admiral Jellicoe's statement about the last war: "The allies had floated to victory on a wave of oil." This wave, he thought, would never reach the shore. The motors were cut to minimum ahead. The tanker was bearing down. Everyone aboard could feel the thunderous pulsing of the ship's powerful engines. The sound man took his headset off and rubbed his ears. Her bows loomed high in the periscope.

"Torpedoes one through four, stand by for submerged fire."

Werder, in the forward torpedo room, pulled a lever, activating a servomotor that flooded the tubes, equalizing the outside pressure and allowing the doors to swing open.

"Boat balanced." Chief Sammann checked the trim.

Prien, pressed into the rubber, ordered, "Switch on tubes one and two." Obersteuermann-navigator Spahr held a clipboard in one hand and a stopwatch in the other. "Enemy course one-zero-five green, speed twelve." Endrass fed the figures into the torpedo data computer. "Set for sixteen feet . . . hydroplane station—bow right, angle sixty . . . follow change . . ."

The computer clicked and buzzed, sending its calculations in spurts down and forward, through a cable and a waterproof contact that fed into the deadly eels.

"Enemy angle one-zero-ten . . . and holding . . . follow . . . follow . . . torpedo one . . . *fire!*"

The boat's bow rose slightly as the G7e 2,500-pound eel spurted from its lair whose hatch was labeled "Rozmarie." Spahr counted: "Thirteen . . . fourteen . . . fifteen . . ." Anxious glances were exchanged. Too long; should have hit by now. The commander cursed under his breath when he saw what had gone wrong!

Then it happened. A muffled ba-room.

All hands cheered.

The commander didn't have to explain *just then* that he'd forgotten to change the magnification of the periscope to standard from 1.6 diameters. A little luck was always welcome!

The wet, metal-clad eye inched up, dropped, then feathered along at minimum speed, just enough to hold course against the ocean current. Had it eyelids, it would have blinked at the sight! Blinding white-hot belching flame—hundreds of feet high!

"Fast screws approaching red twenty!" The sound man.

"Down scope; crash dive."

"Sounds like destroyers," Steinhagen shouted from his niche. The depth-gauge bubble decended: twenty meters . . . thirty . . . Everyone waited, hoped, expected—and then it came. The first retaliation of the enemy. Since wars began, first it was the stone hurled back, then the spear, then, from the unseen adversary, the arrow. Always, even with the advent of guns, the enemy had at least been *spotted* by the quarry. But now there came an impersonal projectile, a silent messenger of death . . .

EEYOOOM.

They missed!

EEYOOOM. The boat shook. Again . . . closer! Then a silence that was magnified, distorted, eerie. The next one, if on track, would be closer. The commander ordered hard right rudder. It was pure instinct—an automatic animal reaction. *Veer. Hide!*

EEYOOOM EEYOOOM EEYOOOM.

Shattering glass, popping light bulbs, paint chips

raining from the white ceiling, gurgling in the vents. Hands went for conduits and bulkheads. Red emergency lights flickered on and off. Diesel Mate Böhm held onto the WC bowl below him. He'd been caught; he'd taken a chance when they were on the surface but had lost.

Oberleutnant Wessels, in charge of damage control, asked for reports via the intercom. As in exercises, the reports came in sequence, starting with the most important sector.

"Engine room, all secure."

"E-motors, three bulbs broken."

"Forward, two manometers damaged, two bulbs broken."

"Wireless, line fused, emergency in operation."

Eeyooom. Sighs of relief . . . farther away! Steinhagen reported all clear on his hydrophones. The commander called for full ahead.

Römer, the chief electrician *Obermaschinist,* pushed his motor handles as far outboard as possible, and the armatures whined as *U-47* picked up speed. The petty officer watched the voltage surge on the meters over the stainless motor drums. He would find that extra power and use it, for everything could depend on it. He knew by the sound, by the tickling vibration of the nonskit metal plate he was standing on, that the boat was doing better than its maximum: eight knots!

A rumble far away as a pattern of wabos, or *Wasserbomben,* detonated. Prien decided it was safe to take a look. The hydroplanes tilted up like flippers on a sea monster pushing against the water, and the boat rose to periscope depth. The captain chose the attack instrument again. It was now night; he had forgotten the stories of 1915's commanders. Depth-charge attacks were eternities quickly and wantonly forgotten. He pressed the foot pedal, and the *Seeröhr,* or sea tube, rotated toward a glow. The captain's pulse quickened at the sight: a dome of fire—like a blazing city. The etched range calibrations in the periscope field indicated that the inferno was 1,500 feet long and as high as a thirty-story building. Twice as broad and almost as high as the Great Pyramid. Secondary explosions hurled burning oil and debris in all directions. Then he thought of the men inside that hell, men who, like him, were simply doing the thing they did best. These men did not deserve such a fate. He felt a kinship; then he heard a voice within. It was his father, whom he hadn't seen since the divorce—when he was only ten. His father, sitting up high in his judge's robes and booming down, "Günther, there is only *right* and there is only *wrong* in this world. . . ."

The commander felt a pang of guilt as he stepped back, allowing Endrass's eager eye to apply itself to the rubber. He threaded his way down, past Spahr's outstretched hand, and acknowledged the pats and plaudits of the control room watch, then ducked into the wardroom corridor. He nodded at his telegraphers and the hydrophone operator before drawing his curtain. It occurred to him that he had killed. Not *a man,* but a score . . . perhaps as many as forty souls. He shook the images out of his sandy, short-cropped head.

Prien took his little book out of the mahogany ledge drawer and pulled the reading lamp chain under his locked cabinet. He sat on his bunk and leaned over the next blank page.

A familiar vibration signaled that *U-47* was surfacing. It meant they'd eluded the destroyers. They were safe. They'd cut their teeth on war. Veterans now, the next time would be easier.

First, he entered the date, the approximate position, the wind direction, and the sea conditions. These were his confidential notes, separate from the official log, which he supervised in the control room every two duty hours. Then he described the day's routine action: the test dives and torpedo inspections, the flak and deck gun exercises. Next, the war action—the performance of the men under stress, weak as well as strong. He jotted a note about the second watch control room mate. Very young, perhaps *too* young. Had he lied about his age?

Then he penned some numbers: "5,000–6,000 tons." He added this mentally to the others. His third sinking. He was over 10,000! But it was hard to tell. Certainly over 9,000. He hung his white-crowned cap on its peg, then kicked his seaboots off and stretched out on his leather-covered bunk. The diesels were now throbbing, sending reassuring caresses through the pressure hull and into his shoulder, his body, snug against the wood-paneled bulkhead. It was cozy, here. It was safe—almost like being unborn, still in the womb.

TEN

Major Claus Krupp slammed the throttle of his twin-motored He-111P-2 back, and the black-speckled olive bomber slowed down and descended in a lazy, wide arc. The odometer swung from 390 down to 310. Next, he flipped a switch, and the wing flaps angled downward. The Daimler-Benz inverted-V liquid-cooled engines whined as they dipped into a sea of cumulus.

The copilot navigator, Lieutenant Michalski, closed his chart folder and formed a ring with forefinger and thumb, the universal sign of affirmation. The sun sent shafts of cold light up through cloud breaks in the distance: a portent of the long arctic nights to come, the dark days.

They'd left three and a half hours earlier from a blacked-out Luftwaffe strip near the town of Husum in Scheswig-Holstein 50 kilometers south of the Danish border. Claus had brought the Heinkel 850 miles, 100 miles farther than its normal range with a full bombload. But there were no bombs. Instead, it carried a triple fuel load in special interior tanks in addition to the normal ones, extending the range to about 2,000 miles. The square-jawed "Aryan" zipped up his flight jacket. They were almost at the sixtieth parallel, level with Oslo and Stockholm, and it was cold.

Suddenly the ominous, angular bird, emblazoned with crosses and swastikas, broke through the cloud layer, and the startled crew of four instinctively threw up their hands as shields against the blinding rays of a low-hanging sun. The altimeter hovered at 12,000 feet as they leveled off—a safe margin over unexpected antiaircraft fire.

Michalski pointed over the side with his big leather mitten. Claus banked the aircraft and squinted at the islands ahead to the left. A smile spread across his face, and he tipped his service cap to the navigator. Sergeant Walther Loos took the cue and swung his 7.9-millimeter Rheinmetal machine gun to the side of the acrylic-paneled nose compartment. Then he unzipped a fitted bag and took out an aerial camera, which he inserted into a flexible fitting on the underside of the nose housing.

It was the pride of Zeiss. The incomparable German optical firm had perfected a sixty-inch focal-length lens, twice as powerful as any the English could muster. The scientists had made possible aerial photography from a safe altitude.

And Scapa Flow would be the first victim!

Claus had been briefed: Make three runs at 12,000 feet over the southwest coast of East Mainland. He looked at his chart of the Orkneys. The entire main island, or Mainland, appeared like a bow tie when it was approached from this angle. At the narrows there would be a city: Kirkwall, the northern terminal of the run. What a piece of cake, he thought and wished he'd carried bombs instead of photographic film. He wondered whether his father's influence ever left him. Would he have made major so quick if he hadn't been born a Krupp?

"All set, sir"—a shout from the sergeant.

"Over there, Claus." Michalski lowered his binoculars. The sharp-eyed one had spotted St. Magnus Cathedrel, its red- and yellow-hued sandstone tower catching the oblique sunlight. The twelfth-century Romanesque building towered over the tiny gabled houses of Kirkwall.

Claus checked his note pad: . . . *Tower: 133 feet. Plan: cruciform.* He nodded at the lieutenant, then turned and looked up at Corporal Krafft. Satisfied that the dorsal gunner was ready, he spoke into the intercom: "Franz!"

"Ready, sir." The boy corporal closed his fingers nervously on the grips of his 20-millimeter belly cannon.

"Bearing?"—the major to the navigator.

"Three-two-seven."

"Reciprocal?"

"One-four-seven."

"Keep your fingers crossed, we're going in."

Kapitän zur See Karl Dönitz moved an enormous magnifying glass back and forth along the glossy black and white coastline of Scapa Flow. The prints had been joined to form a continuous aerial view. A flare of light moved along under his glass.

"Fantastisch! Look here, Commander. Even the searchlight!"

"Just like the drawing." Korvettenkapitän Eberhardt Godt leaned over the display. "That midnight sun casts nice reconnaissance shadows."

But the staff officers at Toten Weg, headquarters

of U-boat Command in Wilhelmshaven, all had seen it: the passage into "impregnable" Scapa Flow. There was enough water for a fast, low boat to slip in between the shore and the blockships . . . at night. The channel showed clearly, a dark, undulating snake against the light, sandy bottom of Holm Sound. Just a three-mile run through the sluice. Even against an eight-knot tide, a VIIB would have a nine-knot advantage, provided she got up enough speed for steerageway, provided a few small details were taken care of. The darker, the better. It would be the night of a new moon. It would be new moon in a week.

Too soon, perhaps next month. Yes, next month, they agreed. October 13. That the thirteenth was a Friday did raise the communications officer's eyebrows, but he quickly recovered.

The officers passed magnifying glasses around and fairly salivated at the shapes of English battlewagons and cruisers lying so vulnerable, so unexpectant, so calm.

Godt suggested that they first send a small coastal submarine to lay off Pentland Firth submerged and record the tides and currents, perhaps spot the defenses as they would appear from the sea. This would be done in daylight, as well as dark. Dönitz agreed.

A young lieutenant, just promoted from ensign, feverishly took down the notes and orders of this most secret meeting. It was all very new and exciting. He hesitated upon writing the name of the headquarters. Toten Weg. It didn't seem to bother the others—perhaps he'd get used to it, too.

But *Cemetery Road*!

ELEVEN

Alexander S. MacCowan, for a man in his middle fifties, handled his twelve-foot dory like a young Jack Tar. It was important to know the eccentricities of the tides to fish Holm Sound. Many a boat had foundered between Glims and Burray. The tide was a woman: capricious and unpredictable—unless of course, one knew that woman, as the major did.

He pulled hard on his starboard sweep to come to the lee of a rock off Lamb Holm. Tide was starting to ebb. It was late afternoon, September 21, 1939. It struck the major, or Sandy as he was also known, that he'd been fighting the ebb for almost exactly twenty years!

It was 1919 when he had come back from the war and a year's occupation duty in the Rhineland. He'd already had fourteen years in, so he'd applied for home duty to fill out his time and had drawn this godforsaken end of the world. He had hated it so much that he'd volunteered for a second three-year stint in the Orkneys and had then retired there. In St. Mary's by-the-sea. That he'd married an Orkney lass was one consideration, of course, but his fish-and-chips restaurant, thanks to retirement pay, had weathered the stormy Depression, and there was new hope. Someone had to feed the antiaircraft crews outside their regular mess. Someone had to keep up their morale on this bleak island. Sandy's Sea Specialties on the Six-mile Road between Netherbutton's wireless masts and St. Mary's Holm did just that. Sandy was getting the business from battery HQ at Borrowstone Hill, just this side of Kirkwall, and the naval air station at Hatson, as well as from Skaill and Foubister. Another installation was being built on Burray, across the sound. MacCowan would be ready when the hungry troops got off the ferry. It was getting around that Rowena MacCowan's fish batter was lighter and tastier than Smoky Joe's in Kirkwall's Junction Road.

Sandy pulled hard for Kirk Sound, past the two-masted wreck, sunk as a blockship, then the cement-filled hulls, barely underwater, of the blockships *Thames* and *Soriano*. The flat bottom of his dory scraped against connecting chains and wires. Sandy, a resourceful man, kept his boat's bottom free of barnacles by this method.

One of the three fish sliding in the wash between Sandy's boots, a three-pound haddock, was still flapping. The others, whiting, had expired. The major would allow himself one afternoon per week to pursue his quest: the elusive halibut. He had an interest in one of the commercial boats that unloaded every two days at the Holm wharf, sufficient to supply at a fair discount the needs of his business.

The record halibut caught on a commercial line was more than 600 pounds and measured better than nine feet. Individual rod and line records were in the 100-pound range. Sandy *knew* there was such a fish in the flow. He had once seen it, fighting the eight-knot tidal bore through the skerries. Magnificent fish with its ring speckles all over the broad, flat back. Leopard of the Atlantic deeps. Sharp-toothed predator of the sub-Arctic. With the onset of winter it would venture south to the Orkneys again, and Alexander MacCowan would be there—with his Allcocks' Leviathan reel and 400 yards of eighty-pound test braided line! With a dozen live herring in seawater as bait and a dozen number 12 tempered, barbed hooks!

A hundred pounds—reflected A. Schmuele MacCowan, Simpson on his official records—would, dressed down, make 150 portions of pure profit! He scratched his red-tinged sideburns and nearly dropped an oar, pulled a crab, and lost way.

It bothered him that even with a discount he had to pay too much for his fish. He cursed the middleman but then realized that he was the middleman. Then he cursed the slovenly trawler gangs. Perhaps he should buy out the others. With a few large halibut of his own . . .

He suddenly caught himself. His father's side again, always popping up. But then it was because of his ancestral merchant history that he'd been picked for the job.

Supply officer for the king's army all those years! Now unofficial general or commanding officer of his sector's Home Defense Battalion. And home defense was mainly a problem of logistics, of supply.

Making his painter fast to the wharf cleat, he wondered whether he might inquire for assistance through some of the more affable young seamen from the old *Iron Duke*; symbolic and senile battlewagon lying as a fleet memorial and emasculated flagship—two of her five turrets removed—of Sir Wilfrid French, admiral commanding Orkney and Shetland. It was *Duke* that had led Jellicoe's Grand Fleet from Scapa to Jutland in 1916. Now a depot and transit ship, much as *Hamburg* in Kiel, she was moored in the flow, the deceased admiral's blue frock coat and plumed hat propped grimly in a glass case aboard.

"General" MacCowan made a mental note as he wrapped his catch in newspaper: Inveigle Sir Wilfrid to strip off a couple of three-inchers so the Home Defense could mount them over Kirk Sound to be manned by a volunteer twenty-four-hour watch. If a halibut could buck the tide, so might a submarine.

"Rowena, m' lass"—Sandy unwrapped his catch on the gutting table—"if you want to catch a fish, you've got to think like a fish. . . ."

The cowbell on the door jangled briskly. Mrs. MacCowan wiped her hands of the batter she'd been mixing and scurried into the dining area. It was more a lunchroom and store than a restaurant. Who would want . . . at this hour?

"That's a beautiful Regulator, I mean the wall clock."

"Why, thank you." Rowena watched with fascination as the handsome blond officer set his watch at 4:15. She admired his blue uniform—such a welcome change from olive drab and dull navy. And his accent: so romantic, like in a movie. He ordered fish and chips with wallies as he sidled onto a counter stool.

"Such a fine view you have, and a perfect bicycle road."

Rowena rustled the haddock in bubbling beef drippings. Her heart was thumping. If only . . . Then she realized she hadn't answered. "It's all right, I guess, but I'm so tired of looking at boats."

"And I don't blame you."

She reeled at the officer's reply. Now here was a gentleman, not like the others. She hoped Sandy would take his time in the back, and she hoped that no more customers would come in for a while. "Are you visiting?"

"You might say that. I'm staying at the Kirkwall."

"It's the best, they say." Rowena wondered what it would be like to stay at a fancy hotel—with a handsome officer. She wished she'd done her hair; she avoided his eyes as she set the steaming plate before him. She tingled all over at the aroma of after-shave lotion. Such a change from fish.

"I'll bet the fleet comes here." He smacked his lips.

"You should be here when they get paid."

"No, thank you." He laughed at the idea. "By the way, how late are you open?" The officer stirred his coffee slowly.

"Weekdays, til six—except Fridays we close past ten. Saturdays about nine, and we're closed on Sundays. . . ." She'd busied herself behind the counter for a while so as not to appear too forward. When she turned around, all she saw was an empty plate and a shiny coin. She ran outside with three shillings' change, but there was only a cloud of dust where the road bent. She took two shillings out of her purse and put them in the cash drawer.

Then she fondled the silver crown and slipped it into her bra when the back door creaked open.

TWELVE

Sturmbannführer Erich Knochen, a cynical smile on his scarred lip, handed the file card to his typist, Gefreiter Ursula Pregler. "Here's a funny one for your *M* list."

She looked up from her Adler, green eyes piercing her thick eyeglasses. Ursula snarled inside; she didn't like to be interrupted in the middle of a list page. Now she'd have to recollate. Enough, those long lists for Neuengamme, for Bergen-Belsen and Buchenwald. But the commandant, Gruppenführer Peschke, had rewarded her brilliant logistics efforts with a promotion. After being a female work leader of the National Labor Service for three years, she was made an honorary corporal in the SS with full SS man's pay, privileges, and uniform. How she just loved her new uniform. *Black*, like the scar-lipped major's. And she was so proud of her little silver death's-head insignia on her service cap next to the typewriter. She shone it with special polish every day. How it glistened, her *Totenkopfchen*!

The file card waved a second time in front of her eyes, and she reached out, took it, and read:

MacCohen, Deckname (alias) *MacCowan*; Major Ret. St. Mary's, East Mainland, Orkneys.

Ursula's prim, wide mouth quivered in one corner. "God, won't they *ever* learn?" She riffled through a sheaf of papers. "We've already got a Magowan and a Macohon. . . ."

"And it seems I remember a Macoenė. . . ." Major Knochen took his SS dagger out of its sheath and examined the steel point. "That *Cohen* is a chemistry professor."

"The one who managed to buy his way out of St. Petersburg?"

"Corporal"—he knew she loved to be called that—"stick with me, and you'll make sergeant."

"What do we have on this one?"

"Ah, yes. After 'Retired,' insert 'Agent.' He's in charge of resistance on his little island."

"The ancient Home Guard again, armed with pikes from Admiral Nelson's flagship." Ursula typed a correction strip, then slit the proper *M* sheet and inserted the addition, backed up with cellophane tape. The major giggled over her absurdity.

"Corporal, you do slay me."

"It's true!" Ursula didn't bat an eyelash, and the major went into a giggling fit. An idea occurred. Why not a little asterisk or other symbol for the Cohen types? But then the sheets were predominantly . . . anyway. She counted seventeen Meyers on one sheet alone. The buxom spinstress straightened her brown hair bun with one hand while she took a file box down from a shelf over her desk.

The spine bore the code designation GB-1.

She privately called it her Arrest List.

THIRTEEN

"Lieutenant Commander Benjamin Mount, United States Navy."

"Ah, yes, Commander. Your room is reserved through tomorrow night—and of course—the morning. Check-out time is noon."

"That's fine." Mount signed the register.

"I suppose you'll do a little sight-seeing about our fair islands before you board your ship?"

"Who said anything about a ship?" Ben replied sharply.

"But all naval officers—Yes, of course. Your bags." The balding, skinny desk clerk tapped the bell button, and a young man limped toward the commander's bags, taking the room key off the desk as he passed by. He picked up all three, in spite of his affiction, and started to hobble toward the lift.

"Come on now, son." Mount pulled the heaviest bag from the bellhop's grip. "Now you lead the way."

"Name's Danny, sir." The boy set the bags properly on a stand near a closet, then drew the curtains. "You know the regulations, sir—about blackouts, sir?"

"Call me Ben, and yes, I've got my war handbook *and* a gas mask."

"Wouldn't be proper, sir, to call ye that."

"Danny."

"Sir."

"You're a British subject."

"I am, and right proud, sir." He straightened the bedcover.

"And you're a civilian."

"I woulda been the first to join up, sir."

"I'm sorry, Danny, I didn't mean *that*. I'm trying to tell you that I'm here as a tourist—an American tourist—and I don't want to be called sir. Got that?" Ben winked and flipped a shilling to the boy, who snapped it in midair.

"Got it, but in front o' the others—I mean, in the lobby . . ."

"It's a deal, Danny."

"Okay then, Yank, I'll call ye Ben."

"That's better. Now don't just run off. If you had little more than a day, how would you spend it around here?" Ben opened the casement window and looked out over Kirkwall Harbor.

"Would ye rent a bicycle?"

"Great idea, Danny. I need the exercise."

"Okay. I'd ride the coast road down to St. Mary's, then come back by way of St. Andrews. You'll get a good lay of the land—the flow and the Mainland sounds. Then I'd go out to Finstown—they've got a fine country pub; it was frequented by some Orcadians who fought in your Civil War. One of 'em was related to your famous General Cursiter, a man of Orkney descent."

"Cursiter?"

" 'E was the man called Yellow Hair who made the famous last stand wi' all those bloomin' savages."

"Do you mean *Custer*?"

"Aye, that's American for Cursiter! . . . The pub's called Pomona Inn, but most of us still think of it as the Toddy, from its original name, The Toddy Hole. Say, if ye get out to Finstown tonight, I'll be at the Toddy, an' I'll shout you a pint. It's my Saturday night off. The men get together after five thirty."

"If I do, I won't have a uniform on. Sweater and knickers."

"And the food's fine, too—not to put the Royal Hotel down."

"I'll have breakfast here in the morning. Now, how about lunch—It's about ten. If I cycle to St. Mary's, there must be a place I can have a decent lunch. I've heard so much about your Orkney seafood. . . ."

"Say no more, Ben. I can recommend a place on the Six-mile Road. It's called Sandy's Sea Specialties. If yer of a wont fer fish 'n' chips, ye won't find a better meal. Ye go past the searchlight battery, an' it's the first store on th' left after the gun emplacement. Can't miss th' sandbags."

"Danny, you've done a man a great favor. Even though it's against my upbringing to drink whisky, I'll make a special effort to turn up at the Toddy."

"I'll have a bike in front o' the place in ten minutes, Yank."

"I can't promise, Danny, but I'll try to make Finstown."

Benjamin Mount slid onto a stool at the counter. The bicycle ride had whetted his appetite. Eight miles he'd made, including a stop-off at the pier. He'd watched the activities—the Navy barges flitting back and forth from the capital ships at the anchorage. He'd especially noted the barge that sallied out to the carrier. To HMS *Courage*. To *his* ship, to the ship that he'd been assigned to as radar observer, as representative of the most potent nation on earth —and the most unprepared, considering its resources.

"Afternoon, sir." The body swabbed a rag over the varnished wood counter. The body's blouse was loose at the body's bronzed breast. Ben watched the curve of her breasts as she wiped the bar, oblivious of her angle.

"Good afternoon." Ben gulped as he saw a silver Star of David between the breasts. He pointed at the wall menu. "Fish and chips, please."

Ruth MacCowan turned and bent over the bubbling vat. Ben watched her: the nylons . . . the näiveté. For a moment he thought he was back in Brooklyn—sitting on a bench on Ocean Parkway. It excited him. Why? He was tired of erudite British hostesses and wives of members of Parliament. He wanted warmth.

"I say there, lass." Ben, in his creamy knit cardigan and tweed knickers, was in a mood for fun. "I'm a traveling salesman, not used to these parts, and since it be Saturday, I was wondering whether you could advise me of the local synagogue."

Ruth's color left her, and she tore at her necklace, covering up the pendant. Nobody'd ever asked that of her before. She blanched and looked down. A button was missing on her blouse. My God, what had the stranger seen? Ruth collected her wits; this was rare!

"Excuse me, sir . . ." Ruth played blasé, clasping her blouse.

"Where can I find a Sabbath service?"

"This is a restaurant."

"Yes, I'll have a fish and chips, but tell me, where is the local synagogue? Oh, yes, you can draw me a beer . . . please."

It was the "please" that did it to Ruth. The RAF boys never said "please"; neither did the searchlight crews—or even the swaggering petty officers from the *Royal Oak.* They were interested in only *one* thing: woman as a . . . as a repository for their baser instincts. But this man seemed different. What was it Father had cautioned her about? Traveling salesmen were the worst, he'd said. For all ye know, they've got too much family at home . . . Ruth was interested; this was different; it spurred something within her, something she'd been used to—before it happened. Before her mother left the house—the house her family shared with the others in Jaffa, where she was born. Her father had fought the Turks at Gallipoli and served with the Royal Desert Mounted Corps under General Allenby in the campaign that drove the German-led Turkish armies to retreat. Her father's unit was part of a cordon that ringed Jaffa, Haifa, the major Palestinian seaport, having been captured early in the war. Her mother and father had met in the orange groves where her mother worked. Ruth remembered the fragrances of the groves, where as a child she'd helped gather and pack the fruit for shipment around the world on the freighters that moored off the port. The orange groves compensated for the squalid ancient seaport.

Then there was the Arab market, with dancing bears and prancing ponies—and there was the sea where she loved to swim. Where her father swam underwater and pinched her toes, then explained that it was not *he,* but the descendant of the legendary sea monster, the bones of which were taken by a Roman governor to the seat of Empire, where it was acclaimed by Caesar and Pompey.

Ruth smiled at the stranger and, not knowing what

to reply, prepared the chips and drew a pint. Two RAF boys were seated at the far end of the counter; she was glad they had not seen the Star of David hanging from her neck. Her father forbade her to wear it in the dining saloon or in company at home. The gold star had belonged to her mother. When she drowned, near the rocks that Andromeda was said to have been chained to as a sacrifice, Ruth had torn the star from the cold body, knowing that her father would have sold it. Lieutenant MacCowan was an English officer, he'd say, even before she died, and there was no room for driveling religion in a world of cordite and shrapnel. Besides, he'd say—to the dismay of the *others* at the table—that he'd stand a better chance of promotion without *such* encumbrances and, in turn, might be of more value to the cause.

After the tragedy her father transferred to a regiment in Edinburgh, where she attended a proper school and learned of the finer things: the arts and sciences. Her mother's dreams for her daughter came true; she was allowed piano lessons and even went to the Royal Opera with her classmates.

One evening her father, having finished the dinner she had cooked, made a pompous announcement: "Ruth, now that you've had your education you'll want to find employment in what you do best. I'm retiring from the Army, and I've bought interest in a restaurant near Kirkwall in the Orkneys. It'll be a booming area soon, and you'll never regret working for me. Nothing like a family business." The rest of the family was Rowena Sinclair, a widow of one of Allenby's Desert Corps officers.

Ruth combed the foam from the stein and set it before the sweatered stranger.

"I'm sorry, sir, but I have no answer to your question. You see, I'm not religious." She fingered her closed blouse at her budding breast. "It was my mother's, but she drowned."

"I'm sorry." Ben lowered his head.

"It wasn't your fault—I'm not supposed to wear it . . ." She caught herself, and Ben looked up, perplexed.

He studied the girl: her raven hair, curls on roseate high cheekbones, very dark eyes and brows that could be trimmed and shaped. Her somewhat chubby forearms glistened as the low noon sun caught the fine down. She was a change from the fair-haired elegant ladies of Cayenne's circle in London. She was almost Spanish in cast and demeanor, perhaps Minoan, reminiscent of terra-cotta profiles on ancient Mediterranean pottery. Ben felt he'd seen her before —*somewhere*. He felt sure he'd seen her in New York, at the Metropolitan Museum, perhaps—or downtown in Brooklyn, under the sparkling marquee of the RKO Albee on a Saturday night.

Then it came to Ben! The waitress reminded him of his mother—the wedding photograph on the sideboard at home. He was suddenly tempted to say, "What's a nice Jewish girl like you doing on an island like this?" Instead, he asked her how long she'd been working at—he read the menu masthead—Sandy's Sea Specialties.

It's my father's establishment, sir. Major MacCowan started the place after retiring from the Army; he was in the cavalry, though he doesn't care for 'orses anymore. *Too dusty,* my dad always has said. He's out fishing now; goes out middays on Saturdays because e'll be on late tonight. We close past nine, what with all the service personnel so famished and no place to go after the movie's out. I work the slow hours, and my stepmother comes to help if we get a crowd; she's in the back. We live behind the store, and we've got two rooms upstairs. We can take in one guest—the room, it has a view of the harbor, is unoccupied and costs six bob a week, and you'd share a loo—"

"I'm afraid I'm already staying at the Royal, and I won't be here for a week anyway."

"Too bad." Ruth pouted. "Are you a professor?"

"Do I look like one?"

"You forgot your gas mask; professors are always absentminded."

"Very true. Sometimes I wish I were a professor, and I may be one after the war. My field is science."

"Are you after the *Scapasaurus*?"

"Excuse me?"

"You've heard of the Loch Ness Monster?"

"I believe I've even seen a photograph, however fuzzy . . ."

"*Scapasaurus* is the Orcadian cousin. My father's heard some stories about fishermen seeing a strange sea serpent in Deer Sound, mostly on foggy mornings. . . ."

"And after a few tots in the wee hours." Ben chuckled.

"The Scots are very superstitious; there are many ancient cairns and ritual stones on these islands."

"So I've been reading; elves and fairies behind every rock."

"If you're not a teacher . . ."

"I'm in the American Navy—a kind of holiday."

"Oh, then you're in mufti."

"That's a short long word."

"My mother had many books in Jaffa."

"Palestine?"

"Are there any other Jaffas?"

"There's a *Cape* Jaffa near Melbourne."

"Australia?"

"Do you know of any other Melbournes?"

Ruth giggled as she brought the steaming fish. "I like games like this. My mother always played word games."

"Your father doesn't?"

"He's interested in only two things. *One* is the infernal halibut he almost caught, and *two* is the Home Guard unit he's trying to start."

"Then he can appoint himself general."

"It's not that easy. The men have no weapons, and he's tried many ways of getting some. All they have are axes and the like."

"Your father seems an interesting man."

"Come by after six, and he'll be here."

"If I do, it'll be after dinner, more like eight."

"You won't say anything about—" Ruth touched her blouse.

Ben stood up and finished his pint, then plinked a bob on the polished mahogany counter. He leaned over and whispered, "My mother *and* my father wear gold stars."

She watched the slim cardiganned cyclist through the multipaned window, each pane crossed with white tape. The sill hid all but the handlebars and the American from his elbows up. First he waggled and stopped. He turned and waved, sheepishly, set his chin determinedly, and glided out of the frame.

"Honored to meet you Mister Mount."

"Call me Ben."

"Would that be for Benjamin?"

"It would, Major. Thank you, miss." Ruth combed the foam from his tankard and, averting his twinkling eyes, set it on the varnished counter.

"'E's a Yank—from Brooklyn, in New York." Danny Hobbs lifted himself onto a warm stool after making sure it was not a gift, that the patron was indeed leaving. "Ben and me are real *pals*. We jus' come from th' Toddy Hole."

"As you can probably tell." Ben feigned a hiccup.

"Then you've already had supper?" Sandy MacCowan turned condescendingly as a trio of sailors swaggered in and shooed Ruth to clean up a corner booth as he ushered them in.

"Ye'd be on a holiday, Ben?" MacCowan's beady eyes searched the newcomer up and down from his tasseled golf shoes to his nose to his Irish knit sweater and back to his nose. Then the major absentmindedly felt his own.

"Sort of a holiday, yes." Ben studied the menu. "We ate earlier, but I could go for a little *lox*."

"Eh?"

"Smoked salmon, or is salmon not considered a sea specialty?"

"Aye, the fish migrates, but—"

"There's a bit in the kitchen icebox." Ruth scampered away, apron tails flying.

"And there's precious little on this island; besides, it's no' on the' sign."

"In that case I won't deprive—but your daughter . . ." Ruth slid a plate with a generous slice of pink before Mount.

" 'Ow'd ye know she was m' daughter?" The major touched his nose again.

"Her mouth, delicate yet firm. The classic stiff upper lip . . ." Ben winked at Ruth as she drew another brew for Danny. "Just like yours."

"Now come on, eat," MacCowan laughingly slapped Ben on the back. "Danny, m' lad, I like your pal. Ben, I was only joking. It's on the house."

"There's no price on the sign either, so ye' can't charge him anyway."

"Hmmppht." MacCowan evaded Danny's taunt. "What did you say you did in America?"

"I didn't."

" 'E's a top Yank naval officer—a commander." Danny slurred his words. "Sorry pal, I shouldna . . ."

"It's okay, Danny. It's not a secret."

"Well, then, welcome *Commander* Mount. I happen to be *General* of our local Home Guard and I'd be pleased if ye would be kind enough to have a word with me in private—with Danny, of course—back o' th' store before ye leave. The organization has a favor to ask of ye."

"Top secret?" Ben whispered.

Sandy MacCowan stared at his harpoon, hanging above the wall menu. He nodded gravely.

FOURTEEN

"I hope you don't mind, Theo, but I didn't want tourists about." Nielson appeared much more sinister than at St. Andrews. The shadow of his sharp profile flickered over the runic inscriptions on the stone slab wall of the Neolithic burial chamber.

"Not at all." Theo's palms were moist and shaking slightly. "I've never been here at night, though I must say, the keeper thought it very peculiar that I asked him to open at this hour."

"I'm sure you gave him a good reason."

"A serious archaeologist can take rubbings only when he is not jostled by undisciplined children and gawking fools." Theo unrolled a sheet of rag paper and taped it over a wall-incised knot of serpents. Then he took a small kerosene lamp out of his Gladstone trunk bag, lit it, and turned up the wick. "Batteries are devilishly hard to get." He blew the candle out, then snuffed it with his fingers. "The *war*, you know." Theo tried to laugh, but it wasn't very funny. He laid out his rubbing tools on the stone floor. "Why all this cloak-and-dagger?" Why was he so nervous? Can't the man say something? Why is he standing there with that grin? Theo started his rubbing.

"As you said, Theo, *the war*."

"If it's got to do with clocks or chronometers, I'm afraid my current contract with the Royal Navy—"

"Not even close," Peter interrupted. He reached an inside jacket pocket and drew out his billfold. "Do you remember our little dart game at the Royal and Ancient?"

"I got hell from my wife. Skunk drunk I was." Theo turned, curious about what Nielson was leading up to. The Swede carefully unfolded a square of paper.

"Remember this?" He held it down near the lamp.

Theo leaned over and adjusted his bifocals. He read aloud: "R and A, 1754." Then, next to the green calligraphic script, he saw something very familiar. "Where did you . . ." Theo's eyes bulged. Next to his signature was a crudely drawn map of Holm Sound. The captions were in his handwriting, little slashes instead of dots and periods. Kirk Sound . . . Glims . . . no question about it. Even the blockships were indicated. And the dotted line leading in from the North Sea . . . past Rose Ness . . . between the last blockships under the Six-mile Road. Even the searchlight and the guard positions were marked. . . ." *"Ach, mein Gott."* Theo lapsed into German. The rubbing chalk dropped from his fingers and shattered on the floor slab. He reached for the napkin, but it retreated. Theo studied it again. The dotted line turned at St. Mary's Point and ended in an *X*. Beyond was the crude outline of a ship's hull, crossed by a second *X*.

Theo felt nauseated. His whole world, his life paraded quickly over the ancient symbols on the sepulcher wall. A walrus mocked him. A Norse dragon belched flame at him, at his business, at his possessions. A sycophantic smile crossed his thin face.

"Please, give me that."

Peter tongued his cheek and shook his head.

"What good is it to you? Besides, it's all wrong anyway. I made it all up. Just a joke. We all do things like that when we have a drink or two, eh?"

Peter didn't answer.

"What is this *venture* you wrote about?" Theo tried another tack. He started his rubbing again, affecting nonchalance.

"I'm so sorry to have to ask, but I need a little favor from you, my friend."

"Go on."

Peter drew up behind Theo and whispered, "As a former officer in the Kriegsmarine you must have mixed feelings about this war. . . ." Theo trembled as he rubbed. Snake's heads were beginning to appear. "All *we* want you to do is be at a certain point at a certain time . . . and perhaps cut one little wire. . . ."

Theo's mind raced. "Who is *we?*" he asked faintly.

"Do you want to be on the losing side?"

"You're a . . . an agent!"

"Thank you, I don't like the other word."

"What if I . . ." Theo stopped. Out of the corner of his eye, looking down, he saw the napkin, shimmering near the lamp. "If I agree—" Theo whirled and snatched the paper out of Nielson's fingers, then crumpled it and tried to stuff it into the lamp chimney. He burned his hand instead. Then he popped it into his mouth and chewed it up. Nielson, after a token struggle, watched quietly as Theo gulped and swallowed.

"Thank you very much." Nielson shook out a cigarette and lifted the lamp to light it. "I didn't want it found on me anyway."

Theo stared at the Swede quizzically, then regained his composure and started packing his equipment.

"I guess that finished our *business* meeting, Lieutenant Nielson. Can I give you a lift back to your hotel? The buses are infrequent after nine."

"Theo"—the voice became steel—"you're going to finish that picture for me."

The older man started to untape the rubbing.

"Theo, have you ever heard of the *camera?* Do you think I'd be foolish enough not to make copies. I brought the original because the paper is more soluble than the prints."

The watchmaker's arms dropped limply to his sides.

"And then there's always the poor little tart. You did mumble something about *burying a bitch* at . . . at—another *B.* I did some research this afternoon. Brogar, wasn't it? Just up the road. That's how I found out about this tomb. It may be nothing at all. But then there's always *in vino veritas.*" Peter put his hand lightly on Theo's bony shoulder.

"I don't believe it. This is all some hallucination."

"I'll take that ride now. Drop me off, if you will, at the Kirkwall. We can go over the details tomorrow, in my room. After that, perhaps the round of golf you owe me . . ." Nielson carefully and proudly rolled up the rubbing.

FIFTEEN

"Günther, what's wrong. You've hardly touched your dinner. . . ."

"I'm sorry, my love—and my favorite potato pancakes!" Oberleutnant Prien started cutting the cakes voraciously. "I guess I was daydreaming again."

"Understandable." His wife poured more coffee. "You've hardly had any time for yourself."

"Nor for you, and Birgitchen; I tried to get home before she went to bed—"

"But something important happened again!" Ingeborg Prien smiled knowingly. "What was it this time?"

Günther was quiet. This worried her. He was always so ebullient; normally he'd answer with a joke —or sing one of the hundreds of sea chanteys he knew by heart.

"Routine assignment." His pale blue eyes stared out the window toward the Kiel-Wik shipyards. "It'll be only a few days."

"I'm so glad, Günther; it's not like it was—before Poland." She set the Sunday newspaper before him.

"Yes, war was a game. My God, Inge, I'd forgotten what day it was." Prien leaned over, sipping his coffee.

"Seven days shalt thou labor in the Navy . . ."

"Next Sunday, I promise . . . Hello, the British are still denying that *Ark Royal* was damaged. . . ."

"The Warsaw garrison has marched out, and we've arranged a boundary with Stalin," Ingeborg reported.

"Ugh, politics and marching soldiers are so dry. Give me a boat any day. Just wait till this is over; we'll buy a proper sailboat and go to the South Seas: Maracaibo, Zamboanga, Samoa! Just the three of us—or as many as we are *then*." He moved his chair closer and took her hand in his.

"It's hard enough to feed *one* today. . . ." She blushed.

"Tell you a top secret?"

"Please!" She kissed him below his ear.

"In a few weeks you may meet a dashing *Korvettenkapitän*."

Ingeborg squealed with delight. "Do you think my husband will be jealous? I pity the poor officer. Do I know him?"

"All too well." Prien helped with the dishes, and they went into the bedroom to look at their baby daughter.

"We're so lucky, Günther," she whispered. "This house . . . so close to your base." She started to undo her blouse.

"Darling." He embraced her.

"For how long?"

"I'm just going to pick up a few papers and bring them home. You go to bed now. I'll be back in half an hour, and I promise to wake you when I've finished a certain report."

"If you don't wake me by midnight, I'll come out and get you. I'll set my clock."

"I promise."

* * *

Senior Lieutenant Prien retraced his walk to the pier and caught the motor launch back to the old *Hamburg,* anchored across the bay. Once a proud cruiser, the ancient ship had been stripped of armament and served as a depot ship for transient Kriegsmarine personnel. Kapitänleutnant Prien, though still in command of *U-47,* had temporary usage of a cabin on *Hamburg* because of the extraordinary events that had taken place in the past week.

Even Ingeborg had not been told. For the first time in their short marriage he had kept something from her. This was not a war *game.* It was something big—and dangerous.

Prien was piped aboard and escorted to the deck officer's room, where he was assigned an armed marine who took him below. While the marine waited, Prien unlocked a desk and removed a thick file of charts and envelopes.

It was past nine when he spread out the assorted sheets and envelope's contents on his writing table. He was thankful that Ingeborg and the baby were asleep.

For several hours he pored over the charts and studied the minutest details on his charts with a magnifying glass: each sounding, each buoy and marker, the shoals, the obstructions, and the strangely spelled Anglo-Viking names of the Orkneys, a group of some fifty islands off the north cape of Scotland.

Sneuk Head, Skaill, Eynhallow, Tankeness. The large islands of Hoy, Mainland, and Ronaldsay. These were the ones that nestled a bay among them.

A bleak, flat, cold bay called Scapa Flow.

Scapa, Prien thought. Curious name. What did it mean? "Flow" was *flow*, obviously. Muckle *Skerry!* Corn *Holm!* He looked in his *Kleine Brockhaus*, a desk encyclopedia. On page 616, below an engraving of a *Saxophon*, he found a short paragraph under "Scapa Flow." Nothing of the word's derivation. The paragraph ended with: *1919 versenkt: 10 Linienschiffe. 5 gr., 5 kl. Kreuzer, 46 Torpedoboote. . . ."* Prien clenched his teeth. All those fine ships. The old *Hamburg* was lucky. She had been badly damaged at Jutland and wasn't considered worthwhile war booty to be interned in the flow.

He set the book down, and its pages flipped to the *H*'s. Prien tiredly studied a color plate of *Himmelskunde*. Another chart. He looked at the October segment of the northern sky map. Arcturus would be high on the fifteenth. Then he saw it. A good sign: the Hunting Dog, just south of the Dipper. *U-47* would follow that star north in the flow to the British fleet anchorage. He turned the page. The other side showed a color diagram of the earth's motions and the solar system. For a moment he became engrossed in a drawing of Mars. What curious "canals." The *red* planet he'd so often marveled at, far out to sea. It was his planet now. War was red, too. Then he examined the tidal diagrams. Prien, he said to himself, you're a professional sailor, a warrior. No time for the romance of astronomy. You made your bed a long time ago. You went to sea instead of school.

He flipped to the next page. This was like a dessert after more than two hours of grueling study. A little play—A name on the bottom of the page caught his eye.

Hitler, Adolf, Politician . . . Nazi party . . .
Munich putsch . . . jailed . . . freed Dec. 1924.

He chuckled—smaller paragraph than Scapa Flow—then turned to the title page: 1925, and, coincidentally Leipzig, his home. Printed two years after he'd gone to sea. He would have liked to have seen the newest edition, what they'd done with Hitler's little paragraph since.

One more bonbon. He turned nostalgically to the *U*'s. *Unterseeboot.* He remembered the cute little diagrams he'd first seen in another edition of the *Brockhaus* when he was fourteen, in the seamen's school library at Finkenwerder.

Still there! *Querschnitt, Längsschnitt!* "Cross section, longitudinal section." How small, how like a toy it appeared in simplified diagram: seven watertight sections. *Kommandoturm,* literally "order tower." *Bug und Heck,* "fore and aft." *Hinterschiff,* "stern." *Vorschiff,* "forecastle." He strained his memory for the English equivalent of *Zentrale,* tried to visualize the captions on that chart in commanders' school two years earlier. Ah, yes, control room.

So placid on the page. So simple in diagram.

So deadly! So infinitely complex.

He read on. ". . . Built in Great War: 360. Lost: 199."

Six thousand sailors dead. The 1915 boats were smaller; carried thirty. His boat, a new VIIB, had a crew of forty.

Prien closed the book wearily. How many would die in German iron coffins in *this* war?

How many Germans would die in all services?

In all countries?

An aircraft droned over his house. He felt an unusual vulnerability. As if he *and* his family were the quarry.

SIXTEEN

The force 8 gale boiled up the sea; bubbling foam and spindrift blew in white streaks toward the full-rigged ship *Hamburg* as she dipped her bowsprit like a rusty narwhal charging into the waves. Captain Oelkers pulled at his red sideburns and signaled his first mate to shorten sail.

"Strike the royals!" Bosun Stoewer screamed above the wind's roar. "Up ye go, Prien. You, too, Staabs, or I'll fix ye t' stay Moses till ye rot."

The sixteen-year-old cabin boys followed the older seamen up the swaying ratlines. Up, up, up. There were sounds like pistol shots and snapping whips high above.

"The t'gall'nt," Stoewer shouted, "she's split, get on up an' secure it." Up, up, up. Günther Prien was afraid to look down. Far below, the rattling of chains and creaking of windlasses; above, the mad flapping of slackened square sails.

Finally, they reached the yardarm and shuffled out on the footropes, 160 feet above the tiny white deck with the ants looking up.

Hamburg dove into a mountainous wave, and she heeled hard to starboard. The rats in the rigging grabbed for handholds as the wavetops came up to meet them. Again and again the snarling wind drove the wet sails into the seamen on the topgallant yard-arms of three masts. Suddenly a high-pitched scream to the right of Prien. Staabs had been blown off the footropes by the madly bucking white canvas stallion, his feet swinging frantically over the white-tossed waves. Burly Witaschek sidled along the rope and, in the nick of time, reached out and got hold of poor Staabs's shirt collar. He was ordered to the crosstree to wait as the sails were secured.

As the sailors descended something strange happened: The gale weakened, then fell off to a warm breeze; the spars righted like soft saplings, and the sails fluttered and hung limply. Way was lost, and the rusty old hull turned its side with the tide. Swarms of purple and indigo umbrella-sized Portuguese men-of-war ebbed against the fouled waterline, streaming white tentacles on the azure sea.

A flight of screeching fork-tailed gulls swooped through the shrouds at main yard level and threaded the limp jibs.

"Galápagos forktails," shouted the old man. He disappeared into the aft companionway singing "Praise Be to the Lord."

"We must be crossing the equator. I've heard strange things happen when you cross." Balkenhol rubbed greasy paws on his swilly apron before scratching himself with them, ladle still in hand like a pharaoh's effigy.

A scratchy melody wafted eerily from the captain's cabin. With increasing intensity it walked under the decks and emerged triumphantly. The old man's "Stradivarius"! He was proudly fiddling his favorite: "Ein' feste Burg ist unser Gott."

"And it's not even Sunday." Zippel made a face.

The old man dropped his bow momentarily. "We're

between Galápagos and the Esmeraldas. Temporary doldrums. Soon as we're under way again, we'll head in for Guayaquil." He went off in a stepping jig and struck up his tune for a trip around the decks.

"Shore leave." The crew shouted as one.

"Hoch, hoch, hoch," they cheered from all quarters below and spars aloft. "Three cheers for Saint Pauli. *Hoch, hoch hoch.* Three cheers for Guayaquil . . ."

Ingeborg Prien snapped bolt upright in bed at her husband's *Hoch, hoch, hoch.* The first seemed a snore; then by the last she'd recognized the naval cheer. Günther had kicked off the comforter, and she could feel him, still in a dream, pulsing spasmodically. She drew the cover over him and wondered what submarine commanders dream about.

"Fogbank to starboard," from the forward watch.

It rolled in over the calm water like a phantom. The air became heavy and yet more humid. It was April, and the rains were almost ended.

Then it dawned on the crew. April what? they asked, and the captain, dancing by, now wearing bowler and gray spats with black frock coat, answered, "Thirty, m' lads, thirty."

"Walpurgisnacht," moaned the old ship.

The horn sounded, low and gloomy. Not a foghorn, thought the cabin boy. He looked at his sleeves. Two broad stripes and one narrow stripe in between! What was this? Another hallucination? A trick of the tropics? The tunic was too large; his boyish hands were still up the sleeves.

Günther scrambled below to the head. There, in a round, magnifying shaving mirror, hung bearded

Prien. Bearded as on a patrol. A bearded boy with a big head and a small body! He felt his brass buttons: yes, four on each side. He felt his neck. What was he doing wearing a scarf in the tropics?

"Craft approaching; I can hear the sweeps." Stoewer strained his eyes into the steaming fog.

Another horn, a wailing sound similar to the long horns of the mountains. A strange form eased out of the fog like a gray swan. Long, low, and lapstrake, it headed toward *Hamburg*. Its heavy, wooden stem curved up sharply, and the bows obscured its crew. On it came as if weightless on the river Styx, a millipede of muffled sweeps in perfect unison, hardly dipping.

It carried a short mast and an angled spar. Some silhouettes could be made out aft. The fog was following as if reluctant to give up its charge. Little by little the sleek craft drew clear of the fog. *Hamburg*'s crew, to a man, stood mesmerized and becalmed. Not a word. Only breathing.

"Boat starboard sweeps." The order came from the aft platform, from the silhouettes, one of which raised an arm. Smoothly the craft eased alongside, starboard oars vertical. "Boat larboard sweeps." The forest of nude wood oars pointed up at the crew lining the rail of old *Hamburg*.

A curious lot they were! Dressed like savages—or were they Vikings? Yes, with horned helmets and animal skins, with cymbaled shields and broadswords on the thwarts.

One of the aft people put a huge conch shell to his mouth and startled *Hamburg*'s crew.

"Who be you, and where bound?" A powerful figure thrust a three-pronged weapon toward the captain.

The old man took his cap off and, trembling, gave the information as best possible. "Your Majesty," he implored, "please honor our ship. Come aboard." He shot a glance at the bosun, which meant "Set up the boarding plank." Stoewer picked a detail, which included the two Moseses and piped the visitors aboard with his silver whistle.

The first—the most important—personage to board *Hamburg* wore a mask of exotic bird plumage. There was something very proper and nautical about the man with the trident. He acknowledged the first officer, Pfeiffer, with a curt salute. It was *Neptune!* Who else had a trident and wore a garment that trailed octopus's tentacles? He was followed by two blackamoors carrying a throne of shells and braided seaweed. After Neptune's entourage came a series of familiar people. Little Günther leaned on the rail and identified them, one by one: old Miss Kleewitz from Leipzig, where he'd grown up, his mother, carrying a painted wooden ham; a skeleton dragging chains across the deck; a beautiful Inca princess with copper necklaces; Seaman Fliederer flailing at a large rat with a capstan bar; a German naval officer with gold epaulets on his summer white dinner jacket stepped briskly aboard. The uniform was odd: of course, the kaiser's era, 1915. Properly tropical.

There was a low moan of the conch shell from below, followed by a multivoiced chant. They came aboard in pairs: Inca priests carrying effigies—magnificently robed in rich silver cloaks, with dazzling rings of fine gold on their heads. More than a score, the chorus chanters lined up aft of the wheel against the deckhouse in a semicircle.

"They sing to the sun's glory. . . ." The princess spoke softly to Prien. "They will raise their voices as the sun rises toward noon; then as the sun lowers, so will they chant lower . . . until sunset, when all will be quiet. . . ."

The copper- and purple-clad vision brushed the boy with her silks as she danced past and left him with the fragrances of lupine and fuchsia—ambrosias of the past that drugged his senses once more. *Once more!* It was Raua—the trip down the west coast. He'd met a beautiful Indian girl in the marketplace in Guayaquil. He called her name. She smiled and beckoned him to come to her.

"Remember, Günther, I told you I was descended from the mountain legends. . . ."

"That's how you knew about Ingapirca!"

"I knew you would come. My fortune paper told me that a white bird would fly from the north. I saw your sails from the temple and hurried *baja* Andes. Down to lie in wait. To abduct you. To show you beauty . . . and love. You said you'd return. I waited, and still wait." She was sobbing lightly.

"But the times got worse. I got my captain's ticket, and there were no jobs. I went to Hapag, Slomann . . . then to Reidemann. They all told me it was a bad time."

But Raua was gone.

Neptune's court was boarding. Two slaves carried young Triton, the merman fishtailed son of Neptune, as Amphitrite, the mother, followed. Triton brandished his twisted seashell with which he could induce calm or raise the ocean waves. A bevy of giggling nereids scampered to places right and left of the chanters.

Günther tried to sneak away but was stopped in his tracks by a command and another trumpet-conch fanfare. The sun was at its zenith, the chanters at their loudest, when a high-pitched voice screamed from the boarding ladder: "Attention for the *Oberbefehlshaber der Luftwaffe.*"

A wooden horse's head appeared on a pole. It was white with brown leather ears, a black mane, and shiny black buttons for eyes; its mouth was open in a toothy grin. Small, pudgy suede-gloved hands raised the toy over the gunnel. Then a Luftwaffe cap raised itself slowly until a sinister, smiling Göring appeared beside the hobbyhorse.

The bemedaled hippopotamic hulk raised himself in a grand gesture and inserted the hobby pole between his jodhpurred legs. He struggled through the gate and stood on the deck, impatient for the next boarder, an SS drummer; his instrument emblazoned with death's-heads, his drumsticks tipped with gleaming white skulls.

"Captain, bring your fiddle and follow us," Göring ordered as he broke into a lumpish gait on his hobbyhorse, singing "Ev-ery Thing That Flies Belongs to Meeee . . ." The SS drummer picked up the cadence as he fell in, and the old man brought up the rear, fiddling madly and strutting his gray spats in unison.

A work detail of blackamoor slaves had erected a sham decorative gun carriage on the aft bridge deck over the chanters. It was drawn by merry-go-round seahorses and flanked by a winged Mercury on one side and a white polar bear on the other.

The bear assisted Neptune and his bride into the carriage, where they sat high on white ermine pelts and under slave-held swaying palm fans. There were a few civil words between Neptune and the captain, who then told the bosun to set the crew at ease.

Mercury, brandishing his caduceus, read aloud from a scroll. He urged the crew to admire Amhpitrite and her offspring, to obey Neptune's laws and be fair to all creatures of the sea. There was a cheer of *hoch, hoch, hoch.*

The sun by now was low in the west, and the Inca chorus hardly a murmur. The captain ordered a detail to set torches around the binnacle and up on the poop deck in addition to the kerosene lamps. As a precaution he ordered the anchor dropped, then sent Prien down below to help Balkenhol prepare delicacies from the captain's pantry. Prien commandeered Zippel and then scoured the ship, looking for Raua. Instead, he found his father. In the brig, wearing his judge's wig and robes. "My son, I would be at the tribunal also—but I can't face your mother. . . ." Back on deck he thought he'd heard the bowsprit nets rustling, then a splash. When he looked over, he saw glowing phosphorescent rings on the water far below.

The boy lay on the sprit and looked up at the stars. It was such a night, long before the war, before the Führer mattered. When the sea was all things to him. It was on such a night that he first saw the twinkling lights of Guayaquil. He was an able seaman on *Pfalzburg*, a large freighter out of Hamburg. The year was 1926, and he was only seventeen and working for his master's certificate. He'd worked hard, drawing double duty. The captain had given him a two-day pass for his efforts, to the envy and jealousy of others. Especially the beachcomber. Mayland was his real name. A tattooed brute.

It was good to get away after hauling coffee, castor-oil seeds, tagua nuts aboard at insect-infested ancient ports from the Panama Canal to Ecuador in return for water closets, picture frames, and tools from Germany. Young Prien went ashore dressed in his best

Sunday shirt; his mother had made it and insisted on small ruffles about the neck and sleeves. Trousers still had fresh press, and shoes hadn't been out of his locker since home port.

A bright morning with high thunderhead cumulus over the Andes. Prien skipped merrily along the teeming dock, sidestepping goats and chickens with all the agility of unfettered youth let loose. He carried a small satchel, a sort of doctor's bag made of fine, stout blue-gray ticking with vertical navy stripes and a strap closure. The handles were real whalebone.

Guayaquil was surrounded with lush jungle, right down to the edge of the Pacific Ocean. The seamen had marveled how the navigating officer had drawn a course so precise from lanes that were so far out. There were precious few buoys, even inshore. Twenty miles out all he'd seen from the crow's nest were the snowcapped peaks of volcanic Chimborazo and Cotopaxi. He knew what pranks mountains could play on position plots and vowed to study the dreaded celestial tables with fresh vigor. He would. Because eventually he'd have to compete with university graduates.

Prien stopped at the marketplace in San Penas and turned around. No more forest of masts and funnels; he'd walked several miles, first along the Malećon Simón Bolívar and then west on Avenida 9 de Octubre to the Guayas River district. He wanted hills after much flatness, lush, verdant hills bursting with myriad flowers. About to go up a stone stairway, he became intrigued by a crowd of townspeople in front of an adobe stand. It was a happy crowd, and he walked over, picked a spot and easily looked over the clamoring Indians and mestizos. Prien wasn't very tall, but the Guayaquileños were very short.

A chattering monkey hopped excitedly up and down on a shipping crate, waving a small piece of crumpled paper. Its handler cajoled the monkey with a banana, then ripped the paper from the surprised animal's hairy fingers. With a mouthful of banana, the entrepreneur read from the slip of paper: "*Se dice que mi amigo vivaré setenta y cinco años . . .*"

A *huasipunguero*, or poor landowner, slapped his adolescent son on the back, smiling with stubby blackened teeth as the proprietor pocketed a centavo and entreated the crowd for more customers. Günther, with only a smattering of cargo language terms, was perplexed. A crude sign hung on the thatch. It was in two languages: Spanish and one he didn't recognize. "Su fortuna corriente de simio." He reached into his bag for his pocket Langenscheidt and flipped to the *S*'s.

"Your instant fortune by a monkey." A mellifluous, but broken, German. He wheeled and looked down into animal-brown sensuous eyes. She was sandaled and wore a loose peasant blouse of starched linen and a full, florid skirt. Her eyes flickered, then looked down ashamedly. "Excuse me for helping . . ." Günther tenderly touched her warm chin, lifting her gaze to his.

"You spoke German. Where did you learn?"

"I work for rich mans and his lady. They have *gran* villa—" She pointed to the hill. You are *alemán,* no?"

"Sí," he replied, and they both laughed.

"Today is my holiday," she said proudly, then acted as if she were interested in the monkey's antics.

This gave Günther a moment to look at her: long jet black hair to her shoulders, iridescently sparkling in the sun; high cheekbones of the Indian, cocoa-soft unblemished skin. She strained to see over the crowd, and her blouse fell open to Günther's young eyes. He retreated, but when she remained intent on the monkey, he returned and savored. Hardly a woman's breasts. She couldn't have been over fifteen, he thought. Yet he felt a surge within and blushed for it.

"Are you all right, señor?" The girl startled him.

"Er, yes . . ." He changed the subject. "Do you have a holiday every Thursday?" Günther spoke slowly.

"*Sí*; most Thursdays." She squirmed her body.

"The people you work for"—he pointed uphill—"are from Germany?" She looked perplexed. "Er, what is their business in Ecuador?" The surge had not abated.

"*Abogado* . . . lawyer."

"I guess there must be many Germans—here?"

"*Sí. Muchos.*"

"What is your name?"

"I hope you ask me." She turned to him on tiptoes, her glistening chalk white teeth in a wide, impish grin. "Raua." She seemed to growl it. "And yours?"

"Günther." She cocked her head like an animal. "That is very hard to say." She tried to repeat it, and it came out *Goonta*. "Is that what people call you all the time?"

"No. Günterchen."

"You are a *duende*. I'll call you Duende."

"What's a *duende*?"

"An elf. You have an elfin smile. Up to tricks!"

"I feel the same about you—but I like Raua."

"Then it's *Raua und Duende*. Now we are both immortal."

"I don't understand. I'm just a poor sailor."

"My name is from the ancient tribal legends of Ecuador." Raua's forest eyes sparkled mischievously. "In the beginning of the world there was Ayar Manco, the sun-god—and his three brothers. Manco carried a mahogany bird in a basket. It had powers to tell the future—"

"It didn't need slips of paper like the monkey!"

"No, it was a noble wood bird. Manco's brothers were Cachi, that means salt; Uchu, which is pepper" —Raua pantomimed a sneeze: *uchuuu*—"and Auca. I am a descendant of Auca and his sister-wife Raua." She drew her blouse taut against her breast.

"What does *Auca* signify?"

She plucked an errant thread from his sleeve. "Pleasure."

Günther was at a loss. Was this *it*? *Was it* going to happen halfway round the globe? But he truly liked her. He'd never enjoyed talking or being with a girl as much as this. But where should he go? It *was* up to him, a seaman, to solve this. Wasn't it? He would have something to crow about back on *Pfalzburg*. It would get the "beachcomber" jealous. Raua rubbed his arm like a wild kitten.

"*Duende*, could we talk to the monkey?"

"Of course; let me pay." Prien dug into his pocket.

"Not for me. *You!* The monkey and I have already talked."

Günther knew he'd been captured, and he liked it. And he felt genuine pleasure in making Raua happy. The monkey chattered and came up with a paper scrap. The entrepreneur read in Spanish: "*Gran gloria veniré . . . y . . .*" He crumpled up the paper.

"*Gran gloria veniré*! he shouted ceremoniously and took the centavo.

"Great glory for *el Duende*," Raua repeated as she tucked her hand under Günther's arm and led him up the stone stairs. "You don't mind Raua walk with you?"

"I want you to." His callused hand found hers.

They stopped at a level where two cannon pointed over the river, and she told about the pirates who used to sack the city as far up the river as Babahoyo. Raua pointed out her employer's house, and they walked among the lush flowers, the lupine and the fuchsia, past lakes abounding in water hyacinths and through scents of vanilla and coffee. She told Günther the legends and history of her people: of Atahualpa, and how this last Inca king was tricked into ransom and death by Pizarro: how 5,000 unarmed warriors were slaughtered by the Spaniards' firearms after Atahualpa came peacefully to Pizarro's camp for a debate; how Atahualpa, a captive, filled a large room with gold, yet was garroted for his "crimes" against the Catholic Church and his people; how a Catholic priest got the third highest salary after Pizarro and his lieutenant in a grant from the emperor of Spain for their deeds in Ecuador. She told him about the riches of Quito and Cuenca.

At a roadstand on the Guayaquil and Quito railroad they enjoyed roasted guinea pig and bean cakes for lunch, and he bought her a bottle of German beer, which, though she had only half, made her tipsy and sexy. They looked at a display of brightly painted children's coffins and decided they were not ready to buy. Suddenly the two-car train chugged to a steaming halt, and she enticed him to board with stories of Ingapirca, only a two-hour ride through the mountains and deep rain forests. She'd been there and offered to be his personal tour guide for "no charge." The train was almost empty, and she fell asleep in his arms. His own, his first kitten. The jungle, the steep drops, and dizzying bridges built by two Americans from the state of Virginia, who were both killed in the process, according to his Baedeker, transformed him. His animal instincts took over—with the help of several bottles of Beck's. His hand strayed, and she pulled it snug against her breast. The heat, the dampness, the remoteness, and primeval mysteries, the exotic bird sounds and cheetah's shrill screams enveloped him, and he slipped his hand inside her peasant blouse.

They got off at a whistle stop near the ruins of Ingapirca at quarter past three and were advised by the conductor to catch a return trip in two hours. Prien set his watch, and the couple watched the old locomotive sputter on toward its terminal at Cuenca.

After exploring the ruins and playing like children, Raua led Günther to her favorite place, a stone battlement high on a knoll overlooking a deep rain forest valley. The neatly fitting stones, some as large as an automobile, were overgrown with flowering vines and shrubs. They lay down on a bed of jasmine and hyacinth, under swirls of lupine. A rain cloud swooped past towering Chimborazo into the valley below them. Lightning and thunder to the north as the cloud hung before Cotopaxi, the world's highest active volcano. They felt safe in each other's arms.

An ozone freshness pervaded the valley, and the night sounds began. It was unusually warm, yet pleasant as the twilight gave way to lush night. The train was long gone, and Günther looked out over the valley toward the sea. The moon was whitening. Chimborazo's shadow crept over the jungle as the night sounds echoed below: screeching, gaudy parrots, snarling pumas and jaguars, clouds of flapping bats; the chattering of spider monkeys and rasping of anteaters and grunting of the collared peccaries; the squeaking of chinchilla.

Immersed in images, Günther hardly felt her hand on his back. "*Duende,*" she whispered, "I have often wanted to sleep here as my sisters have. They've told me of magical things . . . romantic things that happen on such nights when the moon is full and the warm wind comes from the rain forest." Raua's hand snaked slowly around his waist; he felt her body, warm against his back. "But Raua never stay because of no boyfriend that she like. Now, if we stay . . ." She hesitated.

"I want to stay." Günther stared stoically ahead, trying to hide his desire.

"I can feel your *corazón,* and that is good. For years I dream of this night with *el Duende del Norte* . . . ever since the monkey told me in Riobamba. I have dream many time that on first night with man it happen like with gods and sisters. Like Auca, son of Manco, and his bride, Raua . . . in the *montañas,* smiled on by the moon-god. We play Raua's dream?"

"What shall el Duende do?"

"*El Duende* wait till Raua call him." She took off her sandals and placed them daintily near the stone in front of him. He heard the rustle of fabric. A flock of white egrets glided below, catching the bright moonlight.

"*Duende,* close your eyes and walk to me."

He turned and felt his way past a flowering hibiscus.

"Over here."

Young Prien shuffled toward the voice, apprehensive of what might happen. Slow, short steps; he felt the softness of grass beneath his Sunday shoes.

"I command *el Duende* to stop!"

He smiled an elfin smile, eyes closed, and saluted. "Able Seaman Duende, at your service."

"Bequem, Herr Matrose!"

Prien struck the at-ease stance.

"Offnen Augen!"

Günther blinked his eyes. No Raua! Then he looked down. He was transfixed at what he saw in the moonglow of luminescent tropical blossoms. There, at his feet, lay a body. Nude and primeval against a blanket of cyclamen, clematis, lupine, and gentian—all in full bloom. White hibiscus petals were strewn over her lithe fawn figure—spread as a breathing, impatient cross. The petals, pearl and interspersed with lavender and madder, ran in rivulets between her breasts, across her lean middle, and over her silken moonlit mound.

He knelt over her and devoured her beauty. She lay still and deliciously innocent and open—a jungle orchid. Raua, knowing the shyness of poetic young men, feigned sleep lest the spell of manhood be broken. It was thus with the sisters of her gods.

The young virgin sailor slipped out of his blouse, hung it neatly on a branch, biding for time. Time to collect himself, plan the approach—appear experienced and in charge.

Now nude and restrained, unused to the night sounds and alien surroundings, he slowly descended on her. A flapping shadow on her breast made him draw back on his haunches. His vision of fear abated when the shadow, an opalescent butterfly, alighted just above the silken mound. Günther, enthralled, as if by omen, as if now allowed closer, took advantage and examined the glorious winged jewel. Ephemeron that it was, it darted away. It was such a night, and he, bewitched, kissed her *there*. . . .

"PRIEN, PRIEN, PRIEN." Captain Oelker's shouts reverberated through the jungle. The Inca stones changed to rusting metal and neglected wood, the lush vines to hemp hawsers, the moon to a glaring flashlight.

"Prien, you're wanted aft and on the double." The bosun delighted in shining the blinding light in the boy's sleepy eyes. Prien's attention was caught by strange figures aloft in the spars. Incas wearing chessboard costumes of red and white squares, on the main yardarms, the lower t'gallants, on the crosstrees, and dangling in the shrouds and ratlines. They watched him walk aft, with their birdlike eyes, their flashing gold *orejón* disks, glittering on earlobes distended to their shoulders. An aviary of attendants from the sixteenth century. Prien marveled that these scores of people had come all from one longboat. Surely a magic boat.

The boy was halted by a whiteclad guard, who blocked his path with a silver battle mace. Young Triton sounded his warped seashell as a gold and silver palanquin, carried by four cerulean-robed blackamoors, was lifted over the gunnel. One of the bearers slipped on the deck, jarring slightly the sungod within. The bearer was quietly replaced by a reserve and by the ancient Inca laws was swiftly and discreetly beheaded.

The monarch, seated on a pure gold throne inside the purple-plumed palanquin, wore silver robes and, on his head, the symbol of his station, a scarlet-trimmed *borla*. His necklace of emeralds, the size of songbirds' eyes, glinted green fire. The Inca was carefully carried up the companionway to the poop deck, where he was set down next to Neptune. Attendants removed the palanquin sides, and Mercury proclaimed from his scroll:

"O mighty Atahualpa, sun incarnate, most brilliant ruler of Cuzco, Quito, and all provinces of the greatest and noblest kingdom of the Western Hemisphere . . . I welcome you in the name of Neptune, ruler of the equally splendid, infinite kingdom of the sea, and in the name of Amphitrite and in the name of His Majesty's Auspicious and most Righteous Tribunal."

Another blast of Triton's horn.

Mercury continued: "We have concluded the preliminaries, having collected silver from the polliwogs and summarily doused the initiates, those unworthy sailors who have crossed your domain, El Ecuador or Latitude Zero—"

"All but *one*." Father Neptune's booming voice shook the ship. "Bring the unfortunate host aft, and lash him to the binnacle."

Young Prien was carried by two mace bearers and lashed with strips of peccary leather to the copper and brass binnacle. Neptune looked down from his perch and fingered his feathered mask before speaking. "Herr Prien, you are charged with avoiding the sacred mandate of our court, and for that you will be blindfolded, shorn of your hair, and keelhauled—" He stayed the polar bear, who already brandished an immense pair of scissors. "But that, owing to other, more heinous transgressions, as brought to the attention of this court, is balefully not all." He signaled Mercury.

"You are charged, Seaman Günther Prien—or *Commander,* if it fits—with banishing a young comrade from the youth camp at Hundsgren—for stealing a ham. You *were* a party leader and then a group leader in December of 1933?" Mercury pointed his caduceus down at Prien. He nodded yes. "Speak up."

"Yes, but—"

"No *buts*; you may get your chance later." Mercury descended the companionway slowly, in flickering torchlight. The checkered aviary watched keenly. "Did you know, Prien, that the young boy from Dresden, the one you threw out for stealing a ham, was destitute? That his father was out of work and his mother was ill? And you *threw* him out?"

"Let him answer." Neptune stood up, trailing his octopus tentacles, breastplate gleaming. Suddenly he ripped off his mask and stared at the prisoner.

Neptune was the Lion, Commodore Karl Dönitz. An Iron Cross clanked against his armor as he sat down on the gun carriage.

"Your Excellency," the boy intreated, "the Dresden boy broke the camp's law. He had to be punished. There should be no exceptions. . . ."

Prien's dream became even more preposterous and symbolic. His mother had been an artist in Leipzig, eking out a living as an artist during the "evil" summer of 1923. Inflation was rampant. The streets were gray, dirty, and unswept. Three blue envelopes lay on the mantelpiece of the walkup. Bills! "The worst is the dentist's." She'd brought in three bowls of barley soup. Liese and Hans, pale and hungry, devoured the meager dinner.

Atfer his mother had cleared the table, she told Günther to take the box of lace she'd got from her sister and bring it to Kleewitz and Bramfeld in Neumarkt. He did his homework for school and went to the shop afterward. A small, dried-up woman with a pointed nose complained about the merchandise, then gave him a few coins from the till. Her sour face changed when a customer came in. Big smile for those above, and kicks for those below. The way of shopkeepers.

He went to sea for eight years, got his captain's ticket, and couldn't find a job. It was 1932. When he returned home to Leipzig, penniless, his mother had turned haggard and gray. Instead of painting hams and sausages in still lifes, she'd been constructing hams and sausages of wood and painting them for shopwindows.

Commodore Dönitz pondered young Prien's answer, then conferred with his court. The poop deck, to Prien, had changed into a gigantic wooden ham, properly painted in high gloss colors. His mother was laboriously painting in cloves as large as her head. Neptune-Dönitz's court was still in session like so many figures out of a Hieronymus Bosch painting, oblivious to the other goings-on atop the ham.

Mercury stomped his caduceus on the wooden ham. "We have reached a verdict; we find the accused *guilty*—"

"Of doing the right thing!" Dönitz clapped heartily.

As he clapped, a bizarre happening stunned the boy; with each clap, the commodore's head spun half a turn, alternately displacing his face with Adolf Hitler's, marked by cries of *Heil . . . Sieg Heil* from the chanters and the chessboard aviary.

"And," Mercury went on, "what say you to this charge—communicated to the court by one Frau Kleewitz of Leipzig? She claims that in August of 1923 you did willfully, in her dry-goods shop in Neumarkt, say things untoward—"

"He called me a cheap Jew," Frau Kleewitz shrieked so, that she woke up the chorus.

"And what do you say to that, Herr Prien?"

"Your Excellency, her prices were unfair; everybody said so."

"Hmmm." Dönitz conferred with his advisers. He looked sternly down at the prisoner, and his head started rotating like the cherries in a slot machine. A staccato bell rang, and Hitler's mustached face shuddered to a stop.

"*Guilty as before.*" The dictator screamed.

"One more charge before sentence is passed." Mercury motioned that Atahualpa take the floor. The splendid Inca rose majestically from his throne; his constituents, including a group of Indian concubines who were distributing a sparkling drink called *chicha* to the crew, as prescribed, fell to their knees.

"Mr. Prien, you are the one called *el Duende* by my people?" The sailor answered positively. "I am told that you were the *first* advantage taker of one of our princesses, that you lay with her at the sacred temple of Ingapirca on the night that you called *Walpurgis* and that you vowed to return. Thirteen harvests have been made, and still, you do not keep your vow."

"You may speak, Herr Prien." Dönitz had rematerialized.

"At first I wanted to, but then I thought it better not to . . . despoil the purity of her race. She, Raua, was a descendant of Manco . . . and I was only a common seaman."

"*Guilty of doing the right thing.*" Hitler again.

"The court will recess and agree on a sentence." Mercury stomped his caduceus three times on the deck, the ham having dissolved.

"*Chicha* for all." Atahualpa slapped one of his favorite concubines on the rump. He turned to Neptune-Dönitz with a toothy grin. "Always trying to live down my name. It means 'sweet virility.' "

"Everything That Flies Belongs to Me." Bemedaled Göring galloped his hobbyhorse onto the poop deck, followed by the SS drummer and the ship's captain with his fiddle. The corpulent former flying ace and commander of Richthofen's Flying Circus snatched a jug of *chicha* from a passing concubine and downed it in one long swig. "Hah, I wish I'd brought my pills." He leered at the enormous emeralds around Atahualpa's neck. "Aren't you the gentleman who was ransomed for a roomful of gold?"

"The same. But I was executed anyway."

"Bloodthirsty Spaniards."

"I was baptized Juan before they garroted me; at least it was better than slow death by burning."

"The loot was divided, I heard." Göring nuzzled his hobbyhorse's leather ear. "Is it true that every Inca king had a treasure of gold that was secretly buried at his death?"

"Yes, Señor Göring. The succeeding son of the sun has to start from scratch. There were twelve rulers before me."

"Twelve rooms of gold!" Göring's mouth quivered. "Perhaps we can work out a deal. . . ."

Just then the conch shell wailed. Mercury stomped his wand and called for order. "Gentlemen, have you decided on the sentence?"

"We have." Dönitz stood up, tentacles trailing. "Release the prisoner to hear the sentence." The guards obliged.

"By decision of this tribunal, the Court of Neptune, upon consultation with the sun-god and various other personages, we hereby sentence Herr Günther Prien, in addition to the keelhaul to be . . . *given a chance to redeem his misdeeds* by performing a most dangerous mission. . . ."

"Kapitänleutnant Günther Prien, you will take these documents to your quarters; you will study them. You will make a decision. I want your answer in twenty-four hours."

Prien saluted, did a smart about-face, and took the folder of documents and maps down the main companionway. He realized, suddenly, that his jacket fitted. He had hands again.

The ship's company, the Incas, the personages, the chorus, and checkered Indians all melted into a fog, all but Göring and Atahualpa. They sipped *chicha* and discussed gold and women and politics. "I hear," slurred the German, liquid dribbling from the corners of his crooked smile, "as a militaristic regime, as an expanding empire, you are interested in *Lebensraum. . . .*"

SEVENTEEN

Headquarters,
FLAG OFFICER, U-Boat Command, West
7 Oct 39
U-47, scheduled for Atlantic Patrol, grid *BF* on 4/10 has been reassigned. Will be replaced with standby . . .

Admiral Canaris held the photocopy over the nearest candle. A brown spot appeared on the reverse of the note. He dipped the corner closer to the licking flame. The spot turned black, then glowed and burst into flame. The poker-faced head of the Abwehr lit his cigar with the makeshift taper and reached over the espresso urn to light Nielson's Gauloise.

"We're not supposed to know about this." The admiral blew out the flame and stubbed the charred paper into a crystal ashtray. He picked up the wine list, squinted, then took his platinum-framed reading glasses out of a blue velvet case.

A stern-faced elderly waiter appeared from nowhere as the admiral pointed to an entry. The waiter nodded, spun in a military gesture, and evaporated as quickly as he'd arrived.

"Soon,"—the white-haired officer smiled—"we shan't have to pay for Napoleon brandy!"

Lieutenant Peter Nielson puffed nervously as he looked around the smoke-filled cabaret. Hänschen & Sarah's, on Knesebeckstrasse, was Berlin's notorious gay trysting nest. Canaris had explained that he was *amused* by the proceedings there, and outside of his dachshunds there was little relaxation in his life. Of course, he would never have frequented such an establishment had he been a uniformed admiral. For all purposes he could, to the staring young men, be an industrialist or a surgeon.

Peter wondered about the admiral; he'd heard stories about the party intrigues at the Turkish baths, the Kleist-Kasino, and the Silhouette. Could there be continuations of murdered SA Chief of Staff Ernst Röhm's circle of the early thirties? And the "Italian soirees" of General Göring! Was the head of the Abwehr part of this? He seemed on in years. He had been in the Great War, an officer aboard the cruiser *Dresden* when it was scuttled off Valparaiso in 1915. There were rumors that he had been a lover of Mata Hari in Madrid in 1917. Was it true that Canaris's wealthy parents had nicknamed him the Peeper because of his childhood penchant for spying through keyholes? Was *this* part of the deal arranged by Krupp? A joke?

"William." The voice trilled.

Peter turned at the young man's salutation.

A woman smiled down at him. She wore a white boa over her low-cut lavender chemise. She snapped her bony fingers, and the waiter set the Napoleon brandy before the admiral, who inspected the label and nodded approval. The woman placed a capacious snifter before each guest. Her boa tickled Peter's left ear.

"On the house. Where have you been keeping yourself, Willy?" She leaned her hip on the admiral's shoulder, rested her jeweled hand on the crimson leather of the booth behind him, and ogled Peter.

"My apologies, Sarah. This is Leutnant Peter Nielson of the Royal Swedish Navy. He's in Berlin as an observer."

"What would you like to observe, darling?" Sarah batted her green-tinged lashes facetiously.

"I asked for that."

"No harm in trying." She leaned toward Peter. "I just adore your uniform; such a nice shade . . ." Peter's face reddened.

Sarah had hair on her chest!

The waiter, having poured the brandy, started to leave. "Emil," she shot, "my stinger, please." He brought it from the bar while Sarah edged Canaris over and slid into the round corner booth.

"I've always wanted to go to Sweden; they seem so *advanced* in many ways. They do such good things for the body—the Swedes are all so healthy. . . ." She sipped her drink suggestively.

"We have our vices." Peter ground his cigarette into a bird-shaped white glazed ashtray. He felt uneasy in Sarah's presence, and she knew it.

"One of these days I'm going to try a sauna—"

"Dear William, saunas are *Finnish*."

"Originally, but Sweden, especially Norland, has its share. Even Germany—There's a good one at the Luftwaffe command training center just a few miles from here, in Bernau."

"But, Admiral, would I be allowed—like *this?*"

"You'd have to become an officer first."

"You can make me one, can't you?" Sarah giggled. "All those men, sitting there, on boards." She picked up her drink and slithered off the seat. "Must be off now; come again, Peter—when you have more time." She dragged her boa past his cheek and left the table.

Canaris tilted his sharp nose into the snifter, keeping his penetrating eyes on Nielson. "It takes all kinds to do a job like mine. One never knows where information can come from, and one never *cares.*" The fifty-two-year-old shadow admiral, known to his inferiors as Father Christmas and *der Alte,* swirled the amber liquid that had been bottled when he was still a crawling baby. He breathed in the fumes, nostrils quivering slowly, then raised the snifter, still looking at the young Swede across the table.

"Leutnant"—the admiral sucked in the cognac—"you are a stallion—I can feel your emanations, so *don't* interrupt. I've been *there*—South America . . . Spain . . . Morocco . . . I know what it's like. I detect a sympathetic feeling; we are of the same mold. It's been said that old Canaris is guilty of a shortage of *Sitzfleisch.* You know, it's true!" Canaris played his whitened tongue inside the snifter. "I think you are like me. I think you are searching for something. Oh, you may say, '*Der Alte* is drunk,' but what's wrong with being *tipsy*—and I warn you, I'm not, or you might think that the admiral is, shall we say, *playing his role?* But I must assure you that I know what I have to do. Fair?"

"Fair, sir. I know about *submarines.*"

"All right. So I don't have to apologize about Sarah?"

"Understood."

"Very well. Why don't you light up?" Canaris slid his Gauloises across the tablecloth. "I think you'd ought to relax before the *mission.*" The mufti admiral tore a corner from his wine list. "I suggest that you call this number. Tell whoever answers that Navy Willy recommended you. I guarantee that Sweden could not do better." He slipped the scrap under Nielson's snifter.

"For Gawd's sake, Kitty, another one?"

"Not just anyone. Remember the *count?*"

"The stud with all the ribbons?

"You didn't do too bad."

"Considering I don't know Italian." Vera Lubienski, leaning backward against the gilt-edged vanity, snapped her hosiery catch on her garter belt. She stood there, cigarette dangling from the corner of her raspberry mouth, booted legs forward. Her frilled pink blouse touched the bony white projections of her pelvis. Her left hand rested on the vanity, an inch away from an empty schnapps glass, and the other, flat against her milk white thigh, clutched a pair of sheer black panties with an embroidered miniature red rose.

"Vera, this is special." The blowsy madam was mesmerized by Vera's thrust-forth black forest.

"How special."

"Bubi called. He's with Reinhardt; he said you should use the Green Room."

"Partial payment for that room . . ."

Kitty reached into her pocketbook and drew out a 100-mark note. She folded it into a thumb-sized rectangle and put it between her yellowed teeth. Vera spread her stockinged legs wider, then fingered her forest to a clearing and thrust it generously out.

Madam Kitty fell to her fat knees and, grasping

Vera by the buttocks, pushed the engraved rectangle into the wet valley clearing. Tilting her hennaed head, she tongued it home.

Vera pressed a button near her knee, on the underside of the purple sandalwood Ch'ing table. The button was of the same shape and pearly iridescence as the border motif of the seventeenth-century inlaid tea table. Adjacent, under the fretted, lacquered peonies, another button, a petal, was set into a hidden plastic receptor and connected in series to a cherub's wooden finger—part of an idyllic walnut frieze on the headboard of the bed, modeled after a fourteenth-century Apocalypse tapestry that showed an elaborate bed occupied by Albrecht Dürer and four unidentified young men. It was authentic even to the trellis of leather straps that supported the mattress. Its four posts shaped as sacred ibises, supported a green japanned canopy on their needle beaks. In the headboard, behind the cherubic digit, was a switch box out of which a brown wire ran down, invisible in a wood groove, then through a baseboard conduit into a small, unmarked service room. The wire was spliced into three leads on a metal tabletop. One led into a scrambler radiotelephone, another into a recording machine, and the last snaked into an amplifier and was, in turn, attached to a receiver. On the receiver were two buttons, one marked *Sprecher,* and the other, *kopfhörer*. The latter button was depressed.

On the headboard wall, beneath the canopy, a mirrored Art Deco entitled *"Zeus in Schwanengestalt und Leda"* reflected Nielson and the prostitute as the door opened in response to Vera's button and a fresh champagne cocktail replaced the spent. Vera smiled at the servant girl who renewed her spritzer; somewhat plain, she, but why take chances on turned heads?

The artwork, snug against a brocaded wall, portrayed Leda in triangular and curved interlocked roseate mirrors while the swan was in standard beveled clear mirror. The tabloid-sized pastoral canted down suggestively on the oversized French four-poster: roseate Leda, standing and guiding the spread-winged, clawing Zeus, courtesy of the National Museum, Athens, Antike Marmorplastik.

In the service room, a niche cut out of the common wall held an ashtray on its sill; a smoldering cigarette butt emitted gray, curling wisps toward the invisible ceiling of the windowless room. Windowless but for the bright two-way glass swan.

The edge-lighted admiral, acknowledgedly deficient in *Sitzfleisch,* peeped through the swan every ten seconds. It would be a shame to miss anything—one of the fringe benefits of his position. He mumbled a curse against the cumbersome naval headphones that irritated his noble ears. He felt his way past the table and made sure the door bolt had rammed home. On the table two green dials glowed: one on the Braun recorder, the other on the amplifier. Only the transmitter was cold to his sensitive hands. The alien emerald instrument light picked up the machined contours of Canaris's Sauer M38 auto pistol, lying in perpetual readiness.

Old Father Christmas, still trim at fifty-two, brushed the cold steel tabletop with his thigh and shrank back instinctively. Except for his earphones, he was nude.

He expertly adjusted the headphone volume control. *Donnerwetter,* he'd instructed Vera to talk louder from the far side of her lair. . . .

". . . Peter, I suppose you know many beautiful girls in your country, but I've heard their love is cold."

Nielson stretched his legs out on the alpaca rug and settled back comfortably on the tufted cerise love seat as Vera leaned over her drink and displayed her pink-tipped charms above a tucked-in white orchid.

"Yes, our style of lovemaking is different; without great passion we are spared great disillusionment. But I am part German. In fact, the part is from the South." He closed his eyes and sighed.

Vera looked at the porcelain pendule clock on the marble mantelpiece. Already twenty minutes and *nada,* as her first husband had always said. She thought about the doubling factor: the tip that was forthcoming *if* the admiral enjoyed the show.

Nielson seemed tired; perhaps he was toying with her. She'd also heard that Scandinavian men were often embarrassed about showing too much affection for women. His attitude began to interest her.

"Come on, you can just as easily lie on my comfortable bed." Vera tugged at his shirt sleeve, but he didn't move. Perhaps she'd rung too often for the champagne. Sometimes a sweet drink put seasoned drinkers and strong men to sleep. "Please, Peter." She loosened his necktie and slid it off. He refused to move. Undaunted, Vera rolled the table away and turned the three-way light to its brightest. Then she sighted, like a surveyer, the angle and distance to the swan mirror, making sure that the bed drapes and canopy would not obstruct the view.

"You are an important man to know the admiral." Vera sat beside Peter and unbuttoned his pants.

"He's a brilliant man."

"You are mostly Swedish or you'd be in our Navy,

no?" She reached inside his pants, then pressed a second button with her left hand.

"I applied to the naval academy, but was turned down because of a small problem."

"I hope it's not *this.*" She drew out his penis and started stroking it. "He's okay. Vera will make him okay." She contorted her arm for the swan's benefit. Nielson sighed and put his arms behind his blond crew-cut head.

"You *hate* the English?" She increased her tempo and changed hands. He grew and grew, glistening by the combined light of candles and 200-watt bulb.

"I want to kill the English." He wiggled his pants and shorts down. Vera let go and slipped out of her shift and panties, leaving her bra, garter belt, and stockings on. She slipped his shoes off and pulled his pants down, hung them neatly over a side chair.

"Vera will make him okay again." She got down on her knees and leaned her head on his lap as she resumed her specialty, careful, in her new position of the viewing angle. Knowing about apogee, she stopped and inserted the sculpture into her carmined mouth, swarming her black tresses around it simultaneously. After a few moves she knew he was ready; she could feel the pulsing; she could sense the timing.

Vera got up and turned her back to the swan, then straddled Peter, black-stockinged knees into the cerise tufting. She pumped into him, guided him. Pumped and rode him.

"You'll kill the English?"

"I'll kill the English and fuck their women. . . ."

Vera slumped, exhausted as the Swede expended.

The mirrored swan was covered with condensation on its other side.

EIGHTEEN

The mural dominated the large, high room in a building on Zeyestrasse, a block from where *U-47* lay, taking on last-minute perishables: boxes of oranges, crates of apples and grapes.

A combination of Art Deco and Walt Disney, cute pink and baby blue fishes danced on their tails among fanciful sea plants and applauded with their fins as a nude "Aryan" couple cavorted idyllically while rising toward the glistening ocean surface. The male, fortunately, was spared a leaf by portraying Triton, the fishtailed merman. With his left hand he blew a shoal of bubbles upward from a barnacled mollusk while his right caressed the sea damsel's waist as she rose, arms reaching up—a symbol of Nazi truth and beauty.

The sea floor was obscured by a grand piano's upright lid and a throng of uniforms, smoke, white ruffled blouses, and a seven-piece dance band. The nattily dressed male vocalist, eyes closed, sang rapturously of Berlin:

> If you walk along Unter den Linden,
> That's where the girls will be,
> And you'll find your own treasure . . .

Seaman Peter Plauen rolled up his jumper sleeve and turned away from the bar. He was tired of sitting; there were several empty beer bottles and schnapps glasses by his elbow as he bared his tattoo to a sultry *Mädchen* who he thought had given him the eye over her partner's striped collar. As they danced closer on the crowded floor, the stocky *Obermaschinist* flexed the lascivious red and blue nude on his forearm.

"Peter—don't!" His buddy from another submarine jostled him. "This is no time to get into another fight."

"All I know, pal, is that it's last night in port"—Plauen slurred his words—"and on last night this sailor always gets laid—'speshully when 'e's goin' on a fuckin' patrol the next day." He inhaled a half inch off his cigarette in one long drag, then lit another. "Here comes the little twat again; I tol' ye she and me are gonna make it. And that pansy destroyer yeoman is dragging her. I can tell she wants me to cut in. Watch this."

Plauen drained his Kümmel and slammed the glass on the bar, breaking it and cutting his right palm. He spun on his stool just as the couple glided by and stuck out his tattooed arm. Just then the music tempo changed and the thin yeoman whirled the *Mädchen* around and stopped, face to face with Plauen. He looked down at the tattoo and read the inscription below the nude; then the girl read it and also turned away, embarrassed. Peter unclenched his fist, and blood ran over the caption and the figure.

The next thing he felt was a glancing blow off his ear. The young yeoman had gallantly responded, but missed. The band had stopped; a cordon of naval police with their polished metal breastplates pushed through the entrance. Before they could reach the brawl, Peter had picked up the yeoman and thrown him over the bar, smashing and scattering glass and ashtrays everywhere.

Several hours later, in a naval cell, he'd sobered up enough to realize what had happened. He hadn't started the fight, but his tattoo had. The inscription under the nude: *Meine Nutte*! He shook his head; he'd get the book for this. Damn, he was so used to the tattoo that he took it for granted. The fancy script couldn't be read by him because to him it was upside down. He'd forgotten that it said "My whore."

Plauen looked up as he heard a key click the lock; the bars slid open. "You can go now, sailor." The marine guard handed Plauen his billfold and papers.

"What happened? I mean—"

"Seems you have some pull in high places." The corporal escorted Plauen down the corridor.

Back at the dance hall, the trombonist picked up the tune; debris had been cleaned up, and cheek-to-cheek was in full swing again.

"Kurtchen," the pianist whispered between beats, "she must have been pretty good; you were gone over an hour. But the boss is going to be mad. . . ."

Kurt smiled around his mouthpiece as he blew a high, long note. The boss wouldn't want to mess with the Abwehr—especially with Canaris.

The lights went out in a lavish room of a town house in Berlin. Two dachshunds snuggled back against the old man's feet under a down comforter. "There, there, my friends. There has been a little problem, but there won't be any more calls to wake us again tonight."

NINETEEN

"Give us an eel," the torpedo mechanic, Kurt Bleeck, shouted up through the torpedo hatch, his hands resting on the skid frame. The Mercedes truck operator swung his crane slowly into position, then lowered the long, grease-covered projectile to *U-47*'s deck, stopping just short of the skid.

"That's it, hold it . . ." The torpedo detail of four crewmen eased the eel into the skid tracks. "Let 'er go." The PO waved at the truck on the dock as a cable was attached to the aft steel band and winched tight. The hoist tackle went slack and was removed; then the deck winch was eased and the twenty-foot, 2,500-pound messenger of death disappeared into its pulsing womb.

Below, the protective nose cone was removed, and a warhead primer locked into place. Serial numbers were noted and recorded. A clanging of overhead chains was accompanied with a chorus of "heaves" and "ho's" as the G-7e was rammed home into its forward tube, one of four. It was the newest model, electric-driven, with no telltale bubble wake, and popular with U-boatmen.

"All right, now," Endrass, the first WO and torpedo officer, called out, "Rig for forward deck loading." Meanwhile, Walz had switched his galley radio to a music program and, per requests, had upped the volume. The captain, wearing the standard shore overseas cap and carrying a package, had just boarded from the loading pier. It seemed like a musical spoof for a moment: torpedoes being loaded, several, simultaneously, with each background men's chorus refrain—"La Paloma!"

Content that preparations were in good hands, Prien went below to his curtained nook. The captain unwrapped his package, taking out a British naval ensign, which he quickly tucked, still folded, into a wall locker. Bosun Ernst Dziallas, happening past at that instant, blinked at what he had seen. An enemy flag aboard meant one thing: deception in the case of emergency. German gunboats disguised as freighters had used deception flags in the Great War, as had others. But who'd ever heard of a submarine in that context? No—this was not going to be the usual patrol.

Bleeck waited for the command to load the fore upperdeck torpedoes. Instead, Endrass called for the gun details to load 8.8. shells and belts of 2-centimeter ammo for the flak gun. The torpedoman rolled his eyes at his mate, Scholz. It seemed obvious that this would be a patrol that would not be interested in moving the spare deck torpedoes below. Word got around.

Leutnant Sohler waved from the bridge of *U-48* as it glided past its sister ship of the Flotilla Weddigen. It was Saturday, October 7—the day that *U-47* had originally been scheduled to be off the coast of Ireland, but for the new assignment. Sohler was late because of repairs to his diesels. As he left, *U-40,* commanded by Kapitänleutnant Barten, was coming in from a trial run. Barten shouted, "Pruentje, is Onkel Karl sending you into the lion's den?" Spahr, standing on the bridge with Prien, was embarrassed at the apparent breach of security, but the captain, performer that he was, joked back at Barten.

Gerhardt Hotzer, just finished with cleaning the armatures of his electromotors, had to go to the Mathilda, as he called the head. He had started to go forward, past the galley, when he noticed the galley-head door was open. He peeked, then went in and closed the door. With all the perishables loaded on this last day before leaving Tirpitzmole, he shook his head in disbelief. It was the first time in his several years' service that the second Mathilda was not off limits—filled with boxes of canned food and sacks of flour. It bothered him so much that he couldn't *go.*

Well rested and eager, after several days of indecision, and having finished trimming and runs, the duty crews topped up the oxygen cylinders, renewed the air purifier cartridges, and loaded the obligatory demolition charges.

Endrass surprised everyone with new orders: The "A" torpedoes were to be unloaded, and some of the fuel and provisions as well. That the saddle tanks were still flooded with water instead of diesel fuel was already an indication of the patrol's duration. Seaman Willy Loh, for one, sported a smile at the prognosis.

At nine o'clock the next morning *U-47*'s thirty-seven ratings stood muster on the slatted wood deck while three officers manned the bridge. They were wearing their Sunday best: gray leather pants, royal blue peacoats, deck boots, and ribboned caps. Church bells chimed over the sprawling port from the medieval cathedral tower of St. Nicholas, as a warm sun glinted on the copper flashing atop the lofty spire of Kiel's Town Hall on August-Viktoria-Strasse.

Kapitän zur See Hans-Georg von Friedeburg and his adjutant walked with Prien up and down the pier. It was a time for last words, no words, or sudden insights.

Friedeburg broke the silence: "*Kapitänleutnant,* that was an excellent idea of yours—reduce weight to reduce wetted hull area and gain speed on the surface."

"It's a standard sailboat racing consideration."

"And the old Navy is used to power."

"In this case, Captain, even half a knot . . ."

"Exactly—"

A rakish white sports car spun out, turning onto the dock, and raced toward the officers. Endrass instinctively grabbed for the voice tube cap—but there was no one below to bring up a machine pistol.

The type 328 BMW left tread marks on the pier cement as it screamed to a halt. An SS major hopped from behind the wheel, envelope in hand, which he proffered to the adjutant *Leutnant*. The letter was passed around. There was no doubt that the signature was that of Grand Admiral Raeder.

The passenger, a blond man, wearing the standard *Unterseeboote* clothing, approached the other three. He carried a small seabag. Prien looked him over, somewhat suspiciously, then tapped him lightly on the shoulder and told him to report to the first watch officer on the bridge. Friedeburg assured Prien that

BdU knew nothing about adding a meteorologist to the mission.

Prien saluted from the bridge as the linesmen cast off, aft and springs amidships. "Minimum *ahead* port," Endrass called out, and the stern warped slowly away from the tarred pier pilings. "Stop all . . . cast off bow . . . minimum astern *both* . . ." *U-47* moved backward, toward the main channel. Friedeburg, tallest of the three on the dock, waved. He'd worn his frock coat for the occasion—and besides, it was Sunday.

"Diesels ready." The call was relayed to the bridge.

"All stop . . . switches off . . . go to diesels . . . clutches in . . . half ahead both . . ." A cloud of blue smoke swirled out of the exhausts, obliterating the pier and its farewell committee. When it lifted, the pier had shrunk and the committee seemed like insignificant ants.

"Come to two-eight-five."

The helmsman repeated the order as he looked up through the open hatch. He pressed his starboard button confidently, even though he had no view or sense of location except the maze of instruments before him. Once the ship was on course, his sensitive fingers pushed lightly on each button, like steering a wheel with two fingers on a straight road.

The *Kapitänleutnant* lifted his binoculars toward four immense girdered sheds surrounded by gantried cranes. One of the sheds had large white letters painted on its facade: K-R-U-P-P. Prien scanned the docks around the Germaniawerft complex. Yes, there was a spawn on new U-boats, workers crawling over them —even on Sunday.

He took off his glengarry shore cap and went below, leaving the watch officer to worry about the Kaiser-Wilhelm-Kanal traffic. He would have a word with this Nielson—in his cabin.

TWENTY

" 'Ere's a letter fum yer brother." The postman tipped his helmet and rode off on his bicycle. Nigel Mulford brushed an errant wisteria vine from the garden bench and gently set his bagpipes down. He selected the proper blade from his birthday present and neatly slit the left side of the lightweight envelope. Stamp collecting was another pursuit at which he excelled.

5 Oct. 39
Dear Nickie:

By the stamp you can tell whence this was mailed. When you get this letter, I'll be far gone. If it goes through a censor, he might block out my "possible" destinations. I give you two, because it would also confuse an enemy agent and therefore the censor may be lenient: Malta or Alexandria.

I hope you're enjoying your Swiss knife. Even an eighteen-year-old bandsman second class aboard a battleship might want to open a bottle occasionally.

I'm glad you've had to learn a lively instrument. The bloody piano deserves a rest.

I can tell you that I expect a command; it'll be sweet to get back in the thick of it. I wasn't made for shore duty, tho I must admit I'd rather dock with a lusty tit than a tubful of Nocky boys.

Talking about bitches, there's a beauty might come over from the States, and she's got a kid sister I'd like to plug as well, but I'll save her for you. Her name is Arabella. You should get your bowsprit out of books and into something juicy for a change.

I'm writing on the run.

Love to Mum and Dad.
Moxie

Nigel went into the cottage and set Moxie's letter on the fireplace mantel for his parents to see when they got home, his mother from a gas-mask factory in Sighthill and his father from Vicker's yard in Leith, where he was a diesel engineer.

The lean young man then packed his pipes carefully and tucked personal effects and clothing around the instrument to protect it during the train ride to Thurso, the northernmost port of Scotland. He set a newly bought biography of Rupert Brooke and another of his favorite Elizabethan composers aside—to pack them in accessible hand baggage for reading during the seven-hour trip.

Occasionally he would stop to admire the photo of his big brother, so dashing in pips and uniform on the bridge of his last command. He chuckled. One mustache like *that* was enough for a family of five. At least his sister didn't have to make decisions on beards and such. Nickie had come as a surprise package to his parents during the Depression that followed the Great War. Consequently he was much younger than Pamela and Moxie and treated more as a baby than as a brother. Little Nickie this, baby

Nickie that. It used to drive him blotto, especially as the terms had stuck and even accompanied him to primary school. A touch of asthma, since cleared up, did not contribute to his masculine dreams, though it was agreed that his absence from the dusty cricket fields was an attribute to the development of his latent talents.

It was not a time for music, or the university for that matter. Nigel wanted to belong to the times. Many of his friends had enlisted; so had he during the heat of August. If war had not come, he'd have been out in two years, having had the benefit of seeing the world, or at least part of it. The recruiting officer had promised him an exotic Asiatic station should the world come to its senses. His visions of Indian sitars and Japanese samisens were shattered by the invasion of Poland, just five weeks earlier.

He wrapped the scarlet Swiss combination knife in its white lanyard and set it down on the books. Nigel flexed his fingers and was tempted to lift the piano keyboard lid, but then he noticed something extraordinary: His wrists were tan. Six weeks of boot training, and he'd lost his pallid ivory white. His forearms felt strong, almost muscular. It was a good feeling, to feel like a man. It would be better to compose music after getting a taste of the world, of its people, of the enigmatic species called woman.

It was almost five; his parents would be home early to see him off. Dinner out and all that. Pamela would meet them at the Victoria Bar. Pity her man was in Malaya. Lastly, Nigel put his orders snug in his billfold. He read them again.

Curious name for a battleship—HMS *Royal Oak.*

TWENTY-ONE

Nigel sat on his small steamer trunk near the bow of *St. Magnus,* approaching the Orkneys. He held the top of his seabag tight against his rump lest in his rapture of sight-seeing, some blackguard, as his brother would put it, would *'elp 'imself.* He'd bought a postcard from the ship's store and would mail it from Kirkwall, assuring his parents that he hadn't been torpedoed in the Pentland Firth. Then a second card for the girl he'd met in the canteen on the train. She was from Aberdeen, and it was she who'd noticed him reading a poetry book. He hadn't expected anyone to know. By the title it could have been anyone: an explorer, a soldier, even a financier. But then, he was a soldier—sort of. Rupert Brooke: that's all it said on the dust jacket. He'd written her address inside the jacket. Brooke was one of his favorites, and she'd heard of him. He'd promised to write to her in a week, after she was settled with her aunt in Thurso. She was going to work at the children's camps in the Highlands to the south. Tens of thousands of children were being evacuated from the industrial centers of Britain. Her name was Craig. Carole with an *e.*

He held the postcard up, navy blue sleeve and gaudy rectangle against the somber sky and hues of Hoy Island. There! Nigel recognized the famous Old

Man of Hoy, an isolated rock column of gray shale capped with crimson sandstone. An attenuated Easter Island caprice of erosion, it conjured up Orkney's mysterious prehistory, dappled with stone circles, sepulchral mounds, and extinct civilizations. There he stood, an old guard sentry in the firth, 450 feet tall, afternoon shadow falling upon the high, sheer cliffs of St. John's Head, Isle of Hoy.

Thirty miles behind, to the south, rose the Highlands of Caithness, beyond the fishing port of Scrabster, where he'd boarded *St. Magnus*. He tried to picture Carole reading his postcard—no, it would be a letter—having put down her book of Keats on a green slope over Loch Shurrery.

The boat veered around the head into a tidal rip, into a northeast Arctic-tinged breeze that flared the bow ensign out trimly from its staff and startled Nigel smartly. His face hollowed. For a moment he felt oddly vulnerable.

Bandsman Second Class Mulford was first through the disembarking gate. He hadn't meant to be, but he was ushered ahead by the few passengers. Nothing too good for our lads of the Home Fleet. Quaint cottages looked down on the port of Stromness from the bleak heights of Harray, watching the travelers disappear into shops and alleys off narrow, cobble-paved Login Street—watching, as they had, in the eighteenth century, strong, young Orcadians embark on Hudson's Bay Company ships to carry the flag of the vermillion cross and four beavers into rich, virgin forests of the New World, to provide the muscle and endurance of northmen for bewigged French financiers and noblemen.

Nigel, on the combined services lorry, glimpsed the neolithic Stones of Stenness at high speed with screeching tires. There was hardly time to digest the *Blue Book* references:

> . . . the Stone of Odin, which stood till 1814, 150 feet N. has vanished. The latter stone is recorded in Sir Walter Scott's 1822 epic "The Pirate" as having been pierced by a hole, and an oath taken with hands joined through this hole was deemed more binding than any other.

The khaki lorry squealed past the church of Stenness, and the young sailor leaned out an open window, straining for a view of the ruins of a famous house where the Earl of Haverd was murdered by "his wicked wife Ragnhild (c. 980)."

Past Finstown, he observed the northern islands—Wyre, Egilsay, and Rousay—while the sailors and airmen were reading penny dreadfuls and vying for the attention of a flock of WRENS.

His guidebook prompted him to take notice of Rousay, with its eerily named bay of Eynhallow, a portent for the eleventh child of emigrants to America, author of "The Legend of Sleepy Hollow," Washington Irving, who was born on the passage.

At Kirkwall, Nigel posted his letters, checked his bags, and, since he didn't have to report to his ship till the next morning, decided, like the other tars, to stay in town for the evening. A salty bosun had advised him that once aboard, he'd wait a fortnight before setting foot onshore again. After a herring sandwich and a glass of Orkney's celebrated milk, he checked his gear, took his Mercury half-frame camera, clipped the lanyard of his Swiss army knife to a belt loop, and set out to explore the waterfront. It was hardly a mile's walk and all downhill from Kirkwall to the tiny port called Scapa on the flow. There were ships lying at anchor. His blood raced at the sight of an aircraft carrier. It was only three weeks earlier that the news had broken on the wireless while he was on leave at home in Braid Hills: "HMS *Courage* sunk by U-boat. Seven hundred men are rescued . . ."

Save 700. That meant 500 dead!

Nigel scurried mentally through the books in Moxie's room. Moxie had long since left and married, but it was still his room—even though it had been usurped by a musician. The copious books about the world's navies . . . Was it *Furious*? No, the converted cruiser had a turret forward of the superstructure—and a 1915 battle cruiser bow at the waterline. . . .

Two fleet marines, with white-belted Wembley .45's, stopped and eyed Nigel's shoulder-hung camera. "I'm not . . ." He pointed at the harbor. The marines laughed and continued on their rounds.

Recognition was a challenge to Nigel. He wanted to prove to his Royal Navy brother that a peaceable person could, when necessary, convert his energies to the exigencies of war. "Too bawd, Nickie," Moxie would say, "tha' a mind lak yourn canna be used in life!" He scoured his memory, flipping the horizontal pages of *Jane's Fighting Ships, 1938.* If he could memorize a musical score—Then, in a flash, it came: "massive stern overhang." The recognition factor. Moxie had pointed it out to him. Just like a swallow; one could tell by the tail. It was probably *Ark Royal. Hermes* and *Eagle* were smaller; *Illustrious* and *Formidable* had been launched but were still being fitted out.

He walked out on Scapa Pier and surveyed the boats, mostly fishing trawlers, bucking each others' gunnels a dozen deep out from the bollards. It was no wonder the steamers went to Stromness—

"Damn, damn, damn!" The exclamations flew from below. Nigel peeked over the edge of Scapa Pier's south side. A feisty red-whiskered dwarf under an oversize tam-o'-shanter was tugging insanely at his dinghy's painter.

"Can I be of help?" Nigel's fleet cap and boyish face appeared over the pier beam—upside down to the reddening dwarf.

"The scurvy rats," Major Sandy MacCowan pealed skyward, "have belayed me fast." He tugged again and sat down on a thwart, defeated. "Hov got to get bock wi' th' haddock." A galvanized round bathtub lay propped against the bow. Green flies were darting about the tarp that tucked into the ice beneath.

"Would ye believe?" Sandy tore at his sideburns as he hovered over the maze of tide-taut hawsers that tangled his three-quarter-inch bowline at the grimy iron bollard above.

Nigel tried his musician's fingers and broke his index nail. He retreated in pain and surprise. A casualty already! Determined to overcome what Moxie had referred to as his "fairy digits," he whipped out the red-sided birthday present. "Would this be of help?"

Sandy's eyes puckered under his scowling brows. "Thot'll do foine, lad; I dinna brung a sharp knife . . . now mind ya, I canno' afford more'n six inches off the end o' m' spliced painter—spliced it m'self at th' bow shackle I did. Now listen t' Sandy: Cut as close t' m' knot—nay, cut through m' knot—get under th' bloody hawsers, son."

The sailor, on blue knees, sawed and sawed with his prized many-bladed knife. He would write Moxie about this when he received the new fleet address. *Fairy digits,* my butt!

No sooner had the line parted when a whistle startled the roosting gulls from their pilings. It tooted again—and a third time as its owner, a low-hulled red trawler rammed its blunt bow through the lapstraked flotilla and tied up at the pier.

A trickle of townspeople grew into a torrent as shouts shunted from skiff to dory, from fisherman to purveyor, and then from monger to customer. Shops were closed as the Orcadians came down from Kirkwall, from St. Andrews and St. Mary's to the south; by foot, by cycle, and in antiquated Rovers.

The eleventh-century bell of St. Magnus rang *once,* out of consideration of the new air-raid codes banning a sequence.

The lemming citizens converged at Scapa Pier.

One by one, they walked out on the stout oak planks, a continuous wake of determined folk: children, gray-haired elders with grizzled cheeks, snappy tars and airmen on furlough, painted lasses and representatives of the Volunteer Home Guard. The chunky tug had tied up near Sandy's dinghy. He and the fleet bandsman were the first to see.

She seemed a proper white lifeboat, snugged up to the tug like a blanched child. There were hand ropes about her rail and artifacts lying in her bilge; the ropes were mottled with dun scarlet-brown and a child's rag doll floated facedown in mucky black oil under a thwart. A broken oar sloshed against a grimy life jacket; a woman's high-heeled patent pump glinted absurdly in green sea slime.

They walked slowly past—the long, the short, and the tall—as they read the charred gold letters on the lifeboat's bows: *Athenia.*

TWENTY-TWO

WREN Yeoman Second Class Pamela Doughty was thankful for the overcast weather. The blitz had let up enough to get some work done. She was weeks behind with her files.

On her desk at the Admiralty in London a framed assemblage of snapshots emerged from the stacks of reports and letters. One photo, a five by seven enlargement, was of her husband, a sergeant of infantry, stationed in Malaya; the smaller ones were of her Royal Navy brothers, Nickie and Moxie. She wished that Rod was Navy, too; at least he wouldn't have been sent into those awful jungles, with snakes—and Japs.

"Pam, will you pull the Metal Industries file, please?"

"Right away, ma'am," she piped up brightly, adding under her breath, "if I can find it."

The WREN lieutenant handed Pamela a flimsy to file. As she inserted it, something caught her eye: "Scapa Flow." She read it.

> Commanding Officer . . .
> Admiralty . . .
> from Commanding Officer, HMS *Scott* . . .

26 May 1939 . . . [and here it was late September]

> . . . no risk at present exists of submerged entry of submarines by Holm or Water Sound in Scapa Flow, and that entry on the surface would be extremely hazardous. Their lordships doubt if further blocking measures proposed would be final or could be relied upon to provide 100 percent security against a determined attempt at entry of enemy craft on the surface, though such an attempt is considered extremely unlikely. It has therefore been decided further expenditure on blockships cannot be justified. . . .

Pamela noticed the letter had been routinely approved by the assistant chief of the Naval Staff, Admiral Burrough. She filed it chronologically next to another letter, one from Metal Industries' chief salvage officer, dated in mid-June:

> Commanding Officer . . .
> Admiralty . . .
>
> It is fully recognized that the navigation of the sounds, even now, presents difficulties, owing to the strong tidal streams and existing obstructions, but it is safe to assume that an intrepid submarine officer, in wartime, would take risks which no discreet mariner would think of taking in peacetime.
>
> . . . if the entrances are left as present, a hostile submarine could enter Scapa Flow . . . and the fact that any such craft successful in

> passing through one of the sounds could be within torpedo range of capital ships in fifteen to thirty minutes makes it of vital importance that the sounds be efficiently blocked. . . .

Pamela felt a cold chill, thinking of the last month's tragedy. The aircraft carrier *Courage* had been torpedoed, with half its complement of 1,200 lost! Pamela inquired of her commanding officer and was told that Admiral French had persuaded Admiral Sir Charles Forbes to approve additional blockships. During July and August, three more ships had been sunk in Kirk and Skerry sounds, and the final one, to plug Kirk Sound, replacing an array of hawsers and wires between the concrete-filled *Thames* and *Soriano,* had sailed from Cardiff on September 22 for Rosyth. It was expected that *Lake Neuchatel,* after being prepared at a navy yard, would reach Scapa by October 15 and be scuttled in place by the twentieth. There had been much price haggling about another ship, *Cape Ortegal,* two weeks earlier, but the Admiralty refused to pay the "absurd price" asked by its owners.

Pamela walked over to a window and looked out on Whitehall. It was almost noon. From the Quadrangle she could see the wind direction cock atop the old building. The relic had turned, and the sky was clearing. Would the bombers come today?

29 Sept. 1939

COMMAND MATTER—*SECRET*

Operations
BdU
Toten Weg

U-10, U-20 STANDING OFF OPERATION "P" AFFIRM. MAIN BODY HOME FLEET OBSERVED AERIAL RECON

Commodore Dönitz handed the message to Commander Godt. "Eberhardt," he confided, "Admiral Raeder has given us the go-ahead."

"Then I'll ring up Prien at once."

Chief Quartermaster Wilhelm Spahr signed his name to a written secrecy oath, then handed his pen and the form to Lieutenant Endrass. As *U-47*'s navigator he'd brought the charts to Prien's cabin on *Hamburg*. Prien locked the door and spread a chart of Scapa Flow on the bunk. He pointed at the ocean handbook and a set of navigational and hydrographic volumes.

"We're going into the flow. I want each of you to prepare your own recommendations for the best date and time." He handed paper and an envelope to the surprised duo.

Assignment completed, they agreed on the night of October 13–14 and were told by Prien that the crew was not to be informed until the boat was well under way. It was to be a new moon attack; there was no quibbling about if. Both periods of slack water would occur during the selected hours.

Prien then conferred with Dönitz. The wizened submariner agreed. The new moon would decrease chances of northern lights, of being spotted and blasted by the shore guns that had been observed in the reconnaissance photographs; of being blinded by the searchlight, the *Scheinwerfer* that had been installed on a bluff overlooking Kierk Sound. The commander of *Unterseeboote* studied the wall calendar. He tapped the new moon engraving on the bottom of the *Oktober* page. "See, *Leutnant,* how it smiles on us."

Then he looked at the date: 13 . . . "Good, it's not a *Friday,* and defenses are usually weakest on Saturday nights. . . ." His eye strayed to the following week. The new blockship would be too late. Canaris had come through. He'd gotten, somehow, to the owners of *Cape Ortegal,* offered more money than Whitehall. Dönitz was pleased that Prien had come up with the right timing. It was proper that the Abwehr stay in the shadows. It had done its job.

Now Onkel Karl would do his.

TWENTY-THREE

They talked very quietly; there was no place on a submarine that was really private. Prien poured more coffee into Nielson's cup.

"So, you were in the Swedish Navy and applied for a transfer."

"It helps to have connections," Peter replied.

"If it weren't for these orders—" Prien laid the letter open on his pull-down desk.

"One does not question the grand admiral." Peter reached into his shirt pocket. "Is it all right to smoke?"

"We're not that rigid." The captain was staring at Nielson's hands. "Meteorology doesn't develop calluses."

"Nor does command."

"Are you to be carried on the ship's roster?"

"My connections would prefer that I wasn't."

"I thought so." Prien took a cigarette out of Nielson's pack of Muratis. "Don't smoke very often." Peter lit it with an expensive-looking gold lighter that did not go unnoticed."

"Of course, I will stand watch."

"Your rank means you'll mess with the petty officers, *Herr Obersteuermann* of the atmosphere."

"I'm glad we understand each other, *Herr Kaleunt.*"

"I'll have Spahr, our navigator, introduce you to the crew by rotating your noon mess. You'll join me for supper in the wardroom and meet the bridge."

"Delighted."

"You speak an *educated* German."

"I was lucky to have gone to school in your country."

"University?"

"That, too."

"Then why weren't you an officer in the Swedish Navy?"

"Did I say I wasn't?"

"Touché, Herr Nielson." Prien hesitated and grouped his thoughts. The Swede was a worthy adversary. "I watched you come down the conning ladder before. A submariner couldn't have done it better."

"We have submarines in the Swedish Navy."

The commander tried another tack. "Is there anything *U-47* can do to facilitate your *meteorological* duties? I didn't notice you bringing much equipment aboard, and I didn't see any such items on the loading manifest last week." It was cat-and-mouse time.

"I have a few small balloons in my wallet."

Prien couldn't help laughing at the quip. "Very good, Nielson; at least we ought to have a good time."

"But, seriously, I do have a packet of authentic instruments, and I've done a bit of homework. At one point or other I'll send up my one orange weather balloon."

"Do it when we're surfaced, which may not be often."

"I'm also good at nocturnal observation." Peter

grinned enigmatically. "Thank you for the excellent coffee."

Oberleutnant Endrass guided the boat past a moored timber freighter flying Swedish colors, slowed down abeam of Scheerhafen, where a light cruiser was taking on stores, then turned to port at the Holtenauer locks, entrance to the *Kanal*. The submarine held against the tide and waited for the locks tower to post a green signal to indicate the Kiel-Wik ferry had passed.

Once under the Prinz Heinrich Bridge, the crew relaxed to normal Sunday off-watch routine. The next fifty-three miles would mean eight hours of running at 6.8 knots, eight boring hours because of the forty-foot high banks on either side of the *Kanal*. There would be nothing to see till they reached Brunsbüttelkoog at the *Kanal*'s terminus on the river Elbe. The control room mate noted in the log that a speed of 6.8 knots was precisely in between the highest and lowest speeds allowed by the *Kanal* authority.

Nielson took the afternoon watch along with Leutnant-Junior Hans Wessels and two ratings. It felt good to be on a submarine bridge again. In this case there wasn't much to do except maneuver through the bridges and compensate for the swells pushed up by tankers and freighters. Nielson was proud of being on *U-47* and returned the salutes and hand waving of the inbound ships with great enthusiasm. He was, however, apprehensive of Wessels's ability and, at times, was tempted to call out orders to the helmsman. He found Spahr to be a jovial and dedicated petty officer—and, to his chagrin, qiute versed in meteorology as well as navigation. Peter made a mental note to send up his balloon when Spahr was below. At four o'clock the next dogwatch took over.

The trim low craft powered steadily through the 145-foot-wide passage across the Schleswig peninsula, invisible because of the deep banks to the townspeople of Rendsburg on the Eider, for ten miles which it ran parallel with. It passed under four railway bridges, three autobahns, and one river viaduct before reaching the broad Elbe, gateway of Germany through Hamburg.

Young boys looked down from the footbridges, 130 feet over the canal, and delighted in seeing the bridge watch wave at them. They counted the triangular white pennants that fluttered from a line tied to the attack periscope head, running diagonally aft and down to the *Wintergarten* railing. "One . . . two . . . three . . . four," screamed a child. "It's sunk four enemy boats!"

Prien, after having a word with the pilot, looked up at the pennants. He knew them by heart. Each one bore a number indicating the tonnage sunk: *Gartavon,* 3,000, the first official kill of the war, September 5; *Bosnia,* 2,500; *Rio Claro,* 4,800; and another, as yet unidentified, a night casualty, 3,000! Over 13,000 tons for Pruentje, as he was called by the other commanders. He had consulted the *Weyer* ship's registry. British battleships varied in tonnage from 25,000 tons to mighty *Hood* at 46,000. This little boy who had never finished school was determined to make his mark over the smart ones with their airs and polish, with their *connections.* He'd had a good start toward becoming the first 100,000-ton ace. Now he was being handed the chance to make it come true. He envisioned his father, in Lubeck, the seaport of his birth, sitting at his high desk, white-wigged and presiding over the court. Proud of his son! He looked at his watch; it was almost six. Time to inspect the log.

Obergefreiter Friedrich Walz wearily raised himself through the conning hatch, still wearing his cook's apron. "I need a coffin nail." He offered one to the watch officer, who declined. Gustav Werder, binoculars hanging limp, snatched one out of Walz's pack. "I swear, one of these days somebody will cook *me* a meal. In fact, next liberty I'm going to a fine hotel and order all three meals in bed." Walz inhaled deeply.

"It would be about time that you ate something *nourishing* in bed," Gustav piped up.

"I'll ignore that vulgar remark and enjoy the . . ." Walz looked aft. "What happened to the brass bands at Brunsbüttelkoog? What happened to Brunsbuttelkoog?" He squinted into the haze.

"You missed it. We've had a good tide with us. Dropped off the pilot twenty minutes ago," said Werder from behind his glasses. The twinkling lights of the small river town disappeared as *U-47* came abeam of Cuxhaven, to port. The boat was well out in the channel and bearing toward Elbe lightship III.

"Oh, my God—the strawberries!" Walz streaked down.

"Engine room, full ahead both." Liuetenant-Junior von Varendorff snapped the voice tube cover shut after he'd heard the repeat.

Walz's china plates vibrated as he ducked and carried two coffees into the wardroom. He'd rather serve and have Sporer wash the dishes aft in the tiny galley. The boat's screws rumbled over a swell as the speed increased: eight, ten, twelve knots. The cook picked up a stack of dishes that the officers had heaped for him, and he staggered through the control room, a drunken juggler.

The surge of power brought the boat to life. It was felt through cork-soled sea boots, in sleeping bodies pressed against wood laminates, through hands and arms touching, manipulating and holding onto railings, levers, and valve wheels from stem to stern. It was seen as sausages and hammocked bread loaves swung from the myriad conduits and overhead fittings, and as coffee cups slid aft on the green linoleum wardroom table and clunked against the plate rail, splattering Nielson's shirt sleeve and eliciting a chuckle from the commander, who preferred full uniform on all occasions.

"Must be out past Cuxhaven." He glanced at his Rolex. "We've made good time." He turned solemnly toward the two officers, the navigator and the Swede. "This is it; we're on our way!" Prien observed Nielson for any telltale reaction. Did the Swede know? Spahr and Endrass had sworn to secrecy. Wessels didn't know; nor did Varendorff, who was on the bridge. He thought he saw a cunning turn of the Swede's lips, not realizing that it was a permanent idiosyncrasy—a legacy of Alfried Krupp von Bohlen, a face to wear at the Prussian Embassy in the Vatican.

The engine room tachometer swung toward its limit as the two diesels, each with six five-foot pistons chugged to develop almost 3,000 horsepower. Twelve rocker arms were working in perfect firing sequence as the individual cylinder explosions, driving the crankshafts, melding into a continuous roar, converted the fuel's energy into rotary motion.

The power was felt on the bridge, and Varendorff called for oilskins against the briny spray, and the lookouts cussed the water dripping from their binocular lenses. Steinhagen scampered up and took down the little white pennants, while forward and aft, the deck bollards retracted, and the fenders were secured in compartments under the wood slats. The small "white bone" bow wave had grown into a slashing cascade of foam as the 750 tons of tempered steel, carrying 3 tons of muscle, bone, and brain, as well as 5 tons of high explosive in twelve torpedoes, charged into the Atlantic swells. The force was heard on the bridge as the supercharger ducts roared and drowned out the diesels. . . .

The power, the rising and falling slapping of the bow were felt by one of the "lords" in the forward bunks. He swung himself out and yawned, then reached behind a reserve torpedo, took a protective blanket off his accordion. His mates joined in and sang.

It was *time,* once more!

The strains of "Must I Leave" wafted aft, rising and descending to the rhythm of the boat. The traditional departure chantey was picked up by the forward intercom and transmitted aft.

In the wardroom Captain Prien, no slouch in chantey verses, which he knew by the hundreds, led his group:

Must I leave this town,
And you, my treasure, stay behind . . .

The music poured out of the bridge hatch, and the aft watch did a short jig around the flak gun on the *Wintergarten*.

Hebestreit, the radioman, tapped his feet as he received a message, and the sound man swayed and hummed in his niche.

In the galley, Walz stirred potato soup while singing:

> *Must I leave*
> *Even though I know I've strayed . . .*

Aft, the E-motor mates and diesel stokers imitated a barbershop quartet:

> *Must I leave,*
> *When I want you so . . .*

While, in the stern, Machinist's Mate Ronni Roth, spanner in hand, tightened a hex nut on a torpedo's fuel line, singing with each stroke:

> *When I return, when I return,*
> *I'll stay with you. . . .*

Prien signed the day's log. He noted that the control room mate had entered "2300 Helgoland Bight, Wind SE 1. Cloudy."

Then he turned in and went through his papers and orders, making sure that all secret information had been destroyed. He took off his six-button blue fur-lined coat and boots, then his leather pants and stretched out on his green foam rubber bunk, alone behind his drawn curtain. He took his diary from a hiding place behind the single shelf of nautical data books, opened it, and he tried to compose something interesting, something worthy of his command. They would ask him, later, onshore, and he wanted to be ready. He'd kept notes for years of his maritime travels. Perhaps now he might have to write a book—if things went well on the mission.

Prien flipped back the pages: to September 7. He read what he'd written about the freighter that had been wheel-lashed to ram him; and his reactions at meeting *Gartavon*'s captain: "We were very polite to each other, like knightly opponents in a novel. But behind this formality lay an icy hatred, the hatred of two peoples who are facing each other in the last decisive round. . . ."

Knightly opponents. He pondered the picture. Yes, in the days of the Teutonic Knights, he would have become one, too, in spite of such things as lack of position and money. He would have gone off with the armies of the Crusade as a page to a famous knight. And returned as a full-fledged knight on a black stallion. Now *U-47* was that black stallion, and he was going to Albion to slay the English dragon. It bothered him that unlike the British and the Americans, the Germans did not allow submarines to have names; only impersonal numbers. He remembered *Sebago*; peculiar name. The boat had been lost, then raised and salvaged. He'd found out that "*Sebago*" was a salmon variant. The Americans named their boats after fish. And so did the Swedes.

Prien was amused at the English. They called their submarines after highbrow words, like the O class *Oxley* and *Oberon*, the P class *Pandora* and *Parthian*. It was the same with their line ships: HMS *Dreadnought*, HMS *Renown*. Pansy names, effeminate names. It was common knowledge that the tommies had more queers amongst them than other countries' armed services. And then there was *Ark Royal* and *Royal Oak*. Like parlor word games! He'd often got the two confused until Spahr enlightened him. There once was an English king who ran and hid from the enemy during a losing battle. He hid in an oak tree, which became known as the royal oak!

The "old man" of thirty stared at his blank diary page, then turned off his light.

"Shhh," someone admonished outside Prien's curtain, "he's asleep." The crewmen tiptoed past. Then a voice rang out, stopping them in their tracks.

"The captain never sleeps."

Halfway to Helgoland *U-47* test-dived and trimmed for the 600-mile trip. She lay on the bottom and perfected a routine that would put her at peak efficiency at midnight, the planned hour of attack in Scapa Flow. The crew were served their three eggs, toast, and jam at 2300 hours rather than 0600. Meat and potatoes were set in the messes at 0400 instead of 1200. The majority of the crew changed sleeping hours to daytime, though it was apparent only when they surfaced to recharge the batteries and dump refuse in weighted sacks. This was done only at night, since chances could not be taken of being spotted by either hostile or neutral vessels in the shipping lanes between Scandinavia and Spain.

On Monday, October 9, she surfaced at 0900 and slipped behind sandy Düne Island and into the "Gibraltar of the North Sea," Helgoland. An island, surrounded by a steep rock platform, it had been given to the kaiser in 1890 in exchange for Zanzibar and some East African territory. The British had wrested it from Denmark during Nelson's time. By 1914 it had been honeycombed with underground tunnels and armed with coastal guns. The harbor included naval piers and a dry dock. Stripped after the Treaty of Versailles, the facility was rebuilt by the Nazis.

Captain Prien, in his cabin, read the top secret Enigma message he had decoded with his special key insert that had activated the fifth roller of the machine. Yes, it was true: He had been ordered to let off *one* man while tied up at Helgoland. And that man was the "meteorologist." He shook his head in disbelief, then crumpled up the specially treated Enigma paper. He dropped it into a cup of water—and watched it dissolve!

At dusk, after Nielson had returned, the U-boat moved out and proceeded, at periscope depth of forty-five feet, southwest—in the general direction of the English Channel. Bets were wagered by the "lords" in the torpedo room. Gefreiter Herrmann took a five-mark note out of his billfold. "Even money that we go after some tonnage out of Amsterdam and Rotterdam. For all we know, they're sneaking their oil reserves to the Allies . . ."

"You might have something there, Herbchen . . . with all these Jew businessmen in Holland," said a voice from a top bunk.

"Maybe we should board some of those Dutch and Belgian ships in case they're smuggling diamonds out." Meyer's eyes lit up.

"I'll put my money on Portsmouth," Mantyk chimed in. "That's the big limey naval base. We just lay out off the Isle of Wight—"

"How so?" came from behind a sunbathing magazine.

"The fact that we're not carrying the foredeck reloads"—Leading Seaman Mantyk had the floor—"means that it'll be submerged fire only. No time to surface—"

"And be seen by the whole fucking English fleet," added Meyer.

The control room mate drew a china pencil red line on the celluloid chart overlay. It started at a vertical line that was marked "8" for time of day, and continued to the next line, marked "12." In four hours the boat had run eight miles submerged at a speed of four knots, then two hours after dark on its diesels, making an additional twenty-four for a total of thirty-two nautical miles. *U-47* was now abeam of one of the East Frisian Islands, called Spikeroog. At twelve knots it would reach Borkum, the last of the chain of seven islands, by daybreak when it would submerge again.

The second watch spotted Juist light, at the mouth of the Ems River, and bets regarding destination were once more laid. There was great consternation among the wagerers when the helmsman swung the bow from 242 southwest to 312 nor'west and the boat submerged to spend the dangerous daylight hours on the bottom, southeast of Dogger Bank minefields. The boat snuggled into the sand at a depth of 175 feet.

The next day, Wednesday, October 11, they'd made 180 miles by sunrise, then submerged and by 0800 were comfortably settled on a shoal near Devil's Hole, the deepest spot in the North Sea.

"Hey, Spahr," the crew had joked with the navigator as the manometer bubble dropped to 350 feet, "Devil's Hole is around here somewhere, and it's eight hundred forty feet deep—that's a hundred forty feet deeper than the pressure hull is guaranteed for!"

Obersteuermann Wilhelm Spahr told them that if his plotting was erroneous, he'd buy them all beer *if* they got back to port. What he didn't tell them was that the new electric fathometer had picked up the shoal.

The crew, in small groups, stopped and looked at the red line on the celluloid. If one sighted over the chart along the line, there was no question where that line was going. By nightfall the next day, after a short run of about 100 miles, the VIIB took its last prolonged breather 60 miles off Aberdeen and a night's run from the Orkneys. The log entry for Thursday indicated the wind at "SE 7-6" under overcast skies. There had been little variation since Spahr had rigged his diopter on the bridge and taken his last land bearings off Helgoland.

TWENTY-FOUR

12 October 1939
Extract from the personal diary of a lady in London:

We've yet to hear an enemy aircraft. Our beautiful horizons are so tranquil. We are getting used to the pachydermic blimps which shimmer in the evening . . . caught by sunlight against the firmament. Our cousins in the country, bless them, are not as fortunate; the planes roar on high, by day and night. . . . The autumn has been spectacular—pheasants screeching in the suburbs—and pop, pop, pop; our men at their grand pursuits. I certainly don't miss those evacuated children, though I never wished it upon the dears. . . . They have ample play centers and communal feeding, and Lord knows, there are now fewer parental transportation problems!

I'm so happy about horses. Dear, old pensioned ponies are now back in their revered paddocks. Ancient governess's carts are once more called into action. It's really Gilbert and Sullivan again, much as I abhor music hall. But I must admit that a certain *shoddiness* is on the proverbial *wane*. Since the butcher and grocer are only—owing to petrol rationing—coming out on Mondays, we've had to reevaluate certain ideas. I just love to see the lady of an Ascot manor wobble a bicycle out of the garage to go to tea!

Extracts from *The New York Times:*
Blackout Test Sunday

NEW YORK, Oct. 12—World's Fair visitors on Sunday night will get a taste of what a wartime blackout is like when, as part of the maneuvers accompanying observance of Coast Artillery Day at the fair, a mock air raid will be staged over the Court of Peace. . . . At 8 P.M. the fair's exterior lights will be extinguished and air-raid warnings will be sounded over the amplification system as a squadron of bombers from Mitchell Field sweeps in from Montauk Point. The bombers will try to drop illuminating flares before the defending ground crews can sight them and bring their guns into action.

The only difference in the Saturday night demonstration and an actual air raid, fair officials said, will be that interior and streetlights will be kept on and the planes will not carry real bombs. . . .

BERLIN, Oct. 13—Chancellor Hitler indirectly asked President Roosevelt early today to intervene in the European war by advising Britain to meet Germany in conference. Failure of the United States to do this, the chancellor indicated, would result in his unleashing "a war in earnest" against Great Britain and France, producing the "most gruesome blood bath in history."

LONDON, Oct. 13—Three German submarines were destroyed today, the Admiralty announced tonight in a marked departure from its usual custom of keeping secret the results of the Navy's campaign against underseas raiders on British commerce. . . . The British Navy is jubilant. . . .

PARIS, Oct. 12—Coinciding with the failure of Chancellor Hitler's "peace proposals"—a failure clinched by Prime Minister Chamberlain's speech in the House of Commons today—German aggressiveness on the Rhine-Moselle front, which had increased each day since Sunday, brought about first-line actions along the entire 120 miles. . . .

AMSTERDAM, Oct. 12—Eight days of running without lights, dodging the British blockade through mist and cold under a commander who preferred to lose his ship rather than surrender her, were described here today by a cook on the disguised queen of the Reich's merchant fleet, *Bremen*, now in Murmansk, Russia, since the hazardous trip.

Lale Andersen, daughter of a German sea captain from the East Frisian Islands, had just rerecorded "Lilli Marlene." Originally set in "slow, syrupy waltz time," it was now the sprightly theme song of the nightly German armed forces record program. Radioman Steinhagen put the program on *U-47*'s loudspeaker system every night at 2200 hours. Another consolation of running on the surface at night.

It was against BdU regulations to hang lascivious pictures in submarines, but this order was circumvented while at sea, as long as the evidence was removed before they tied up in port. Lale's photo was displayed in the forward torpedo room and the aft E-motor room along with the usual cheesecake and nudes. Prien made a point not to go into these areas. Women were not a prime interest with him.

Endrass, however, was of a different bent. He'd had some art training and was quite good in drawing, though the idea of being an artist didn't as yet appeal to him. He, like many professional soldiers, was repelled by the bohemianism that had pervaded Germany during the twenties. Art to Endrass had to be idealistic, not depraved and ugly. He kept a reproduction of one of Adolf Ziegler's works as a bookmark. Ziegler was also a favorite of the Führer's. It didn't bother him that the anti-Nazi underground called this painter "the master of the pubic hair."

Engelbert Endrass looked at his pocked face in a stainless steel mirror. But for his *Leutnant*'s cap on the bunk, he might have been taken for a young journalist or a graduate student of paleontology. The officer was constantly immersed in books. Endrass's forte was mathematics; he had excelled in gunnery and torpedo calculation in officers' school prior to being assigned to Prien's crew. It was he, as torpedo officer of *U-47*, who had actually, with Spahr at the tracking table, figured and fired the eels that were responsible for Prien's success. That he was standing in Prien's shadow gnawed at him, but then, the captain was nine years older. There would be time for him to get his own command. Just a little more experience; perhaps this would be the mission that would win him a command.

So Endrass did Prien's bidding perfectly. He never let his true feelings about his captain be known. To the crew he was dedicated and single-minded, the most loyal officer aboard.

The *Oberleutnant* turned to a page marked by a color postcard-size print of the work of another "national realist" artist, Academy professor Sepp Hilz. The painting was titled "Rustic Venus" and showed a young blond girl, nude except for one striped woolen sock which she was about to remove as she leaned on a medieval chair in front of a Bavarian decorated bed. Endrass touched his face, then admired the girl's clean, sunlit "Aryan" skin and features. He was impatient because his beard, unlike that of the other officers, was hardly noticeable. With a command of his own, the beard would not matter as much—to rustic Venuses!

In a few hours they would leave the Devil's Hole area on the last leg of the trip. He flipped the postcard over and continued poring over his calculus textbook. For Endrass, the most important thing was numbers. They kept his mind—and his nervous but sensitive right hand—in perspective.

Numbers! The next day would be Friday the thirteenth. He wasn't normally superstitious, but he was glad that physically the darkest hours of night were the first two *after* midnight. This could be shown graphically on a clockface: If sunset was at 8:00 P.M. and sunrise at 6:00 A.M., a line drawn from between those two numbers, 7, through the center of the clock would end at 1:00 A.M.

And 1:00 A.M meant the fourteenth—which was twice 7!

The fair weather at the embarking from Kiel had deteriorated as a low-pressure area grew and moved across northern Scotland's Highlands into the Moray Firth. The westerlies howled up to force 5 and oilskins were broken out for *U-47*'s bridge watch. Abeam of Duncansby Head, according to the red chart line below, the barometer dropped sharply while the wind rose to gale force. The sea reared up and thrashed the iron chariot, spilling tons of salty Atlantic on the staggering foredecks, twanging the green-terminaled jumping wires, and sloshing into neck collars and sea-boots.

The foam-capped swells merged with evening, obscuring everything beyond a boat's length to the eye-weary charioteers, now shackled to their safety harnesses, fearing the wave that, on occasion, had left the tower unattended.

Endrass pointed a gloved hand to port. "If we turned hard, we'd make the north cape of Scotland in less than two hours. . . ."

Shielding his eyes from the drizzle, Nielson, on starboard forward watch, rested his binoculars on the wood slat lining below the rail. "At this heading I would expect to pick up South Ronaldsay in the same time." He balanced the glasses, as prescribed by regulations, on his fingertips and resumed scanning his quadrant.

Prien, noticing the Swede's perennial smile, chose this point for his sally: "Herr Nielson, would you like to take over? Your geography surpasses even your meteorology."

"Thank you kindly, sir, but I'm not accustomed to night sailing as yet—especially without a moon."

"The Swedes have never worried about moons, Herr Nielson; they've never been in a war where it mattered—"

"Point off the port—land!"

"So it seems, Bertchen. The squall's lifted north of us, or we'd have run up on the Pentland Skerries."

"I think I can make them out, too, sir."

"Good thing. Another fifteen minutes, and we'd have had no light." Prien dried his watch crystal on his right sleeve stripes.

An undulating, ominous black ribbon lay ahead of the plowing, pitching bow, shredded, tentacled clouds grasping down. Endrass cupped his gloves at the commander's ear. "Are we going to visit the Orkneys, sir?" Prien enjoyed the joke; it was intended for the Swede.

The gale bit furiously at the yawing craft, cowering the watch and making a shambles of the galley china. Even the heavy iron chart chest slid on the control room deck.

"Let's go in and take a fix," Prien ordered. "Then we'll lay off and get some rest."

> 12/10/39
> Reached Orkneys approximately 2200 hours. Came in close to SE coast in order to fix exact position. At 2230 English are kind enough to switch on all coastal lights so I can obtain a precise position. We are correct to within 1.8 nautical miles despite the fact that since we left Channel One, there was no possibility of obtaining an accurate fix, as I had to steer by dead reckoning and electric soundings. . . .

Gerhardt Hänsel, leading seaman, focused his glasses on the low-lying islands. "Sir," he commented to Endrass, "looks like a tough place to find one's way into."

Also on the wet bridge, Spahr and his mate, Dziallas, took bearings on Rose Ness and Copinsay lighthouses. They looked for Anskerry, but gave up because of a fogbank in that direction. The cool evening was refreshing; it found its way down through the hatch and was welcomed at all stations, especially tube six, the head. Nielson climbed up and inhaled deeply. "Ah, just like the nor'land from where I came."

"Bring your balloons?" The captain descended and went aft at the behest of Oberleutnant Hans Wessels, the engineering officer. Nielson laughed accordingly and looked toward shore.

"What kind of weather are you predicting for tomorrow?" Spahr was buoyant over his accomplishment.

"If I could predict as well as you reckoned the course, I'll become a magician or a radio weatherman after this is all over. I hear you were less than two miles off—after five hundred miles."

"The stars were good to me most of the way." The navigator searched the islands methodically, noting down the contours, as possible against a faint northern glow. "Such somber silhouettes, those islands—we're—"Spahn stopped in mid-sentence.

"Coming in on the same heading tomorrow—same time?"

Spahr ignored Nielson's remark. He'd vowed secrecy, and even as obvious as the mission might be by now, he was not going to be the one to break his oath.

"I'm expecting a message at midnight, Wilhelm. BdU's sent a weather picket boat out into the Atlantic. It should be about three hundred miles west of the Hebrides by now. It's an experiment, but we might as well take advantage of it."

"Is that why you went ashore at Helgoland?" Spahr

adjusted the ocular of the diopter and jotted down a bearing.

"You were worried about my function?"

"Well–it *is* a tight ship," Spahr snapped back at the equal-ranked messmate. "Does Hebestreit know about the message?"

"Yes, it's in a special cipher key–part of the experiment."

"Well, this is easy for a change; beats astronomical fixes by far." Spahr unfastened the bearing diopter from its pedestal, gathered a sheaf of notes, and went below, moving aside the light deflector. Tomorrow there'd be no regular lights–only ghostly red ones, and red-tinged spectacles beforehand.

Endrass came vaulting topside, face eerily underlit from the bridge instrument red lights. "Helmsman," he called through the hatch, "ring up the motor room; let's leave quietly. Bosun"–he'd uncapped the brass voice tube–"prepare to dive."

"Antenna depth," repeated Hänsel at his helm buttons.

In the control room against the port pressure hull, the hydroplane duo did their fingertip ballet, hands inside the emergency stainless wheels, pressing down on the servo-assisted brass knobs. The manometer water column rose steadily behind the horizontal hairlines as the plane pointers wavered with the trim.

"Antenna raised."

"Thirty feet; antenna clear."

"Steady trim and hold it on thirty." The bosun went from valve to valve around the control room.

"Someone should invent an underwater aerial." Nielson leaned into the radio room.

"It would need a very low-frequency receiver." Hebestreit turned on his transformer. "Countdown, thirty seconds and standing by." The radioman snapped his earphones on and tuned in on the cipher frequency. "Both minimum forward," rang the telegraph.

Prien and Endrass passed through the *Zentrale.* The elfish one turned as the taller one ducked through the round, vertical pressure hatch. "Nielson, why don't you join us in the wardroom after you've decrypted your meteorology message?" The blond one snapped his arm aloft in a quasi salute.

Steinhagen set the metal lid back as they crowded around the typewriter-sized wooden box in the compact radio room. He pulled a latch, and the front gate opened, unleashing a complex of crisscrossed switchboard cables. Impressed into the back of the hinged wood gate was an ellipse, containing a trademark name: Enigma.

The device looked like the insides of a slot machine combined with an ancient Underwood and augmented with an electric-shock apparatus. Hebestreit turned a Bakelite knob to *D,* for *decipher,* then pressed a test button. A glow lamp lit behind the letter *H* on a panel behind and above the keyboard. Good! The *Oberfunkergefreiter* nodded his crew cut.

Nielson moved the key wheel lever to his special code number, activating a slide bar to push its variable cam gears into four drums; digital rings clicked and revolved in response to the input signal. Steinhagen read off the triple-grouped letters from the original transcript as Hebestreit typed in sequence. Impulses were shunted through the rotors, then through a myriad of wires, and the output letters glowed one by one. The smiling one took down the terse message and folded it.

"Thank you, gentlemen. Please send a confirmation on my key, care of cipher asteroid. When received by asteroid, my key will be nullified and replaced with a new sequence."

Nielson went forward into the officers' wardroom and sat down at the fiddle-edged table. He laid the message on the green linoleum in front of Prien, who read it quickly and passed it on to Endrass.

"I don't know whether that's good or bad news. Clearing skies may make us more visible—"

Endrass and Spahr exchanged glances; they knew the captain and his wily games. He was toying with the Swede.

"The Orkneys have a *cabalistic* beauty." Nielson relished the word, but the captain did not betray the fact that he did not understand the term.

"To me they're a group of islands north of Scotland, inhabited by farmers who like to fish and chickens that lay millions of eggs. I've seen prettier islands."

"De gustibus non est disputandum."

Prien ignored Nielson's parry, nodded as if he might have understood, knowing that Endrass *did,* and changed the tack. He was losing, and he didn't like to lose.

"Obersteuermann Nielson, I must assume that your *connections* have told you what this patrol is all about. I don't know why you're aboard, but I do know that we've got to pull together. I have no choice but to believe that the grand admiral must have very good reasons, however expedient, to have included you without telling BdU."

"Sir, he *had,* and if we make it through this war, I'll buy you a drink and tell you the story."

"Good enough, Nielson. I may take you up on that—even if I don't drink very much. I hope the weather boat is right about light winds. There's not much room between the blockships."

"I think we'll need the visibility—even a large ship could easily be lost against those overlapping contours." Spahr sipped his coffee. "Even Hänsel didn't like the looks of it."

"Perhaps we ought to take a quick daylight recon." Endrass watched as his idea burned into the captain's brain. That was the job of the second officer—to suggest ways, come up with solutions, then let the captain implement them.

Compressed air hissed and blew the Atlantic out of the forward tanks as *U-47* rose and scattered a flock of storm petrels into a batlike frenzy, screeching and mewing into the bubbling diesel wake in anticipation of galley scourings.

"Zero-eight-five," acknowledged the helmsman, eyes riveted on his compass as the twin diesels roared and bypassed the exhaust vents in blowing the main tanks.

"Both ahead full," replied the chief stoker, and the gray wolf leaped toward the deep, safe waters east of Copinsay, to wait, to rest on the sandy bottom. The time-hallowed ritual common to man as he hesitantly picked up his weapon—a stone, a sword, a musket—and prayed, or reveled, to gather courage for the next day.

"0437 hrs. Lying submerged at 90 meters, 38 miles east of Rose Ness. Rest period for the crew . . ."

Prien closed his logbook. There would be a general muster at 1600—to tell the crew, all the officers having been told first, a matter of precedence even if certain young officers were less valuable than certain petty officers. Why not, he thought, do as Endrass had suggested—go close inshore at 1530 and lie off Copinsay, come to periscope depth below South Nevi, and get a good daylight look at the contours of Holm Sound? Spahr would memorize it, note the approach bearings in relation to Copinsay light, and *presto,* child's play to go in by compass.

Hänsel was right. Endrass was right. And Leutnant-Senior Prien was not one to overlook his crew's talents. Seventeen years at sea had taught him that. He knew he had the drive, the stamina, to gain what had been denied to him in the shore arena, and he would spare nothing to gain that end: to prove that his way was as good as his father's. He would be to his mother what his father hadn't been. Prien made notes on scrap paper to help him remember. Time was telescoping, shrinking.

"Get in closer . . . run submerged from 1230 to 1600 . . . eight knots . . . cut the attack distance from thirty-eight to ten miles . . . thirty-meter hole SSW off Nevi Point? Yes, a shorter run, especially with the port diesel acting up. Damn, why *now?* Prien grabbed his intercom and called Wessels to his cabin.

"Sorry, sir. Doesn't look too good. Seawater must have gotten in during the overhead lube transfer. There should be another valve on the conduit or a bleeding scupper—"

"Hans"—the captain fidgeted with his fountain pen—"can't we fix it *afterward*?"

'It's over seven percent seawater, sir." Wessels avoided looking his commander in the eye. "We'll make it into the flow at slack tide, and we'll maneuver into the anchorage all right—but in case of trouble, a call for top speed . . ."

"Or even against a nine-knot tide—" Prien interjected.

"The seawater might turn into steam and clog the jets with salt!"

"And then— a *stall,*" Prien lamented. "Well, *Herr Ingenieur,* it's all up to you now. But we'll go in *regardless.*"

"I'll do my best, sir." Wessels slipped through the curtain.

TWENTY-FIVE

Nickie Mulford, in blue coat, fur hat, and Royal Stewarts, marched on the seaward side of *Oak*'s five-piper phalanx, black drone pipes high, and chanters fingered to the sprightly tune "74th's Farewell to Edinburgh." His left arm was pumping hard on the bag, with goatskin sporran and tassels swaying to the gait. Behind, two drummers boomed and swung their muffled sticks in rhythmic loops.

Leading the contingent of the battleship's musical complement of seven bandsmen, Boy First Class Frost, one of the thirty-two sixteen-year-old apprentice seamen aboard, carried a square white silk banner proudly before him. Blue gilt-edged embroidery heralded:

HMS ROYAL OAK
PIPE
&
DRUM
CORPS

The parade had stepped off at St. Mary's Holm at 1000, and was due in Kirkwall, six miles up and off the coast road, at 1130. From the capital it was scheduled to march down the hill to its terminus at Scapa Pier.

The massed bands had come from Caithness, across the firth, and from Lerwick in the Shetlands, as well as from antiaircraft detachments and RAF units in the Orkneys.

There were green plaids from Argyll, sienna Chisholms, and light tan MacPhersons; there were yellow MacLeods and bright reds from Skene and somber tartans of Clan Douglas. Silver clasps and trimmings flashed the sun back at the gabled windows above the crowds that lined the waterfront road.

Young lasses from St. Magnus's Sunday school twirled and danced over toy swords, fancy kicking their argyled legs with splayed hands o'er heads to the tune of "The Shepherd's Crook." After them marched an assortment of town elders and robed priests, swinging holy water and smiling benevolently right and left.

The procession's climax was flanked by a rear echelon of middle-aged home guards in tight military uniforms of all kinds. A milk cart, bedecked with flowering thistle and late nemesia garlands, rumbled behind a Shetland roan pony, led by a wee sailor lad. Atop the cart and rising out of the flowers like a vertical glass casket called to heaven was the case, borrowed from the afterlobby aboard the defunct depot ship HMS *Iron Duke* that displayed dead Admiral Jellicoe's full-dress frock coat. The twelve brass buttons and gilded epaulets glittered on the headless, handless coatmaker's dummy, black cravat on the truncated white neck. The cart wobbled crazily on the ballast-stone road, animating the manikin, while a ragtag knot of urchins took turns jumping on and off the tailgate—occasionally bouncing a pebble on Lord Jellicoe's tinkly case.

One of the more interested onlookers, Major Sandy

MacCowan, ran a few steps along with puff-cheeked Nickie Mulford as *Royal Oak*'s Corps drummed past his restaurant. "Nickie, m' boy . . . cum down fer a sandwich oon th' house before ye leave. And a brew if ye want . . ."

Young Mulford nodded as best he could, with the blowing pipe numbing his gums. One didn't say no to the major, especially when his daughter was with him. Nickie waved quickly at Ruth MacCowan of the black hair and deepset eyes, reminiscent of biblical engravings. Bandsman Second Class Nigel E. Mulford, by virtue of his Swiss army knife, had become part of the MacCowan family. There was nothing in Royal Navy regulations that could keep a sailor from staying with folks ashore at night, provided he made morning muster.

The festive cortege wound its way into the shadow of an early-nineteenth-century converted mercantile countinghouse that sported a black panel sign with stark white bank script lettering:

Robertson & Drahn Ltd.
Fine Timepieces s. 1912
Purveyors to H.M.

The granite building's windows were covered with white crisscross tape, and the interior blackout drapes had been drawn, allowing the watchmakers and office staff a view of the parade. The second floor, north corner had been refurbished in glass brick for the executive offices. There was a small clear window on each facade. A face appeared; it was graying and balding and wore wire-framed spectacles. Its left cheek twitched spasmodically as the *Royal Oak*'s banner passed below. Its eyes squinted out over the anchorage and noted the carrier getting up steam. Earlier it had watched the battlewagon *Repulse* weigh anchor and leave the flow through Hoy Sound, escorted by three destroyers.

Theo Drahn was glad that the deal with Nielson had not included a shortwave radio. The Swede had finally given in to Theo's fear of being caught by transmission fixes. The watchmaker was aware of English advances in radio ranging. Let the Luftwaffe do its recon sorties. There was no point in showing one's hand.

At six the plant workers would have punched out. Theo had told Claire about a new contract he'd have to go over, meaning not to expect him home till late, if at all, that night. The night watchman had happily accepted a holiday with pay, so all that remained was to call Brenda. She always made a good alibi. Fill her with booze, ravish her, and let her sleep it off. She'd swear that Theo hadn't left the building in case something went wrong. As it was, he'd said he'd drop in on Sandy's little party back of the store about midnight.

Theo was proud of his plan. He'd suggested the idea of a good-luck party on the night of Friday, the thirteenth. It coincided with his wife's weekly visit to her mother in Birsay anyway. Sandy had invited the searchlight crew and its eight-pounder gunlayers in for a snort or two, starting at quarter of. That would leave only one position shorthanded for half an hour, *one* position out of a dozen or more around Holm Sound.

He watched the milk cart rattle up the road toward Kirkwall, then went downstairs into the tool cellar, where he selected a wire cutter, an insulated one.

* * *

In Kirkwall two rugged men looked out of separate barred windows in adjoining cells behind the police station. They heard the bagpipes but were unable to see the parade as it thundered past Tankerness House on Broad Street and stopped in front of St. Magnus for a benediction. The sailors had been temporarily jailed, pending a declaration of property damage in a pub on Castle Street. The commandant of Royal Marines aboard *Royal Oak* had been notified and agreed to bring a tender in the morning and wait for the constable to deliver the culprits, with the charges, to Scapa Pier. They would then be locked up in a cell flat aboard the *Oak,* with pay deducted to cover damage claims, and would await the next courts-martial.

Like a black bug-eyed rubber crab, the infrared binoculars rotated on Hänsel's vertical fingers. To the heat-sensing glasses, water, being cold, appeared black. A flight of gulls swooped over the pitching bow and, as warm objects, stood out bright white against the midnight sky. Hänsel grabbed the interior hand-rail as *U-47* was tossed high over a rolling swell; he waited for the bow shock and the resultant torrent of water and spray to subside while he shielded his glasses inside his oilskins. He wiped his eyes and five-day beard, then resumed his forward port quadrant scanning. The first watch officer, Endrass, fresh from his eight hours off, searched the starboard forward sector while a PO and one seaman scanned aft.

Below, in the red-lit control room the assistant navi-gator's brass divider points "walked" across the gridded chart, and its forward point stopped at Latitude 58°25′ N, longitude 1°52′ W. The course line headed nor'nor'west at 330 degrees true.

Abruptly Hänsel riveted. A ribbon of white smoke —warm smoke—danced off the port bow. He lowered his objective lenses, following the smoke, and saw a faint gray mass. Still focused, he noted the bearing in relation to the radio aerial on the spray deflector, in case he lost it, then reached over with his free hand and tapped Endrass on the left shoulder. The officer followed Hänsel's point with his own glasses, then nodded and bent to the voice pipe.

"Captain to the bridge . . . tanker two points off the starboard bow . . ."

Prien, roused from a deep sleep by his orderly, slipped into his preferred foul-weather gear. "Sloppy weather upstairs, sir."

"Spotted something?"

"Tanker, sir . . ."

The captain scrambled up the ladder and past the helmsman.

"About two miles dead ahead." Endrass handed his glasses to Prien, who declined them.

"How big?"

"Seven or eight thousand."

"Let's get back on course," Prien barked, and slipped down through the hatch without another word, closing it behind him.

"That's the second time this patrol that we've turned tail and run away," shouted Obermechanik Plauen from his station.

"I'll have no more of that, Plauen," Endrass replied coolly. "If you've got a gripe, bring it up when you're asked. Helmsman, go to three-three-zero." He snapped the voice tube cap shut and watched the luminous rudder angle indicator swing to port. The temperature was dropping. Latitude 58, he remembered from the large chart, was quite far north and ran through Greenland's southern tip and Alaska. He took another turn on his blue-gray woolen scarf and warmed one hand in his leather pants pocket under his oilskins. The telegram—it was still in his pocket, folded and refolded. It had been run down to the pier at Kiel last Sunday: SYBIL VERY ILL IN HOSPITAL CRITICAL. He'd been tempted to jump ship and fly to Hanover, but he was loading officer—and he'd taken an oath. Instead, he'd said nothing. Duty had to come before personal problems. He knew that Prien would have done the same: honored the knight's oath. Endrass drummed his wet, shriveled fingers on the voice pipe housing, counting the minutes, the wave splashes, the twangs of the jumping wires—anything to get his mind off his fiancée and back to the task at hand till the hatch opened once more and he could find the sanctuary of sleep.

A flock of white-throated great cormorants, perched on the low-tide reefs off Corn Holm, were drying their outstretched black wings in the afternoon sun. The wind was light and offshore as the sleek dark shape slipped quietly into the thirty-meter shallows. A ponderous halibut shook the sand and gravel from its flat brown back and slithered toward a deeper spot where it would be camouflaged in the swaying kelp beds.

There was a frenzied flapping of wings as the periscope suddenly spouted its white plume, turning slowly in response to the captain's foot pressure on a pedal below the metal saddle.

"Steady as she goes," he cautioned the helmsman beside him. He stopped scanning at a 272 bow bearing. "Land at two-seven-two red," he called, eye into the rubber. Then he pushed the magnification lever. Two little islands glimmered into the lens field. Prien waited for the condensation element to work, then focused. His hands suddenly gripped the crossbar tight, and he exhaled audibly.

"Take 'er down—fast." He clapped the scope bars up and slid down the ladder, hardly hitting a step, then motioned Endrass to come into his cabin. "All stop," he added, and drew his curtain.

"I don't believe it!" Prien slumped onto his bunk, wide-eyed.

"What's wrong? The HE is negative." Endrass was upset.

Prien rubbed his stubbled beard. "There's a fucking fisherman up there, and he's rowing right at us. Came out from behind the tiny island . . ."

"The one south of Corn Holm?"

"I guess so. He must be heading for the low-tide reef. Another few minutes, and he would have spotted our scope."

"We'd have to—"

"To surface here would be suicide." Prien slammed his fist on the bunk. "Why the hell did I come in here?"

"A chance in a million—a fisherman, rowing!"

"The crew needn't know about this; they're on edge enough as it is." Prien uncapped an apple juice bottle, took a swig, and handed it to his exec.

"It would look strange in the log." Endrass drank. "So, we lose a little time, then take another look?"

"No good," Prien whispered. "Let's get out of here."

Endrass knew better than to argue. He went aft

into the *Zentrale* and called the navigator, told Spahr to set up the electric depth finder. "How much water?"

"Ninety-six feet." Dittmer read the Papenburg at the hydroplanes.

"Checks out on the chart," Spahr added.

"Any reefs?"

"Yes, but I don't have that good a fix; maybe I can take a bearing upstairs." Spahr was curious as to why they'd dived.

"Skip said our asparagus could be sighted from here." Endrass covered up, and Spahr let the subject drop.

Suddenly everyone turned as a clunk sounded aft, then a scraping of metal on metal. Walz came running forward, shouting, "It's a mine! I swear it's right over my soup." He waved a stirring spoon.

"Walz!" Endrass's eyes burned into the cook.

The captain and Wessels, the IO, or engineering officer, came ducking into the control room. Prien's look spoke to Endrass. It couldn't be! Or was it? The fisherman's anchor!

"Didn't sound heavy enough to be a mine." Peter Nielson stuck his head through the circular forward hatch.

"I suppose you've been in situations like this." The captain was irritated at Nielson's interruption.

"Well," the Swede replied, "it could just be debris . . . a piece of steel cable with a fitting . . ."

A rasping, grating noise echoed through the welded hull, as if a metal-fingered sea monster were clawing at the saddle tanks. Varendorff whispered to Wessels, "The Loch Ness Monster out here?"

Prien shot a glance at his number one, then left.

"Take 'er up a few meters."

"Aye, sir." Sammann eased a lever, a hissing of air.

The depth-finder indicator shivered, then sprang to life. "Got a reading." Spahr was hunched over the instrument. "Three meters."

"Stand by, port motor," Endrass ordered. "Trim boat."

"All trimmed, sir."

"Port motor, slow astern."

Spahn nodded at Endrass. A good move—when unsure of the bottom, always back out the same way you came in.

U-47 picked up way.

"Five meters, sir." Spahr was exuberant. "We're in the channel."

"Starboard motor, small *ahead*." The boat, props in opposition, slowed to a creep and spun, as if on a turntable.

Major Alexander MacCowan had just gotten a good bite. He cranked his reel excitedly, the rod tip bending almost into the calm swells. He'd trailered his dory to the ramp at Foubister, four miles from his establishment, determined to leave no shoal unfished in his quest for the "ultimate halibut."

The record halibut caught on rod and line weighed in at almost ninety-five pounds. It had been caught off Duncansby Head across the firth. It was a rare fish, very few anglers having ever caught more than one. Sandy had hooked a possible record a year earlier, only to have his terminal tackle break. This time he was ready—with shark tackle and a new multiplying Allcocks' Leviathan reel. The live herring had done its job—delivered its number 12 double-barbed blue-steel hook.

The major leaned back, pulled the anchor rope. There was play; then it snagged. Good. If it was a large halibut, a man might be hauled, dory and all, out to sea. The fish, taken by commercial methods, had been known to reach over 600 pounds. Whoops—whatever it was sounded again, dipping the dory's stern and activating the reel ratchet. Sandy tightened the drag wheel and forced his stout hickory rod tip up. Then strange things began to happen. The islands of Copinsay and Corn Holm had swung away; he was now looking at Rose Ness. Whims of the tide, he thought, and was again reeling in furiously as the line slackened. He turned around and confirmed that all 300 feet of his anchor line had been let out, giving him a three to one scope, a minimum angle for ground tackle such as his patent plow. The rod tip sprang down into the water once again, and the wiry Scotsman rose to the occasion. It was man against the unknown, and man with his multiplier reel was prevailing. Grunting and huffing, with the rod's butt driving painfully into his crotch, next to his jewels, he inched the eighty-pound braided line in. The reel was almost full, the runs were getting shorter—and at last he saw that flash of white below the surface that signaled the fish's tucked-up turn of belly. It was large, larger than Sandy had dared expect. The sweat ran into his fatigued red eyes, stinging salty. His clothes were sogged and cold from runoff and spray; his fingers, shriveled, as he locked the reel drum and reached over the side for the glinting wire tackle. Holding it with a wrag-wrapped hand at a swivel connection, he reached for his landing hook.

It was a beauty as it churned its pale-blotched sienna trunk against the dory's lapstrake bottom. Two gelatinous eyes, the size of cricket balls, both on the same side of the fish's head stared up at Sandy's reaching gaff hook.

Just as the hook probed the half-moon pulsing gill, a jolt threw Sandy on his back, into the sloshing bilge along with the upturned barrel of live herring. Stunned, he crawled back over the center athwart, rod still in hand, though the tip had been smashed. The fish, the fish; that was all that mattered.

But there was no halibut; instead, he was sprayed with a bubbling foam from the bow. The line was slack and flailed straight out toward Copinsay, and the wake was one worthy of a powered craft. It was awhile before Sandy's head cleared enough and he realized he was under way. In fact, the dory was planing like a racing skiff in the newsreels.

He dropped his precious rod to the floorboards and crawled forward, new bait knife in hand. It would have to be done—there was no other choice. He'd hooked a sleeping whale. Yes, that was it. The finbacks were migrating—or had the monster escaped from Loch Ness? Bracing himself, one hand on the gunnel, he reluctantly slashed at his anchor line till it parted and the dory was abruptly stopped by a strong current. He cursed the whale into the wind's face for loss of his halibut and ground tackle, then set his back against the oars and pulled for shore. It took him an hour to reach Foubister, an hour during which he'd made his peace. He would have a whale of a story for the midnight randy.

* * *

"Nigel," Ruth cooed, "it must be wonderful to be so talented." She handed him another helping of batter-fried haddock. "You *did* bring your sheet music?"

Nickie shook his head as he bit into the steaming fish. "Owww." He burned the roof of his mouth and jiggled the mouthful around like a hot coal. "It's okay now. Really."

"I made it too hot."

"I ate too fast." He almost dropped the ice water she thrust into his hand. "I should know better." He laughed.

Ruth leaned on her elbows and watched him: so dashing in his dress blues. He was different from the others—those *animals* from the air station at Hatson . . . and from the batteries on Burray and Flotta. They all acted as if they'd never seen a woman before, coming into the store and playing up to her so!

"Did you have it tuned?"

"Daddy, Nickie's going to play for us, aren't you, Nickie?"

"Let him eat his dessert first!" Wise Sandy peered over the top of the Orkney *Herald*. The banner front-page headline read:

FINLAND CALLS UP RESERVES

"Dear, I have to leave now. I just rang up Mother; she's feeling worse." Rowena slipped into a foul-weather slicker and took her gas mask off the wall hook. "I'm sorry, Nickie. I'll hear you play another time, I'm sure—and don't you two stay up till all hours . . ."

"I'll have to leave at eight."

"Oh, Nickie!"

"I've drawn duty tonight. The graveyard watch."

"Well, at least Ruth will get a good night's sleep for Saturday's rush. Toodle-oo all."

The major put his newspaper down. "Too bad, m'lad. We're to have a little party tonight, and I wanted ye to meet some o' the boys—but I know whut yer up agin, having been there many times myself." He leaned back in the easy chair. "There was the time in Rangoon—"

"Daddy!"

"Yer right, lass; I promised."

Ruth made sure the coffee was just right by tasting it herself in the kitchen before she poured it. She tried the whipped cream as well, since she'd had a tendency to overweight, like her mother—at least as she *remembered* her mother. She was jealous of her stepmother, her trim body. She could eat anything she wanted. But she was glad her dieting had worked so well. Dieting? It was closer to *fasting*. For a moment she remembered fasting, with her mother, many years ago, it seemed.

She poured carefully; she decided to be quiet—not to push. This boy had Daddy's blessings, as well as hers. Visions of Edinburgh warmed her very being. The opera . . . the ballet . . . How she hated this cold, bleak island.

TWENTY-SIX

"There's a letter—no, we've got two for ye, Nickie boy." Corporal James Rollings, Royal Marines Band, tossed the envelopes on the steamer trunk that doubled as a table between the two tiers of hammocks. Rollings, having shone up his cornet and left it on the trunk, closed his copy of the ship's weekly and smirked at Mulford.

"For a young lad, new at this business, ye seem to do pretty well. But for watch tonight ye'd be snuggling up to that little Jew tart, wouldn't ye now?"

"But they're not religious, so what difference does it make?" Mulford wiggled out of his jumper.

"Look, lad, take it from a man who's concerned about you—why, I could be yer father, I'm that old, almost. Yer a talented boy, and ye oughta go far—provided ye dunna get sidetracked by some cunt. Now, having been there, I full know of what I speak . . ."

"I'm listening." Nickie jumped into his bunk and opened one of the envelopes—the one with the military postmark—then waited for his friend to finish.

"I've had fish and chips at the major's establishment, and they're top-ho. Fine. But I've seen what is happening even if you don't. The major's daughter is a typical culture-hungry cunt. I tell you, Nickie—

if ye don't watch it, yer gonna get the short end of the stick. Before ye know it, ye'll be hooked as sure as I was when I was your age. For me it's all over, and m' kickers will suffer, bless 'em. But there's no need for a bright lad like Nigel Mulford to throw away his musical career for a bowl of chicken soup and a toss or two in the hay."

"What makes you think I'm serious with the major's daughter?"

"That's just it, lad. You've not given it a serious thought, but mark my words, *she* has, and she's just the type that will roll you up like a fly in a spider's web. I know. Old Jimmy's been there. Since you say yer not serious, I can give ye a few of my own observations. Firstly, have ye noticed how standoffish the bitch is with the troops? They're not musicians . . . or poets. No, mon! This pushy wench knows what she wants all right, and what she wants is something that she is not. Get the picture, lad?"

"I've got other *ladies*." Mulford sniffed at the second, unopened envelope.

"So, that's fine if you have, but this godforsaken end of the world will play tricks on you. One doesn't know for sure whether it's night or day, summer or winter up here—but believe me, the bitches know. You know, laddie, the Orkneys are practically Scandinavia; you've tried to pronounce th' names, I'll bet. It's bad enough to get speared by a native Viking lass, but beware this one. She's the type who'll never be happy. Religion or not. She's got it bred into her. Beware, my lad. Beware."

Nickie didn't say anything; he knew better. From here the conversation would go into races and subhuman races. Into Wagner and his *Nibelungen* with all the trimmings, when all he wanted was to enjoy life, to enjoy people, to find out for himself which road was best for *him*. The strapping sergeant of Royal Marines took out his pipes, blew each drone in succession, then unscrewed and laid them out on the trunk top. "Cum oud, ye little reedies; it's time fer ye cleanin'. You've got another recital on th' morrow, and Nickie boy is achin' to 'ear fum 'is pussy."

He opened his brother's letter first.

9/10/39

Dear Nickie:

You can tell by the date that I went to the far place of the two mentioned last letter. Unfortunately I drew a desk instead of a boat but have been promised a command for next spring. In the event that your admiral lets you off in Rosyth within the next few months, I ask a favor. Please stop off at the Naval Hospital and look up a close friend who was badly burned when *Courage* got the hammer last month. We worked together at Dundee this summer. He's a Yank—Lt. Cmdr. Benjamin Mount—and the best Jew I've met in a long time. Cheer him up, he's gone to hell and back . . . should be off the critical roster by now and allowed visitors. I've told him about my brainy and talented kid brother.

Meanwhile, the native women are quite fetching from what I've seen my first day ashore. The only skin a man can see is what's between their flitty eyes. Eternal mystery of the unknown and uncharted! It seems that by the time a bloke has unwrapped one of these prizes he may have very well forgotten what he was looking for. He may even find out she's not a female.

I've written home.

Keep your pipes up,
Moxie

Nickie folded the letter crisply, jotted the new address on back, and slipped it into a notebook. He always saved letters. Noting that Rollings was immersed in his cleaning compounds, he held the other envelope up to his nose. It was perfumed; he expected such of Carole. Again, the small blade of Moxie's present prevailed.

11 Oct. 39

My dear Nigel:

Auntie Grace is as anxious to meet you as I am to see you again—to find that you're not an illusion—someone I dreamt of on the train to Thurso.

I loved your letter, especially your description of the harbor and the fisherman you met right off. I'm sorry that you won't get much liberty, but should you, you can stay over in our attic. It's insulated, and the Highlands are as colorful, Auntie says, as any time she can remember. She said it was because of the unusually lush summer. Perhaps the summer knew there was a war coming and did its best before the bombs and horror.

We're very busy with thousands of energetic brats from the industrial cities. I look forward, at dusk, to taking a book to my favorite stone bridge and reading a bit. I managed to find some of Rupert Brooke's works, and though I like his concern with life, he seemed to end up often on a negative note. I had to search between his negatives to find this:

These I have loved:
    White plates and cups, clean-gleaming,
Ringed with blue lines; and feathery, faëry dust;
Wet roofs, beneath the lamp-light; the strong
    crust
Of friendly bread; and many-tasting food;
Rainbows; and the blue bitter smoke of wood;
And radiant raindrops couching in cool
  flowers . . .

But my personal favorite lines, at least *now,* are:

    Jane, Jane,
    Tall as a crane,
    The morning light creaks down again.

and . . .

  Nobody comes to give him his rum but the
  Rim of the sky hippopotamus-glum
  Enhances the chances to bless with a benison
  Alfred Lord Tennyson . . .

and one more:

Feathered masks,
Pots of peas,—
Janus asks
                guess who?
Nought of these . . .
In among the
Pots of peas

Naiad changes—
Quick as these.

Please come
to Loch Shurrery c/o Redfern
It's only two hours by train from Thurso—
or I can meet you anywhere
provided it's on a Thursday
my day off—
Love, from
Carole

P.S.: I'm sorry Rupert Brooke died from sunstroke, but at least it was on an idyllic Aegean island, the same one where Achilles dressed up as one of the king's daughters to evade an oracle's portent of death in Troy, only to die at Scyro's gates.

Nickie picked up his fountain pen.

13/10/39
Dear Carole:

Just received your very entertaining letter. Brooke's early biographers didn't know the whole story. He was bitten by a scorpion, the effect of which was complicated by a weakness caused by coral poisoning in Tahiti—will continue this letter after I get back from the midwatch. We call it the *graveyard* watch. . . .

TWENTY-SEVEN

Endrass had drawn his curtain and was snoring, nose through the white ladder bunk railing on the starboard side of the officers' wardroom. Both bunks above his were empty; Varendorff had relieved him on the bridge, while Wessels had gone aft, forsaking his sleep, to be with his oily bride in the engine room. The second officer's white-shriveled nails dug into his checkered mattress cover in a dreamless twilight narcosis. An occasional click and murmur entered his ears between snores, tempting his autonomic rise to station, a flexing of the neck muscles, then oblivion . . . pure, sweet sanctuary of the womb *within* the iron womb.

Threatening his bony, bare left foot peeking from behind his aquatic pullman, a locker door was open, swaying side to side. Neat shore clothing was stacked inside, sparing no corner. Between the dress jacket and trousers was tucked a bright vermilion book. The title, upside down, read *Diesel Segeljachten.*

In the next compartment the captain jotted down notes for his impending speech to the crew. His personal diary lay open and unattended on his bunk.

13/10/39 E of Orkneys. Wind NNE 3-4, light clouds, very clear night, northern lights on entire horizon. . . .

Through the "lion's hoop" pressure hatch, the control room, dimly lit, seemed like a steel mausoleum crawling with angular metallic serpents. The silence was occasionally broken by a sharp snap after a hand had dipped into the hazelnut barrel in the shadow of the heavy chart chest.

Quartermaster Spahr, almost an officer, imagined his own U-boat on the blue and brown chart grid "Anton Nordpol": the most eccentric of all sixty-nine Kriegsmarine mercator sectors. It was distorted to include the entire east coast of England and the perimeter land area of the North Sea; its only adversary in number of corners was "BG" or "Bruno Gustav," a partition of France and Germany. He slid his ebony parallel ruler onto the course and extended it to cross the compass rose intersection. He motioned to his assistant navigator.

Soon a buzzing, then a circular motion in the oscilloscope; a cluster of luminous blips hovered near the numeral 70.

"We're picking up the canyon," Spahr whispered to the twenty-year-old watch officer, Varendorff. He held his chronographic wristwatch under the ruby chart light. "Another six minutes."

U-47 had run fifty minutes at her top underwater cruising speed and made five miles, leaving a reserve before battery charging of an additional sixty submerged. The blips moved steadily deeper.

"Quite amazing." The neophyte *Leutnant*-Junior wiggled out of his red-tinted spectacles. "I would imagine a whole new book of rules with that instrument of yours." He studied the six-mile-long finger of the North Sea that pointed through the coastal shallows at the entrance to Scapa Flow.

"I had a professor of navigation at Kiel who wrote a paper on the subject of submarine canyons. He'd been an oceanographer before the war. Strange name . . ." Spahr mused a moment and noted the depth finder indicated eighty meters. "Eighty . . . *eight—Oct*, Oct . . . *Octavius*! Leutnant Octavius Kunert; queer duck, but he sure knew his oceans. Indentations like this one are formed, according to his theories, by a combination of current and sand shifting and are the ocean's continuations of land features. Kunert said that every river outlet and estuary in the world had its canyon—"

"Somewhat like a well-walked dirt road."

"Or the carpet that Onkel Karl paces up and down on. . . ."

Nielson entered the *Zentrale* and picked a nut out of the hooped barrel, cracked it, and set one of the two halves on the chart of Scapa Flow. "Please," he offered. Spahr speared it with his dividers and carefully popped it into his mouth. "Steady on the helm," Nielson called up the ladder.

"That's about it," Dziallas called out.

"Put her on the bottom, please."

"Aye, sir." Chief Sammann took over. "We'll find a nice, soft spot for the engine artificers, sir."

"What do *you* think, Sammann?" The young officer's voice broke falsetto. Recovering, he added, "Can we fix it?"

"Well, sir." The chief petty officer bent over, big hands on the tandem shoulders of the plane operators, and watched the Papenburg bubble descend. "No offense, sir—but I don't get paid for thinking. Notice that both m' . . ." He held up crossed fingers.

Grimy and tired, Otto Strump grunted as he tightened the port overhead lubricant wheel valve. Nothing wrong there. He traced the white-painted conduit under, around, and over its thicker and thinner companions. He checked the saddle tank inlets, the daily fuel usage tank, and the overhead reservoir gravity feed to the fuel pumps. "Sir." The chief machinist rubbed the peephole glass clear of grease so the demarcation between oil and water was visible. "There's not enough water to account for even a tenth of what we found in the funnel drain." Otto tested the system again; he cracked the compressed air line, and the fuel pumps drove the lines full. He listened as the indicator taps clicked and hissed. He pressed his better ear against the warm block and heard a dampened gurgle, seemingly from the fifth- or sixth-cylinder area. He sidled aft ten feet and listened again. Intermittent but persistent. He motioned to a stoker, who closed the lubricating pump lever. The hissing stopped, but the gurgling, now alone, could be isolated.

Otto drew an *X* at the approximate location of the fifth cylinder below its fuel injector. "Sir," he called again to Oberleutnant Hans Wessels, who'd been engrossed in the diesel blueprints and handbook, "I think we've got it; Emil is sick—" The chief named his cylinders after the German naval code. The port motor's Emil was Red Emil, while his starboard twin responded to Green Emil.

"Good work, Otto." Wessels's face brightened. "Do you think it's the cooling chamber?"

"From the sound of it, I'd put my dough on the lining; even if we don't find a crack, it could be an invisible porous section. . . ."

"Not enough binder." The *Leutnant* opened his handbook.

"The asbestos fiber might have parted; all it takes is a few square inches, then some condensation . . . and you're in trouble."

"How long, Otto?"

"An hour to drain, while we take the head off . . . a couple more to strip the accessories and the exhaust and inlet headers. Then we've got the connecting rod to tackle. If we can get some help—get someone building a bypass gutter . . ."

"The captain gave me full authority."

"Then wake up Roth and get him started on a drain ring. All cylinder casings are the same. Tell him to find a seven-inch can in the galley for a template."

"I get it; then I build it and cut it in two sections, shim them on the casing, and run off the seawater before it goes through."

"Right, sir. We'll funnel the runoff through a new tap so it can't steam and burn off around the bearings. I think we can get a drill bit into the bedplate housing. Can we spare the juice?"

"We didn't use much in the run from Copinsay."

"So far, so good, sir. I'll need five more volunteers."

"You've got 'em, Chief. I'll *organize* your detail, sleep or not." Wessels ducked through the forward bulkhead, where the galley steward was dozing over his potato peels. "I know we can count on you, Strump. . . ." The officer's adulation went unanswered.

Otto Strump was a man of action; he'd managed

a diesel repair shop in Wilhelmshaven before being called up. Emil was a challenge, and challenges were his forte. There was a time to stop talking—a time to pick up the wrench.

Cook Walz broke out a bag of fresh coffee beans and ground them, turning more than one nose in the engine room next door. The musky roasted tropical fragrance of the bean prevailed over the fetid stench of bodies, fuel oil, electricity, vomit, and urine swilling in the bilges under the cramped, stifling compartment.

Six mechanics and engine room artificers had been shaken out of fetal slumber to fix the Achilles' leak in the otherwise invincible plan, and it was the cook's task to keep them reasonably content, especially with such emasculative restrains as a twelve-hour ban on smoking and using the head, which was all but inoperable at depths greater than twenty-five meters. Military science was yet to cope with the effects of deep-submerged deprivation on the skills and morale of man. Captain Prien had decreed that Walz spare no rations—except the chocolate bars—to inspire the mechanics.

Dim red battle bulbs in wire cages cast grisly shadows among the myriad veins and organs of the humming, welded serpent. Fore to aft, all hands slept. A pair of slippered feet attended the oxygen flasks, then shuffled and noted the trim indicators; entered data in the control room log.

In contrast with the tomblike corridor, the diesel engine room blazed—a bright arena of stainless handles, polished brass gauges, and glinting glass dials, twenty-one feet long, thirteen feet wide, and seven feet high. The two massive engines occupied about twenty percent of the total cubic area of the room, each one rising over the floor plates to the height of an average man and, like icebergs, extending below-decks, anchored on reinforced mountings braced on the long ballast keel.

A floor plate lay aside as Obergefreiter Winzer, still rubbing his drowsy eyes, fed a power cable into the bedplate access compartment below. At a signal Machinist's Mate Stolz threw a switch, and a grinding purr ebbed low and rose high in the bilge, as Schmidt's carbon steel drill bit into its starter dimple. The slight sailor's trigger finger faltered as something scurried over his bare right calf, partly immersed, as he knelt is the putrid, swilling bilge. The slimy rat sat on a steel frame rib under the diesel, baring its needle white teeth below flaring nostrils and savage orange eyes at the alien that had invaded its rank domain.

The seaman swung his drill at the seething creature only to be grazed by the rodent's razor incisor. He shrank back in horror and swung the heavy drill again, this time stunning the gleaming rodent. Hand bleeding into the slime, Schmidt grabbed the scaly long tail and dragged the groggy black rat out of the bilge water and propped it on a rib, head up like a kitten on its back. He jammed the whining drill bit between the rat's teeth and rammed it through the tiny gray brain and ground bone into the steel rib, scattering skin and winding the screeching carcass around the bloody drill chuck and handle.

"What the hell is going on down there?" Winzer called, and played his extension light on Schmidt.

"Nothing," he screamed, and continued his drilling while the lube oil drain splattered beside him and the rat floated aft as the keel shifted slightly in the English sand.

A cordon of sweating attendants crawled atop and behind the ponderous patient; the head was off, and Emil was divested of his rocker arm, exhaust header, and fuel injector. The orderlies attacked his push rod and removed his air header duct in their quest for the afflicted organ deep within his complex glistening chest. They snaked wires and conduits through his apertures and laid out his parts and bolts on oily rags in sequence of dismantling. Viscous yellow and greenish fluids dripped and slunk from rods and cams, then onto bearings and into the black-boweled oil pans below the nonslip textured deck plates. *Dlop-plik . . . dlop-plik.*

Two orderlies scuttled fore and aft, one with Walz's specialty based on the ingredients taken on at Kiel: strawberry tarts; the other, with a bucket quite the opposite of galley crockery, which catered to the baser necessities of the crew.

Walz appeared with his second batch of cakes, held high on a tray. "It's a good thing there's a wall between my stove and your engine. I've been slaving over these tarts for hours; I think they're more successful than the first batch. I've added extra kirsch to the apricot to kill the *slight* lubricating oil flavor. I'll put it on ice now, after adding some luscious whipped cream. Captain said you could have seconds *after* you fix up Emil."

Fritz," howled a gruff voice from the bilge, "I want some now or I'll drop a dead rat in your next pot of liver ball soup."

"You *can't* because the recipe says my tarts have to cool for *two* hours. . . ." Walz whistled his favorite tune, and the mechanics picked up the lyrics:

A dog came into the kitchen
and stole an egg from the cook.
The cook then grabbed a ladle
and bashed the dog kaput. . . .

Nielson leaned out of the galley with a bottle of apple juice in his hand. He'd been unable to sleep because of the excitement of the mission. It would take more than a few days to get accustomed, like these *veterans*, to the regimen and abandon of war. The Swede watched with admiration as the chief mechanic orchestrated the drama, cueing first a mechanic, then an electrician. He imagined Strump as a doctor, the engine room as an operating room; an emergency operation was in progress:

Dr. Strump conferred with Dr. Schmalenbach, who recommended a specialist. Dr. Römer was dragged, yawning, from his bunk and consulted regarding the dissection of a stubborn generator, then was rewarded with a cup of "night watchman," whereafter he stumbled through the circus hoop hatches toward his quarters.

Nielson wondered whether it was the fetid heat, the depth, or both that had affected him and induced hallucinations. The mechanics' leather clothing had changed to white, and Emil seemed to be breathing, attached to bottles, tubes, and life-support indicators. He had no reason to suspect that his paranosmia was triggered by a combination of musky apricot and burned diesel oil, that the illusion was a result of the added factor of pressure changes, and that instead of a crossover odor perception, the aroma had been short-circuited into a bank of optical receptors near the olfactory bulb, the impulses changing gray to blinding white.

"Seawater drain secured, sir." Schmidt's voice cracked hollow from below as the power cable was retracted, followed by a blood-sotted arm, a heavy duty drill, and a drawn face.

"Damn. Fuck." Expletives rang out as the last bolt on the fifth-cylinder casing access plate did not respond to a spanner.

"Easy, now, son." Strump pacified the nervous intern and took the sweating tool from him, knowing that a slip—a contortion of the plate bolt—would be fatal to the husky patient. Motion stopped—and all watched breathlessly. The chief was among the best surgeons in the Kriegsmarine.

After handing the spanner to his orderly, he held his right palm out—"Small monkey wrench"—eyes riveted on the patient.

The tool was slapped, handle first, into his waiting hand. His nimble fingers closed, found the regulating screw, and the metal jaws winched down to a small aperture. Strump carefully applied the wrench onto the hex-head bolt. He called for more light, then tested the handle clearance from a plate lug. Satisfied, he called for the rust oil and squirted a few drops on the plate over the afflicted bolt; the acrid, thin brown liquid ran down and around. Next, he tightened the jaws, pressed flat against the plate.

"Wood hammer."

Heavy breathing as the crew craned for a view.

The chief deliberated about *clockwise* and *counter*. Good—the wrench was correctly poised. Jaw up and at two o'clock, the wood-sided grip had purchase allowance for better than a vertical, upward mallet swing. He poised, took a breath, then tapped sharply. The handle moved, not much. Two or three millimeters at best. Strump tapped a second time, then handed the mallet to the intern.

"It's yours now."

To adulating glances, the chief stepped back as the bolt was slipped out and the plate taken off. The cylinder lining was handed to Römer, who'd been impatiently waiting to fit his bypass gutter which was jigged in a machine vise around a pickle can.

The six-inch diameter gleamed, bared inside Emilport like a chromium heart; Nielson's illusions were waning.

Otto Strump picked his china mug off the engine block and drank, ignoring the rainbow spread of oil on the dark coffee surface. When he set the cup back on the housing, it almost eclipsed its ring: formed in grease, when the cook had first placed it there, steaming—almost six hours earlier.

TWENTY-EIGHT

"Now we can count on *both* engines." The commander cracked a hazelnut and popped the fruit into his elf mouth. A chart lay flat on the iron case; one-quarter inch to the mile, it was a hydrographic contour study of the southern Orkneys. Prien looked up, beard catching the red glow of the chart light. "Sammann, have the crew stand to at sixteen hundred hours, but let the diesel gang sleep if they want to."

"Aye, sir; they've done the impossible."

Spahr bent over the table and traced the coastline of Ronaldsay with a round magnifying glass; a ruby pip of refracted overhead light traveled across Hoxa Sound, rested there. "Nice of the Royal and Ancient Yacht Club to lend us this excellent chart for our pleasure boating weekend."

Prien grinned, then cocked his head inquisitively. "We're not going in *that* way—are we?"

"No, sir, I was just thinking about *UB-One Sixteen.*"

"Poor bastard; Emsmann's still on the bottom."

"Do beards grow on dead men . . . *underwater?*"

"Here, Caligari, have a nut for your cabinet."

"Thanks, but you know what really bothers me," Spahr whispered as he heard footsteps behind him.

"BdU said we didn't have to worry."

"Even with much improved hydrophones and more lethal mines?" Prien raised an eyebrow, and the navigator set the aerial recon glossies in a circle on the chart around Holm Sound. He picked up the magnifying glass, and the red pip moved to Rose Ness, the first landfall checkpoint; slowly the light moved along the coastline of Kirk Sound. "There's enough water right up to the lighthouse—we can hug the shore, seems free of rocks after the turn. Unless the lighthouse keeper is having a lawn party . . ."

"They'd all drop their Scotch whisky." The commander coughed on his nut as he tried to laugh at the image. "The keeper will probably be dead drunk or asleep by the time we pass."

"We can send him a postcard with our thanks."

Prien memorized the approach once more: Holm Church . . . the Tower of Clett—landmarks to spot against the night sky.

"What about the *Scheinwerfer*?" The red pip hovered near St. Mary's Pier, then over a glossy showing the unmistakable shadow of a searchlight installation.

"They've got *that* worked out, too . . . and there's an abort plan in case the fleet is out. Something Emsmann could have used. Onkel Karl didn't let me in on it—if he knew."

"I see . . ." Spahr played mental skat, his favorite card game, and came up with a possible trump. "Nielson?"

Prien smiled quietly.

The crew, some in skivvies and all wearing specially issued soft slippers, filed through the *Zentrale* toward the bow torpedo room where twenty-six permanent residents were already waiting. The upper and middle bunks were lashed back. Prien waited for the traffic to stop, then snatched up a few photographs and ducked through the "lion's hoop." The electric-coil heater in the radio room pulsed in cherry shades as he passed and entered the bow compartment.

"*Stillgestanden!*" roared the chief.

"As you were." Prien stayed the sardined audience, crammed around the deadly eels, between bunks, and peering through loops of hanging chain. With a flare honed during his prewar voyages and early naval training days when he'd stood on mess tables and fired up his mates with stirring chantey verses, he probed the anxious eyes, man by man, before he spoke:

"Here it is, mates—we're going *into* Scapa Flow; we're going after carriers, battleships, and cruisers—"

More than thirty hearts leaped and stuttered as the angel of silence careened through the huddled, musty room; a wave of reactions mounted and ebbed. Jaws twitched, mouths opened, and eyes closed.

"—I am determined to get *in*; I am determined to get *out*, and then we're all going home. . . ." A round of cheers echoed. "Here are some recon photos that have helped us choose the safest, surest course—through the blockships and around the minefields. The High Command has given much study to this mission, and they are confident that we *will* get in. You've all done an extraordinary job in getting us here, and I know you'll do even better, once we're in. . . ."

The commander lowered his voice to say, "Thank you," after which he wheeled smartly and left.

* * *

A pall pervaded the slumberous vault, torpedoes' warheads glimming at their handlers. A specter of death colored every whisper, burdened every laugh. Here was a good and fortunate boat—but the *lion's den*! Medals would be nice, pondered the 17-year-old as he rigged his string hammock amid a hanging sausage garden above the reload eel. Iron Cross for sure. A picture flashed through his trilling brain: the fish tank at home, his mother's pride. He'd saved his meager allowance and bought her an expensive tropical rarity for Christmas. Blue turquoise fluorescing through joyous bubbles, adoring faces . . . his mother gently dropped the feathery iridescent two-inch fish in. It streaked once around the cubicular ocean, then dived sprightly after a speck of food, seemingly ignored by the many other, larger and less harlequined finned tenants. *Hemigrammus ocellifer,* known to aquarists also as the head-and-tail-light fish, habitat Brazil, disappeared behind a miniature sea castle.

When it emerged, it was only half a fish, neatly eviscerated by whatever barb or molly had exercised its aquarian rights.

"One gets you four—*if* we get out . . ." Curly Lochig, the Berlin oddsmaker, waved a handful of five-mark notes from his upper berth. "Step right up, mates—the chance of a lifetime."

"What's the point of betting if we *don't* get out?"

"Mr. Moses, Curly will be rich, if only fleetingly."

"Maybe he's not so dumb," Werder piped up. "How about that Union Jack in the old man's locker? There must be a plan."

"Sure, Gus. You carry it ashore and see what happens." The Moses, or youngest crew member, covertly finished his chocolate ration.

"Suppose we *do* sink a carrier or two." Lochig's voice changed pitch. "We'd be way ahead. Right? So we grab the ante, and if we can't get out, we just run the ol' girl up on th' rocks. So we get captured, so what? We did our part; what more does Dönitz's Steamship Company want? I won't mind pickin' potatoes in the Highlands. I like potatoes."

"I say we've got a good chance." Machinist's Mate Werder swung up into his bunk. "The captain has a master's ticket; he's no ninety-day wonder."

"That's *fine,*" ruddy Plauen croaked, "but this ain't th' fucking merchant marine, and I can think of better ports to call on."

"Okay, you guys—enough of that," the chief boomed out. "Orders are to turn in till chow. Bullshit uses up too much energy and air."

"Oh, sir—"

"What is it, curly one?"

"Do *you* think we can get in—if Emsmann and Hennig couldn't?"

"We've got a much faster boat, more ballast for headway, and we know where the mines are. . . ." The chief torpedoman sat down on one of his progeny and wound his watch.

"What about the English hydrophones? I heard the old man and Spahr talking about them. If they pick us up, we're dead."

"Curly, why did you volunteer for U-boat service?"

"For the glamour . . . the dive pay . . . adventure . . . a bride in every port." Lochig, on his back, pantomimed masturbation accompanied with salacious animal grunts.

"*So,* you've got three out of four right now. Not bad."

"True . . . but it could get worse."

"Make it five to one—and I'm in." The chief peeled a ten-mark note out of his billfold.

"You're faded—On second thought the house limit is five." The Berliner gulped while the chief admired a snapshot of his wife and baby daughter.

Walz unraveled a wet newspaper and laid it out on the drainboard as his galley helpers scurried to prepare dinner, a special dinner. He lifted a soggy page, read it for a moment, then slapped it over, revealing a pattern of bright green and a vivid red flower. The cook separated the green herbs carefully, fluffed them up, and spread them out. After discarding a few sprigs, he handed a knife to a steward and ordered him to chop the herbs fine.

He then picked up the delicate flower, sniffed it lovingly, and stuck the long, prickly stem into a water-filled Beck's bottle. By the time the men were seated it would have revived.

Walz jabbed a fork into the bubbling pot: another fifteen minutes for the potatoes. He bent over and peeked into his small oven, gave silent thanks to the inventors of Kassler Rippchen, the paragon of salt porks. All they needed was gravy and a quick searing.

"Smells great." Werder leaned through the forward hatchway.

"You couldn't sleep?" Walz turned the pork, and the pan fat sizzled, wafting such a delicious aroma that Werder's eyes closed.

"I was dreaming about Rippchen—maybe I'm still dreaming. . . ."

"He's sleepwalking; I saw him get out of his bunk." Curly peeked around Werder. "This chowhound could smell roast pork even if he was forward on a battleship and the galley was three decks down under the fantail."

Werder feigned sleepwalking on his knees, toward the oven.

"Soon, soon." Walz pushed him backward and into the dimmed sleeping quarters. "There's plenty for everyone—and seconds!"

"For the *hangman's meal,* I expect seconds."

"You're right, Curly. When a man is served his Last Supper"—Werder became solemn—"not only should he get seconds, but he should be given a menu. . . ."

"I'll give you a menu—" Walz rolled up the wet *Zeitung* and brandished it at the kibitzers. "On second thought, both of you are hereby *organized* as waiters; you can start by stacking those plates. . . ."

"You and your ideas, Werder." Lochig screwed up his sharp features like a weasel picking up a scent. "Tell you what—you take this, and I take the next *two* they get you on. . . ."

Chunky Gus shrugged no.

"How about one gets you *three?*"

Prien couldn't sleep. He closed his eyes time and again, only to have the Scapa Flow chart float before his mind's eye. He tried to imagine his path into the bay with seven inlets, to reconstruct the indentations and irregularities of the coastline. He tiptoed aft and checked out the boat, found a "curious unrest" as bodies tossed and turned heavly, sighing and rasping. A crewman raised his head wearily, then flopped back again, his arm trailing onto the deck plate. The control room mate, feet swathed in oily rags, skated past, throwing a half salute. About to turn into his niche, the captain noticed light streaming over the lockers that divided the officers' wardroom from their sleeping quarters. He found his tall navigator hunched over the charts. He was chanting.

"Skerry . . . Hoxa . . . Harrabrough . . ."

"Abracadabra!" Prien startled the chief quartermaster. "Are you enlisting the forces of darkness?"

"Sir, it's important to memorize the checkpoints *backward* as well as forward. . . ."

'You're right, no question about it." Prien sneaked past a tier of curtained bunks.

"Sir." A hand drew back the curtain, revealing Endrass's schoolboy face. "I can't sleep either, and you can court-martial me if you like."

"Shut up and save the air," Prien shot at him jokingly.

Back in his bunk the thirty-year-old *Kapitänleutnant* spun his white-crowned symbol on one finger. Interesting, he mused, that alone of all services, the U-boat commanders were now allowed to wear the summer cap all year round. Perhaps it was because of the more raffish individualists—like Lemp and Vaddi Schultze, both of whom dressed like coal miners rather than officers. The white cap had become the entire uniform. Not so with *this* officer, who was never out of his stripes, brass buttons, and little Nazi eagle on the right of his double-breasted wool jacket. He kicked his slippers off and whirled the cap faster on his stubby right index finger. As it wobbled, the gold embroidery on the fabric-covered bill seemed to change alternately from one stripe to doubles—the sign of a flag rank officer.

The portent pacified him, and he fell asleep, ". . . but it was a very light sleep with one eye open . . ."

* * *

Lochig and Werder were kept hopping between the galley, three messrooms forward, and one aft. It was rare that forty men sat down at one time to eat on a submarine. But Walz was prepared. This was to be the last hot meal until the mission had been accomplished. Plenty of time and hands to clean up during the run back.

First . . . steaming leek soup—trays balancing over the upturned bearded heads, spoons in hand, to the officers' wardroom. Curly tightroped through knees and drop-leaf tables. An occasional trip and subsequent juggling feat brought on cries of "Bravo for our Laurel and Hardy waiters."

Varendorff was in splendid form—"lively as a cricket," in the commander's log. He spieled a torrent of jokes and stories that for some precious minutes eclipsed the fear and uncertainty that had been mounting to an almost critical stage. The junior lieutenant related his favorites: "What if she is brainy, but ugly? . . . I will drink until she's gorgeous. . . ."

"My compliments to your chef." Nielson held up a potato on his fork. "The pork and kale are superb—but where did your cook find fresh parsley? After six days at sea!"

"The Navy sails on its stomach, Herr Nielson; I searched afar for Obergefreiter Walz. One might say I shanghaied the fellow. But then our humble cuisine could not possibly compare with that of the bigwigs in Berlin. . . ."

"Really, I am a *connoisseur des pommes de terre persillées.*

Endrass hid his amusement behind a napkin at

Prien's reaction to the phrase—which a well-bred officer would know referred to parsley potatoes.

The blood red rose was wired to the white induction conduit above the mates' mess, tables strewn with peaches, *marzipan Kuchen*, and coffee mugs. Walz, thumbs hooked proudly on his apron, parodied the ancient Kriegsmarine song as he looked up at the flower:

> There are no roses on a sailor's grave,
> No lilies on an ocean wave . . .

"So who needs lilies?"

Steinhagen stood up, mug raised high. "A toast for the cook."

"Three cheers for our Fritzchen: *hoch . . . hoch . . . hoch.*"

The signalman reached behind his bunk and drew out his miniature accordion. *"Ja . . . dem Schifferklavier, hoch . . ."* An extended chord resounded through the boat, and everyone joined in, compartment after compartment to a final crescendo.

> . . . the dogs then bought a gravestone,
> and this is what it said:
> A dog came into the kitchen,
> and pinched an egg from the cook. . . .

Excerpt from a report:

Col. H. Piekenbrock
Abteilung I

Section IM; *U-47*, N.

. . . 1840 hours, on bottom, E. of Orkneys

All hands put to battle preparations. Bunks strapped up. China dishes dampened, sandwiches prepared. Torpedo gratings dismantled, loading tracks lowered. Secondary G-7e's lashed in quick load position, tubes 1 & 2. Detonators and hand fire weapons broken out. Scuttling charges set with five-minute delay fuses between tubes and in vital compartments. Enigma and radio codes, secret communications, log and signals lashed to charges. Escape gear checked and in position. Crew's morale and readiness appear excellent. . . .

Commander and officers seem relaxed. First officer and chief *Steuermann* outstanding. . . .

Signalman Hänsel knocked on the commander's bulkhead. He had an idea that would be advantageous in case of capture by the enemy. His scheme approved, he borrowed Walz's poultry shears and went forward into the torpedo room; he would start there and work his way aft. Most of the crew wore classic round caps with streaming ribbons trailing from the back, gilt-lettered with the inscription, in German *Schrift* letters, "*Unterseebootsflotille Weddiger.*" He cut off the "*Weddiger,*" and the crew tied the remaining tails into bows, like those of the English tars. Whether it was of great tactical value, no one seemed to care, but it did relieve the tension somewhat.

Clupea harengus didn't know—or care—what she was classified as by *Homo sapiens.* Indeed, she knew only two things: One, her world was *wet* . . . and that other world above was dry and alien. Two, she was ready to spawn. And to spawn well, she'd have to find a safe object or place for her eggs to cling to.

Once-slim *Clupea* didn't know she was called an autumn spawner by ichthyologists—nor did she know about autumn, except that the alien sun warmed the waters and improved her condition. The ten-inch Atlantic herring, small of her kind, scurried in and out of the kelp beds off Switha Island in Hoxa Sound, the southern portal of Scapa Flow. She'd come a long way—back to her own spawning waters, across the tempestuous North Sea, from a summer in Norway's Björnafjord—the bear's fjord under mighty Folgefonn Glacier—and now she was ready: her first time.

Tail wiggling, she turned; yes, her lover was behind her, skimming through the milky froth deposits of spent males. *Clupea* brushed past a rock, almost disgorging her brood—but she went on, ignoring the shattered seaweed-thronged compass binnacle. There was a cave that intrigued her spawning instincts. She swirled happily in, male at her tail. It seemed a safe place—away from the sand shark and the scavenging sculpins. Joyously she slipped through grottoes and corridors, past strange rocks and plants. This was the place! She relaxed, limp and tired; then the contractions snapped her body. It was now! The male waited, impatiently circling above, lingering and darting among the seaweed-threaded valves and barnacled brass gauges. Then she saw it: white, clean and bright, a curious stone at the base of the cave wall, reflecting the light that filtered through a high opening. She wiggled down to it and rubbed her soft, scaly sides rhythmically back and forth on the hollow "stone," ventral fin fanning feverishly. A stream of viscous amber fluid, mottled with upwards of 50,000 jelly-soft eggs, poured out of *Clupea*'s tiny ventral opening, collapsing her inside sacs. The issue settled on the white stone, slimed into the two large tandem openings, into the triangular one, and sifted between the gold-capped bars of the long curved entrance, collecting in clumps on dark, mossy ledges of the interior.

Clupea, her job finished, sprang lightly up toward the rayed light of the alien world as her male spiraled down to exude a white swirl enveloping the skull of Kapitänleutnant Hans Joachim Emsmann, son of Commodore Emsmann, High Seas Fleet, and honor graduate of Flensburg Naval Academy, class of '16.

TWENTY-NINE

"Battle stations." Prien's command crackled out of loudspeakers in each of the eight compartments of Krupp's iron offspring. The boat snorted and wriggled out of its cozy sand shoal, scattering an army of startled horseshoe crabs from a burrow below the port after diving plane. The propellers whirred sand over the fleeing fossils and mowed a swath through a tendriled kelp bed. The serpent rose and gained headway, forward planes unfolding like flippers of a resurrected plesiosaur. Up and up it ranged, instinctively seeking the sky and the world into which it had been born—the world for which it had been conceived. Inside its brain a green light flashed. . . .

At 1915 hours a wet cyclopean eye glinted red, reflecting the waning west light; it blinked and saw nothing on the ocean's surface, then turned north, rising atop the sleek gray tower as it shook the frothing foam from its rims.

"Surface." Prien's order rang through the control room as he snapped on his oilskins. The ocean gurgled out of the main tanks, chased out by hissing compressed air.

"Down scope."

"Tower clear." The tubular boat rocked as it broke surface, feeling for an even keel. Young Varendorff, first up the ladder, undogged the hatch and thudded it open. A shower of spray leaped through, cascading off the climbers and puddling the decks below. Cool evening air rushed down into the partial vacuum; Hänsel, at the helm, leaned back, inhaled deeply, and through the circular hatch, Pegasus's great square of stars appeared to sway, as if in seesaw battle with its neighbors.

The white-crowned captain, two officers, and the navigator racked their eyes and ears; nothing could be seen or heard—but there *was* something. Something unearthly! The wind had slackened, and a soft swell cradled the slim craft.

"Starboard clear . . . port clear . . . aft all clear." The round of reports mingled with faintly sloshing water through the retracted bow planes. "Ventilate the boat," Prien snorted into the voice pipe, and two raspy fans spun to life, sucking salt air into the bridge duct behind him.

"Diesels ready." The cry had been relayed to the helmsman.

"Stop motors; both engines, slow ahead." Prien had planned a slow, steady approach to the target. *Slow and easy,* the first rule in closing on a port whether in peace or war. In this case the bridge crew's senses would be better honed to the night conditions—the feel of tide and windage—that could not be had on a fast approach. The tiny bow wave, barely visible under the jumping wire connections, indicated a three-knot speed . . . a creeping, steady, stealthy pace like the wild west Indians of Karl May. Prien had slipped one of the German novelist's books in among his sea manuals and occasionally tried to memorize a line or two. One never knew when such knowledge would be handy. He recalled another self-taught man who liked the author's adventure yarns—the Führer himself!

In addition, the slow speed would create a minimum wake and not attract the casual observer on the islands' heights. Three knots for five hours would put Rose Ness's light abeam just before midnight and charge the batteries full to boot.

Suddenly it all came to him! Instead of getting darker, the opposite was happening. The starboard saddle tank had never been so visible at night, never except in moonlight. But there was no moon!

"Northern lights." Spahr broke the silence. "I hope it doesn't get worse."

'Of all the goddamn—" Prien mumbled under his breath.

'September and October are the peak months, sir," the navigator prattled on. "Now we know why Hebestreit got so much static on his last radio check. . . ."

"At least *that's* a relief," Endrass added. "I'd hate to be without a radio on the way back."

'Good evening, gentlemen." A Swedish accent preceded Nielson to the bridge. "My, my, is it morning already?"

"Don't tell me you've never seen aurora polaris." The captain affected a cultured delivery.

"Of course. It's actually a good omen—for Eskimos—ancient superstitions held that it was the clash of armies battling in the skies. But I suppose it does present problems tonight."

"Your weather boat knew nothing of this?" Prien looked up as the incandescences separated into greenish bands, tinged with rose and stretching west to east in tenuous, coruscating arcs—a celestial satin with deep-folded crevasses. He felt like a fish in a glass bowl on the Grosse Freiheit in Hamburg. His peripheral vision caught a shape to port—conning tower's shadow slipping smoothly along!

It was time for a decision. Two figures wrestled inside him. Both wore white caps. One captain told him to submerge and wait till the next night since the aurora seldom lasted two days in succession. The other captain cautioned that the crew was ready *now,* and its efficiency would suffer were the attack delayed.

"Looks like a good night for shooting." Endrass's comment burned into his superior's arena in support of Captain II.

Varendorff whispered to Spahr, "Man, it's going to be sticky tonight." Prien gripped the interior handrail, face ruddy, reflecting the compass repeater illumination. The signs were positive; his men were bolstering him . . . saying yes.

The second-in-command elbowed next to him. "I heard that our boys have all eaten their special chocolate rations already. Walz says that's the *last* of it."

A solemn smile crossed the commander's face. Twenty-one years earlier, almost to the day, Emsmann's boat had been blown up with all hands lost—trying to get into Scapa Flow!

At 2307 (shortly past 11:00 P.M.), Varendorff spotted a ghostlike shape dead ahead, steam trailing low. Once more, the VIIB dipped under, changed course to starboard, taking her aft of the sighted vessel. A green light flashed, indication that the "asparagus" was ready. It rotated; the blue eye below saw nothing.

A north wind greeted the bridge watch; it pushed the clouds south, to port, as the northern lights shone even brighter; orange rays, blue rays—all fanning to the zenith. In Prien's words it appeared as "a magic light on the Day of Judgment."

The islands were now visible: a black ribbon snaking and undulating on the shimmering horizon. Rose Ness light was guiding the enemy in, flashing every seven seconds.

"Jolly decent of the English." Nielson polished his binocular lenses and raised them toward the shore.

"Newest Zeiss design." Navigator Spahr ogled the rubber-covered glasses. "They're hard to come by."

"You can get them in Berlin." Nielson panned the lighthouse peninsula. "Looks very still . . ."

"Most of the commerce goes through Stromness."

"Ah, yes, Wilhelm, another good reason for this approach; it would be a shame to get rammed by a clumsy freighter in a crowded channel."

"Copinsay at green one-forty, sir," Dziallas reported from his station aft of the flak gun.

Spahr noted the compass repeater: Rose Ness was dead off the bow. He looked at his watch. "Land fix, sir—one mile to the point . . ."

Everyone on the bridge knew. One mile at three knots meant twenty minutes till the turn-in to Kirk Sound, the shallow bight that would be the test. BdU said they could get through, and there was only one man of the six on the bridge who knew *why* . . . and that man belonged to One-M, the Abwehr's naval arm.

The lighthouse drew closer and closer: three-tenths of a second flash, 7.2 seconds eclipse, ambiently lighting the faces on *U-47*'s bridge, an animation that flickered like Edison's first moving pictures. So close did Spahr maneuver to land that the ribs of the giant Fresnel lens atop the lighthouse could be seen during each rotation pass. "Motors standing by," was reported.

"Come to three-one-zero . . ." Spahr had memorized the turn bearings. "Right rudder," he added softly.

Sporadic lights appeared, popping into sight one by one as the boat rounded Rose Ness; other, fainter lights above, marked the rolling hills' contours. Endrass ordered E-motors started.

"Good thing," the captain whispered to Endrass, "that those hills are between us and the *verdammte glimmer.*"

"I think we've got shadow all the way in, sir."

"Good work, Spahr, now—what's that? Three points to port. Looks like a blockship." Prien focused his glasses.

"You're right—helm, ten degrees left and steady." The first officer glanced down at the Schmeisser machine pistol propped against the aerial housing.

"Something seems wrong, sir; there's only one channel that I can make out; wait till I check depth. . . ." Spahr slipped below.

"Minimum ahead for steerageway." Endrass cradled the pistol.

"Wrong channel . . . correct to zero-three-zero," Spahr called coolly, his head through the hatch. "Run half a mile and then go back on three-one-zero; we've got to go around that island." The navigator scrambled to his station and pointed at a low, barren shape. "There—head toward that church steeple . . . then there should be a defunct lighthouse a quarter mile farther up. . . ."

"Slow ahead . . . hard starboard . . ." *U-47* wheeled smoothly toward South Mainland Island, deeper into the protective darkness of the south shore.

Prien mumbled about lost time as he piloted his boat into Kirk Sound with a following current; the plan had been to enter some ten minutes earlier, at slack—an easier steering condition.

"Slow ahead both." He waited for Spahr's electric sounding.

"Seventeen meters, sir," the navigator called up through the red-rimmed hatch. "We're abeam of Manse Point; it'll get deeper and then shoal to fifteen in about half a mile. Then we follow the shoreline about fifty yards off."

At 12:19 A.M. the metal shark nosed into the north channel, where the blockships could be faintly seen in Ayre Bay, strung from the night lights of St. Mary's village to Lamb Holm, a desolate grassy dune in midsound. The E-motors whined as the tanks were flooded to gain draft and helm control. Two broken masts jutted up from a sunken hulk dead ahead. The dark bow, responding to its rider's verbal kicks, veered sharp to starboard, almost brushing the schooner's tilted transom. The inshore curls of current boiled though the U-boat's retracted planes as she rounded the obstacle and came back on course.

Ahead lay the cement-filled blockships *Soriano* and *Thames*. There was water between them, enough to maneuver through—provided the wires and chains that drooped from the battered fantails were low enough at their centers. Prien prayed to his God that the new moon tide was high enough, that the chains would sag low enough. He'd just blown the tanks enough to cut the draft from five to four meters; the saddle tanks were halfway out of the water, and he dared not go any farther.

Suddenly the stern swung out—caught by a surface eddy and a puff. "Flood the dip cells." The helmsman ayed and passed the order. Vents opened, and the boat settled deeper by a foot as the twin rudders shouldered into the three-bladed screws' thrust. The commander watched as the rudder angle repeater responded.

On either beam the tide gushed white on the dipping chains as the bridge watch held their breath—waiting . . . waiting.

Electrician's Mate Fritz Schmidt—in the cramped battery room below the deck plates—felt it first, vibrating through his thick rubber seaboots: a rasping of metal against metal, followed by a thumping drum on the ribbed pressure hull.

"Port stop . . . hard aport rudder." The bow swung erratically toward Lamb Holm. *U-47* had been snagged on her ballast keel, but the seasoned sailor knew what to do: Go *with* the skid just like driving on an ice-slicked autobahn. Find the slack, and have it work for you. "Blow the dip tanks . . . both ahead slow . . . hard starboard and come to two-seven zero . . ."

The boat shuddered as the heavy chains sprung and slid aft along the keel. *U-47* broke free and lurched ahead.

"Christ, I thought it was a mine cable—I could feel it!" Schmidt climbed out of the battery compartment and panted into Steinhagen's hydrophone-effect niche.

"It almost blew my eardrums out." The *Funkgefreiter* eased his earphones back on as he turned his big bearing wheel, eyes closed.

"Does that mean we're *in*?" Schmidt's knees trembled inside his shapeless leather pants.

THIRTY

Midnight was one half hour away.

A nervous Theo Drahn set his chronometer bezel to 11:45. He had fifteen minutes to accomplish two assignments, either one punishable by hanging. After leaving Brenda snoring in his office Murphy bed, he light-footed it downstairs to the garage. First checking his toolbox next to the oilskin-wrapped Neolithic ax in the unlocked boot, he got into his immaculate ivory Bentley 4½, turned the key, and pressed the starter button. The coil whined weakly, then died. He tried again but stopped for fear of flooding the carburetor. After easing the brass outside brake lever, Theo opened the cutaway door, hopped out, and pushed the vehicle out of the garage.

He stepped on the starter a second time, then cursed and shook his fist at the infernal "Merry Dancers," as Orcadians called the northern phenomenon of lights. It wasn't the first time it'd played its havoc on the fickle ignition system. "Damn, damn, damn." The thin watchmaker grunted and pushed the classic car several yards until it started rolling. He swung in, hands on the wheel as the momentum increased on the inclined Bay of Ayre Road. Theo waited till the air rushed into his face, then jumped the clutch. The flywheel spun, and the Roots blower carburetor between the chrome headlights wheezed and sucked along with the chugging motor. Theo hit the brakes and stopped to gun the motor, then backed up sharply and spun in the opposite direction. He snapped on his dims and headed north toward Scapa Bay. The first assignment concerned reconnaissance.

"Shout us up another." Self-appointed "General" Sandy MacCowan handed his crockery mug to Angus Muldoon, who passed it on to the keg, where it was topped off by lame Danny Hobbs.

"Too bad yer wife dunna ha' a few more mothers to tend to." Old Tommy, the postman, hollowed his gray cheeks on a long white clay pipe. "By the saints." He slid back on his chair and swiped errant ashes from the purple satin of his father's Crimean War dress dragoon trousers.

"Dandy to throw a randy on Friday the thirteenth, guvnor. There'll be no hobgoblins hangin' round this establishment. We'll certainly see the new day without bad luck."

"Too bad, Danny, about your American friend; the commander wouldn't ha' missed this for sure."

"At least 'e's alive, poor bastard—that carrier blew up like a bloody blast furnace."

"Luck. Pure luck that the Boche came up when 'e did."

"Luck or no"—Tommy leveled his pipe at Angus's faded Turkish campaign ribbons—"over five hundred of our lads went down with 'er."

"It was more than luck." Danny blew foam from his mug and eased his lame leg over the bench. "Those Nazis ha' been practicin' for years for this war; we're only just workin' up—"

"Sandy, d' ye think we'll be invaded?"

"Thomas"—the sideburned veteran waxed worldly —"the primary tactic of a successful campaign is *surprise* . . . and from there on to exploit that surprise, to keep it going—or coming. Look what they're doing in Poland. Do you know that the Wehrmacht produced a blueprint to conquer the world in 1923! I wouldn't put anything past that madman—But if they do come"—Sandy slammed his freckled fist on the table—"we canno' fight without proper weapons!"

"Commander Mount wrote a letter to Whitehall, did he not?"

"I helped him draft it, Tom—but you know how one has to badger those armchair admirals in Whitehall: First you write a *please* letter; then you've got to tell them you know so-and-so and if no action is forthcoming—"

A sharp, staccato tap, tap, tap clattered in the restaurant.

"Someone at the front door, Gen'ral."

"Maybe it's the first wave o' Nazis!" Tom guffawed.

"Draw me another brew"—Sandy went into the darkened front room—"and I'll come back and tell you about the halibut that was big enough to be claimed by His Majesty's ancient law. . . ."

Sandy snapped the door shade up, peered through the glass, and slid the heavy dead bolt aside, opening the door just enough for his young nephew Clyde to slide through.

"Corporal Dorne reporting, sir." The boy threw an awkward salute, hand inside his fatigue sleeve. "Hit's time, sir."

"Corporal, you left your post," Sandy boomed.

"Beg pardon, but I was due to be relieved at midnight, sir—and it's almost quarter past."

"You could have rang us up."

"I ran all the way sir; hardly a minute . . ."

Sandy slung his gas mask pack off a wall peg and slammed his helmet over his reddish hair. "I suppose yer stepfather went to the late flick at the aerodrome."

" 'E said 'e'd send a replacement, sir."

"Too late now." MacCowan scuttled behind the counter and took an antique harpoon from its wall plaque. "Tell one of the boys to drag the blaggard from the cinema. I'll stand watch till he shows." Brandishing the harpoon, Sandy went out into the night.

The long, low Bentley took the curve at ninety with parking lights only. It was still there! The mighty *Royal Oak* was lying under Gaitnip Hill. There was no question—it dwarfed the other large ship north of it. The green-lit dashboard clock to the left of the steering column showed 12:23. Seven minutes left, assuming the Swede had got a good timepiece. The ivory beauty snorted to a stop in the shadow of Clett's Tower.

The watchmaker adjusted his wire-framed bifocals and selected some tools from the fitted trunk toolbox. Then he took out a folding stepladder, opened and locked it, then set it against a telephone service pole. After climbing to the switch box, he tried a ring of keys until one fitted and the metal door clicked open. It was an easy matter to disconnect the trunk line that serviced Ronaldsay, south of St. Mary's, and several military posts, including the searchlight position manned by MacCowan's Volunteer Home Guard.

Back in the car, Theo, wearing a cap, tan leather jacket, and tweed knickers, replaced his bifocals with masklike driving glasses and drove the supercharged animal to a ledge overlooking Kirk Sound, about fifty yards past the unmanned searchlight position. Yes, it had worked: Clyde Dorne's stepfather had taken the bait. A ticket to the aerodrome flick—the late one.

It was 12:28. Drahn counted down to 12:29 along with his chronograph sweep-second hand.

He flicked his headlights twice toward the sea, repeating the sequence for a full ninety seconds. Two shorts . . . wait two counts . . .

Two meant there were capital ships in the flow. Three flashes would have meant "no target . . . abort and return." He slammed the shift into reverse—

Four pair of keen eyes searched the mirror surface ahead, where the blockships lay. Endrass rested his Schmeisser MP44 on the wind deflector as he flicked the safety off, borealis iridescently dancing off the blued steel muzzle and brass thirty-two round curved magazine. Dziallas and Hänsel willed their night binoculars while Prien, in voice-tube touch with Spahr below, guided the sombrous stiletto doggedly toward its objective.

The commander would later log his feelings:

> It is a very eerie sight. On the land everything is dark; high in the sky are the flickering northern lights, so that the bay, surrounded by highish mountains, is directly lit up from above. The blockships lie ahead, ghostly as the wings of a theater . . .

A fifth oilskinned figure held his glasses on the dim shore silhouette ahead to starboard. He recognized the abandoned lighthouse at Clett and focused at its base. It was there, just as he'd retriangulated its sea bearing from the squarish bell tower of Holm Church, now abeam at starboard. Nielson counted down the last minute under his breath. If Drahn signaled *abort,* he would call for a hold and give Prien privately the special sealed orders—written by Canaris and counterstamped by Raeder and Reichskommissar Himmler himself. It would then be a simple matter to come about and slip out to sea again—no one the wiser—to reschedule the attack. There'd been too much footwork to blow the Orcadian's cover for nothing.

And Kapitänleutnant Prien would obey orders!

Nielson's second hand swept past 12. He waited impatiently—a short eternity. Then it happened.

Headlight high beams flashed . . . *twice.* Then twice again.

Prien's white cap glowed. So did the bow cable cutter, the 8.8 deck gun, and the curved front of the conning tower. The watch instinctively ducked behind their chariot's armor. One of them smiled, unseen in the shadow behind the aerial container.

Bootsmaat Dziallas peeked over the wind deflector and saw parked vehicles on a dock and armed sentries silhouetted against a spotlight on a building. He exchanged a glance with Prien, and they both drew deep breaths of the charged air.

It was a miracle that no one had spotted the gliding submarine!

And a debacle.

"Hold it right there." A searchlight popped on, and a barbed harpoon point pressed under Theo Drahn's ear as he hid behind his driving gloves.

"Turn off the motor," commanded Sandy Mac-

Cowan as he jabbed the bronze weapon into Theo's neck, grazing it. The powerful engine cut off, leaving a doomful silence, aurora dancing on the polished chrome headlights and ivory body.

"Show me yer face, mon, or I'll run ye through." Cowering, Drahn turned and drew his hands down, light flashing from his goggle glasses and upper lip scar visible through his thin mustache.

"Well I'll be pitch-kettled—it's the grandee himself. . . . Get out." Sandy swung the door and prodded Drahn. "Hop it over to the searchlight, or it's the end." The harpoon tip, between Theo's coattails, ripped his silk shirt and caught a barb in his belt. "Now both yer hands up, Herr Drahn, and no tricks. I've kicked a few into the beyond in my time, mind ye."

Drahn stumbled over the sandbags and fell on his back, a cornered, cringing rat, wheezing at the harpoon in front of his nose. "I'll have the authorities on you, MacCowan," he squealed. "I'm a subject of His Majesty in good standing—and I know people in high places. I'll have you thrown in jail for this outrage . . ."

The wind veered, a low drone carried from the sea. Sandy cocked an ear, then opened the field telephone box. "We'll just get a few reinforcements—" The drone grew ominously louder. MacCowan put the phone down and leaned over the sandbags for a veiw of Kirk Sound. Was it a boat? It must be, but there was nothing . . . unless— The old soldier sidled around his sniveling prisoner and climbed over the parapet, harpoon now pressed against Drahn's ear. Sandy inched over to the precipice and looked down.

He froze, then got hold of himself and pounced back into the pit. "You bastard, you bloody damned traitor. They shoulda locked ye up wi' the other krauts." He rang up the phone with his free hand. "MacCowan here . . . hello . . . MacCowan with a Mayday—damnit . . . General MacCowan of the volunteers at Kirk searchlight station. A U-boat! It's steaming up the channel. . . ." He shook the phone madly.

"The line is disconnected," Drahn sneered in the half-light, his goggles reflected blues and greens from the sky as one hand groped behind his back. "Look, Sandy—I have money; I can make you a rich man. There are ways that nobody will know. Think of it—" Drahn's sweaty hand closed around a power cable behind him; his beady eyes tracing it under Sandy's seaboots. "You can buy a yacht, build a big hotel . . . have a car like mine . . ."

The drone, ebbing to the north, was replaced by the chugging of a motorcar, its blackout slits bouncing down the road.

"Over here . . . hurry, hurry." The harpoon tip wavered.

Drahn yanked with desperate strength, sending his captor sprawling. He was on him like a cat, slammed a handful of dry earth in MacCowan's bewildered face, and wound the cable a turn around his neck. "Damn Jew," snarled Drahn. The veteran clawed blindly as the cable tightened, then slumped, eyes and tongue bulging in the dirt. Drahn felt cold metal in his hand. The harpoon! He raised himself up over the writhing form, both hands holding the shaft high, bronze barbs downward and glinting, then drove it with all his might through MacCowan and into the Scottish loam.

Theo dragged the corpse down the grassy incline to the water's edge where a power skiff was tied to a float. The German jumped aboard and turned up a forty-pound plow anchor and a coil of hemp line. After roving the line through the stock shackle and forming a bight, he dropped the anchor off the seaward stern and carried the lines back to shore. Pulling hard on both, he set the plow in the mud fifteen feet down. Next, Drahn bent a timber hitch around the corpse's right ankle and tugged the running end taut.

Then he thought of the harpoon. He turned palms up. Should have kept his driving gloves on when he—

He had to get rid of the weapon. Everyone knew it was Sandy's. How stupid of him. Fingerprints! He clambered up the bank and over the breastworks, the gargantuan ribbed searchlight lens staring darkly at him. Just as well! Blood on a sandbag! He grunted and turned the bag over, bloody side down, then snatched the harpoon and slid back down to the embankment.

About to fling it into the sound, he stopped. The long wooden stock—it would float. He got a better idea. Hurriedly Drahn unwound the relic's six-foot lanyard and lashed it snugly against the body.

Then he pulled the loose end of the anchor line. MacCowan slid and jerked, feet first, sprawling . . . into the dark waters. The body, immersed to the chest, snagged on a rock, as if protesting the degrading method of interment, then slipped off, one arm trailing as the waters closed over the corpse.

Drahn hauled until he felt resistance: the body had reached the anchor on the bottom. He laid his line taut underwater and set a heavy stone on it. The incoming tide was slow now—but in several hours the ocean would surge into the sound at eight knots or better, slipping the line from under the rock and through the anchor shackle—freeing MacCowan for his last passage into the depths of Scapa Flow.

THIRTY-ONE

"'Twilight had gone, and night's profound darkness had fallen. Directly overhead sparkled the brilliant polestar, eye of the shepherd of the Heavens. . . .'" Nigel Mulford held a penlight to his book.

"Go on, Nickie boy, you've got a few minutes till you're on. It's the same every night anyway on this antique." Midshipman Alistair Dill-Fraser gazed dreamily over the starboard rail. "A" turret's massive guns cast long shadows on the holystoned deck beyond him.

"I'll just do the good parts." Nickie continued reading from a prewar guidebook's description of the northern lights as seen in 1916 by a dogsled traveler in Siberia.

> . . . an arch of light flashed across the black sky. Along the whole extent ran waves of transparent light, colorless and phantomlike, as in a dream. Suddenly there spurted out a vast, billowing river of multicolored fire; the arch glowed with a green brilliance, and far out over the entire expanse of the heavens, rays of blood-red light were flung. . . . Abruptly the arch was extinguished, leaving only a few greenish points flashing here and there on the horizon. So wonderful

is the sight that one feels the truth of the ancient native proverb: *Who looks long on the heavenly light becomes mad.*

"I can go mad with or without lights on this godforsaken outpost. Nickie, you read like an absolute dream. You know, Nickie—I've talked to some of the fellows in the Sebastian Society; they'd like to have a look at you. . . ."

"What on earth is the Sebastian Society?"

"You've heard of Sebastian Melmoth?"

"No."

"Yes, you have." The haughty midshipman took the guidebook out of Nigel's hands, closed it, and tucked it provocatively into the bandsman's trouser pocket. Nigel squirmed away from the ensuing grope. "It's the name that Oscar Wilde took on the Continent after he got out of jail and went bankrupt. A sort of exile—our secret society." Dill-Fraser withdrew his hand at the sight of the watch approaching. "Why don't you come down and have a look? I'll call a meeting at oh-five-hundred; that'll give you time to freshen up after your watch. . . ."

"But Alistair—I'm . . . I'm not . . ."

"Fiddlesticks, Nigel. No one's *forcing* you. Everyone needs friends. No? I've been watching you. You are very unhappy. Alistair knows all. Bring something to read to the fellows . . ."

"Well." Nigel weakened.

"Good show, Mulford—Nickie." The well-tailored midshipman grabbed Nigel's limp wrist and gave it a squeeze. "Our hideout is amidships, on F deck; it's an empty cordite magazine two decks below the electric room. We'll exspect you at oh-five-hundred."

Nigel looked down at the midshipman's right hand,

still clamped around his wrist; there was something on Alistair's hand, almost lost in the folds between the thumb and index finger.

"It's an anchor." Dill-Fraser let go and brought his hand up for Nigel to inspect the tiny purple tattoo. "Easily hidden, so." He closed the gap. "It's the society's symbol. Almost all of our capital ships have similar organizations, different names of course. But we all have our little anchors—a sort of calling card ashore . . . traveling . . . in clubs and country estates. All it takes is a warm handshake—if you know what you're looking for. You might say the sun never sets on our little anchors—oops, here comes one of those apes from the West End. See you later . . . and make sure the coast is clear when you come down . . ."

" 'Ere ye go, myte." Stoker Jack Makin popped the .303 clip from his Lee-Enfield carbine and handed it ceremoniously to Nigel, who gingerly slid it into the chamber of the weapon he'd drawn from the guardroom.

" 'Ats no wye t' 'andle yer piece, boy; she'll not lock in proper." The jut-jawed giant set his carbine leaning and snatched Nigel's. He pulled out the clip and held it up. "Ye take a firm grip and set it in the opening . . . mind ye, I'm demonstrating in slow motion. Make sure it's in by *feel*, don't *look*, yer eyes should be on the water. Then when ye know yer *in—slam* it home."

The snap startled Nigel; he was glad he'd enlisted in the Navy. The thought of catching his fingers in the contraption appalled his pianistic asperations.

" 'Ere ye go, myte." Makin slapped the carbine against Nigel's chest, knocking the wind out of him. "Practice—and remember: Load yer piece like you were fuckin' a bitch booby. First, ye feel yer peggo in—then ye *slam* it t' th' hilt. And all the toym yer lookin' the cunt stryte in her eye. And now it's toym" —Makin licked his chapped lips with a smack—"to dip m' tin in the king's barrel. And don't forget the syftey lever." He spun with a rubbery squeak and clomped aft, toward the hills of Hoy and the crew's mess.

"Thank you," Nigel called sheepishly after him.

He slung the Enfield over his right shoulder and marched toward the bow, treading lightly for the first hundred feet, marked by the huge capstan. The officers' quarters were on A deck, forward of the turrets and separated from his boots by only two inches of steel. His gait hardened for the next thirty strides, then lightened as he approached the jack staff. Having availed himself of the ship's cross section in the library, he knew that the bow compartment on A deck was the servants' quarters, right up to the stem. And why shouldn't the *untouchables* be allowed to sleep as well as the masters? Expendable, these poor sepia souls, as he recalled a fleet tactic entitled *Ramming a Hostile Ship*. And how on earth could the servants sleep anyway, right under the rattling anchor fairleads?

By way of passing the time, Nigel worked out a system his first time on watch. He counted 70 strides from his juncture with the midship's watch territory and the forepeak; 140 for a round trip. He clocked one way at fifty seconds and would speed up, slow down, lengthen and shorten his gait accordingly to fit the system and come out to his lucky round numbers.

A 4-hour watch consisted of 14,400 seconds, which meant that each round trip took the beautiful cardinal square of 144. He was especially fond of the fact that his system depended so on *sevens* and *twelves*. Such a coincidence with his music! Seven for the diatonic

Western musical scale that dated back to the medieval beginnings of the art of notation. *Twelve* for the dodecaphonists—the dissonant destructors of palatable sound, led by Schoenburg and his radical Viennese *Wunderkinder*: Berg and Webern. As a music student he'd tried to like . . . to understand . . . the *sour notes* that critics extolled. Was Schoenberg saying something important—or was he wailing at the wall, surrounded by press agents?

For a moment Nigel agreed with the Nazis: The *people*—his hardworking parents . . . Moxie . . . Jack Makin—didn't give a hoot about twelve tones. Music was for pleasure, not anarchy. . . . What was it with these people who had so much influence in the arts, in radio, in film that they got exposure far beyond their nominal due. Yes, he thought, the Nazis are bad, but they're not all wrong. They're just too much in a hurry. Nigel wondered whether one of his favorite composers, Gustav Mahler, really knew what his ambitious Viennese protégés were after. It was Nigel's belief that Schoenberg, the son of prosperous Jewish shopkeepers who had converted to Catholicism at a rich refuge in Spain when expedient—and reconverted to Judaism when safe in sunny California in 1934—was interested in one thing, and one thing only: the destruction of a civilization that frightened him. And why not destroy the culture first—if not confuse it—by pounding, pushing, pounding, paying . . . ?

Nigel inhaled the night air and scanned the flow. Quiet. Not even a cormorant drying its wings on a skerry. Perhaps Alistair was right. The brother of Moxie had no friends. Nickie just didn't fit in anywhere. He didn't know what to do with girls, and he was confused about his own sex. The cockney had exited him—and repelled him. Same with Dill-Fraser. Same with Carole Craig and her evacuees. Ditto about the major's daughter, Ruth.

Nigel felt a cold chill from the west, behind him—as if someone, something were watching him. *Fool . . . fool,* screamed the wind, and he shifted his carbine, turned up his jacket collar, and pressed to his task. Sanity on watch at all costs. He repeated to himself: *Do not jump overboard and end it all. It's too easy.*

Hmmm. The Oscar Wilde clique . . . why not? It could be part of a scandal . . . bigger than the one in 1923. What skeletons do these steel lockers hide? Certainly *more* than in the sweet homes ashore! Now *lightly* over the officers' easy chairs. Almost forgot. Consider Trafalgar and all that. This is what ye wanted, O brother of Moxie—or was it? Yea, it'll do—till something better comes up. Hah! I would have loved to have been in the ship's band during those roaring twenties. Imagine two officers losing their commissions and a foggy admiral put on the pension list—all over the old sod's derogatory remarks about *Royal Oak*'s nifty dance band. A free-for-all, the tabloids called it. How precious!

Poor *Oak*! Nigel tapped the jack staff with his carbine's butt and executed a *Pinafore* about-face. Too bad; no footlights. I think that was rather good. He agreed with himself.

Am I going mad? He cocked an eye at the sky's phenomena. No . . . I'm not, he reassured himself. *Press on!*

Poor Oak! It seemed that the old girl's misadventures had received more press than her accomplishments, scarce as they were. One of the five *Royal Sovereign* class battleships, she'd been laid down in 1914, at 29,150 tons, with a complement of about 1,100—

and plagued with misfortune. Soon after her commissioning, her deck was buckled in test firing her bristling midships' six-inchers. Automatic loading systems were faulty—had to be refitted. A seven-ton stern anchor, its chain parted, dropped on a captain's barge, almost killing the crew. Just four years had passed since the sabotage incident; the battlewagon's entire gun-aiming system had been put out of order by the anonymous insertion of a one-eighth-inch-long steel pin in a cable connection.

In the meager plus column, steaming behind Jellicoe's flagship *Iron Duke* off Jutland on 31 May 1915, *Oak* had lofted seven fifteen-inch salvos at the kaiser's fleet—and claimed two hits.

There was something pathetic, yet lovable about the dreadnought. Time had overtaken her; since she was partially obsolete, refitting was difficult and hardly worth the cost. Now she was languishing in Scapa because, too slow, she'd been given a station between the Orkneys and Shetlands while Admiral Forbes aboard *Nelson* led the main fleet to scour the North Sea after a sighting of the *Gneisenau* fleet off southern Norway.

Caught in a heavy gale, the twenty-five-year-old ship had lost her destroyer escorts and returned, port guns inoperable, compartments awash, and plates sprung, to the sheltered caress of the Orkneys—to lick her storm wounds.

Twenty minutes of his stint done, Nigel had counted twelve round trips—when a bright flash of sky viridian haloed the high control tower. He could see lookouts in the slitted maintop as high as a ten-story building. He admired and felt the gallantry of the tripod structure. The watch on the lower compass platform forward of the funnel top waved at him; he returned in kind.

Skirting the double starboard anchor pipes, he looked up at the massive guns of the forward crab-like gray turret, their muzzles plugged with canvas-covered tampions, each one bearing the bas-relief heraldic royal crest of Charles II, the deposed seventeenth-century monarch who had hidden in a large oak tree after the Battle of Worcester—his Scottish invaders decimated for a second and final time by Cromwell.

Nickie whistled a tune from *H.M.S. Pinafore,* content in the peaceful anchorage and thankful that the relentless yawing and pitching of Thursday's gale had finally subsided in his stomach. The officer of the deck turned and was walking the other way when he spied the carbined sailor hop a few dance steps in rounding a bollard. He felt safe; he'd seen the diagrams of the "torpedoproof" bulges that had been fitted lengthwise port and starboard. Watertight, they were designed to explode a torpedo before it could penetrate the original hull.

Sounds filtered forward: creaking of wood; squeaking of blocks; slapping of wire stays aloft; flushing of fluids; a muffled shout from the crew's head, aft; a groan from boweled boilers; the footfalls of the port watch. The boat was alive, though sleeping. This was a city of men—and *oh,* how the boy wanted to be part, a man among men. He would prove it—above all, for his brother Moxie Mulford—or could he?

The west wind picked up, wafting salty oil and rancid bilge trails from vents and hatches that speckled the 620-foot-long floating machine. Then the wind wheeled, came in from the north, and Nigel, once more, felt alone. Vulnerable.

THIRTY-TWO

U-47 made the turn at Skaildaquoy Point.

"Keep a sharp eye for rocks," Spahr called to the bridge. "Howequoy Head coming up . . . bearing to Cava will be two-five-three."

The shark was inside.

The word went around, foc's'le to stern tubes: "We hit those wires, but it didn't stop Pruentje; the captain hit 'em again and again. . . ."

"I swear—he went in like a bull. . . ."

The bull was in!

As Prien would describe it later in his autobiography:

> The shadows of the hills right and left merged and the waters darkened, for the sky's glow had vanished. And then suddenly it was bright again. . . . The bay opened out in front of us—far into the horizon, in which the burning sky was mirrored. It was as if the sea was illuminated from below. *We are inside,* I said.
>
> There was no reply, but it seemed as if the whole boat was holding its breath and as if the very hearts of our motors were beating faster and quieter.

To the north lay the hills of Mainland, sweeping gracefully westward, dipping into Hoy Sound, and rising majestically to the red sandstone summits of Ward Hill on rugged Hoy.

"Diesels both ahead slow." Prien watched the exhaust puffs disintegrate aft—into the low-slung ribbons they had just penetrated. South Mainland . . . Burray . . . Ronaldsay. No splashing pursuit . . . no turmoil among the diminishing shore lights. The commander etched the reciprocal panorama on his mind's eye . . . seventy-two degrees' return bearing was not enough.

The boat moved cautiously, but steadily on the Cava bearing as the bridge watch scanned for a pinlight, nor'-nor'west of the tiny island called Barrel of Butter Beacon. For it was in the good holding ground between Cava and its neighboring Fara, a mile south, that the main fleet usually anchored. Straining his blue eyes through the night-wet rubber-coated glasses, Prien picked up the beacon, then methodically searched southward.

Nothing! His Majesty's Ships had left.

Bending his slight frame to the voice pipe, Prien delivered a running account: "cruising on a calm sea and those Merry Dancers up there have us lit up like a carnival sideshow . . . we're coming about and takin' a look on the other side . . . got to be something in here. . . . Helmsman, rudders to port ten and hold until we're reciprocal. . . ."

"But there *is* something in here." Nielson's accent startled the others.

"You know something that we don't," Prien fired.

"I'm psychic—it runs in my family."

As the boat made its long turn, bow sweeping past Fara and Flotta, two small skiffs hove into view; they were patrolling Hoxa Sound, Scapa's southern entrance where the ill-fated *UB-116* lay, a herring haven since 1918. "Coast Guard," hissed the captain.

U-47 ran three and a half miles on diesels, then switched to E-motors again a mile off Quoy Ribs. Lights danced offshore, making Prien's "blood hammer in my temples." They turned nor'east and closed in. "Tankers," the captain snarled sourly, and pressed on—deeper and deeper toward the blinking tiara of Kirkwall's environs.

Then a long, irregular shape was spotted to port. Another small dune island? Prien changed course and stalked closer . . . closer. Again, from Prien's writings:

> At last . . . over there, close into shore appeared the mighty silhouette of a battleship. Hard and clear—as if painted on the sky with black ink. The bridge, the mammoth funnel, and the towering tripod superstructure. . . . Slowly we crept in. It was a moment that stopped all personal feelings. One became part of the boat, the brain of this steel animal, creeping up on the colossal prey. At such times one must think only in iron and steel—or perish. . . .

"Slow ahead both." Prien's eyes narrowed, nostrils flaring.

"Double turrets, fore and aft." Endrass focused as a leading seaman fitted white-coated aiming binoculars to the *Unterwasserzieloptik* pedestal at his left elbow.

"I think she's *Royal Sovereign* class." The commander wiped his lenses and took another look. "Minimum ahead," he whispered.

Lieutenant Peter Nielson was impressed, about to

be a witness of history. Nielson, the applicant who had been rejected by the Flensburg Academy because of his sense of smell. Nielson, now the clandestine cog in the greatest sea mission of modern times. He was proud. Proud of the weapon forged by Germaniawerft . . . by Krupp–by his father. And his father would be proud of him . . .

"Another ship behind her, sir." Dziallas's eagle eyes picked out a silhouette forward of the first.

"Smaller, perhaps a cruiser."

"Distance plays tricks." Endrass centered the farther warship in the calibrated optic cross hairs of his UZO.

"Take over, Bertchen." The wiry officer locked his hands at the small of his back and sidestepped the optic's field.

"Flood tubes one to four."

The boat edged in to within 3,000 yards of the quarry.

The new shadow was lying parallel to the "southern target"–bow in toward the steep cliffs of Gaitnip. The bridge watch could glean her martial profile.

"Battle cruiser; she's low in the water," whispered Prien.

Endrass nodded and pressed his eye to the torpedo aimer.

"For'ad tubes ready for surface firing," the helmsman relayed as the northern shadow hardened in Endrass's cross hairs.

Water gurgled past the tube doors, and a lever clicked obediently; *U-47* was ogling the battle cruiser –the farthest target. It was simple naval sense: Leave the *duck* for last! Tonnage figures pirouetted under the white cap: *Sovereign* class–29,500 . . . *Renown* class–32,000. . . . The boy from Lübeck's waterfront did his sums. His mind's blackboard screamed at him: *GÜNTHER PRIEN: 100,000! . . . GÜNTHER PRIEN: IRON CROSS . . . OAK LEAVES . . . DIAMONDS . . .*

Forward, in the cramped bow, Obergefreiter Herrmann waited, tensely watching his torpedo mates—sweating and heaving as they straddled the reloads, easing them on tracks toward four white torpedo hatches. The mates' blood raced, and hearts pattered when the humming E-motors cut out. A deadly silence erupted as the boat coasted resolutely toward her destiny.

Swishing water gushed past the open bow tubes—a peculiar, specific sound for the torpedo mates, blind underwater moles . . . no eyes . . . all claws and ears. It was a clarion sound—a call from the gates of watery doom.

"Range twenty-eight hundred meters . . . depth seven-point-five . . ."

Within the complex tubes the messengers of death panted and chafed at their electronic bits, bodies and fins inscribed in grease.

"All my love . . . Bottoms up . . . Hi, Neville. . . ."

"Detonators—one-zero . . ."

"One-zero . . ." parroted Bleeck.

"Fan shot . . . spread point-zero-six . . . two-second intervals . . ."

"Zero-six . . ." The figure was fed into the eels through a contact umbilical connection in the tubes. A series of clicks—

Then silence—only the sea through the diving planes.

An angel flew through the torpedo room—

An angel of *death!*

LOS!

Endrass pressed the bridge button with his palm. PO Bleeck threw the mechanical backup switch below.

A short hiss.

The boat lurched, then rocked gently.

A second hiss . . . and a third.

"Eels running true." Steinhagen adjusted his earphones.

Navigator Spahr watched his second hand slide—and counted under his breath: *two minutes . . . ten seconds . . . twenty . . . thirty . . .*

THIRTY-THREE

"Seventy-seven . . ." Nickie Mulford counted the lucky round trip as he trod past the sheet anchor pipe. He was sidestepping between the bollard and chain when a peculiar spectacle occurred: A length of links, each weighing more than 200 pounds, rose off the deck as if levitated by an invisible magician, then thudded down. The penomenon was accompanied by a low rumble and a shower of salt water. Nickie found himself stunned on the wet planked deck, carbine against the gunnel.

"Air raid," shouted a lookout aloft as acrid yellow smoke curled under the jackstays and streamed out of the hawsepipes.

"Don't panic," barked the deck officer. "Cable slips have parted–"

Nickie dragged himself up. He was glad that it was only the anchor chain . . . it had happened before.

A knot of men surrounded the starboard bower pipe. "The bugger's fractured," a cockney wailed. Nickie could see the links paying out erratically, the cable sliding around the capstan not two yards away.

"Have Commander Renshaw report immediately–" Buttoning up, his four-striped sleeve gleaming, Captain W. G. Benn had come down the armored ladder from his sea cabin, where he preferred to sleep at anchorage. Fifty feet above the decks, he'd felt the boat rock as if hit by a swell. The captain's first reaction was to order air defense procedure from the bridge. Realizing, after a period, that there were no aircraft, he settled qualmishly for an "internal explosion," perhaps in the forward paint stores.

A diminutive but noteworthy passenger, 1912 all-services rugby star, recently upped to a big stripe, Rear Admiral H. E. Blagrove, strode into the foray and went below, spouting expertise. Benn, rank-pulled, followed quietly, harassed by memories of HMS *Vanguard*. In this very anchorage, during the Great War, the dreadnought had lain next to a polished, new *Royal Oak*. On a summer's night in 1917 the cordite magazines had blown up. Only 7 officers and 2 ratings had survived out of a crew of more than 700!

"I heard *Drake's Drums*." The young bandsman wondered why his hammock had swung so.

"You musta had too much brew, m' lad." Corporal Rollings yawned. "Next time we play for the brassy mess, I'll take your pint and give ye 'alf."

"You didn't 'ear the drums?"

"Bugger off, kid. It's not all-hallows yet."

Bandsman Dudley Harrison tripped into the forward flat. "Explosion," he panted, "for'd heads are a mess, the urinals are cracked—everything's flooded . . ."

"I knew yer always was a big pisser, Dud, but—"

A pipe shrilled from the loudspeaker: "*Magazine testing parties, fall in . . .*"

"See," Harrison chided the veteran musician. "Say, where's the sailor?" He shook an empty hammock.

" 'E's got graveyard watch, lucky pup. Ain't missin' any sleep on this queer night." Rollings turned away from the caged bulb.

"Whot's 'at strynge smell?" Harrison's nostrils narrowed.

"Slack off, mate, it ain't cordite."

"Tantadlin tarts!" Leading cook Gaitskill watched in horror as a cordon of cockroaches, shaken loose from the deck-head conduits by the sudden tremor, dropped into a pot of simmering béchamel sauce. Baking tins rattled and clanged as the shock wave traveled midships through the officers' galley just aft of the funnel on A deck.

Gaitskill glowered right and left. Alone! The onetime assistant chef of London's famed Emperor quickly scooped out the intruders with a wooden spatula and stirred frantically. Had he counted four or five of the six-legged devils? He deliberated—was tempted to start the sauce anew. *Rump 'em!* He'd sieve the mush again anyway. After shoveling the sauce into a vat of green avocado paste, he added more gelatin and turned up the burner. Gaitskill was confident that the outcome of Saturday dinner's mousse would not, by a doxy's tit, suffer from the transient ingredients.

Five decks straight down, in the empty cordite compartment between the slumbering Babcox boilers, a sixteen-year-old apprentice seaman, one of eighty-two aboard, lay nude and prone on the nonskid deck plates. His eyes were covered by a black velvet strip, tied behind the ears. An older boy, hirsute and also unclad, knelt over the first, while a bespectacled pharmacist's mate, in sick bay pajamalike whites, leaned on an indecorous Beardsley print that had been taped to the bolted bulkhead door. He trailed a leather lash.

The heavy backbone keel shuddered violently through the deck plates, startling the revelers, sending shivers into the apprentice's white back. He reached for his blind, but the lash stung first.

"He's depleted." The pedantic midshipman sneered as he brushed rust from his knees. "I can't wait for Dilly's bandsman."

THIRTY-FOUR

"Fuck me, baby . . . fuck me." Six sweat-dripping arms pulled as one; the hoist chains jangled and clattered, easing the long, greased eel into tube four. Plauen simpered grimly as he patted the sliding bronze fin and saw the oily fingerwriting: "have a Havana Herr Winston."

Two misses and a possible hit on the northern boat!

Prien was fuming; he ordered *U-47* to come about, and tube five spit out its only enfant terrible. Again, a miss.

The captain's round face warped, and his rabbit mouth sucked in, trying not to betray his anger. Never, in seventeen years of sea duty, had he been this vexed, had the stakes been so high. The precious minutes were mounting. How much longer till a destroyer would be screaming down on him, flailing death? It had been fifteen minutes since the "possible" hit. . . . Damn, how on earth could Endrass have missed? Such close range . . . and a motionless target!

"Tubes one, two, and four ready, sir." The helmsman's eager tone startled Prien. He glared at his torpedo officer.

"Slow ahead both."

The bridge could now make out the battleship's gun deck deadlights. Bit in mouth, the bearded blond bull closed in for a broadside. It was all or nothing. The alternative was to die without a reason—or to slink out, beaten. No, he would rather . . .

"Range, two-six-zero-zéro . . . spread point-zero-four." Endrass had the dreadnought's tripod mast dead center as he pressed the burnished brass button.

"*LOS.*"

THIRTY-FIVE

Nigel's knee hurt. Determined not to falter or complain, he limped back to his post. He'd do what Moxie would have done. Slinging his carbine, he dragged himself forward to the bow and looked over the starboard side. The anchor cable stretched out at an odd angle, snubbed by a jury slip. He'd heard a steward talk of a CO_2 bottle that had exploded, and the port watch had told him that a tender had developed engine trouble and sideswiped the bow near the waterline. He hung over the water and watched it sluice under a Plimsoll number: *28*.

Twenty-eight feet! Four of the six hull decks were below the waterline, behind the copper-poisoned red antifouling paint. Half the complement of 1,100 men slept below the waterline—as did *all* the black rats. He'd heard they were as big as cats and got bigger the deeper down they lived—and blinder!

Below the keel flowed fifty feet of water and, then, mud.

He hiked his limp and looked south toward Holm. Yes, it would be nice . . . Just then the northern lights flared green like the end of a fireworks display, the surge reflected from a tiny object far off the beam. Nigel forgot his pain, squinted into the half-lit bay. It looked like a buoy—grayish green. Perhaps it had slipped its mooring and come north with the current. Yes, he would report it to the sergeant of the guard . . . later.

Tube one's electric G-7e struck His Majesty's Ship in section 19, well under the narrowing protective torpedo bulge. It crumpled "D" turret's understructure and demolished the steam condensers, low-pressure turbines, crew's mess, and gunner's stores, setting off the stacked cordite cartridges and, in turn, the fifteen-inch shells.

The second eel, starboard on the fan shot, with an uncanny homing instinct pierced E deck at traverse section 5 and blew up *Oak*'s own torpedo magazine, as well as the mine stores—the chain reaction buckling and immolating the midshipmen's and officers' flats above.

Churchill's Havana hit almost dead center, lower than the others. It went right through the impregnable bulge, entering the hull at the starboard shell compartment, which, although empty—except for the surprised Sebastians—was backed up by a second, which was full. The detonation knocked out the electrical communications center, ruptured the forward Babcox boilers, and buckled the mainmast tripod.

Cold Scapa Flow waters gushed through the yawning holes—into the warm, sleeping city.

Nickie Mulford couldn't see. It felt like a dream; everything was wet—and cold. He kicked his legs, felt a dull ache, like a cramp in bed. He tried to move his arms; they responded slowly, more slowly than he was thinking. Suddenly something struck his cheek. He grabbed at it and let go. It was a hand, and it wasn't his.

Cold reality set in. Nickie coughed slime out of his mouth and gulped the night air; he was reviving, and that gave him strength. He swiped at his eyes, but they burned all the more. Oil. The taste sickened him momentarily. Plop, an ear opened and sounds rushed in: splashing, moaning . . . a distant klaxon horn. Then silence.

He felt for his knife, found the lanyard, and pulled it out of his trouser pocket. Good old Moxie—he knew!

With renewed vigor he slashed his boots and kicked them off. Ah, now he could tread better, stay up higher. He spit more oil out and slashed his watch coat buttons, reached inside and tore off a shred of shirt, rubbed the oil from his stinging eyes, and blinked clear. Bright lights blinded him; he turned away.

A high red cliff loomed over the young sailor; it was haloed with green streaks. The red sandstone of Hoy? He'd been swept overboard and southwest toward Cava? Nickie started to swim toward the cliff. Then he stopped. The cliff was full of ants, crawling, sliding, and jumping. . . . No, they were bigger than ants. Lemmings? If Sweden had lemmings, why not Scapa? Then Nickie saw the huge starboard screw streaming water as it turned up and out like a gigantic turtle's flipper. Arms were sticking out of the ooze around him, grabbing for sky, then slipping away. The red mountain was turning, lights playing fore and aft.

"Over here," men were shouting.

He tried to swim to the lights—a black moth flapping in a shiny puddle. Rainbows flashing. One arm . . . the other . . .

"Over here, mate . . . this way . . ."

He was in the midst of a group of bobbing bodies. Some were slumped, and some were shouting, grappling with a small launch.

"Bloody rope—dammit."

"Don't get in, she'll go under with 'er . . ."

"Anybody got a knife?"

" 'Ere, sir." Nickie yanked the lanyard loose and held up the Swiss army knife, blade flashing.

"Good show, lad." It was snatched from his hand.

Nickie was proud as he struggled to stay with the men, watched the blade slash and saw at the hemp. A strand parted, then another . . .

"We've got 'er—" The black figures pulled themselves up onto the listing craft. Nickie reached for the transom, along with another rating, as the current swirled about them. "Give me yer hand, lad, we're almost there . . ."

Light shone through the many arms that reached down.

Nickie reached up. Fingers touched—and backed away . . . farther . . . farther. Something was pulling him back. Something—fouled around his neck and under his arms, twined by the mad current. He tugged. It gave. Marshaling all his young strength, he pulled—and a head popped up through the black slime, wrapped and fouled by the same line that was snagging him! Nickie felt for his knife—*gone*! At least *they* were saved. The lights were smaller now; the round red cliff was gone.

Nickie, energy flagging fast, tried to swim, to pull the cold corpse toward shore, toward the flurry of moving vehicle lights. He tried sidestroke, as in the manuals; he tried floating on his back and kicking, but to no avail. The tide had started to ebb, was pulling him south, away from Mainland. Refreshing salt water had replaced the sluggish oil, reviving his senses—but not his body. The floating black corpse tugged and jerked, yawed and dipped to the vagrant currents and rippling junctures of counterflows—sucking the last vestiges of Nickie's endurance.

The broad expanse of Hoxa Sound beckoned as the divergent flows joined in their nocturnal surge to the sea, knowing not of men, caring not but to heed their own primeval drums and pipes.

The boy tugged and drew the limp form to him—or him to it; it mattered not. Specks on the sea. He would free himself with his last whit and gasp. Head reeling, Nickie grabbed the tangled hemp shrouds at the body's breast and heaved. The oil-slicked head snapped like a slack puppet as it jolted up, eyes gleaming white, and rolled back. The rope slipped up.

Another heave—the coils loosened, freeing an arm to pop to the surface.

Enheartened, he heaved with all his might; the body rose, bare-chested, arm tangled and pressing a rope-swaddled harpoon to itself. Nickie let go. Yes, he'd be all right now.

It *was* a dream. King Poseidon, I presume—am I crossing the line?

He closed his eyes . . . listened for, and heard . . . Triton's sad horn.

THIRTY-SIX

Nielson stretched out on top of the floral comforter. A noisy mockingbird had wakened him before dawn. He'd almost fallen asleep again, but then *other* sounds had penetrated deep into his being. They'd left a window open. . . .

The night before, after dinner and a spirited discussion, the three friends had bidden one another good-night. Moxie's room was on the ground floor, behind the living-dining area and adjacent to the kitchen and pantry. Helen had excused herself and gone up the stairway to one of the two bedrooms off the balcony. The atmospheric mantelpiece clock, works visible inside its brass-trimmed glass case, chimed quarter past eleven as she waved at the two men sitting over coffee and brandy before retiring.

The mustached Royal Navy officer and the fair, trim Swedish naval observer fought the war until wee hours: the campaign in Norway . . . the lend-lease destroyers that were on their way across . . . the blitzkrieg over London, and the impending invasion called Sea Lion by the Germans, Nielson wondered whether Sean Russell and Frank Ryan, the prominent IRA leaders who had left Lorient with him on *U-71,* had been as lucky as he, had arrived at their destinations, Belfast and Dublin. They were to be put ashore at Lambay Isle and Ballyquintin Point along with transmitters and sabotage equipment. Russell's activities in Dublin were to be activated by the appearance of a pot of red flowers in a particular window of the German Legation. He thought of poor Theodor Drahn, who had had to use his whole month's ration of petrol to drive an Abwehr agent from Holyhead, Anglesey, to Lyme Bay, across the Channel from one of the invasion embarkation points in France.

The Abwehr had intelligence that the English center of anti-invasion experimentation and tactics was along the relatively uninhabited beaches between the resort town of Lyme Regis and the Chesil Bank, south of Fortuneswell. One of the British officers listed for the defense efforts was Lieutenant Commander W. E. Mulford.

Moxie had been evasive to Peter's questions and suggestions. He was mum on the topic of low-tide beach obstructions and would answer: "Look, mon, m' task is related to keepin' Jerry fum puttin' ashore sappers and infiltrators *from submarines,* and I don't have knowledge of *neap* or any other kinds o' tides. . . ."

Nielson's objective, as outlined by Canaris, was to find a sea floor route into Britain's southern coast for Herr Professor Gottfried Feder's "war crocodiles." Feder was no ordinary crank, but an esteemed senior official in the Reich's Ministry of Economics. He'd planned and presented to Hitler his contribution for the destruction of England. Consisting of a gigantic hollow slab of reinforced concrete, the "crocodile," ninety feet long, twenty feet wide, and twelve feet high, was powered by an engine that would either drive it just below the Channel's surface or, upon touching bottom, transfer the power to caterpillar belts. Each of these behemoths was designed to disgorge 200 armed shock troops or detachments of guns and armored vehicles. Certain terror would be wreaked on the townspeople of Brighton, Portsmouth, and Hastings. The German concrete industry, best in the world, fresh from contracts on the Siegfried Line and building thirty-foot-thick submarine bunkers in Lorient, La Rochelle, and Brest on the French Atlantic coast, would rise to the occasion.

In addition, a legion of amphibian and submersible armored vehicles was being designed. Watertight Panzer tanks were developed, with floating snorkel air buoys, capable of crawling on the sea floor and steering by 100-foot periscopes. The demonstrations in late June had been successful. Sea Lion operations commander Field Marshal von Brauchitsch had already been supplied with adequate converted tanks and supportive vehicles.

Bildhefte, or picture invasion books, had been printed and distributed by the great Leipzig nationalized publishing corporations. Swarms of Messerschmidts and 190's, escorting the Junkers and Heinkel bombers across the Channel, gave the Germans a feeling of invincibility.

Nielson, issue of a country that was *afraid* of war—that had not taken sides in the Great War as well, that had been moving toward a castrated form of socialism—was one of those who was impressed by the new Germany, by the *powerful* Germany.

Nielson listened; the ridiculous mockingbird had gone. Far in the hills behind the cottage grounds, toward Charmouth in the foothills, a shrill chatter was heard. It moved from hill to hill, from tree to tree. The woodpecker's machine-gun rat-tat-tat cleared his mind of the previous evening's revels. He dragged himself toward the leaded glass window of the servant's bungalow and looked through ground fog at the stone and stucco cottage. The second-floor window was now closed. Perhaps the morning breeze had chilled them in their tired nude entwinement. But he had heard, thanks to the capricious mockingbird, the sighs and sounds of carnal love. He pictured them together: Helen McCrary's fair, lithe body lying asleep; Mulford, the "owner" of the borrowed castle, stumbling drunk up the balcony stairs, bumbling into her room. Saying, "Sorry, lass—Oyve made a mistake," as he pulled the lamp cord. And she lay still sleeping and under the delicious sheet. Then Moxie, the opportunist, picked up the corner of her sheet—and whipped out his . . .

Nielson felt his penis growing at the thought of Helen being attacked by the randy Mulford. It was war!

The brandy that had clouded his mind had been whisked away. His body had expelled the poison, and he was now able to remember.

The mockingbird—laughing at him! The girlish sighs; the sobbing, muffled cries from across the lawn. The windborne drunken words: "Easy now, lass."

And earlier—he'd left the hutch, gone out to relieve himself against the hedge, when he'd noticed that Moxie's room was still lit. He hadn't meant to, but he stumbled over to the cottage and fell against the cool stucco. Couldn't help peeking past the shutter. Moxie had stuffed a series of papers and charts into an official-looking portfolio. He tied the closures and took the folio out into the fireplace area, set it on the mantel. He unbuttoned his service shirt and took up that strange Egyptian silver symbol he al-

ways wore on a chain about his neck. He moved th
atmospheric clock to the left and inserted his nec
symbol into a slot. One of the eight seemingly ho
mogenous inset wall panels over the mantel sli
sideways, revealing a metal wall safe. Once more h
used his symbol. The safe swung open with a click
Moxie slid the portfolio in and restored the mante
to its pristine state.

And what about Helen? Nielson reconstructed th
previous afternoon: He'd taken the bus from Axmin
ster, five miles north of Lyme Regis, where Theo ha
dropped him off as discreetly as possible from hi
white Bentley drophead coupe. He then rang u
Moxie at his Charmouth Hills "borrowed" cottage
Moxie told him to take a table at the Three Cups
near the stone pier, put a pint on Mulford's account
and wait.

Peter took a window table and ordered a geneva
Ale was not enough to quaff his jitters. A squeal o
tires preceded the appearance of Moxie's Aston-Ma
tin Ulster racing machine.

She wore her hair up, under a sun-drenched wide
brimmed straw hat. Alighting, she tossed it back o
a scarlet chin ribbon. He watched them as he emp
tied his glass. Helen was out of a fashion magazine
England had been good for her. She primped in th
side mirror as Moxie slid his hand around her waist
she threatened to hit him with her purse, then kisse
him instead.

After enjoying a luncheon of fish bisque and stuffe
mussels, they drove along the shore under the famou
lime cliffs where eleven-year-old Mary Anning, gathe
ing shells to be sold in her father's souvenir shop i
1811, had found the *Ichthyosaurus* fossil that led t
Britain's dominance of the field. Moxie commente

that his brother, had he lived, would have enjoyed the topic. Nielson asked whether his brother was a scientist and what were the circumstances of his unfortunate death. Moxie stared at the speedometer as the needle swung to 100 kilometers, and Helen, behind in the jump seat, pleaded with him to slow down. Moxie, with two pints in him, spun out on the left turn to Charmouth, narrowly missing a rock ledge and stalling in soft sand. He apologized and drove like a priest as Helen leaned forward and told Peter about *Royal Oak* and how the mere mention of the subject changed Moxie into Mr. Hyde.

That afternoon the three went for trout on the Char River up near Yarcombe. Helen was game and kept up with their stone hopping and branch ducking, though preferring not to fish and, for her inexperience with casting, be a dragging liability. "You men and your trout . . . my father told me that the British brass went into the Norway campaign because, with Nazi occupation, their favorite fishing fjords would not be available in May." Without complaining of insect bites and thorn scratches, she prepared an elegant salad from a head of lettuce and a confusion of dusty canned vegetables and fillets she'd found in a root cellar that had been converted to an air-raid shelter by Vice Admiral Sir Lancelot Bryans-Hughes before he was assigned to Australia. Moxie did an expert almondine with the relatively small browns and vowed to get up early the next morning and go for the big one that fed at sunrise.

Nielson lay there, watching the sun incandescing the topmost branches of a high evergreen. He would wait till the next lower one was bright, a sort of tree clock. Moxie was now his enemy, and he hated the Scotsman for possessing Helen. What was it Mulford had mumbled as Peter turned in last night? He was about to talk after finishing half a bottle of Duggan's Dew o' Kirkentilloch, but then he caught himself—advised Peter *never to volunteer,* but he was doing this assignment in order to kill as many Germans as possible because of that unsporting, bloody attack that killed more than 800 men and officers, including Nickie Mulford, at Scapa Flow. He was putting everything he could into this effort.

That bastard Mulford; did he think the British were lily-white? All those years of subjugation and plunder for the Empire, for those bewigged fops and hyphenated snobs. He would get even, as well as succeed in his mission.

Peter, determined, roll-cast his white floating line under the summer-heavy branch of an ancient oak. It was open warfare now: Mulford the king's man against a Viking, against a German! What did Moxie have that he didn't? He couldn't bear the thought of another night like the last one: the vision of Helen, rent open by the uncouth Scot—receiving that pompous martinet!

The red and black coachman streamer dropped under a startled dragonfly and zigzagged across the sparkling, brisk waters of the Channel-bound river. A slim dark dart passed under the lure, catching refracted morning light on its square tail, and disappeared behind a sunken log. Peter let the streamer dally and sink. He counted five and fingered his line in steadily. The lure rose, in short, lively jumps. As it broke the surface, a swift spout of water enveloped it. Then a lash of tail, and Peter's reel ratchet whirred as the line payed out. He thumbed the reel, and the drag tightened until the line was snapping taut on the rippling surface; then, raising his tip, he set the hook firmly. The line disappeared, pulled down by an unseen force that was fighting to rid itself of its terrible technological adversary. The cagey fish, veteran of many years, tried its final trick. The line went slack —faster than Peter could reel it in. In desperation he grabbed the line and pulled long loops about his waders, entangling, but gaining the tautness. The fish, summoning up the last of its strength, made its final charge for freedom—to break the catgut leader, to snag the line, to rip the hooked feather from its jaw. But it was too late; the slack was gone, and the drag drained the last of its fight save one futile jump and a short surface tail dance.

Peter slit the sixteen-inch native brown trout expertly from its ventral opening to its gills, then gutted and washed it in the swift river. It was the fish that Moxie had wanted!

Having heard the last downshifts, Moxie and Helen were in the driveway when the proud Swede, trout in hand, jumped out of the Aston-Martin. "I thought you two wanted to sleep, so I decided to bring home the breakfast."

Moxie approached the fish reverently, examined it —head, fins, tail—and shook his head disconsolately. 'You've beat me out of 'im; you've got m' brownie— poor *downie brownie. . . .*" Moxie hitched up his suntan shorts and went into the house.

"I didn't know it was his pet."

"It's not your fault, Peter." Helen accompanied him to the kitchen by way of the rear door. "Ever since he lost his brother—"

"I understand." Peter lied; he had contempt for sensitivity, which he considered weakness, especially in an officer. His mind was elsewhere anyway; he was alone with her, and he liked the way the sun shone through her summery skirt. He watched her bread and pan-fry the fillets he'd cut, and he stood tall over her, his bare arm feeling her firm breast as she darted around him, supervising his toast and setting the table.

Peter's cheerfulness at breakfast was countered by Helen's guilt and Moxie's confusion with both of them. Moxie was not a man for games, the games that ladies play the morning after, the games that *educated* men play like ladies.

"I've got an idea." Nielson broke the ice. He'd rehearsed it several times as he drove back from the Char that morning. "You know, the root cellar—the one that is partly converted . . ."

"The shelter?" Helen's eyes twinkled mischievously while Moxie stirred his coffee.

"It would make a perfect sauna, and all I'll need is a petrol tin or some container for the stones. You have a garden hose out back which should reach, and there's plenty of wood stacked by the toolshed. . . ."

"There's not enough wood lining in the shelter; the heat won't be absorbed fast enough. Ye'll roast alive." Moxie laughed.

"But I can stack some wood on the shelves and along the floor—away from the fire."

"Do as ye will, mate; ye'll not get us into it."

"But, Moxie, I think it's a marvelous idea. I want to help Peter. I haven't had a good hot bath in weeks." Helen had made up her mind, and Moxie knew it.

"I won't have ye goin' in there wi'out yer clothes now."

"Silly; I have a bathing suit."

"I don't like it one bit. What if—"

"The door's not locked; if it gets too hot . . ."

"Please, Moxie. You've never worn that *smashing* suit I bought you." Helen winked at Nielson.

"Smashing it is; belongs on a pimp on the Riviera." Mulford weakened and struck a coxcombic pose.

"But, darling, I'll love you in it. You're so used to your uniforms and khakis, you should try vermilion for a change."

Mulford set his teeth and grimaced at the ceiling. "Peter, what can you say to a determined lass?"

"Then it's settled; I'll set it up right after I do the dishes." Peter started stacking them.

"You two go along and build it. I think it's time for a woman's touch in this galley."

"The old-time settlers in northern Sweden and Finland used to put up a sauna first, when clearing the land, then live in it until the main house was ready. . . ." Peter stacked the smooth stones into the metal tub as they were handed to him. "The sauna was usually built near a lake or stream for summer usage. Salt water is not good for rinsing."

"But the early settlers didn't have water hoses." Helen held out a stone as Moxie ducked out for more split spruce logs.

"Originally," Nielson continued, "saunas were built to face west, so the rays of the setting sun could stream through the door and onto the front platform. It's such a fine, calming experience, to come out and lie down, without clothes—like the animal man is—and commune with nature before diving into a cool lake or rolling in the snow."

Helen averted Nielson's eyes. She'd known enough men, especially sailors. "I'm afraid the McCrary clan is too proper for such primitive rites." She squatted over the pile of stones pensively. "Are smooth stones granite or basalt? That's what the earth is made of, at least that's what I learned in geology class."

Peter tucked another brick under the makeshift stove and turned to answer her question. "Stone can be composed of any one of the basic minerals . . ." His voice trailed off to silence at what he saw. Helen was examining a veined white stone, her mind temporarily lost in the fine textures and patinas. But she was, as prim women say, off guard. Her front-buttoned skirt, two bottom buttons undone, had hiked open between her knees, which faced the enraptured Swede, while her upper, shapely torso, and her head, obscured by long, sun-bleached chestnut locks inclined toward him. She leaned far over and picked up another stone, spreading her thighs innocently. Peter riveted, heart pounding. Her very brief white panties stretched and slipped, revealing dark, curly outcroppings and the sensuous folds of skin that have always driven men mad. It was an eternity. First, Peter looked away; he'd had enough. He wouldn't be able to hide his excitement. She'd notice, or Moxie would stumble in with an armload of wood. But nothing happened; she squirmed and studied the stones, oblivious to his searing eyes. He devoured her until he was consumed by passion, lust, or both.

She finally got up and dusted herself off.

"I've enough stones," Peter waved her away. "I'll start the fire. Tell Moxie to leave the extra wood outside. Why don't you both go and change? I'll meet you here in an hour. The stones have to be extremely hot."

After Helen left, Peter washed and slipped quickly into a pair of khaki desert shorts. He packed his belted leather suitcase, leaving his summer-weight uniform and its accessories laid out neatly on his bed. Then he slipped a deadly 7.65-millimeter automatic out of the bag's side pocket. He inspected the seven-shot clip and tied the weapon onto a birch branch. When he got to the shelter, Moxie was standing outside, smoking a pipe. The silver talisman hanging over his hairy chest caught the late-afternoon sun.

Peter carried in a tray with bottles of vodka and Scotch, a small pitcher of water, and three tumblers.

"Now that's wot I call service." Mulford poured himself a hefty shot of Duggan's Dew and downed it. "'At's one fer the road, in this case for th' cave." He poured another, set it down, and went outside to look for Helen, to make sure she was properly dressed before committing herself to the sauna.

She wore a two-piece beige suit; for a moment Mulford was startled by the illusion of nudity, but then he decided it was quite all right, better than some he'd seen in the magazines. By the time they had taken their places on the wood benches a little pill had finished effervescing a wispy cloud of bubbles in Moxie's drink.

The clouds of dry steam made Helen sigh and stretch her supple limbs ecstatically. "This feels *so* good, you have no idea. . . ." Then she noticed the birch branches lying below the small window in the wood face of the shelter. "Are you—" She pointed at the branches. Moxie was strangely quiet, sitting stiffly with his unlit pipe protruding under his sandy handlebars.

"I would, but the practice is done by a woman." He didn't want to say "birchwhipping" lest Mulford react too quickly.

"I certainly couldn't do *that*—even if I wanted to," she quipped, looking at Moxie. "Commander Mulford, are you enjoying this as I am?"

He swayed forward, a silly smile on his face. "Lass, I haven't felt like this since I was a wee un. . . ." Nielson's eyes were on the ankh hanging from a chain around Mulford's sweaty neck. Peter turned the hose nozzle, and a superheated whirling cloud obscured the dazed British officer.

"Peter, perhaps Moxie has had enough, he doesn't seem himself. Isn't it about time to go out and cool off?" The sun had lowered into the pine trees, and it was getting dark in the shelter. Glowing embers beneath the stone stove cast an eerie light on Nielson's severe facial features. He pulled a chain, and a bare bulb exploded its light in the tiny shelter. Suddenly Mulford groaned and keeled over.

"Peter," Helen shrieked, "do something." She started for the door. "I'll call for the doctor . . ."

"Sit down!" Peter barked an order.

"Peter, for God's sake . . ."

He tore the birch branch away from his pistol and leveled it at Mulford's prone body. "Sit down, or I'll blast his nuts off—and then it'll be *your* turn!"

"You've lost your mind. Peter, be reasonable." Helen sat down slowly, looking the Swede in the eye like a matador the snarling bull. "Put down that gun —*please*. We've got to get Moxie to a doctor . . ."

"He'll be all right." Peter's voice was softer.

"What on earth do you mean?" She gripped the bench.

"Two years ago Swiss research scientists isolated an acid from rye, then reduced it to other compounds, one of which is a powerful hallucinogen called *Lyserg Saüre Diethylamid* . . ."

"You put something into his drink!" Helen shrunk away from her Scotch and water.

"I wouldn't do such a thing to a pretty lady—like you."

"You, you *fiend*. Who are you; what do you want? All this time you've been . . ." She turned away, toward the wall.

"Who am I? That's easy. I'm a man with an important job to do. What do I want?" He rose from his bench and prodded her to look at him with the snub barrel of his naval issue Mauser entwined in her hair. "I think I want *you!*" He slid alongside and tried to kiss her. She swung around, narrowly missing his head with a stone. He twisted it out of her grip and flung her onto the bench. "What would they think back home? Lieutenant-Senior Nielson killed by a sauna-stone-wielding American beauty!"

Mulford groaned and tried to sit up but fell back again. "Well, if you don't help him, I will." Helen reached for the water hose but was wrestled down by Peter.

He leveled the gun close to Moxie's crotch. "Take off your clothes *darling*, or he'll never be any good in bed again."

"You wouldn't!"

Nielson cocked the trigger. She slipped her top off without a word, then covered her nakedness with one arm. "Now, the rest . . . I don't have much time." The Abwehr agent motioned with his pistol. She obeyed reluctantly. "Keep your hands on the bench." Nielson reached over toward Moxie, gun trained on Helen, and pulled a lanyard out of the drugged man's change pocket. A carmine-sided Swiss army knife tumbled out of the vermilion bathing suit and clattered to the concrete floor. "I've admired this; I think I'll confiscate it. You said he gave his brother—what was his name? Oh, yes. Nickie—an identical one for his birthday? Too bad about Nickie—but they all deserved to die! Fools, we got out of Scapa Flow before you knew what hit you." Nielson's eyes flared madly. "This is *war,* not some garden party . . ."

"Who sez about Nickie—" Mulford strained his body up and stared at Nielson, then at Helen, at her nakedness. He staggered to his feet and was hit by the butt of the Mauser; he fell back again, blood running from a gash on his temple.

Nielson flicked the large blade out of the pocketknife and held the sharp-edged point on Moxie's vermilion crotch, under his bulge. "This might be a more humane way, no?" He jabbed the point under the hem, close to the bulge. "One . . . two . . ."

Helen screamed as the Swede swung the knife in a wide, ripping arc over Moxie's belly. The vermilion fell open. She screamed, and again he slashed, laughing maniacally. Helen sobbed, burying her tear-filled eyes in trembling palms. She envisioned what Moxie called his member in undulating sections, like a fat, wiggling sausage, bleeding and crawling for safety.

Peter, venting his pent-up rage, acted on his innermost fantasies. Nothing to lose now, he was the victor . . . the looter . . . the *rapist.* He set up the framed shelter WC mirror against the wall, opposite Moxie's level, then put the gun down on his bench next to him. "Helen," he entreated, "he's not hurt; believe me." She undulated up, as if in a dream; she opened her eyes and saw Mulford. He was ranting about the Highlands and his first sweet loves; he was lying on the bench, belly up—with an exposed, ample member. She looked at the thick, potent sausage, bearing its silken head and fringed with ruddy forest, and was tingled momentarily within. There was no blood; it was intact, regardless of her fearful images. There was the curl of Moxie, spread before her eyes like a river; hirsute tributaries to his loins, to his hips . . . chest . . . neck . . . and mouth. There was sensuousness in war, and she was tempted to take advantage of this, the Last Supper, when a Prussian voice said, "Excite him . . . take his weapon to your lips . . . stroke it with your jeweled fingers and supple hand. . . ."

Helen McCrary—daughter of Commodore McCrary, USN, Retired; sister of Jack McCrary, goat of the doomed *Sebago* . . . sister of Seaman McCrary, deceased in the flooded aftercompartments of the *Sebago,* late pride of the United States submarine forces —does hereby succumb . . . to forces . . . and orders . . . lacking sufficient strength. . . . She reverted to Helen McCrary of Boston. To Helen of the cocky sailor who smoked his Lucky Strikes while she did something unbecoming to a Radcliffe girl. She took it in her hand, lifted it like the *pietà*-limp figure of Michelangelo's Christ in the Vatican. It reminded her of reclining marble nudes in museums, the ones her schoolmates giggled and whispered about—the muscular marble warriors without fig leaves. She closed her fingers about it and told herself that it was all a dream as she stroked slowly and lifted it, feeling it surge and ebb, then, finding the touches that swelled her fingers, repeated the same until the marble became pulsing muscle and lifted her hand. It grew until she could scarcely hold it; now she used both hands, fingers pulling and smoothly stripping, then one hand down to the root and up . . .

Her eyes were closed, and she hadn't seen Nielson take down the cracked shaving mirror from over the washbowl and set it against the concrete on the bench near Moxie's hips . . . angle it for a position he'd planned on. He was getting very excited now. The spectacle burned into his groin, and he slipped out of his shorts. He manipulated himself in cadence with Helen's movements while standing level with the wide bench. When he was erect, he tapped her lightly on her left shoulder; she opened her eyes wide. Nielson's penis glans was almost touching her mouth. She recoiled and let go of Mulford, but the Mauser was thrust against his testicles, and she resumed her stroking. Peter crawled up on the bench behind her, looked at the mirrored reflection of her kneading hands on Mulford.

"Now," he shouted, "take it in your pretty mouth, and suck; suck for his life—and yours. I'm a desperate man; I have nothing to lose by killing both of you. So don't get me mad. *Suck. Now.* He pushed her down on Mulford, and she did his bidding, coughing as her mouth circled the glistening, throbbing column. Then she found her rhythm varying her motion to allow for breathing. She thought it better to assuage this madman and hoped that it would end with Nielson's masturbating as she'd heard some men did because of inability with the opposite sex, perhaps a fear of failure.

Then she felt Nielson's smooth, strong hands on her hips, grabbing her from behind, pulling her buttocks up; she felt his heaving breath on her back, then his body against hers, hands feeling under her, exploring, spreading her. Fingers feeling, caressing, and entering. Still, she continued, bracing herself on Mulford with one elbow and manipulating him with her mouth and hand. Mulford's torso spasmed upward, thrusting the penis far into her throat, and she gagged, then regrouped. The groping had stopped behind her.

"The drug I gave him should impede ejaculation for a while, so just keep on with it." Helen was frightened by the matter-of-fact statement: the statement of a cold-blooded lunatic.

Peter's erection had drooped, become limp. He had to excite himself again. The time was now, *before* Moxie, before Helen would tire. He picked up the snub-nosed pistol and put the barrel against her ripe, untanned buttocks. He started to erect at his next idea. Spreading her cheeks, he set the one-half-inch round blue steel muzzle against her anus. It shrank taut, and she stopped her motions.

"It's my gun you feel. If you stop, I'll pull the trigger." Peter watched her in the mirror. Satisfied, he pressed the muzzle slowly forward, holding her pelvis back with his free hand. His erection grew, harder than before. Then he pressed harder—and the muzzle disappeared into her. Her body, her mind, her viscera reacted—but her survival instinct prevailed. Her intestines, disturbed, released their gases autonomically into the Mauser's muzzle—and were ejected through the cocked breach. For a long moment Peter's paranosmia was triggered. A stress situation had occurred; electrical impulses were impeded in traversing the mitral cells which spasmodically broke their fibrous bridges to the microscopic tufted cells of the olfactory bulbs in Nielson's forebrain. Infinitesimal short circuits occurred as a specialized mitral axon crossed a wrong receptor. The *foul* sensor transmitted its impulses to the *flowery* and *burned* receptors, and a musky odor tinged with lavender was the sensation that Peter perceived—whereas Moxie, drunk, didn't care.

Magnificently erect at long last, Peter retracted the muzzle and set the automatic down. He grabbed Helen's pelvis and, kneeling behind her, inserted himself and rammed in to his hilt.

"Harder, harder. Now . . . now," he screamed, forcing the flesh machine of three into a frenzy of coordinated undulation . . . mounting, mounting . . . until he saw, reflected in the mirror, Moxie's violent upward thrust, at which he also shuddered and exploded in one final, splitting penetration. He then withdrew, reached over, and ripped off Moxie's *ankh*. Leaving Helen in a sobbing embrace atop Mulford, he picked up his shorts and pistol, then bolted out of the steaming cave. After slamming the door shut, he braced a split log under the door handle, tested it, and raced into his cottage.

He got dressed, threw his bag into the Aston-Martin's jump seat, and tore into the main house. He found a pressure switch behind the mantel clock, the ankh key fitted, and after ascertaining the contents of the watertight envelope, he cut the phone line with Moxie's red knife.

The 1,500 cc motor revved the tachometer to its red line, drowning out Helen's door banging and screaming as Peter swerved out of the driveway toward the coastal highway. He knew one thing; he would drive east, along the narrowing English Channel. Bypassing Bridport and West Bay, he slowed down as the road went through the intersection where he'd noticed a police vehicle the day before. Besides, there was no reason to attract attention. He was a proper Swedish naval observer who had borrowed Admiral Bryans-Hughes's sports car. Driving with one hand, he reached into his inside jacket pocket and drew out a small black address book. He one-fingered the index tabs and opened to the *G*'s. A khaki lorry honked and narrowly missed his right fender. Too used to driving on the right. Peter pulled over onto the left shoulder and cut the engine. He had to be alone, had to think . . . to plan. He looked at the shiny deep greenish envelope. *Royal Oak,* with 830 dead, was one thing—but *this!* The plans of Britain's defenses on the Channel beaches involved a quarter of a million German troops! He had to deliver the packet to Canaris. Or should it be Canaris? Perhaps he would go directly to the Führer. There was something wrong about the Abwehr admiral. Something intangible—but *weak*!

"G.W." It was the code designation for Snow's agent in Wales and Dorset. There were two addresses: one in Cardiff and the other on the Isle of Wight. Peter rummaged in the wire basket below the dashboard. Flashlight . . . driving gloves . . . aha, road map. He spread it out on the green bonnet. Less than two hours, including the ferry, should he hit it right! He would go to Lymington and find the ferry. Peter was especially observant. The Abwehr had briefed him. The English had removed all their road signs as a deterrent in the event of invasion by the Germans. He would make pencil marks, keeping record of towns and crossroads starting from Dorchester, the next large town and county seat.

Once past Dorchester's Roman walls and, to his amusement, the fifteenth-century Church of St. Peter, Nielson became aware of the encroaching darkness. It would be past seven when he arrived in Lymington, fifty miles farther east. Perhaps, in order not to appear suspicious, he should plan on spending the night at Southampton. No, that would be risky—an unnecessary, dilettantish detour, however tempting with Sir Lancelot's car. He stepped on the accelerator. Perhaps G.W., whom he had met as Mr. Brown earlier that year in Berlin, might have managed to spirit Vera Erikson into England. The "beautiful spy," as she was known in the business, had mentioned connections on Wight. He would enjoy exchanging *experiences* with his compatriot from Denmark by way of Stavanger, Norway. He'd been excited about Vera, a rare agent: a Danish subject who'd been born in Siberia! For one, she'd amused him when they'd met in Oslo, through a mutual friend. He'd agreed to accepting the Mauser as standard issue but had declined the flick knife. Not so Vera, who'd said, "If it's free, I'll take it."

Nielson thought it over and decided to take a chance. It was Friday night, and there'd be no services to call on the admiral's cottage till Monday. Helen and Moxie, God bless 'em, would survive on the canned jars and each other, if necessary. He squirmed as he drove. Felt like a lesion on his foreskin. Sore! He took his eyes from the road on a straightaway overlooking a peninsula he assumed was Swanage and looked over the Channel. Somewhere, sixty sea miles south, lay Cherbourg, the French peninsula that reached toward England.

The Aston-Martin pulled up behind an inn. The establishment's sign had caught Nielson's fancy: Anchor & Hope. He took an order of fish and chips, along with a newspaper, to his room overlooking the Lymington yachting station. With renewed dedication he rejected his usual preference, and ordered a pot of black coffee.

JAPAN JOINS AXIS, the banner headline of the Southampton *Times* screamed. Peter skipped the story; he was looking for something else. A lead, anything that might bear on him, on a way to escape. Had they been discovered yet? Perhaps they'd escaped. He stopped at a secondary headline. "LONDON BADLY HIT . . . We down 130 of 600 bombers." Nielson turned the pages. "NORWEGIAN OFFICERS ESCAPE IN OPEN BOAT . . . Rescued by British submarine in North Sea . . . assumed it was a German U-boat and threw code books overboard . . . books were to be used for anti-Nazi underground movement . . . officers said they had memorized code. . . ."

"Fools—those Norwegians . . ." He popped another ketchuped chip in his mouth and had misgivings about leaving England.

Then he saw it, a short article on the next to last page:

> LOCAL MAN BUILDS MINIATURE UNDERWATER CRAFT: 27 Sept. 1940. Mr. George Adams, of Milford, interviewed by this newspaper, was quoted as saying: "My design is capable of descending to 300 feet, and features an airlock whereby a crewman can exit and accomplish rescue operations on disabled . . ."
>
> . . . Mr. Adams is confident that the Admiralty commission at Portsmouth, where his X-2 now lies, will be more than pleased . . .

Peter scanned the rest of the article. It stated that the submerged range was "over eighty miles" and that it was currently "working up" for naval trials. He looked at his road map. Portsmouth was about an hour's drive from the Anchor & Hope. He would forget Snow's man on the Isle of Wight. He set his travel alarm for 5:00 A.M. He would go by the book and use the element of surprise.

THIRTY-SEVEN

Peter studied his reflection as he shaved. His mother had told him that he resembled the international film star Paul Henreid. True, he reminisced, albeit a high-domed Henreid, courtesy of Gustav Krupp. He sprinkled liberally from his cologne; after all, a representative of the Swedish crown should be beyond reproach.

He had done it. What established agents had tried and failed in, he had succeeded. Surely there would be an Iron Cross for him—a *Ritterkreuz,* with oaks and *Brillanten*! It was unfortunate that Ulla couldn't see the Führer decorate him. She would have been so proud—and his father . . .

Nielson arrived in Portsmouth at seven, having driven the long way, around Southampton and down the east bank of the Solent. It was just as well, for he was famished and the best restaurants opened only at that hour. Peter went into Kimbells on Commercial Road, across from the Naval Green, and relished a breakfast of kippers, toasted muffins, and coffee. Should his plan work, it would be days before he'd have a good meal again.

Then, at an adjoining chandlery, he purchased an

array of tinned foods, including pumpernickel, ham, apricots, and apple juice.

It was almost eight when he button-snapped the tonneau cover tight in the Admiralty parking field off Queen Street. Nothing unusual about an admiral's car's being left there—especially over a summer weekend. Good hiding place, too, for the travel bag which he had discarded in favor of a small seabag—there being no need for extra clothes and accessories. The defense plans, now in the form of bracketed 11-millimeter Minox film, reposed neatly in a hollowed-out and refinished walnut shell, one of many in a small paper bag. The Mauser automatic and his trusty Minox camera, giveaways in the event of a metal detection scanner, had been left in the car. Peter was "armed" only with Moxie's Swiss army knife, also in the seabag.

His naval credentials got him through the main gate. Peter told the Royal Marine guard that he'd come from Lyme Regis on Admiral Bryans-Hughes's belated recommendation to visit Admiral Nelson's flagship, HMS *Victory,* refitted and lying as a museum in the Royal Dock Basin. He apologized for being so early, but explained his abhorrence of sight-seeing crowds. Peter agreed with the corporal that yes, indeed, he might be a distant relation of the martyred sailor.

He walked briskly past the illustrious wooden man-o'-war, with its three decks of gunports, decorative stem, and long bowsprit. High atop its mainmast, a long, colorful pennant swirled southward, toward the Continent. Good sign—a following sea is faster.

There were two *S* class coastal submarines rafted at the far end of Number Two Basin. A guard had been posted. Nielson returned a salute and continued unabashedly to the third and largest basin, where a great number of assorted boats were fitting out. After strenuous searching, he came across several curious, torpedolike craft. Peter's heart skipped. If these were the subs, they would never do. Two seats, set on a closed cylinder and open to the sea. He began to sweat—a cold sweat. But then the boats were not operational; still on blocks, they were not yet powered. No propellers. But it seemed he was in the right area.

Then he saw it, bobbing gently against a finger slip. And what luck—the fuel float! The counter on the diesel pump was turning. A duty rating seemed oblivious to his approach, was intent on guiding the fuel hose nozzle into the outboard fitting, aft of the diesel exhaust riser. The pump's whirring allowed Nielson to move behind the kneeling sailor. Peter, with the assuredness of an executioner, cocked his arm behind the unsuspecting figure's neck, measured the distance, then struck a karate blow to the base of the skull at its intersection with the digastric nerve. The worker reached for his ear, then dropped the hose and fell sideways on the dock. Peter dragged the moaning body into the hose shed, wound it up with one-inch water hose, then gagged it with an oil rag.

He kept low, behind the scarcely three feet of hull and deckhouse above the waterline, and fueled it till the diesel oil backed up out of its tank. Dropping the hose, he let go fore and aft lines, grabbed his gear and the midships spring line, and clambered aboard. The aft hatch was open for ventilation; he climbed in, snubbed the spring line on a fitting, and looked for the diesel controls. First, throw the fuel lever! The arrangement was not unlike that on a small power launch. He turned the vapor switch, and the interior lights snapped on. Next, he pressed the electric start button. The diesel turned over slowly. Cold! He counted ten and tried again. It caught, and he gave more throttle. One last look out the hatch; then he let go of the spring. Because the tide was going out, he let the craft ease out slowly as he blew the main ballast tank and slowly slipped below the surface. By the time the forty-three-foot cigar had cleared the slip its electric motor had taken over and the diesel riser was secured. As the two-foot riser went under, the miniature periscope whirred up, and its little prism head scanned the basin.

To the west, one tidal lock was open. The thirty-ton dun gray submersible drifted—caught in the flowing tide. Nielson put the transmission into reverse to get steerageway toward the open lock as the craft, bearing a white "X-2" on its bows, glided under the eight-tubed humpback nose of a new T class sub.

The little bronze eye skimmed through Lock Number One, hidden by the dock, and into Portsmouth Harbor. It traversed the narrows and turned hard aport off uninhabited Burrow Island. Staying far west, away from the wakening naval complex, it made for the Channel between Point Battery and the Blockhouse Fort.

Peter retracted the scope for the half mile run when he was abeam of the railway ferry dock, but not before a final sweep should the ferry be crossing.

Combining its maximum underwater speed of two knots with the full race tide, the commandeered craft slid through the 200-yard-wide sally port and into the sprawling, hazy English Channel.

THIRTY-EIGHT

Nielson set his automatic self-steering device at 190 degrees magnetic according to his memorized chart calculations of the night before at the Anchor & Hope, where in his room he had also photographed the anti-Sea Lion defense plans. He'd calculated the distance to Barfleur Point on the east head of the Cotentin peninsula as about eighty miles. The inventor had claimed an underwater range of eighty-five miles at two knots. Peter, not to press his luck, had planned to surface after running twenty-four hours and recharge his batteries somewhere in the middle of the Channel. France had been occupied for several months now, so no matter where he landed—even on the formerly British Channel islands of Jersey, Guernsey, or Alderney—he would be in safe hands. Provided he wasn't spotted and sunk first. After eleven hours running submerged, he fell asleep.

At 2100 hours he woke up, brought the craft to periscope depth, and checked out the systems. It was dark and overcast, no moon, so he surfaced and ran on the 32 BHP Gardner diesel for an hour. He welcomed the feeling of exhilaration as the X-1 accelerated to six knots on the following sea. It was a fine time for a ham sandwich, and Moxie's all-purpose knife was put to task on the tin. Peter was about to prepare another sandwich when he heard aircraft drone above.

He took the sub down to fifty feet and continued on course. About five hours later a sudden jolt threw him out of the off-duty bunk. The boat was buffeted by strong currents, and he dived to half the gauge-designated limit. He suspected a violent Channel storm and decided not to go up and chance a broach just because of curiosity. Because 100 feet was still not deep enough, he went down to 150. After several hours he ventured up and was driven down again. Peter tried to eat but almost became nauseated. Finally, he slumped into his bunk, in a tired stupor.

The midget boat had been designed for a crew of three: four hours on, four off. He was not the superman he thought he was. The foul air and the tight quarters were affecting him. The X-1 had not been designed for long, submerged trips.

He lay in his bunk, against the restraining bars. It was worth it; there was no need to convince an Abwehr agent in line for decorations and a furlough that it was anything else. Once the festivities in Berlin were over, he'd have his pick of the ladies, for unlike Prien, he was unmarried, and even if he were, it would be all his for the taking. He would be welcomed, somehow, into the Krupp family . . . become a millionaire . . .

The storm subsided. According to the log entries, the boat had been to sea for almost forty hours. The voltmeters flicked nervously in the low numbers. It was time to go up.

Peter found a sextant in the navigation table

drawer and climbed through the hatch. It was past midnight, and he'd expected landfall at dawn. He took a fix on Capella, then cruised another hour and sighted the star again. The conversion tables were plotted on the Channel grid chart. Storm and tide had taken him off course, more than thirty miles east of the peninsula. He drew a line along his parallel rule. The boat was about seventeen miles north of Port-en-Bessin.

At dawn, cruising on the surface, Peter, using "difficult" British binoculars, spotted cathedral towers. A check of the chart showed the town of Bayeux, some five miles inland. He noticed a road leading from Bayeux to Arromanches, several miles east of Port-en-Bessin. He altered course; he wanted to be closer to a large town. Peter had heard stories about the resistance.

He was spotted by a patrol boat that ordered him to beach the craft under threat of blowing it out of the water. The patrol boat sent a radio message, and an armored gun carrier was waiting when Peter drove the X-1 onto a sandbank.

At noon, after a bath, and in a German SS uniform, Peter lunched at an inn across from the Museum of Queen Matilda in Bayeux's medieval quarter with the local colonel of the SS. Monocled Standartenführer Eduard von Felbert arranged a special showing of the famous Battle of Hastings eleventh-century tapestry, courtesy of the museum. He observed that Napoleon had displayed it in the Louvre, as a propaganda device when he was planning to invade England in 1809.

By nightfall a Messerschmitt Bf 110 touched down at Tempelhof airport in Berlin. Admiral Canaris watched it taxi to a stop.

Early the next day Hitler canceled Operation Sea Lion.

EPILOGUE

Lieutenant Commander W. E. Mulford, cap in hand, stood before the historic desk.

"Sit down, Commander." A cloud of cigar smoke hung about the statesman, as if around the summit of an active volcano.

"I shall be brief, as I have a lot of brass and braid waiting in the conference room."

Moxie nodded; there was nothing he could or should say.

The former "Naval Person" thumbed his broad vest and pondered a moment. "How is the girl—the American?"

"It was a shock. . . ."

"Of course it was. War is shock." The prime minister looked down, then, his eyes twinkling, shook his massive head. "When I picture the frogman putting that trout on Nielson's fly . . ."

"He took it all—"

"Spare me the proverbial phrase." The statesman quivered. "Even the advert about the X-1—I should say *article.*"

"It was close, though," Moxie stammered. "When he slurred my dead brother . . ."

"I read the report, son." The Prime Minister rose. "Moxie," the lion roared, "just think of all the brothers . . . the fathers . . . and the sons your assignment saved. . . ." He stubbed out his Havana stoically, then stuck another one between his ruddy lips.

"History will record that your coup in averting Operation Sea Lion redeemed the victims of the disaster at Scapa Flow. 'Out of this nettle, danger, we pluck this flower, safety! . . .' "

Without another word the statesman steamed out of his chambers, leaving the ponderous oak door open.